Mossy Cre

and

Reunion at Mossy Creek

"Delightful."

— Georgia First Lady Marie Barnes

"Mitford meets Mayberry in the first book of this innovative and warmhearted new series from BelleBooks."

— *The Cleveland Daily Banner, Cleveland, Tennessee*

"MOSSY CREEK is as much fun as a cousin reunion; like sipping ice cold lemonade on a hot summer's afternoon. Hire me a moving van, it's the kind of town where everyone wishes they could live."

— Debbie Macomber, *NYT bestselling author*

"A fast, funny, and folksy read. Enjoy!"

— Lois Battle, *acclaimed author of Storyville,*
Bed and Breakfast, and
The Florabama Ladies Sewing Club And Auxiliary

"REUNION AT MOSSY CREEK is down home story telling at its best."

— Jackie K Cooper, *WMAC-AM, Macon, Georgia*

"Colorfully and cleverly portrayed. A wholesome story."

— Harriet Klausner, *Amazon.com's top reviewer*

"The characters and kinships of MOSSY CREEK are quirky, hilarious and all too human. This story reads like a delicious, meringue-covered slice of home. I couldn't get enough."

— Pamela Morsi, *USA Today bestselling author*

"I want to live in Mossy Creek."

— Astrid Kinn, *Romance Reviews Today*

"These southern belle authors have done it again, even better this time."

— Bob Spear, *Heartland Reviews*

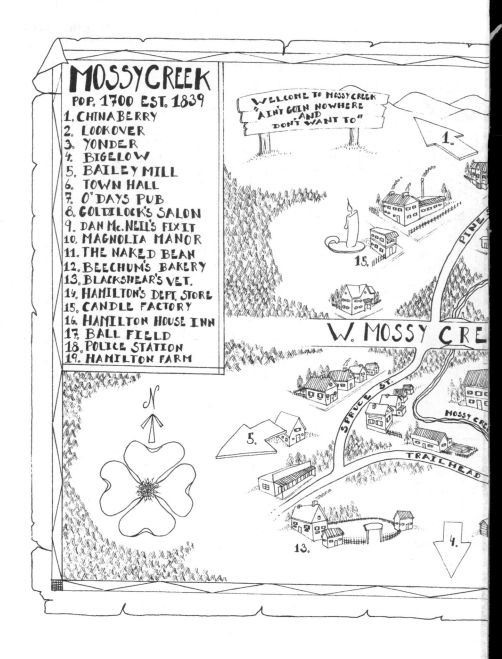

MOSSY CREEK
POP. 1700 EST. 1839

1. CHINA BERRY
2. LOOKOVER
3. YONDER
4. BIGELOW
5. BAILEY MILL
6. TOWN HALL
7. O'DAYS PUB
8. GOLDILOCK'S SALON
9. DAN Mc. NEIL'S FIXIT
10. MAGNOLIA MANOR
11. THE NAKED BEAN
12. BEECHUM'S BAKERY
13. BLACKSHEAR'S VET.
14. HAMILTON'S DEPT. STORE
15. CANDLE FACTORY
16. HAMILTON HOUSE INN
17. BALL FIELD
18. POLICE STATION
19. HAMILTON FARM

Summer in Mossy Creek

A collective novel featuring the voices of

Deborah Smith, Sandra Chastain,
Debra Dixon, Martha Shields

and

Carolyn McSparren, Anne Bishop,
Susan Goggins, Bo Sebastian, Kim Brock,
Shelly Gail Morris, Judy Keim,
Patti Callahan Henry

Smyrna, Georgia

BelleBooks, Inc.

ISBN 0-9673035-4-0

Summer in Mossy Creek

Published by:
BelleBooks, Inc. · P.O. Box 67 · Smyrna, GA 30081
We at BelleBooks enjoy hearing from readers. You can contact us at the address above or BelleBooks@BelleBooks.com

Visit our website— **www.BelleBooks.com**

First Edition June 2003

10 9 8 7 6 5 4 3 2 1

Cover art: Laura Austin
Cover design: Martha Shields
Mossy Creek map: Dino Fritz

Summer in

Welcome from the
Mossy Creek Storytellers Club

Welcome back to Mossy Creek, Georgia, the small mountain town where love, laughter and kindness are facts of life but people cheerfully live up to the stubborn pioneer-era slogan still painted on a grain silo at the town limits: "Welcome to Mossy Creek. The town you can count on. Ain't Goin' Nowhere, And Don't Want To." The namesake creek circles the town like a moat, and people like it that way.

"Creekites" come in every size, shape, color and country of national origin, but they all share a love of small town living and sheer, feisty independence. Whether it's feuding with their snobby neighbors down in the "big town" of Bigelow or one-upping Governor Ham Bigelow, an arrogant native son who wants to see Mossy Creek tamed once and for all, Creekites are always ready for a fight or a celebration.

The writers who contribute their voices to the Mossy Creek Hometown Series think of themselves as The Mossy Creek Storytelling Club, and they tell these Creekite tales with a true love for the town and its quirky people. So pull up a chair on our porch, sip some iced tea, enjoy the sweet whisper of the creek and the view of the Southern mountains, and join us for a warm, poignant, funny, crazy summer in Mossy Creek.

Many thanks to Laura Austin, who contributed the art that graces this book's cover, also many thanks to Lillian Richey for the whimsical "A Guide to the People and Places of Mossy Creek" readers will find in the back this book. Thanks once again to Wayne Dixon, aka Bubba Rice, for contributing recipes so wickedly good only a Southern bubba could have created them, and thanks to Ali Cunliffe, copy editor extraordinaire, who makes sure we don't mess up the spelling for words like extraordinaire.

Happy reading!

The Mossy Creek Storytellers Club

Mossy Creek Gazette

VOLUME III, No. 1   MOSSY CREEK, GEORGIA

The Bell Ringer

A Welcome Note To Our Summer Tourists

by Katie Bell

Ahhh, summertime in Mossy Creek. After midnight, O'Day's Pub and Hamilton House Inn close down and the town goes soft and quiet. The sky in Mossy Creek is coal black, alive with lightning bugs blinking in unison to the pin cushion of stars overhead. You can hear the breeze ruffling the trees and the musical sound of the frogs croaking their mating calls in the Creek. Those of us who live here have always believed our summer nights are filled with magic that clears away the discord and makes the world ready for tomorrow.

Morning starts the bustle of life once more. Those of you who've come to visit in Mossy Creek have met many of our residents. You smile at the cheerful shops around the square and ask how such charm has been protected. The buildings are over a hundred years old.

Not necessarily. From the beginning we've preserved the look of our town. New buildings have been added but Mayor Ida Hamilton Walker and Bert Lyman, owner of WMOS Radio, have worked with Fix-It Shop owner Dan McNeil, who heads the historical district's planning committee, to maintain the ambiance of Mossy Creek. In no way have we forced our more eccentric shop owners to tone down their personalities. Creekites are original and they're stubborn, but we give them lots of help and they love their little town.

Among others, you'll likely to meet Mayor Ida and Mossy Creek Police Chief Amos Royden, who can usually be found somewhere on the town square, often together. If you stop by the *Gazette's* offices I'll be happy to share my column archives with you. You can read my article about retired farmer Ed Brady, who showed us the true meaning of devotion as he cared for his wife, Ellie, until her death, and later when he reconciled with his son Ed, who has returned to Mossy Creek.

I'll tell you all about our local animal celebrities, such as Bob, aka The Flying Chihuahua, Emma the cat (Bob's nemesis), Samson the legendary mascot of Mossy

(continued on page 10)

Welcome to Summer Visitors

(continued from page 9)

Creek High, and even Rose the disappearing elephant. Since last year some new residents have moved in, and some old Creekites have come back home.

Gossip continues to be shared freely, though it can be slightly tainted by the gossiper. So forgive us if we sometimes mislead. And if our local purveyor of secrets (me) doesn't tell all, drop me a note. I'll try to find out what you want to know, and who knows? I might even print it in the *Gazette*.

This summer in Mossy Creek promises to be special. Come sit a spell in the gazebo or join me for English tea at the Hamilton House Inn and I'll catch you up on all the news as it happens.

In days gone by, wealthy people had summer homes in the mountains and winter homes in Florida. They don't do that much any more. Mayor Walker says it's because when they come here, they stay. Maybe, but Wolfman (he's a member of the Foo Club, and one of Miss Ida's cohorts in civic service) says that sooner or later, Florida is going to get caught in the Bermuda Triangle and be ripped off the United States. That means Georgia will have the white beaches and the Gulf waters. Creekites will own winter *and* summer homes then.

This newspaper does not subscribe to that line of thought.

From the rise in subscriptions to the *Gazette*, I'd say there are plenty of folks on the way. It drives Sue Ora Salter, the owner of this fine paper, crazy but there's not a day that goes by that I don't get a call or a note asking for two things: directions and more information about us Creekites. Our readers don't care what goes on in the outside world.

Everybody's polite and none of them call it *gossip* but I think they want to get to know us. It's like meeting your family through the printed word. So, good journalism or not, here goes my capsule report for this week.

Pets are welcome, but we don't have a full-service humane society yet. Though Chief Royden doesn't have many bad guys to catch, he isn't the dog catcher. So he has talked Dr. Blackshear, our local vet, into offering a spay and neuter special. There are those who feel that program ought to include people but that's another column.

I might add that we've long had a policy of adopting stray children, animals, relatives and an occasional husband or two—once they're unattached, of course. In fact South Bigelow Road is like a revolving door used by those who swear they can't wait to leave and then can't wait to come back. Try not to run over each other on the way home.

"A real friend is one who walks in
when the rest of the world walks out."

— *Mencius*

🐾🐾🐾

AMOS and DOG

Chapter One

A good leather recliner.

That's all a man really needs to be happy. I ran my hand possessively over the butter-soft leather arm of my just-delivered chair and leaned back into heaven. The recliner was a custom job, extra long when stretched out full-length. Josie McClure over at Swee Purla's helped me pick it out weeks ago. The start of summer is a strange time to acquire a hot leather chair, even in Mossy Creek, where *summer* and *strange* go hand-in-hand as the temperature rises. I hadn't really intended to buy an honest-to-God-real-leather chair that day. The thing cost more than a month's salary.

But, as Josie carefully explained to me when I balked at the price tag she put on paradise, there comes a time in a man's life when he has to stop living like a bear in a cave. She's an ardent believer in the Japanese art of feng shui as a way to visualize and change your life. I wasn't so certain furniture philosophy was going to change my life, but I was willing to be convinced. A leather chair was the pot of gold at the end of enlightenment. So, I nodded and made hmming sounds.

Sort of like I did now. Mac Campbell was on the other end of the phone, having a great deal of fun at my expense.

"Patty said Josie's worried about you. Apparently you're about one feng shui faux pas away from total chaos."

"You're about one crack away from about a dozen parking tickets."

"Touchy, aren't you?"

"You would be, too. Patty's blowing this all out of proportion. I only agreed with Josie that it was about time I replaced the castoff furniture I've either inherited or liberated from divorcing-couple garage sales. I haven't agreed to anything else."

Mac's hoot of laughter kept me honest.

"Okay. Not much else." I could actually *hear* Mac's grin all the way through the phone.

"Son, you are living in a house with a toilet in the wealth area. You'd better agree to change something. Patty thinks you need to focus on your relationship area first."

"Mac, why do I need a relationship area if I don't have a relationship at the moment?"

"You're right. The first order of business is having your chi all messed up because your back door and front door line up."

"They aren't actually lined up."

"Close enough that Josie made you promise to keep the toilet lid down and avoid opening the back door until she could do a full-scale analysis of the problems—free of charge."

That much was true. Josie had declared a state of emergency and had taken my case on a probono basis. At least for the consulting. The rest of it she charged through the nose for. That first consultation with Josie shocked more than my pocketbook. It shocked me out of denial. She was right, I had to change some things. I had to stop pretending that this job, Mossy Creek and the house were just way stations in my life. That I'd be moving on to bigger and better things eventually. Truth is...I'm not going anywhere and really don't want to. There might be bigger, but I doubted there'd be better. It was time to accept Mossy Creek was *my* town for better or worse, until death do us part.

Especially now that I'd made the supreme sacrifice and engaged a decorator.

"Trust me, Mac. If I'd known what I was letting myself in for, I'm not sure I would have gone through with the consultation. I thought I was just shopping."

"You don't shop at Swee Purla's; you have a consultation. Everyone knows that."

"Apparently not me. I thought it would be easy to get someone to fix up the house for me and save me all the trouble. How long can it take to buy a few pieces of furniture and maybe new blinds? Dammit, Mac, I didn't want a place worthy of some national design magazine centerfold. I didn't want fancy. All I wanted was to make my house feel a little more like home and less like an empty military barracks."

"Hey, I understand. Me and the boys are rooting for you."

"What?" I had a sick feeling in the pit of my stomach.

"Well, you're in Josie's cross-hairs now. Won't be long before you'll be looking at paint chips. Unless you can break free."

"I have to go." *Bang my head into the hallway wall. The one with test paint patches on it.* I hung up.

I had been foolish and naive. I hadn't known anything about feng shui. But my biggest mistake was not realizing that the force was strong with Josie. I was toast. Quite literally.

My idea of color theory is that tan is, well...just tan, and it pretty much goes with everything. Ha! Apparently there is some worldwide conspiracy to fragment the color tan into about a million sub-colors that all look exactly the same but are called foo-foo names like sandstone and harvest wheat and toast. Then—just when you think you've got a handle on the tan thing—the decorator asks trick questions like,

"Which of these three paint chips is closer to your wall color?"

Huh?

My walls are white. Don't get me started on what the decorators of the world have done to the color white! It's actually scary.

If color torture weren't enough, whatever furniture you order has to be delivered to you when it finally arrives—by a big truck with Swee's logo plastered all over it. Every woman on the block now thinks I'm just one big-screen TV short of having a wicked bachelor's pad. That's what happens when you're single and have a new stereo system delivered the day before you have a leather chair delivered.

The combination is fatal.

My buddies thought I was going over to the dark side. The women in town thought I was going over to the dark side. The two groups just didn't agree on what the dark side was.

Sighing, I hauled myself out of my newly beloved chair so I could haul myself down to the station. Might as well give Sandy her chance to comment on my sudden wild streak. She wasn't expecting me until later in the day, but I figured there's no time like the present to get the unpleasantness over with. A little grilling never hurt anyone. Not much. Besides, Sandy could use some cheering up.

🌱🌱🌱

"Hi, Chief." Sandy reached for the pink message slips she had piled on top of the row of file cabinets and walked them over to the counter. When she actually handed them to me and turned back to her filing without saying a word about my new chair or the messages, I began to worry about my favorite dispatcher. She never, *ever,* allowed me to sort my own messages. Hell, I was rarely allowed to touch them.

Looking at the slips in my hand, I had to admit the truth. The effervescent Sandy Crane was officially depressed, and I knew why. Not that I could do anything about it.

Sandy still spent most of her time in the office even though she'd been promoted to "officer." She was having some trouble qualifying on the firing range. With a rifle and a decent scope she can shoot the tail feathers off a hawk at 600 yards, but using a pistol she couldn't put more than two in a row in the kill zone of a paper target. Why? Closing your eyes as you pull the trigger pretty much insures a bad score.

She was shooting herself in the foot...so to speak.

My guess was Sandy's soft nature couldn't reconcile itself to shooting anything that looked like a person. Or she was afraid she'd make the wrong decision when push came to pull. God willing, she'd never have to pull a gun or shoot anyone in a town like Mossy Creek, but I have a responsibility to the citizens and, more importantly, to Sandy. I can't put her on the streets unless she can do the job. All the job.

She either qualifies like every other officer or she works the desk. Even Battle wouldn't have bent that rule. The issue is strictly black and white, governed by state regulations. For once, there isn't even a smidgeon of gray area for me to agonize over.

Sandy doesn't blame me, but it breaks my heart to see the sparkle fading from her smile. She worries that her dream of being a real officer is slipping through her trigger finger. The harder she tries the worse her scores get.

The hell of it is, Sandy was born to be a small town cop. She loves the people, makes it her business to know everyone and genuinely wants the best for Mossy Creek.

Watching Sandy quietly filing our meager stack of incident reports, I knew I'd have to give this problem some more thought.

In the meantime, I had a couple of questions about my messages. I've gotten used to Sandy putting them in context and making sure I had all the important background on the issues. Seeing the pristine, un-annotated messages in my hand was a little like reading a book with blank pages. I didn't quite know what the plot was.

"Hannah called? Someone moving the books in the library again?"

"Nope." She didn't even turn around to answer me. "That whole book moving thing doesn't usually happen for a few more weeks."

Okay, now I was really worried. The old Sandy would have practically bounced as she relayed the info, making plans to stake out the library for the annual *moving of the books* event. It happened every year near the beginning of the summer and near the end of the summer. Well, it had happened for the last year and a half, long enough to establish a pattern of harmless mischief. A mystery. But Sandy wasn't even interested.

"So," I prompted. "Why is Hannah calling?"

"Don't know. Didn't ask. I figure that's her business."

I clamped down hard on my response. Now was not the time to remind Sandy that as our dispatcher it *was* her job to screen my calls. I made a mental note to have a talk with Jess, her husband. Then I asked, "Okay. Next question. Did Dwight say why he needs me at the special council meeting he's calling tomorrow night?"

"No."

"Sandy, I know he wouldn't actually *say* why. That would ruin his little surprise plan. It's always a secret coup with him. But, *you*, you know, right? You've always got an ear to the ground. I count on you for the good stuff. Don't let me down now. What's Dwight's emergency?"

She looked up from her filing, a tiny bit of the sparkle was back. "I think he's tired of the kids playing in the park."

"Because..."

"Little Ida rode her bike past him this morning and rang that fancy bell on the handle bars to warn him. But Dwight being Dwight, he jumped ten feet and splattered coffee all over his new suit." She looked at me speculatively. "And..."

Now *this* was the Sandy I knew and loved, waiting for me to finish the deduction. "And..." I concluded, "Dwight being Dwight, now it's war on kids enjoying their own public park?"

"Right, Chief. That's what it looks like. You know he's been in a bad mood since last fall's reunion."

I would never forget Dwight's expression as he realized his old humiliation could be traced to Ham Bigelow's ambition. Ham had gotten rid of his rival for the state senate by making Dwight look incompetent. Twenty years ago Dwight had been busy barfing in the bushes instead of guarding the high school mascot and symbol of Mossy Creek's honor. That stolen ram was the first link in a chain of events that ended with a fire that destroyed the high school.

The loss of a high school is hell on your political capital.

Probably didn't help that Dwight irritated Battle Royden enough that the former chief finally roared, *"Sorry doesn't get it done. Now does it, Dwight?"* Half the town had quieted down just in time to hear those words. The news anchor from Bigelow heard it, too. Got it on film. Battle's question made a good sound byte.

I tried not to smile at the memory. It just wasn't neighborly, but I couldn't help it. Dwight never had been very good at getting people on his side. "I do have to admit that solving the mystery of the fire was political, if not poetic, justice."

Sandy grinned and slapped an empty file folder against her thigh. "It was a moment to savor. Yes, indeed, it was a moment."

"I imagine another moment will be watching him face-off with Ida over kids using the park."

"The smart money's on Miss Ida," Sandy advised.

I didn't even try not to smile as I headed for the door. "My money is always on Ida."

My thoughts were on her more often than not as well, but I didn't volunteer that information. I considered it "need to know" only. And nobody but me needed to know.

🌸🌸🌸

The town library is a modest concrete-block building without fancy stonework or architecture. It's the hodge-podge kind of building that says, "We spend money on books, not bricks." Still it's a solid building, bigger than a town our size would normally have. Right before I moved home, we were the fortunate recipients of a tidy estate left by the Sisters Grim. The two spinsters, Sadie and Sarah Grim, had reveled in their little literary pun during the last years of their spinster lives and extended the joke by leaving all their money to the library. The town, in turn, reveled in their legacy.

Until the details were revealed.

The terms set the town on its ear. I understand Dwight's were the most irate set of ears in the bunch. I wish I'd been here to see those fireworks. According to the executor of the estate, Mac Campbell, the city fathers and mothers had no control over the money. Every decision about what to spend and how to spend it was given to Hannah Longstreet, our full-time librarian, who'd suddenly become a *very im-*

portant person without ever meaning to.

The Sisters Grim figured that only someone working in the library day in and day out could truly know what the town needed to bring its library closer to the county branch "showplace" over in Bigelow. Then they figured they needed someone strong like Mac to face down the town. And the sisters were right. The town (Dwight) didn't have a clue. He pressured Hannah to make cosmetic changes and improve the facade. Dwight wanted to turn the library into an imposing, impressive institute of learning that would project the image of a progressive and growing Mossy Creek. To give the man credit, he did try to camouflage the completely cosmetic aspect of his proposal by swearing we needed to widen the door anyway for better handicapped access.

Since the library already happily accommodated anyone with special needs—including book deliveries to shut-ins—Hannah ignored Dwight and used the money as she saw fit. She decided we needed more space for a proper children's section and kid-sized furniture. Also on her list were a decent heating and air-conditioning system; serious additions to our large-print and audio title collections; and a computerized system with two terminals for patrons to use for research on the internet.

But her pride and joy took her last bit of legacy money. She had an idea for a "local interest" room, which meant she also needed the archival materials necessary for preserving the important historical records of the area—diaries, journals, old maps, auction catalogs, school year books, newspapers and articles, published quilt patterns, letters home from soldiers, Sue Ora's old first drafts of manuscripts and unpublished stories, and even fund-raising cookbooks from the local churches. Katie Bell's research for Lady Victoria put the bug in Hannah's ear about how important our history was. She wanted anything that related to what it meant to be a part of Mossy Creek. Once she put the word out, donations for the collection had happily exceeded her expectations.

She knocked down a wall and added another eight hundred square feet to the library. The new footage was mostly space for the children and computers, but some of it was for her local room. During the entire renovation, Dwight stood right beside her telling her how short-sighted she was to care about the inside of the building and about whether the patrons were comfortable in the summer heat when, Heaven help us, the outside of the building was just rotting away!

Standing in front of the building, I took a good look. I didn't see any rot—concrete rarely rots—but I did see a number of cars in the parking lot and two pre-teens leaving with several books each. Hannah's plan seemed to be working quite well. In fact it probably irritated the snot out of Dwight. For the second time today, I smiled at his expense.

The girls thought I was smiling at them, so they giggled and nodded as they passed me. I grabbed the door before it swung closed and slipped inside. I'd half expected the call to be about some summer troublemakers with too much time on their hands. At least I was *uncharitably* hoping for some troublemakers. Zeke could use some help weeding the park flower beds. That's where my troublemakers always ended up. I haven't had a kid yet who'd rather have me call his parents down to the station than do community service.

But, today, I didn't see any obvious candidates for our flower-bed chain-gang. There were no children running like heathens through the stacks. No shrieking laughter. No loud talking. But neither was the library deathly quiet. There was a pleasant hum about the place, a quiet purpose.

I scanned quickly for Hannah, found her several rows

of books away and looking down an aisle. She was a bit younger than me and had been a widow for a few years now. I couldn't remember how many.

Her small, black-rimmed glasses were shoved up on top of her head, messing up a short blonde 'do that was actually cut so short the cropped style should have made her look masculine. Except that Hannah Longstreet couldn't look masculine if she tried. Even with short hair and in khakis. No one ever asked me, but if they had, I'd have told them it was her eyes. Enormous, bottle green and smiling. Yep, smiling. And soft. Like she was always glad to see you. No doubt about it. The eyes put her squarely in the "girlie girl" category.

She had a pencil stub tucked behind one ear. Her arm was part-way up, and her finger was raised. I expected her to bring it to her lips and make the classic librarian "shushing" sound at someone farther down the aisle. Instead she slowly turned her hand and crooked her finger in summons. I moved close enough to hear what she said.

"What did I tell you?" she asked the aisle, hands on hips. Nice hips. This was a librarian who worked out regularly and expected an answer pronto. "Well?"

Two voices. One mumble. One whine.

Hannah glanced at me with a half-grin and motioned for me to give her a minute. Then she turned back to her culprits. "Speak up, and don't you be making those puppy-dog eyes at me. Well...what did I tell you?"

The culprits slithered into view. One of them quite literally. On his belly, his head never far from his paws. He was a medium-haired, medium-sized, motley-looking, splotchy-colored mutt. When he rolled over in submission, gravity gave him a kind of doggie grin that made it clear he wasn't the least repentant. I laughed.

Hannah turned on me, not too far from laughter herself. With an effort she managed to look stern and reprimand me. "Do not laugh at them. You will only encourage them."

I straightened up and said, "Yes, ma'am." Librarians almost always had the moral high ground.

"We're sorry, Miss Hannah." The boy wasn't even looking at her. He'd dropped down on his knees to give the mutt a tummy rub with one hand. The other held a book. "I know you said we had to stay in the office if I wanted to play with him, but I saw Caralee nosing around the summer reading books and I *had* to go get my last book before she stole it. Daddy'll be mad if I don't get my reading finished this week. He says I have to work starting next week. Won't have time to read. You know I can't come back much. And if I don't get it done, I won't get to have my name on the fund raiser thing."

When he looked up, the first detail I cataloged was the bruise on his left cheek. Like he'd been backhanded by an adult. The hairs on the back of my neck stood up. I hated it when intuition kicked in without true evidence; always put me squarely in that gray zone I hated so much.

He had to *work?* Intuition kicked me again. I was beginning to feel like a punching bag. Intuition slammed me again. "Punching bag" was a bad analogy in this situation.

The kid was maybe nine-years-old. Freshly scrubbed face, brown hair, a freckle or two and wearing old, but fairly clean hand-me-down clothes. I didn't have kids, but I'd seen enough hand-me-downs in my lifetime to spot them, the way they never quite fit because another body had broken them in, stretched them out in all the wrong places.

Hannah leaned over and touched his cheek. Just below the bruise and casually drawing my attention to it. *Great.* Hannah wanted to be sure I saw it. I wasn't imagining things.

"Clay, sweetie, I can bring books to your house. I take

them to lots of people."

"Daddy don't like people coming to the house."

Well, that settled it. I'd be making a social call on Daddy. Whoever Daddy was. "Hannah, aren't you going to introduce me?"

"Love to, Chief. This is Clay Atwood, my favorite kid. Next to my own little girl, of course." The boy smiled at that. Then Hannah moved on to the dog. "And this is... d-o-g." She spelled it, just like you spell ice cream in front of three-year-olds. "He's why I called. He wandered in this morning like he lived here. No one's ever seen him before. He's as sweet as pie, but I had to put him in the office because he kept trying to herd all the kids into one group in the corner."

"Herd?"

"Yeah. At first I wasn't sure he was doing it on purpose. But then every time I looked up he'd managed to quietly nudge another one of the kids into the growing group in the corner. He was so intent on it and did it so well, and so many times...I did a little research. The best I can tell he's an Australian Cattledog. Or at least enough of one that it's splitting hairs to figure out what other genes he's carrying around."

I looked at the heap of over-grown puppy on the floor. He looked like a mutt, and then again...he didn't.

"Dog?"

Dog bounced up immediately and re-deposited himself devotedly at my side, one paw gently resting on my boot, his eyes watching me intently for a command, any command that he could slavishly perform. I had an overwhelming urge to warn him not to get attached to me—he wasn't staying.

"Look at that, Chief!" Clay said. "It's like he knows he's your dog now. You are so lucky. Is he going to be your police dog and round up criminals? Or maybe rescue people? Here boy, smell my hand so you'll remember me when we have an earthquake. I saw a rescue like that on TV once." Clay was clearly impressed that he might know a police dog.

"I don't think so, Clay. For one thing, we hardly ever have to use earthquake dogs around here. Besides, he's too friendly to be a stray. I imagine he belongs to somebody. Heck, there may be a tourist looking for him right now. Why don't you take him outside near my truck in case someone is driving around looking? I need to ask Miss Hannah a few questions and then I'll be right out. Can you handle that, Special-Deputy-For-The-Day?"

"Yes, sir!"

"Show her your book first so she can check it out."

He held his book up for a split second and then ignored the adults. "Come on, Dog. Let's go catch criminals."

I opened my mouth to caution him, but Hannah put her hand on my arm. "Let him go," she whispered. "He won't get into any trouble. Not here."

So, we were back to the bruise. "I think we need to go in your office, Hannah. Have you got a minute?"

"Sure. I have my summer intern covering the circulation desk."

I followed her. "You wiggled budget money for an intern out of Dwight's tight-fisted little hand?"

"No, I think Ida and Sue Ora beat it out of him."

"Ah." I grinned. "Makes sense. I hear there's likely to be another showdown at this special council meeting he's called."

She waved me into the small office and shut the door. "I hate that I'm going to miss it. Got to go over to Bigelow for a library services presentation. I need the continuing ed hours."

I waited for her to scoot around the desk before I took a seat in the old, oak school chair nearest me. On the wall behind her squares of fabric clung to a flannel sheet tacked to the wall. I'm not an expert but I've seen a few quilts in my day. This was some kind of quilt—in pieces and on a wall, but it was still a quilt. As quilts went, this one was pretty snazzy, bright colors and patterns with oddly blank patches—more sandstone than toast—scattered evenly over the design. "I'm going to go out on a limb and guess that you're a quilter, Hannah."

Laughing, she swiveled around to survey the collection of fabric on the wall. "Yeah, that's a quilt in progress. It's my summer reading program reward. If the kids read all the books on my list for their age group, they get to put their name and a favorite quote on the quilt."

She reached to straighten one violet-colored piece and then turned back to me. "When all the spaces are filled, I'll finish it up. Then we're going to display it in City Hall for a month this fall and auction it at Autumn Fest as a fund raiser for the library."

"Clever."

"I liked the idea." She pulled the glasses off her head and tossed them on the desk. A signal that she was ready to get down to business. I jumped right in.

"Clay's afraid his Daddy's rules will keep him from getting a spot on the quilt."

"Right."

"Most parents would dance naked in town square if it'd get their kids to crack a book. And this guy is putting up road blocks for his kid. How often is Clay bruised?"

"Not often enough for me to report it."

"But too often for you to be comfortable?"

"Yeah. And it's the location of the bruises. I can't quite explain it. I see other kids with bruises. I have one of my own—the sweetest, clumsiest child on God's green earth. I know kids, but something about Clay worries me. Once he had some bruising that I would have sworn was from fingers squeezing his arm. I did ask him about that one. He said an old window fell on his arm while he was filling up the bird feeder outside it."

I leaned back and thought for a moment. "That's a pretty good lie for a kid his age to come up with. May turn out that the reason it's so good is that he was telling the truth."

Her eyes narrowed. "I don't think it's the truth or even *his* lie. And neither do you."

"I don't think anything yet, Hannah."

"Yeah, you do, or you wouldn't be talkin' to me. Clay's not clumsy. Never bangs into anything when he's here. I've got high hopes for him as an intern when he hits junior high."

"Okay. I'll check around, but I'd appreciate it if you wouldn't mention this to anyone. This is an informal investigation at best. I don't even know if the Atwoods are in my jurisdiction yet. If my checking comes to nothing, I don't want a family smeared by gossip."

"Understood. I'll leave it to you." *To fix.*

The unspoken words hung in the air. She was leaving it to me *to fix.* She was way too confident for my peace of mind. I used to see that kind of faith in Battle. People thought nothing about dropping their suspicions in his lap and leaving him to untangle the threads of the problem. No one ever gave a thought to whether Battle had the authority. They just expected him to handle it, and he did. With or without bending the law.

Now they were looking to me.

I stood up to leave. "Any other problems you want to hand me while I'm here?"

She grinned. "Nope. That pretty much clears my list for today, but I can probably think of a few more by tomorrow if you have some slack in your schedule."

"Uh huh. I just bet you could." I let myself out.

❦❦❦

Peels of laughter rolled over me as soon as I exited the library. Dog and Clay were catching criminals by wrestling in the small patch of grass bordering the front shrubs. Dog was winning, poking his nose into every uncovered tickle spot Clay had and sending a new scream of laughter into the air with each poke. As soon as I stepped onto the walkway, Dog's head came up. He put a paw on Clay to hold him there and looked straight at me.

Woof? (Do you need me?)

Hairs on the back of my neck stood up. I understood him as clearly as if he'd been speaking English. He wasn't my dog. I shouldn't be able to decipher his barks. He shouldn't be that aware of me. I didn't like this at all.

"Dog, you are going out to Hank Blackshear's place until we find your owners."

He looked down at Clay. *Woof.* (We're going.) Then he trotted over to me and sat beside my leg waiting for direction. Clay dusted himself off, a smile lingering on his face as he reached for the library book he'd perched precariously on one of the boxwoods. But the smile faded as he said goodbye to Dog.

"Well, I gotta be gettin' home."

"Where is home?"

"Out at the Bailey Mills Trailer Park. It's not one of the double-wides, but it's big enough for Daddy and me."

The Bailey Mills area wasn't my jurisdiction, technically. It was just outside the incorporated area of Mossy Creek. That's where my badge ended. "You meeting your mom or dad in town?"

"No, sir. Momma died a long time ago. Daddy's at work. I walk it. Takes a bit of time. That's why I can't be doin' this all summer."

I fought to keep the flash of anger off my face. An eight

or nine-year-old had absolutely no business walking miles of road by himself. Hell, he had no business riding a bike that far, but he didn't seem to know it. Jurisdiction or not, Daddy and I would be having a little chat.

"I tell you what. Police officers worry about kids walking that far alone. It's our job. And since I'm going out to the Blackshear place, it's just a bit farther to drop you off. So how about I give you a lift this time?"

"In the police Jeep?" His voice all but squeaked.

"Yep."

"Yes, sir!"

I flicked my arm at the Jeep in a signal to Dog, who not only knew I wanted him to move off my foot, but correctly interpreted the direction of my "flick" and waited by the Jeep for me to let him in. I shook my head. "You have got to be someone's dog."

"Wouldn't it be cool if you got to keep him?"

"Uh huh." But I silently gave Dog a warning look. *Do not get your hopes up.*

❦❦❦

Clay was a great kid. Ready smile. No complaints. Didn't chatter on constantly, but he wasn't silent either. By the time we'd arrived at the trailer park I'd begun to hope that Hannah and I were just jaded adults, jumping at shadows. The kid seemed well-adjusted, was even supposed to check in regularly with his neighbor while his dad was at work. Maybe his dad just needed a few parenting pointers about child safety.

Dog made the trip with his body curled in the back seat floorboard and his head resting on the console beside my elbow. Clay leaned over from time to time and kissed Dog on the head. Dog's tail thumped happily in response, but he didn't move.

I stopped when Clay said, pushed the emergency brake and scanned the area. There looked to be thirty or so trailers. Everything from an almost elegant double-wide to one trailer so small it could be easily pulled behind most trucks. Clay's trailer was on the smaller side of medium. I guess to a kid, it looked bigger.

The tiny yard around the trailer was a mess. Grass hadn't been mowed. If there'd ever been a flower bed there was no sign of it now. The trailer itself looked to be in reasonably good shape, at least on the outside.

From a chain inside his shirt, Clay produced a key. "So I don't lose it." Before he went inside, he hugged Dog and said, "You can bring Dog around to visit sometimes, right?"

"Clay, I'm pretty sure he belongs to someone." Two pairs of puppy-dog eyes drooped. Sighing, I said, "But we'll see."

He let himself in, and I walked over to the neighbor's trailer to let her know Clay was home and to...snoop. This might not be my jurisdiction, but I was already here. Earlene Hardeman lived in one of the tiny trailers. She was retired, no family. Living in a trailer and collecting a few dollars a week for "watching" Clay let her stretch her social security.

By the time I left, I knew more than I wanted to know about Samuel Atwood. He was a hard man, who ran a tight ship. Only noticed his son when he had to. Couldn't confirm the bruising but Earlene's comments painted a picture of borderline neglect. *A gray area if I'd ever seen one.* I'd be back. I left my number in case she ever needed to reach me.

🐾🐾🐾

"Hank Blackshear, I can't believe you are telling me to take this dog over to the Bigelow pound. They euthanize after fourteen days, for God's sake." I raised a brow and gave him my best official glare. The one that says: You and I both know I can't make you do this, but you don't want to irritate me.

Hank squared off and stared me down for all he was worth. And he's worth a lot. Solid man in the community. Solid marriage. Solid career. Solid values. Besides, when you play softball with a man, it's hard to intimidate him. He raised his brow right back at me. "I am *not* telling you to take that dog to Bigelow. I'm telling you that I don't have room for him here."

I snorted. The Blackshear Clinic was old but in first-class condition. When Hank took over, he brought everything up to the most modern standards. He'd added buildings and kennel runs so he'd have enough room for a proper large and small animal practice. I was looking at all that extra room over his shoulder right now.

"You had room to take care of Possum when Ed Brady needed you. Hell, Hank, I'm looking at two empty kennel runs!"

"Casey needs those. They're the closest to the house. When I'm out on a call, she can't be rolling all over the place trying to find a spot to put a dog when a client drops one off. And I can't ask my clients to handle their own dogs and walk to the back forty. No."

Damn. Casey's wheelchair trumped my need to get rid of this dog. What was I going to say that wouldn't sound completely insensitive? Even if I thought Hank was lying about needing *both* runs? Every instinct I had told me Hank could take this dog if he wanted to. Why on earth wouldn't he?

Dog had taken up residence by my side with one paw

on my boot again. I flicked my hand at him to tell him to get off and down. He did. I shook my head. Hank could see Dog would be no trouble at all, so what was Hank's real problem?

Couldn't be money. Ida had set up a small per diem for any animals Hank cared for at the request of the town. It wouldn't cost him anything.

Ida. I smiled.

She had lots of room. I had to talk to her about the council meeting anyway. She liked animals. She'd take Dog.

"Okay, Hank. You can't take him. I'll figure something out."

"Good man. You'll enjoy having him around. He's about the best-behaved Cattledog I've ever seen. It's like you trained him personally."

"Whoa. I'm not taking this dog in. My next stop is Ida's."

Hank smiled. It reminded me of one of Mac's smiles. I didn't like it. He thumped me on the back as I turned to leave. "Tell Ida I said hello. And don't forget to come out to the ball game Friday night. Casey wants you to coach third base for her girls."

I had to laugh. "The Blackshears, who just turned me down for a favor, now want a favor from me?"

"I turned you down. Casey wants the favor, and you're welcome to go tell her no. God knows *I* can't, but maybe you won't have any trouble with it."

Shaking my head, I declined. You don't tell a ray of sunshine that you're going to rain on her parade. "Tell her I'll be there. Get in the Jeep, Dog."

He obeyed. This time he plopped himself right in the middle of the passenger seat and grinned at me as I got in.

"You have not won, you mangy mutt." I leaned toward him to make my point.

He poked my nose gently with his and then looked out the window.

❦❦❦

As the crow flies, Ida is actually quite close to Hank and Casey. But getting there in the Jeep meant I had to circle around Trailhead Road. Dog enjoyed the scenery. I used the time to check with Sandy. The answer to every question I asked her was a resounding, "No." No one had called in about the dog. No one had placed a lost dog ad in the paper. No one had put up any fliers around town.

Time for Plan B. I turned onto the long drive up to the Hamilton place, and reached out to scratch Dog's ear. "You'll like it here."

Woof. (Uh huh, sure.) Then he promptly laid down on the seat in a sulk.

I was still laughing when I saw Ida walking up the drive toward the Jeep. I hit the brakes a little too quickly. Dog slid to the floorboard with a thump, and now I did feel like a jerk. "Sorry, Dog. I'm not used to a dog in the car."

He crawled back up on the seat and mumble-growled a scold at me. I cut the ignition and got out. He followed, perking up as he saw cows through the rail fence. Every muscle in his body tensed.

"No! Sit. Stay."

His butt hit the ground, but he wasn't happy about it. On the other hand, I felt quite clever. Nothing like saying just the right thing at the right time to avoid disaster. I sure didn't want Ida to realize this was a herding breed until I was halfway back to town. *Then* Dog could herd all he wanted. Right now I needed him to sit and be charming.

Ida had on some old jeans. Hers, not hand-me-downs. I could tell because they fit in all the right places. Her faded navy t-shirt was a fairly short one, the bottom edge slightly askew—like she's used the end of it to dry her hands. As she approached, she eyed Dog for a minute, then me.

Ida is a woman who, despite all her contemporary thoughts, still does something old-fashioned. She "takes stock" of a man. At least she took stock of me from time to time. I wasn't yet sure what her judgment was. As a chief, I passed muster. As a man, I realized the age difference was giving her fits. She couldn't put me neatly into a category. I wasn't a young friend of Rob's. Or just a town employee. Or a good neighbor.

I wasn't young enough to be completely out of the question, but I wasn't old enough to be acceptable to the logical side of her brain. I hadn't once crossed the line of acceptable behavior. I'd never given her cause to slap me down, to settle this issue once and for all...never given her the chance to politely decline my attentions.

The all-seeing, all-knowing, completely "together" Ida Hamilton was treading water, and she didn't know which way to swim for land. I certainly wasn't giving her any sign posts. I behaved myself, and let Ida draw her own conclusions about if there was or was not a little spark of chemistry there.

She was the fine upstanding mayor of Mossy Creek. A woman of principles and substance. Ida didn't want to get her fingers burnt or be gossiped about—unless she was orchestrating the gossip. And by now, she knew that nobody orchestrated me. What Ida couldn't control gave Ida pause.

I decided I liked her that way—uncertain but damned if she'd show it. I grinned as I realized that I wasn't the only one holding some "need to know" information close to the chest. Ida had herself a little problem, too. Explained a lot about why her relationship with Del hadn't progressed to something serious.

Ida broke the awkward silence first. "So, what brings you by today, Amos?"

I laughed. "Since you're meeting me on the road, I'm guessing Hank called you and you know damn well why I'm here."

She rubbed the back of her neck to lift her hair off it in the heat. "He did. I do."

"Did he tell you he refused to take this stray?"

"He didn't have room."

"We pay him to have room."

"We pay him when he has room."

This time both Dog and I snorted. How stupid did Hank and Ida think we were? "I've still got a problem."

"Why?"

"Because I have to park Dog somewhere. He can't stay with me and I don't have time to go all over town looking for a foster home."

"Keep him."

"Ida, I don't have a fence. He could be run over."

She cocked a hip and crossed her arms. "Do you see a fence that will hold him around here either?"

I looked back down the long drive to this spot and then forward to where I still couldn't see the house. "Hell, Ida. He'd have to pack a lunch and make a day of it to get to the street."

She laughed. "Point to you. But I can't take him in. This is prime growing season. I haven't got time to train a new dog where he can and cannot urinate. And Heaven help me if he digs in the beds. The Garden Club is counting on me this year. An untrained dog can do a lot of damage."

Stepping away from Dog I spread my hands like a magician showing off a trick. "Does this look like a dog, who's hard to train?"

"No."

"So, what's the problem, Ida?"

"He's a *herding breed* for God's sake. The entire time we've been talking, he's had one eye on you and one on the cows. You don't expect him to lie around all day twiddling his paws, do you? I'll be fetching him out of the pasture morning, noon and night. He'll herd my geese until they're nervous wrecks."

"All right. You're a hard woman, Ida. Remind me not to get on the wrong side of you."

That brought her up straight, sputtering. "What you mean by that?"

I signaled Dog back in the Jeep. He gave the cows one more soulful look and then vaulted into the driver's seat. I waved him over to the passenger side then hooked my hand on the door frame before I got in. When I turned to her, Ida was still waiting for my answer. "What I mean, Miss Ida, is that I feel sorry for poor Dwight. He hasn't got a prayer in hell if this council meeting's about the bike incident that ruined his suit. There's not a soul on his side and hasn't been since he lost that damned ram."

Fire flashed in Ida's eyes. I thought maybe I'd gone too far this time and that Ida-the-Mayor was going to take a chunk out of my hide. Instead, Ida-the-woman snapped her open mouth shut on her argument. She sized me up again, and then said, "You're right. I'm not happy about it, but you're right. Someone has to take the first step. And since you seem to think I'm the one who needs a little character improvement, it'll have to be me."

My eyebrows elevated. Ida Hamilton had just admitted she cared about my opinion of her. This was turning out to be some day.

She half-turned to walk back down the drive, but called over her shoulder, "You just be there, Chief. I'll bring the crow."

🐾🐾🐾

"We're home." I swore. "No. *I'm* home. You're visiting, and if Josie finds out you're here, we're both in trouble."

You're in trouble already. You're talking to a dog like he understands you. Had been all day long. What was I supposed to do? Ignore him? He'd been with me all day long because Sandy'd suddenly decided to clean the office. Said she couldn't have the dog around the cleaning chemicals.

So Dog made calls with me. Even lay quietly beside my chair when I stopped by O'Day's on the way home for a consolation beer. Michael wouldn't hear of him being left in the Jeep. Any decent Irish pub allowed dogs. But even with all that high-and-mighty-dog-lover rhetoric Michael wouldn't take Dog home. That was the last straw. I accepted my defeat.

But I wasn't going to suffer in silence. I put my gun and my keys on top of the old-fashioned, bench-seat hall tree that was about the only thing to survive Josie's purge of furnishings. She said the patina of the oak was "fabulous" and I liked the framed top that functioned as a shelf. There weren't any kids running around to grab my gun, but I felt better with my work gun up the minute I walked in the door.

Business taken care of, I turned to Dog, who waited as patiently as always for some command. "Who *are* you? An alien? Stray dogs don't act this way, buddy. Okay. Let's do this." I began the tour of the house.

"Are you familiar with the movie *Turner and Hooch*?"
Woof.

"Good. Then you'll know what I mean when I say, 'This is *not* your chair...'"

🐾🐾🐾

By the time the council room began to fill, I was tired of explaining about Dog. I'd brought him with me tonight for the same reason he'd been with me all day: new cow-leather chair. I had a mental image of Dog trying to herd the damned thing and then nipping at it when it wouldn't move into the corner. So Dog was my new best friend. He went everywhere with me, because I couldn't leave him in a closed car in the summer, and "stay in the Jeep" was the only command he didn't seem to know. Dog thought it meant, "Wiggle out the window and quietly dog my every step."

Clay wasn't the only kid in town who fantasized about Mossy Creek getting its very own police dog. Kids in the park wanted to see his badge. Patty Campbell had hustled right over to the station to make sure I had the proper collar and leash.

Right now Katie Bell wanted to know if it was true that we had a drug lab in town and Dog was here to sniff it out.

Woof. (Oh, puh-lease.)

I bit my lip and told Katie, "No." Then I shook hands with a couple of the council at the table, raised an eyebrow at Ida, and took a seat as close to the back as I could get away with. Looked like every kid in town had shown up in support of Little Ida, who sat primly in the first row, a militant look on her face. I smiled. Blood will tell.

Dwight bustled in and skidded to an unhappy halt beside me as his consciousness registered the number of people in the room under four feet tall. Then he mentally counted the stern-faced parents with them. You could see his head move as he counted.

I don't believe I've ever seen a man with a face more pinched and sour than Dwight's. Probably knew he'd already lost. Dog felt sorry for him and gave him a nuzzle of encouragement. It was more of a goose really. Dwight squeaked, glared at me, and then mustered his dignity for the walk to the podium. Once there he fumbled through his coat pockets, his back pockets; rummaged through his briefcase, and then did it all again. The more he scrabbled around, the more stressed he looked. Even the other council members were beginning to give each other questioning looks.

Finally Dwight drew himself up and narrowed his eyes. "Okay. Which one of you took it? Well, it doesn't matter. I'm starting this meeting gavel or not!"

Crunch, crunch, crunch. Gnaw, gnaw, gnaw.

Slowly, like a condemned man I glanced down to my right and then closed my eyes. Dog was happily making splinters out of Dwight's precious gavel. I'm many things, but I'm not a coward.

"Excuse me!" I picked up the dog-slobbery mess with two fingers and held it up. "I...uh...I think I have the gavel." I walked it up to the podium. The crowd was howling with laughter, but I noticed that Ida hadn't snickered the first snicker.

I mumbled my apologies and the promise of a new gavel as soon as I could order one. Dwight just stared at his symbol of office with disbelieving eyes. I didn't blame him. I didn't want to touch it either. Gently, I laid it on the table and returned to my seat. Most of the laughing had subsided by the time I was silently promising Dog horrible retribution.

Ida stood in the silence and shushed the crowd further by waving her hands downward. "I'm going to break protocol tonight and open the session instead of our esteemed Chair, Mr. Truman." She looked straight at me. "I'm also going to do something I should have done a long time ago. I'm going to tell you about a man who never gives up. Someone Mossy Creek can count on. Someone we like to ignore because he's our conscience in many ways. He watches our pennies. He pushes us to be more. He tells us when we're wrong."

She scooted around her chair to stand next to Dwight.

I was hoping she'd catch his jaw because it was about to hit the floor. She laid a hand on his shoulder. "Oh boy, does he tell us when we're wrong.

"What we forget is that Dwight was raised to be a pillar of the community. His Daddy decided Dwight would follow in his footsteps. When other kids were out playing, Dwight was being tutored in civics or enrolled in one of the hundreds of community service projects his Daddy thought were important for Dwight's moral fiber and work ethic."

She looked around the room. "It worked. Dwight has never shirked a responsibility in his life. Certainly not when it came to Mossy Creek civic duty." A hushed murmur of agreement issued from the audience. "It's my opinion that Dwight could actually use a little time to enjoy the Mossy Creek he's helped build."

The kids didn't know what was going on, but the parents clapped and agreed. You could see several of them looking at Dwight with new eyes. Not a one of them had thought about the fact that someone had had to do all the things Dwight did. Sometimes it takes more courage to paddle against the flow.

Even Dog woofed a couple of times. Dwight looked downright shocked. While he was composing himself, Ida signaled someone in the doorway. Rob Hamilton wheeled in one of the sleekest adult bikes I'd seen in a long time. Wheeled it right up in front of the council table and flipped the kickstand.

"Councilman Truman," Ida said, "the citizens of Mossy Creek would like to thank you for all you hard work through the years and present you with this token of our affection. May you ride it in health and good fun."

Everyone else was clapping for an overcome Dwight, who looked pleased as punch and red as a box of Valentine candy. I was clapping for Ida. She knew it. I gave her a little salute. Dog and I went home. There wouldn't be any more council business tonight.

🐾🐾🐾

The Friday night ball game crowd included one young man I was particularly interested in seeing. Clay Atwood sat in the bleachers. By himself. When he saw Dog, he vaulted off his seat and met us halfway to the field.

"I was hoping you'd bring him. Heyya, boy! Remember me?"

Dog's reception was obviously one of an old friend. The wrestling commenced immediately. I hauled the two of them apart and asked Clay where his dad was.

"Said he had some business and I should stay here until he got back."

"Uh huh. Tell you what. Why don't you sit in the dugout with the team and hold Dog for me?"

"Really?"

"Sure. You have to be nice to the girls or Casey Blackshear will have you scrubbing out the kennels. No poking, teasing, or arguing."

"Aw! But Caralee's on the team. She's mad at me about the library reading books."

"Sorry. Either you agree or you sit in the stands and Dog is lonely all night."

Dog whined and cocked his head. He did a right nice job of begging. I appreciated it. I wanted Clay in the dugout with the team so I wouldn't miss meeting his father. I handed Clay the ball bag I was carrying for Casey and watched them scamper over to the bench.

Casey rolled up beside me. "You look worried."

"Girls with softballs scare me."

She rolled her eyes. "It's more than that." But she didn't push it. She had a game to coach. I imagined I might get another question or two from her on the subject of my worry after the game.

Fortunately, I didn't have to mention Clay to convince Casey I had troubles on my mind. Like Laurie Grey. New to town, an interesting woman and, according to Sandy, a woman who was more than a little ill with no support system in sight.

Casey's girls played a great game against one of their arch rivals—the Big Sky Ravens, rich little girls with fancy equipment and the best coach money could buy. But our team has an unshakable desire to win. They believe that they can beat any team. That's Casey's gift to coaching.

We'd have won, too, if it hadn't been for that unfortunate incident in the last inning. Score tied. We had two outs. I had a runner on third, a bunt on the way, and the opposing pitcher on the move.

Everything depended on my runner getting home and the pitcher fumbling that ball. I did what any base coach does. I signaled run, shouted, yelled and encouraged. I did lots of things, but I am *all* but certain I did *not* signal Dog to streak out onto the field and grab that softball.

Not that Foxer Atlas, the game's umpire, cared. He threw me, the dog, Casey and our girls out of the game for willful interference. Foxer and I were chest to chest for a while there. I don't like being called a cheat; the parents were screaming for my blood. I could see Katie scribbling for all she was worth.

"Foxer, for God's sake. I'm the Chief of Police. I do not cheat!"

"Well, your dog does."

I threw my hands up. "How is this possibly my fault? I wasn't holding his leash, and he's *not my dog*."

"You'rrrre outta here!" You could tell Foxer was enjoying himself immensely.

My lawyer muscled between us at this point. As big as Mac Campbell is, I couldn't even see around him to give Foxer a piece of my mind. "Give it up, Amos," Mac ordered. "Dog is your dog. He's with you 24/7."

"He's not my dog. He'd eat the chair if I left him at home. Besides that, this is all Hank's fault. He wouldn't take him."

"Then take Dog down to the Bigelow pound or give him away."

"You keep missing the point, Mac. He's not mine to give away. His owners are going to want him back."

"His *owner* needs to wise up and smell the dog hair."

Woof.

I looked down. When did this happen? When did Dog become my dog? I smiled. Maybe it wouldn't be so bad. But our softball signals could use some work. I leaned down to scratch his ears. "Huh, boy?"

Then I frowned as I realized Clay and his father had gotten away without my noticing. Okay, tomorrow. First thing. Dog and I were making a house call.

🐾🐾🐾

"This is still not your chair," I warned Dog as we tumbled in the door from the ball game. Tonight he didn't wait for me to tell him it was okay to roam the house. "And you are going to have to figure out a way to make it up to all those girls. And Casey. You have to apologize to her."

He stopped on the way to the kitchen to look back at me. *Woof?* (Again?)

"Yeah. And you'll keep apologizing until she starts speaking to us again."

I noticed the light blinking on the answering machine. "That's probably from Casey, and I'm not defending you. You're taking the rap for this."

The machine whirred through its process and announced the message time in a monotone. Barely a few minutes ago. "Chief? This is Earlene Hardeman. You told me to call. About Clay Atwood and his daddy. He's hit him this time. Backhanded him into the trailer. I hope this is you. I can't read these tiny numbers that well. If you get this, you come on now."

"Dog!" I grabbed my keys and my gear off the coat rack. I could hear Dog's nails scrabbling for purchase as he turned the corner out of the kitchen.

I had Mac on the phone and caught up on the details before I'd pulled out of my driveway. "I don't care what you have to do or who you have to wake up. I'm bringing that boy back. I want him in emergency care with a family in Mossy Creek. He's not going through family services over in Bigelow. I want him here where he'll feel comfortable. Cut the corner off a circle if you have to, but you call me back in five minutes and tell me it's done and I have the authority to pull that child out of that trailer."

That done, my next call was to the sheriff's department to let them know I was rolling on this call and would advise if I needed assistance. The chances of a county car being any closer than me were slim and none. As I suspected, they were more than happy to let me handle this.

Most of the trailers were dark by the time I pulled up to the park. The Atwood trailer was one of them. I saw Earlene look out her window as I got out of the Jeep. I nodded. The curtain winked shut.

Dog trotted alongside me to the Atwood's. I knocked. No one stirred. I knocked louder. This time a complaint rumbled through the trailer, followed by a begrudging and gruff, "Hold your horses."

The light flared on. Samuel Atwood pulled open the

aluminum door, but left the screen door closed. He'd pulled on a hasty pair of pants, hadn't bothered with the snap. His t-shirt was clean.

"Mr. Atwood?"

"*You?* No need you coming around here. I already disciplined the boy for letting the dog loose."

"Could I see the boy?"

"What for? I already told you I took care of it. I'd think you'd have better things to do than come around here rousting us out of bed over a little mix-up like that ball field thing."

"Mr. Atwood, let me make myself a little more clear. I'm not here because of what the boy did. I'm here because of what you've done and to be sure the boy's all right after your discipline. We've had a complaint. I need to see Clay. Clay, you in there?"

Dog whined.

"Who complained? That old biddy?" He pointed at Earlene's trailer. She can't see squat without her glasses on, and she goes to bed at eight o'clock. You just wait. My boy'll tell you he's fine."

I shifted back from the door. "Fine. Get him out here or I'm going to need to come inside and see for myself."

For the first time Samuel began to look impatient. "Well, he ain't here. He run off. I gave the kid a little swat, and he run off. That's what he does. Runs off and has his sissy cry and then comes slinking back."

Anger has no place in law enforcement. It clouds the judgment. I did my best to shove mine as far inside as possible, but it pulsed insistently. "How old is Clay?"

Samuel shifted back and forth on his feet, he could feel the noose tightening. "He'll be nine come September."

"You let a nine-year-old boy go off, unsupervised, in the middle of the night? And you went to bed?"

"I was just restin'. There's nothin' to worry about. He'll be back. He always comes back. Just ask that old biddy over there."

Part of me wanted to haul Atwood out of the trailer and down to jail, but Clay was my first priority. Without taking my eyes off Atwood, I asked my partner for help. "Find him, Dog. Go get me Clay."

Like a greyhound off the mark, Dog streaked away. He'd been quietly whining and leaning toward the woods on our right. I had a pretty good idea that's where Clay was, probably curled up against one of the old-as-time trees and feeling guilty about hating his father. He didn't know he wasn't alone in that.

While I waited, I stared at Atwood. Sometimes the silence is palpable this far out from town. Any little sound carries in the stillness. Soon enough Dog began barking and I heard a faint but definite exclamation from a surprised kid. Atwood huffed. "Told you."

"That's good. That's real good. Here's what the deal is, Atwood. I'm going to go find those two, and when I get back here, if you're still here, I'll be arresting you. Child endangerment, neglect, abuse and anything else I can make stick."

"What if I'm not here?"

For the first time in what seemed like hours, I smiled. Atwood wasn't as stupid as he looked. "Then if I ever find you, I'll be charging you with all of that plus abandonment. But one way or the other, that little boy will not be hit again. Not while I'm drawing breath."

A second after Atwood shut the door, I heard the sounds of cabinets being opened and drawers being slammed. I grabbed the high-beam out of the back of the Jeep and went hunting for the boys. They met me before I'd gone more than a hundred yards. Clay ran at me so hard, I stumbled when I caught him. I hugged him close and made room for Dog, who seemed to think it was his due as a hero.

Clay seemed content to hold up in the middle of the field and collect himself. I kept an eye on Earlene's trailer in the distance. I didn't want Samuel causing any problems. On the off chance that Sandy might be right where I needed her, I pulled my walkie and keyed Mossy Creek dispatch. "Sandy?"

"Right here, Chief."

I leaned the walkie against my forehead for a moment. Then I keyed again. "I do not know what I'd do without you. Over."

"Not nearly as well," she informed me. "Mac called. Said you might need me. Over."

"I do. I need you to haul out to the Bailey Mills trailer park." I described Earlene's trailer and asked Sandy come out tonight and get a full statement while the details were fresh.

"I'm on it, Chief! And Mac said to call him pronto. Over."

"Yes, ma'am. Out."

❦❦❦

A couple of hours later, Clay and I stood on Mac and Patty's porch saying our goodbyes. Mac had not only cut every bit of red tape he could find, he made sure that Clay landed on their doorstep. In barely more than an hour, Mac had had them approved for emergency foster care. Since they'd already been approved for state adoption, it was a pretty small leap to emergency foster care. Especially when you have a father who's a judge and willing to call in favors.

Clay had taken to Mac and Patty like a duck to water. There's a whole lot to like in Mac and Patty. Great house, great dogs and a lot of love saved up waiting. Even so, he wasn't quite ready to let go of my hand or Dog's neck. Patty whispered for me not to rush him and took their labs back inside. Maddie, the pale yellow one had been reluctant to leave Clay's side, but after giving some sort of doggie instruction look to Dog, she allowed Patty to drag her back inside.

Before Mac closed the door, he said, "Son, you just knock when you're ready to come in. We'll be here."

I nodded and waited for Clay to tell me whatever it was he'd been working up to all night. He kissed Dog on the head, then looked at me. "He didn't want me."

"Maybe he was just scared. He may be back."

"No." Clay's eyes were bone dry and his voice didn't so much as quiver. "I mean he didn't want me before. So I don't want him now."

I wasn't sure if I was supposed to argue or agree that it was okay to feel that way. This was Patty's job. Not mine. I didn't know what to do, especially since it was my fault his father was gone. Battle would have been proud of how I handled this one. I sure as hell nudged it the way I wanted it to play out.

"Hey," I said, "why don't we give it some time?"

He nodded, kissed Dog again and knocked on the door. Just before it opened he said, "I'll be okay."

Patty gathered him in. I don't think I've ever seen her look happier. Clay is definitely going to be one of her visionary pieces if everything works out like we've planned.

Dog followed me to the car, looking over his shoulder once or twice. As we reached the car, he balked and sat down.

Woof. (Do you need me?)

In that moment my heart sank, because I knew exactly what he meant. My dog was asking me to be a hero. "Do I need you? Like do I need you as much as a scared young boy who's just lost his father?" I took a couple of deep

47

breaths. I sure as hell didn't want to cry on the phone to Patty. And then I dialed her number.

"Hey, I need a favor. I need you to take Dog."

"What? Why?"

"Clay needs him more than me." I cleared my throat. "Just open the door and let Clay's dog in."

She did.

I went home to my leather chair and discovered that you need a lot more than a leather chair to be happy.

From the desk of Katie Bell

Lady Victoria Salter Stanhope
The Clifts
Seaward Road
St. Ives, Cornwall TR3 7PJ
United Kingdom

Dear Vick:

Hello from the Assistant Editor of the Mossy Creek Gazette. How do you like my new stationery? To bring you up to date since last fall, when we solved the mystery of who burned down our old high school (The Fang and Claw Club will never have secret initiations again) plans are being drawn up for the new building. But the wheels of progress turn as slowly as an old grist mill when Mossy Creek is running low, which is "not at all."

But Ida Hamilton Walker, known for being the only gun-toting mayor in the mountains of north Georgia, is primed and ready to prod her nephew, Ham Bigelow, the governor, if he doesn't get moving. Chief Royden is watching her closely "to prevent violence." He says that with a grin, but we all know that it's Ida he's sticking close to, not her guns.

This may be the hottest weather we've had since 1954, when the mercury down at Pop's Garage popped right out of the thermometer. Mossy Creek occupies a cove with two-thirds of it cupped by the mountains like a hand shielding it from the north wind. That works well in the winter, but with the conditions just right, in the summer it's like having the top on a teapot with the flame on high. We cook supper early in the morning.

Most folks call the evening meal "dinner" but here, if you're over sixty-and I'm not—"dinnertime" is still at noon. But even those over sixty have microwaves to heat up their food when it's really hot. The children head for the creek and those of us lucky enough to work in air-conditioned offices stay late. But the old folks sit on the porch with a paper fan and talk about the past.

You remember what I told you last fall? That I've asked Creekites to share their stories about friendship with me. Well, after reading Amos's story you know why I've learned to take a pocket full of tissues when I conduct the interviews. In fact, I'm going to run a feature story every month. Let me know what you think.

Your sentimental friend,
Katie "True Confessions" Bell

"My friends are my estate."

— *Emily Dickinson*

❦❦❦

OPAL and the SUGGS SISTERS

Chapter Two

I'd seen a lifetime of late summer mornings like this one. After a week of scorching temperatures, last night's rain had swept cool air into the Blue Ridge range of the Appalachians. The sun struggled to peek over the south slope of Colchik Mountain, as if it were already exhausted from its vain attempts to clear away the smoke which hung like a gray blanket above the valley that sheltered Mossy Creek. The filmy layers cut off the Suggs farm from the rest of the world. No breeze stirred to help the sun on this cool September morning. The air was so still, you'd think it had died.

Weary just from getting out of bed, I leaned my forehead against the cool windowpane as I felt the loneliness of the empty farmhouse close in around me.

"It's a good day to die."

"Oh, hush your mouth, Opal May Suggs. You're no more ready to die than I was at fifty-nine."

My head banged against the glass, and I turned to glare at the completely empty room. "LordaMercy, Ruby. You might warn a body before sneaking up on them."

"If Opal wants to die, she can."

"Thank you, Pearl." I headed downstairs to make breakfast, not bothering to hide my sass. "Nice to have your permission."

51

"We're not talking about permission," Amethyst said. "You can die just by hankerin' to. Remember how Mama passed? After Daddy went, she missed him so much, she decided to follow. She up and died a year to the day after Daddy."

"Wasn't a thing wrong with her," Garnet added. "Doc Campbell said so. Mama was strong as Colchik Mountain until the day she died."

I could almost see my oldest sister nodding sagely, but somehow the Garnet I pictured was around twenty, the one I knew when we six sisters lived at home and were thick as thieves and gossiped about everything and everyone in Mossy Creek. The Six Suggs Sisters, we were called. If they have the option, people always opted for alliteration. But the tag didn't matter to us. We were best friends, and swore there would never be a time when we'd be apart.

Time has a way of making liars out of us all.

"Mama always said she was rock hard, just like the mountains."

I was wondering when my fifth sister—Sapphire, the shy one—was going to chime in.

Rocks had been a continuing theme with Mama, as her children's names testified. Her daughters were each named after a birthstone, though not necessarily their own. Mama started with Garnet, January's birthstone, then went down the list from there, skipping several she didn't think were proper names, such as aquamarine and peridot. There'd been a problem naming the only boy in the family, born fourth in line, but she and Daddy had finally settled on Jasper. I was the baby of the family, so Mama had made it only to October before she stopped conceiving. Fortunate probably, since topaz and turquoise were the only choices left.

Although, I always thought my life might've been different if I'd been named Topaz. Bright, sparkling and golden, instead of milky white.

"Opal can't die yet." Ruby had always been the bossy one. "She's still got business to attend to."

I was concentrating on making legs that didn't always work right take my old body safely down the stairs, so I reacted to Ruby's bossiness rather than her words. "I can die if I want to."

"Why do you want to die, Opal?" Sapphire asked.

"I'll be seventy-nine-years-old, next March, and I feel twice that. I can't half-see to read Katie Bell's column in the *Gazette*, and forget watching reruns of *Little House on the Prairie*. I get the misery in my back every time it rains. And this cough won't leave me be."

Ruby harumphed. "Heck's underbritches, Opal, you still put up enough sweet corn from your own garden every year to feed an army. You're healthy as a horse."

I focused on the four steps remaining, as if lowering my head could hide the emotion in my eyes. Would five spirits—even five upstanding Christian spirits like my dear, departed sisters—understand the loneliness of a woman who'd outlived her usefulness? A woman who'd never had much usefulness to begin with? A woman nobody but the preacher and the police chief came to see? Even though I was the baby in the family, I'd never been spoiled. I'd always been the practical one, the sister whose feet were planted firmly on the ground.

I snorted with more than exertion. So when did practicality include talking to ghosts?

Even if they'd still been flesh and blood, my sisters wouldn't understand. Especially not Ruby. She didn't have a sympathetic bone in her body...or lack there-of.

"Heck's underbritches yourself, Ruby," I said. "I'm talking to ghosts, aren't I? To my five sisters who haven't all been together in one room since the night after Sapphire's wedding in 1948. Isn't living in the past a sure sign death's come knockin' on your door?"

Ruby laughed. "Not all the time. Sometimes it just means you're crazy as an old hoot owl."

I wanted to stick my tongue out at her, but there wasn't much point.

Tittering laughter echoed down the stairwell. I'd long since ceased being surprised that the dearly departed still enjoyed a good joke.

"Living isn't fun anymore," I said. "Might as well join my sisters at the Pearly Gates." I paused at the bottom of the stairs to catch my breath. Only then did Ruby's earlier words catch me. "What business do I still have to attend to?"

"You have to—"

A scrambling of panicked voices shushed Pearl.

"You can't tell her," Garnet insisted.

"She's got to figure it out for herself," Amethyst said.

I could imagine Pearl's hands fluttering, like they used to when she got flustered. Pearl had always had the prettiest hands of all us sisters. "Well, if it's fixing up the homestead, I don't care how much money y'all help me win, it won't be enough to coax construction workers this far into the mountains to fix a run-down old farmhouse. Not decent workers, anyway. The good ones all head for Atlanta where they give 'em decent pay. What's the point, anyway? Isn't as if anybody wants this old place."

"Your business on earth ain't the house," Ruby said.

"*Isn't* the house," I corrected automatically.

"Well, la-de-dah, *Miss* English Teacher," Ruby said, working in a reminder of my prim, unmarried state. I was the only unmarried Suggs sister, which was why I still lived in the house we'd all been born in.

"Your business is related to the house," Amethyst explained. "But all we can tell you is it's coming soon, so be on the look-out."

"*It*, huh? Not he or she or they. So *it*'s a thing, this business of mine, not a person."

"Maybe so, maybe not," Garnet said. "Can't say."

I harumphed. "Y'all sure are full of yourselves, and about what's happening in the days to come."

"'Farther along, you'll know all about it,'" Amethyst said primly. "Like the hymn says."

There was a chorus of amens among the sisters, ending that line of discussion as effectively as a prayer. I'd already tried cajoling information about the future out of them, but they were forthcoming on only one subject.

"So you can tell me who's gonna win Sunday's NASCAR race, but you can't give me any useful information."

"Winning all that money ain't useful?" Ruby asked. "How else are you gonna fix up the house?"

"It isn't useful unless I can find somebody to fix it," I said. "Besides, I mean spiritually useful. Spiffing up the house is an earthly concern. At this stage in my life, I'm more concerned about fixing up my mansion on a street paved with gold."

"Don't worry about that," Pearl said sweetly. "Your mansion is all—"

"Time to go, ladies," Garnet announced.

"But Pearl was just about to tell me—"

"Hut Stricklin in Daytona this coming Sunday."

I blinked at Amethyst's change of subject, then as quickly as I could, reached for the chalk hanging from twine on the chalkboard next to the telephone. "Hut? What kind of name is that? Is he a new driver?"

No answer. Not that I thought there would be. Information about the weekend's race was always the last thing said. Amethyst, whose husband had been an avid NASCAR fan, always whispered it to me right before my sisters skedaddled for the day.

I glanced at the clock on the stove. Six-thirty. Couldn't call the bookie in Atlanta yet. He'd already yelled at me once for getting him out of bed before noon.

I started the coffee and meandered onto the porch as the brew began to percolate. The sun now touched the roof of the barn, but there was no glare from the rusted, warped tin. An early hawk circled the walnut grove up the hill, its overgrown state even more obvious since last night's rain had perked up the knee-high weeds.

"That's one thing I *can* do with all this money, I suppose," I muttered to no one in particular. "Hire some kid in Mossy Creek to mow the weeds. If he can get Daddy's John Deere to start up, that is."

Watching the hawk dive into the trees after his breakfast, I sighed.

This was the loneliest time, when my sisters had just left. The few minutes between missing the camaraderie we'd shared growing up and convincing myself I was hallucinating. Although if I was, I sure was good at picking NASCAR winners, something I knew nothing about. The bookie asked me once how come I was so good at it. When I told him my dead sister told me who was gonna win, he reacted the way I thought he would—like I was a crazy old hoot owl.

"And I reckon I am," I said out loud. "Comes from ghosts being the only friends I've got."

With no other destination, my words drifted down the deeply-rutted, muddy gravel road winding down the mountain...to the world that passed me by.

Feeling tears sting my eyes, I turned impatiently. No sense feeling sorry for myself when there was a day's work to be done. Even if I couldn't climb a ladder to put a new tin roof on the barn, I could polish Grandmama's silver tea service and sweep the...

My thoughts trailed off as I caught a movement out the corner of my eye. Thinking it was probably a fox or stray dog, I glanced over my shoulder.

There about a hundred yards up the hill was a young man, carrying a dead rabbit toward my barn. He saw me two seconds after I saw him. Both of us froze, like deer sizing up the situation, deciding if we should run. Everything about the young man looked underfed. He was short, dark and skinny as a fence post. His clothes were thin, too, even considering the past week's hot weather.

Had the boy shot the rabbit? If he had, that meant he had a gun.

I did, too, but my granddaddy's loaded Smith and Wesson was in my nightstand drawer upstairs.

Should I lock the door and call Amos Royden? Technically, I was out of the Mossy Creek Police Chief's jurisdiction, but he'd get here quicker than a sheriff's car all the way from Bigelow.

Even as the thoughts ran through my head, the young man started down the hill. As he came closer, I could see he was of Hispanic origin. The world outside Mossy Creek had been overrun with illegal aliens from across the southern border. I knew that from watching the evening news on one of the two channels my old TV picked up. A few may have passed through Mossy Creek, but I didn't go into town much anymore, so I'd never seen one up close and personal and didn't know anything about them.

"Stop right there," I shouted when he was just outside the back gate. I heard the panic in my voice and cleared my throat. "What do you want?"

He looked tired and scared and very, very young. I could see now he was as much a boy as a young man. He held up the rabbit. "Please, ma'am, don't call police. I pay you for..." His face contorted as he struggled for the word. Finally he gave up and supplied the Spanish. "...*conejo*."

His offer took me aback. Seemed like a painfully honest thing to do. Was it a trick?

"That isn't *my* rabbit," I told him. "That's one of God's creatures."

"This is not your land?" he asked.

"Well, of course it's my land. This and the two hundred thirty acres surrounding it."

He nodded solemnly. "Then this is your rabbit."

I was dealing with a smart young man, one who listened closely and learned quickly. "How'd you kill it?"

He seemed surprised at the question. "I set snare last night. This morning, rabbit caught."

"And just why were you taking it to my barn?"

He glanced guiltily over his shoulder.

"You sleep there last night?"

He took an anxious step toward me. "Please, ma'am. I come in from other side. We— *I* think nobody live here."

My ears were sharp enough to catch his slip. "*We*, huh? Who else is hidden up there?"

His head dropped.

"Do I have to call the sheriff to find out?"

He looked up in panic. "No! Please. I..." He glanced up the hill, back at me, then turned and emitted a shrill whistle. A couple of seconds later, the barn door opened slowly and two dark heads peeked out.

The young man waved them forward, and two young girls slowly walked toward the house.

"What in tarnation...?" I peered closer at the young man. "How old are you, son?"

He straightened his shoulders. "Fifteen, ma'am. These are my sisters, Consuela and Inez."

Realizing I still had a death grip on the door latch, I let go and turned, adjusting the glasses sliding down my nose. The young girls were as skinny as the boy. One looked as if she was several years younger than her brother, maybe around ten. The other was a few years younger than that. "LordaMercy. Y'all are just kids. Where are your folks?"

"Folks?" the boy asked, clearly confused.

"Your kin, son. Your parents. And what's your name, by the by?"

"I am named Arturo, ma'am. Arturo Sanchez. Our parents are..." He glanced sadly at his sisters. "They are gone."

"Gone as in run away, or gone as in dead?"

"Our parents have gone to the Blessed Virgin, ma'am."

"LordaMercy, you're on your own?" Before I knew it, I'd taken a step off the porch. I stopped myself. Didn't pay to be too trusting in this day and time. Was I really crazy as an old hoot owl? I was about to invite them into my house.

I searched their young faces, pinched and anxious. When my eyes fell on the youngest, she scratched her leg, drawing my attention to the mass of bites covering them.

"LordaMercy! Y'all are eat up. Come on in the house and let me put some Calamine on you."

They didn't move.

At that moment, all my doubts fled. These were good, honest children, scared and alone. "I was about to fix breakfast."

The possibility of real food perked them up, and the girls glanced hopefully toward their brother. The older girl, Consuela, said something to him in Spanish, and he snapped back a reply. She lowered her head.

Arturo straightened his shoulders. "We have not come for charity, ma'am. We are on the way to Mexico, to our grandmama."

I'd been an English teacher at the Mossy Creek High School until it burned down over twenty years ago, and had known native English speaking kids his age who wouldn't have been able to come up with the word "charity." Arturo and his sisters had obviously been forced to take enough hand-outs during their short lives to be well acquainted with the word. "Tell you what, son. I'll share my breakfast with you, if you'll share your rabbit with me. I'll make a nice rabbit stew, if you'll dig up some carrots and potatoes from my garden."

Arturo hesitated. Connie—I'd already nicknamed

Consuela—said something to him again in Spanish. Arturo didn't reply this time, just gazed at me steadily, as if trying to find the hidden charity in my deal.

"Do you know English, Connie?"

The girl's eyes widened, but she knew who I was talking to. "*Si*...I mean yes, ma'am."

"Then please use it, all of you," I said. "It's rude to speak in Spanish when you know the other person can't understand. It makes them feel like you're talking behind their back."

"Yes, ma'am."

"And call me Miss Opal." I pulled the screen door open. "Y'all coming in or not?"

Inez took a step forward, then stopped, glancing at her brother. Arturo nodded once, though with obvious reluctance.

I tried not to show my relief as Connie opened the back gate for Inez. "It'll take me a few minutes to take care of your sisters' bites and get breakfast on the table, Arturo. Why don't you go ahead and clean up that rabbit?" For his own sake, I knew I needed to make him work for their food.

"*Si*, Miz Opal." He winced. "I mean yes."

"That's all right, son. I know what '*si*' means. Come right on in when you're done. No need to knock."

"Yes, Miz Opal. And..." He visibly struggled with the words.

"Si?" I prompted.

His face relaxed into a smile. "*Gracias*."

🐾🐾🐾

The girls looked around in wonder as they came into my house, as if it were a palace. Knowing it was no such thing, my heart went out to them even more. How had they been living, to consider this rundown, hundred-year-old farmhouse a wonder?

But their awe made me look around with new eyes as I ushered them toward the medicine cabinet in the bathroom. I'd been feeling sorry for myself the past couple of years, but maybe I was richer than I'd thought.

I quickly discovered that Inez was a little chatterbox, freely mixing Spanish words with English. I could mostly keep up with her meaning, though, and when I couldn't, Connie interpreted.

What I learned nearly broke my heart. After their father died on the job in Raleigh, North Carolina, their mother left, determined to return to her family in Mexico. They had an old car, which Arturo drove and kept running. Their mother had been sick before they left Raleigh, and the summer heat made her worse. Because they were not legal aliens, she feared what would happen to her children if they stopped to get help so she wouldn't allow it. She died soon after they'd entered the mountains. Somewhere south of Asheville, as close as I could make it. They buried her there, deep in the woods, a crudely fashioned cross her only marker.

Connie cried because her mother hadn't received the last rites.

Arturo had pushed them on the same day. The car died a few days later, on the lonely mountain road that wound its way around to the Suggs farm, then eventually down into Mossy Creek. They'd been living in the car for a week, with Arturo scrounging for food. He'd found my barn yesterday evening, and had led his sisters there after dark.

My eyes filled with tears as I blew on Connie's legs to dry the Calamine. Such hardships, for girls so young. I'd grown up poor, too, but nothing like them. At least I'd had the wealth of two healthy parents who put a roof over my head and food on the table three times a day.

I hugged them both, then led them into the kitchen to make breakfast. I'd spent enough time soothing the girls' bites that Arturo should've been there, but he wasn't. Hearing a loud banging on the back porch, I opened the door to find him tacking up the screen that had come loose on the side.

He turned guiltily. "I found the tools inside."

Suddenly, it was like the clouds had parted, allowing a beam of light to reach me from Heaven. I knew what my business was here on Earth. I knew why my sisters had provided me with money.

To emphasize the point, a cool morning breeze wafted through the screen. As it tickled my ear, I heard Garnet's voice whisper, "'Yes."

Overcome with enlightenment, it took me a moment to recollect my voice. "Good. I see you know how to use them."

He straightened proudly. "My father teach me. I help him sometime, on jobs."

"Exactly how good are you? I've got enough work around here to keep you busy for a month of Sundays, but some of it's pretty involved."

His dark eyes lit up. "You have work for me? For wages?"

I nodded. "Plus room and board for you and your sisters."

"Thank you, Miz Opal. I am so young, no one would hire me. And..." He looked down at the hammer in his hand. "I don't have green card."

I placed an arm around his shoulder and hugged him. "We'll see what we can do about that. Meanwhile, we'll also see about the best way to get you to your grandmother's."

He hugged me back, fiercely, like a boy forced into a man's responsibilities but suddenly allowed to be a boy again. "*Gracias!* I mean..."

"Don't worry about it." I winked at the girls watching from the door. "Now, let's get something to eat."

❦❦❦

"So you figured it out," Ruby said.

I stood at the door of the room she once shared with Sapphire and me, watching Connie and Inez sleep on the double mattress. They looked so young, so innocent. I already knew they were sweet, and precious, and wonderful.

I pulled the door to. "Hush, Ruby. You'll wake them."

"Don't be silly," Pearl said. "You're the only one who can hear us."

"And that only because I'm crazy as an old hoot owl," I replied as I started toward my bedroom.

"Owls are wise," Garnet reminded me.

"Especially the old ones," Amethyst added. "That's how they get to be old."

"Not so ready to die now, are you?" Ruby asked.

I stopped in the doorway of my room. I glanced up into the empty air. "I usually hate it when you're right, Ruby. But not tonight." I smiled as I remembered the sweet, sleepy kiss Inez had given me before she'd crawled under the covers. "Not tonight."

❧❧❧

The weather turned warm again over the next several days, during which I pondered the situation. I had no idea what all was involved in transferring orphaned children home to their grandmother in Mexico. I considered calling the sheriff to find out, but Arturo had had such a panicked response the one time I mentioned calling the authorities, I knew he'd bolt if he knew they were coming.

The children had been with me a week when Amethyst suggested I call Amos Royden, the Police Chief in Mossy Creek. Since he had no jurisdiction way out here beyond the city limits, he was no threat to Arturo.

I liked her idea, partly because of its good sense, but also because I'd had a special relationship with Amos ever since I'd been his English teacher the last year of Mossy Creek High School's existence. The angst he felt trying to become his own man while at the same time trying desperately to please his Police Chief father came through in his essays. He and I had several long talks about it. I must've helped him, even if just a little, because he made a point of checking on me every now and then.

Amos wasn't in when I called. Before I knew it, Sandy, the operator, wheedled most of the information out of me. I cut myself off when I realized what she was doing, asking to please have him call me back. Instead, he showed up that very afternoon.

The sound of a vehicle driving up my driveway was so out of the ordinary, I hurried to the front door to meet him, thankful that Arturo was in the barn trying to coax the tractor into running. Connie was helping Arturo, but Inez—bless her heart—wouldn't leave my side.

I watched from the porch as Amos unfolded from his Jeep and looked around carefully. He nodded when he saw me, scrutinized Inez, then started toward the porch.

"You didn't need to come all the way up here, Amos," I told him. "I just need to ask your advice about something."

His sharp eyes examined the new spindles on the railing, where Arturo had replaced rotten ones. "Who did you hire to do this?" He glanced over the front of the house. "Hel...er...umm...Sorry. Looks like you've had a lot of work done."

"Arturo Sanchez," I replied. Arturo's work was one thing Sandy Crane had not tricked out of me.

Amos's bushy eyebrow lifted. "The Hispanic boy?"

"The young man, yes."

Amos ran a hand along one of the spindles, then tugged at another one. "This is good, solid work."

"I know. But that's not why I called you. Come on in, and let me get you a glass of tea."

"Did he make this shutter?" Amos asked from the window at the end of the porch.

"He certainly did." I heard the pride in my voice, though why I should be so proud of the work Arturo had done, I didn't know. But I couldn't have been prouder if I'd done it myself. "He hasn't painted it yet because we don't have any paint. We're waiting on the delivery from Mossy Creek Hardware."

Clearly impressed, Amos stepped into the house, removing his hat as he did. "Hate to be nosy, but do you have the money for all this work?"

"Yes, Amos, I do." I wasn't about to tell him how.

Inez and I took him back to the kitchen where I served him some tea and told him about the children's predicament.

As I finished, I heard the screen door open. A second later, Arturo stopped dead in the doorway. Connie bumped into him from behind, then peered around to see what had stopped him.

Amos started to stand, but luckily, I was close enough to press a hand on his shoulder.

I watched as shock was rapidly succeeded by panic on Arturo's face. A checked movement told me he considered running. Probably the only thing that stopped him was that his sisters wouldn't be fast enough. Finally, his gaze settled on mine with confusion and more than a little accusation.

"Arturo," I said with forced confidence. I didn't think Amos would hand the children over to immigration, but I hadn't yet had time to make certain. "This is the Police Chief from Mossy Creek, Amos Royden. He's here to see what we can do about getting you home."

"Come over here, son," Amos said.

Arturo set his chin, then walked stiffly over to the kitchen table.

Connie scurried around the kitchen table to my side. I

put my arm around her shoulders.

Amos stood slowly, then held out his hand. "Nice to meet you, Arturo. You do real good work, for one so young."

Arturo's eyes widened. "You not going to take me in?"

"In where?" Amos asked patiently.

Arturo glanced at me, his dark eyes wide with confusion, then back at Amos. "Jail?"

"Have you committed a crime in Mossy Creek?"

"I never been to Mossy Creek, sir," Arturo answered.

Amos lifted one of his broad shoulders. "Then I have no reason to lock you up. Shake my hand, son. My arm's getting tired."

Arturo shook Amos's hand, but didn't relax until Amos sat back down. Amos asked Arturo to sit, then began questioning him about where his grandmother lived. Arturo didn't have an address, just knew the town in Mexico where his mother had said she was from. He and his parents had left Mexico when he was five, and he had no clear memories of his birthplace.

Amos wrote down the information. At one point, he glanced sharply at me.

"What was that?"

"What was what?" I asked.

"You didn't...?" With a frown, he peered around the room.

"What's wrong?" I asked.

Amos shook his head. "Nothing. I thought I heard...something, is all. Couldn't have, though." He ran his little finger around his left ear as if it tickled. "Now, Arturo..."

Several minutes later, Amos stopped writing again. After a moment of stillness, he looked at me.

"Your TV on?"

"No," I said.

"Radio?"

I shook my head, my eyes narrowing. Were my sisters

talking to Amos? No. They told me no one could hear them but me. Still, I watched Amos closely as I asked, "Do you hear something?"

"Must be the wind." His eyes swept the room again. "Although..."

"Yes?"

He shrugged.

"Nothing." He clicked his pen closed and folded his pocket-sized notebook. "I've got enough to start asking questions." He stood.

Arturo stood, as well. "How soon, sir? I still have work here, for Miz Opal."

Amos paused a moment to study Arturo's anxious face, then he peered over at me. I still sat at the kitchen table with a black-haired girl leaning against each side, my arms around them both.

Amos's face relaxed into a smile. "I have no idea how long all this will take, son. But I do know that the wheels of the federal government turn real slow. Go ahead with your work. And if you finish with Miss Opal's, then I've got a few things around my house that I can't seem to find the time to get to. You interested?"

"*Si*, Mr. Royden, sir."

Amos smiled at Arturo's enthusiasm and shook his hand. Then he gave me a brief salute. "Don't get up. I'll let you know what I find out. Probably take awhile."

"All right. Thanks, Amos."

"Meanwhile, you might want to think about getting these kids in school."

I blinked. "Can I? They're not citizens of the United States, much less Mossy Creek."

"Consuela and Inez born in America," Arturo said. "I am the only illegal."

Amos placed a hand on the boy's shoulder. "That's the first thing we'll fix. But we're not going to deport you as long you're here supporting your sisters. And doing a da...er, real fine job of it."

"Have you children ever been to school?" I asked.

"Consuela and Inez go to school in North Carolina," Arturo said. "But I help Papa."

I nodded. "Perhaps I'd better home school them for awhile. Until I see how far along they are."

"You're certainly more than qualified." Amos grabbed his hat. "I know the way out."

🐾🐾🐾

That night another storm broke as I pulled my cotton nightgown over my head. Thunder had been rumbling around the mountain for several hours, growing ever louder, agitating the evening air. It was a relief to finally hear the rain.

Smoothing the tiny handmade tucks down the batiste bodice as the hem settled below my knees, I wandered to the window and watched as lightning streaked across the sky. Storms seemed so much more violent in the mountains. Daddy used to say it was because we lived closer to Heaven.

"I don't want to go to Heaven," I shouted at him once, "if it's full of thunder."

I was terrified of thunderstorms then, and remembered scampering into this very room during the worst ones, burrowing into bed between Mama and Daddy.

"Heaven is the calmest, most peaceful place you can ever imagine," Daddy had replied to my outrageous comment. "But you can't know what peace is unless you know the opposite. So Heaven is surrounded by thunder. Otherwise, you won't appreciate how marvelous the love and peace is when you march through the Pearly Gates."

Daddy was the wisest man I ever knew. He was a supple willow that contrasted with Mama's rock hardness. Yet somehow their differences complemented each other, and made our family strong.

"No matter what any of us children needed, one or the other—or both our parents—could provide it," Garnet whispered.

I wiped away a tear that slowly found a path around the wrinkles in my cheek. "I miss them...and y'all, as well."

"But you're not alone anymore," Amethyst said.

"No." But my brief smile quickly faded. "At least, not at the moment."

"You know..." Garnet stretched out the second word. "You don't have to send them back to Mexico."

I started, and reached out to catch myself on the dresser. "I don't? You mean I'm supposed to raise them? How in tarnation? I'm almost eighty. I'll be dead before they even finish—"

"Oh, hush up," Ruby said sharply. "You're strong as an old mountain goat, and just as stubborn. You aren't going to die anytime soon, and you darn well know it. Heck's underbritches, Opal, you're gonna live until you're—"

Several voices shushed her, but not nearly the chorus I'd heard in the past weeks. "How many of y'all are here?"

"Just us three," Garnet replied.

I realized then that I hadn't heard from Pearl since the kids showed up, or from Sapphire in the last several days.

"They're not babies," Amethyst pointed out, bringing us back to the subject. "They're strong, healthy children who will soon be adults."

"Strong enough to take care of you in your declining years," Garnet said.

I sniffed. "As if I'm not on the downhill slope now."

"You're only as old as you feel," Garnet said. "And young people make you feel young."

"Besides, I would never take those children in just so

I'll have nursemaids when I'm old. The very idea!"

"Of course you wouldn't," Garnet said.

"You'll take them in because they need you," Amethyst said. "Desperately. And not just the money we provided. They need *you.*"

"And you need them," Garnet added.

"What about their grandmother?" I asked.

"Miz Opal?"

Startled by the physicality of sound waves from actual words being spoken, I turned to see Inez standing in the doorway, one arm around a ragged sock monkey I'd made over thirty years ago, the other hand gripping the doorknob. Even in the darkness, I could see that her dark eyes were wide. Had she heard me talking to my sisters?

"Yes?" I asked. "What is it, sweetheart?"

"I...Miz Opal, I..."

I could see the white cotton nightgown—a legacy from one of my sisters— shaking around the young girl's ankles. "Are you afraid of the storm?"

With a sob, she bolted across the room and threw her arms around my waist. "When will it stop?"

I hugged her close. This one, the youngest, was so much like me. "Probably not for awhile. Would you like to sleep with me in my mama's magic bed?"

She went still, then drew back to look up at me. "Magic?"

"That's right. Lightning has never struck this bed. Not once. Ever."

Inez studied the bed, as if she expected it to pull rabbits from its own hat. After a thoughtful moment, she asked, "You won't tell Arturo, will you? He already thinks I'm a baby."

I couldn't help smiling. I'd had an older brother, too. "I promise I won't tell a soul. It'll be our secret."

She sniffed loudly. "Then, *si*, please."

I settled into bed, then tucked her along my side. I told her about my own secret, how I'd fled to this very room when I was her age, for the very same reason. And I told her about my daddy's description of Heaven.

Only after Inez fell asleep did I realize I was already living in Daddy's version of Heaven. There was love and peace filling this old house, with thunder all around.

"The Voice Of The Creek"

Good morning, Creekites! Bert Lyman and Honey Lyman here. I'm the brawn behind the voice and she's the brains behind the engineer's control board. Okay, Honey, I'll quit talking and start working. Folks, listen up:

FOR SALE: Mamie Brown's house is still for sale. It's a quaint 2 bedroom, 1 bath with beautiful flower beds and access to fruit trees and pecans. Private—there's only one neighbor. Contact Ed Brady, Jr. newest member of Mossy Creek Mountain Realty.

SEEDS: Even though it's only summer, it's never too early to stock up for the winter, says Tom Anglin at Mossy Creek Hardware Store. He's got fifty-pound sacks of sunflower seeds on sale for half price, since the hawk spotted over town last week has scared off most of the summer birds around the square. On a related note, Bob the Chihuahua hasn't set foot outside Beechum's Bakery since the hawk showed up.

SPECIAL PROMOTION: Pick yourself a free mess of greens, beans and tomatoes in Joe Peavy's garden when you buy your gas at Peavy's Gas Station, just off Trailhead Road. The gas is for your car. None of the veggies should be blamed. If you're just visiting Mossy Creek, don't call the station and ask what a "mess" is. Only true Southerners know the answer to that question.

FOR SALE: Two rams, descendants of Samson, the Mossy Creek High School mascot who helped start the trouble that led to the burning of the high school twenty-odd years ago. Can dye to your specifications. Call Russ Green. He's in the book.

SPECIAL NOTICES: The library now has *The Wedding Dress* and no, I don't mean the wedding dress that Millicent Hart *borrowed* from the Mossy Creek Theatrical Guild again. I mean the book by best-selling author Virginia Ellis. Librarian Hannah Longstreet also says the library has more copies of *Alice At Heart* by Deborah Smith and also the author's newest book, *Sweet Hush.*

BOOK PATRON'S PICKS OF THE MONTH: *When You're the Only Cop in Town...* by Debra Dixon. Chief Royden says it's the best book about small-town police work he's ever read. Also recommended: *Atlanta Live* by Carmen Green. Mrs. Eula Mae Whit says it's the best book she's read in a hundred years.

"Anybody can sympathize with the sufferings of a friend,
but it requires a very fine nature to sympathize
with a friend's success."

—*Oscar Wilde*

MAMIE and GRACE

Chapter Three

"Appreciate what you have, Emily Sue. You don't always understand it but, remember, what goes around, comes around."

My grandmother, Grace Peacock, always said that. I never quite understood until now. I always thought it had something to do with fences and pecans. But I've come to understand that it applies to many levels of life, starting with family and ending with friendship—the obvious kind and those that are a bit different.

My mother and daddy lived with my grandparents. It was a common occurrence for families in Mossy Creek. When I was born it came down to a larger house or separate dwellings. By then she already knew that Daddy was a wanderer with his rainbow just over the next hill. And she shared his search. Since my mama had no intention of staying in Mossy Creek, she voted for a larger house—big enough for her to come home to, but one where she was not responsible for the bills and the upkeep.

At any rate, that's how we came to live next door to Mamie Brown. Granddaddy bought the two acres next to her and my daddy built our new home, his only and final contribution to the family finances. And, pretty much as my mama expected, she and daddy came around, dropping in through the years when things didn't go well. That's another place where my grandmother's saying comes into play. The Generation Xers of today are doing the same thing—coming home when things don't go well. Back then it was considered family looking after family. Now, it's family sharing failure.

Every time my folks left for the next great opportunity, I listened to Granny Grace and stayed put in Mossy Creek. But, even in close families like mine, there are some things that aren't discussed. My grandmother was the sweetest, most gentle person on the face of the earth except when it came to her neighbor, Mamie. Then she turned into a sneaky, conniving woman who spent her bean-snapping, pea-shelling time trying to figure out how to get the best of Mamie and enjoying every minute of it.

Mamie started their relationship on the wrong foot by sneaking across into Granny's blackberry patch without asking. We didn't live there yet and Granny's patch had more berries than she could every use but to her, it was the principle of the thing. They weren't Mamie's and she didn't ask permission before she picked them.

Mamie's next crime was my daddy's fault. When he built the house, he ran the water line into the bathroom but that was as far as it ever got. The toilet and drain pipes were leaning against the back of our house, directly in view of Miss Mamie's screened-in back porch with the most spectacular iris and caladiums planted just beyond. Miss Mamie pointed out to everyone in the church that the trashy folks next door had ruined her lovely garden. But people in Mossy Creek loved my granny. They'd come by and sit on the front porch with her at night. While the children and I caught lightning bugs in mason jars, they'd talk about their family's part in the Great War and the Depression before. Until I reached high school, I actually thought that Roosevelt was a chicken farmer. When Mamie didn't receive the support she'd expected, she bricked in the screens and moved her flowerbeds to the front.

Finally, Granny held out the olive branch, took Mamie some new bulbs for her garden and granted her permission to harvest all the berries she wanted. Mamie was not appreciative. By now, Granny was beginning to question the value of her efforts at friendship.

But it was Buck, my daddy's best hunting dog who elevated Mamie's nose to the next level. Buck had the run of the neighborhood and covered most of it. As if in support of Granny, Buck moved his private potty place to the middle of Miss Mamie's front yard.

War was declared.

Miss Mamie's bedroom windows, formerly open to catch the summer breeze, turned into white shaded squares that looked like two cartoon eyes glaring at my Granny Grace's bedroom.

We never had any livestock. Chickens we had, but they had their own private yard. Granny Grace stared at those windows for a few days, then insisted that Granddaddy fence in the back yard.

We assumed it was to restrain Buck. It wasn't. She never intended to stop Buck's freedom of choice. In fact, the fence kept him out of the back yard—until Battle Royden, the Chief of Police back then, came to call one afternoon and suggested rather strongly that Buck reside in our dog yard or face jail. For once, Granddaddy agreed and put Buck inside the fence.

The incident became a new salvo from Granny Grace, and she didn't even have anything to do with it. Buck didn't like having his freedom curtailed and told the world. If you've ever had a male dog who considered himself a stud separated from the ladies in his area, you can imagine what he did. He howled at the moon, at the sun, even at me. Then he dug a hole under the fence bordering Miss Mamie's side and escaped—several times.

Mamie complained to Battle. "My yard is not his bathroom. He's killed my grass. It looks like a yellow and green polka dotted apron." Battle talked to Granny Grace who was so apologetic. "Why Miss Mamie is such a good neighbor, I can't imagine why the dog doesn't like her. But you know animals," she said, piously, "they are better judges of people than people are."

I'm not sure how ugly the Buck situation would have gotten if Mother and Daddy hadn't come home for a visit before opening a wilderness fishing camp in the Florida Keys. When they left Buck went with them. Our bathroom was finally installed. I went away to Atlanta and worked my way through Georgia State University. I got married and divorced but I swore I wouldn't move back in with Granny. It was a matter of pride. This was a new world. I wasn't my mother. Moving home meant admitting failure.

Then Granddaddy died while mother and father were operating a fishing boat somewhere in the Gulf. I was the one who had to go home to make the arrangements. That's when I learned that it takes ten years for pecan trees to produce fruit, and one good crop of nuts to start a not so friendly feud between Granny and Mamie.

The tree was on Miss Mamie's side but the limbs grew equally from each side of the tree, guaranteeing Granny her share of the nuts. "You always plan ahead, Emily Sue," she'd say. But I never realized how seriously she took that until the pecan tree began to bear fruit. That's when the war broke out in earnest. If we had any squirrels, they had to find another source of food. The two women were out before the sun was up gathering the nuts. Miss Mamie on her side of Granny's fence and Granny on the other.

There was only one problem, Miss Mamie's arms were

longer and slimmer. She could reach right through the fence squares and get the nuts my granny considered to be hers. Eventually, Granny figured out that if I climbed the tree and shook it at just the right angle, she would be guaranteed a better harvest.

After the funeral, Granny and I sat on the front porch and discussed her situation. She'd be fine, Granny swore. Her sister, Aunt Frank, had decided to come and live with her. They'd share expenses and it would give the two sisters someone to share the chores with. I wish Granny had shared a little more with Aunt Frank—like the neighbor situation.

You have to understand that the only people who knew about the intensity of the ongoing feud over the pecans were Battle Royden, me and Miss Mamie. When Aunt Frank learned about the "fuss," she decided that the whole thing was foolishness and she'd just put a stop to it.

From what I can piece together from the various versions I've heard over the years (Aunt Frank, Granny Grace, Miss Mamie and the new police chief, Battle's son, Amos— who all tell a different tale), this is what really happened.

From what I can tell, Aunt Frank marched over and announced that she was living with Grace now and she'd already instructed Grace to stop arguing over the nuts and Miss Mamie should do the same. "There's plenty for both of you."

Miss Mamie apparently didn't smile and agree with Aunt Frank like Granny did, so Aunt Frank was prepared to go even further as a messenger of good. "By the way, one of the ladies from the church said you play the fiddle. I brought my pump organ. Grace plays, you know, and I can pick a mean tune on my auto harp. I'm thinking that since we're in the mountains now, we could get together once a week and play and sing some good mountain music, like the Carter family. You know, the one who had the girl that married Johnny Cash."

That's when Miss Mamie demonstrated the force of the anger that had been simmering for twenty-five years. "I play the *violin* and I am not interested in playing or singing *anything* with you."

Now suddenly, Granny Grace had a partner in crime. Except it wasn't as much fun with Aunt Frank coming up with new plots and trying to run the show. In fact, after six months of living with Aunt Frank, Granny decided she knew why Frankie's husband had divorced her long before that became a common practice. Aunt Frank just plain didn't know how to share the fun. She had to run the show, which was Granny's job and Granny didn't appreciate it. What Granny did finally appreciate was my divorce. She jumped on that divorce like it was one of the opportunities my mama and daddy were always chasing.

She announced to Aunt Frank that I was divorced now and would be moving back home—just like all those other children who spent all they made and had to have help. That, of course, meant she needed her house.

Nothing could be further from the truth. But when she pled her case to me, what choice did I have, but to agree? After all, Granny Grace had given me a home all my life, I was obligated to repay her if that's what she wanted. But I decided I needed to check out the situation in person before I altered my future. The next morning, I headed for Mossy Creek. As I drove up to the house, I passed Aunt Frank driving her Ryder truck packed with family heirlooms. She didn't even wave goodbye.

Granny Grace was sitting on the front porch fanning herself with a paper fan from the newly opened Heaven's Rest Funeral Home. "Come on in, Emily Sue, have a seat and listen to the quiet."

"Listen to the quiet?"

"Yes. No dog barking. No violin music and, thank the Lord, no more Frankie. You know I didn't invite her here. She invited herself then thought she'd take over. I found out something. In spite of Mamie being so high and mighty, she taught me a couple of things over the years. I don't need you to come home. I don't need a keeper. I can look after myself."

"You always could," I said, thinking that it was too bad two widows living side by side weren't friends.

For the next few years, Granny Grace got frailer but that didn't stop the pecan war. Even using walkers to compensate for a mild stroke on her part and a broken hip on Mamie's didn't stop them.

In fact, it was an act of God that interceded in the form of a freaky late summer storm that came in from the south, rounded the foothills and hit Mossy Creek. But I didn't know it at the time. When I made my weekly Sunday evening call to Granny Grace, there was no answer. When I still couldn't reach her the next morning, I left my office and went home.

The power was out and the house was empty. Granny's Buick was under the shed. But no Granny. Finally, I bit the bullet and knocked on Miss Mamie's back door. "Miss Mamie?"

There was a stirring inside and the sound of metal tapping on the linoleum kitchen floor. Granny Grace opened the door. "Emily Sue, what are you doing up here?"

"You didn't answer your phone and I came to check on you." I looked around curiously. If Granny Grace had ever been inside Miss Mamie's house, I didn't know it. "Why are you over here?"

"Well, we had a little problem," she said. "A storm came over the mountain like a mad woman dropping hushpuppies into a frying pan full of hot grease. Lightning was flashing everywhere. One bolt hit the pecan tree and ran across the ground into Mamie's house. I came over to check on her. Didn't you see the tree?"

I'd walked past the fence and the pecan tree without realizing that it had been hit. As if the bolt were a sharp knife it had sliced down the middle of the tree. The tree had parted like a wilted plant, half the limbs across Miss Mamie's yard and half leaning over the fence into Granny Grace's.

"Come on in, child," Granny said.

I felt like The Cowardly Lion as I made my way through the dark kitchen into the room Miss Mamie had converted into a side porch. When I saw her I realized how old and tiny she'd become in the years since I'd been away.

"Come in," she said. "All Grace has talked about is Emily Sue. I figured you'd sprouted wings."

"How are you doing?" I asked.

"About as well as your grandmother, I expect, except she gets around better than me."

"I always did," Granny said. "Had to buy one of those chest freezers to hold all those pecans I picked up."

"Yeah, but that was before you had that stroke, Grace."

"And before you broke your hip, Mamie."

Mamie leaned back in the chaise lounge and sighed. "Reckon between the two of us, we might make one good woman."

"Reckon you're right," Granny agreed.

"You're both better off than that pecan tree," I said. "The two of you battled over it all this time, then lightning comes along and settles the fight by cutting it down the middle."

Mamie let out a cry of dismay. "The tree is dead?"

"Not yet," I answered, "but it probably will die."

"So be it," pronounced Granny Grace. "You want any more coffee, Mamie? There's more pecan pie."

"If I never see another pecan pie it will be too soon for me," Mamie snapped.

Fearing a physical confrontation, I interrupted with a

question. "What do you need me to do, Granny?"

"Not a thing, Emily Sue. You just get on back to Atlanta so you don't lose that job. And stop by the power company on your way through town. Tell them we need lights before tonight. I want to watch *Wheel of Fortune*."

"Only if we watch *Dirty Dancing* afterward," Mamie announced.

"Humph! And I suppose you have it in mind to watch one of those porno channels, next."

I left the two of them squabbling, the pecan tree forgotten in their new-found differences. Like children, I thought. Or friends.

Still, the two of them couldn't be left alone and it fell my fate to come home and look after them. I went to work for the mayor as her administrative assistant and found out I liked living in Mossy Creek as an adult a lot more than I thought, even if I was hungry for a friend who could carry on an intelligent conversation.

Last year Mamie moved into Magnolia Manor Nursing Home and put her house up for sale. A few months ago Granny broke her hip and followed. The only vacancy available at Magnolia Manor on short notice was—you guessed it—in the room with Mamie.

After Granny moved I walked through her house. I stopped to put on a Bruce Springsteen tape and stepped out into the back yard where Granny had poured a sidewalk between her back door and Mamie's. The fence was still there, though an opening had been cut at the end of the sidewalk. In the center of the opening, two new pecan tree limbs had sprouted, one on Mamie's side and one on Granny's. At the bottom they bowed out like a fat-bottomed vase. But as the limbs grew toward the sun, they'd wrapped around each other as if in support.

I looked at those limbs a long time.

❦❦❦

Granny has given me her house and I've decided to stay in Mossy Creek. Not in failure but seeking something that has been lacking in my life—a place to belong, someone to belong to. I remember Granny's famous prediction. *Appreciate what you have, Emily Sue. What goes around comes around.*

She should add, *Be careful what you wish for.*

I wish I had. As I stood looking out Granny's windows the other day, I saw a strange man with a long braid of black hair walking up the drive to Miss Mamie's house. He stopped to pull up the for sale sign, unlocked the door and went inside. Moments later the shades went up and the windows were open. What came next filled the air with sounds I couldn't begin to describe.

Music? No. Drums began to beat, accompanied by the stomping of feet and a melancholy chanting that rose with the intensity of the drumbeat. I soon closed the windows on my side and pulled down the shades. All afternoon and into the night the noise continued, vibrating through the night air. By midnight I decided it had to stop. I'd have to shut off that yowling or I'd never get any sleep. I'd call Chief Royden. No, I'd take care of this myself, just like Granny had.

Moments later I found myself marching across Granny's sidewalk as a nighttime thunderstorm began rumbling in the sky. I knocked on Miss Mamie's back screened door and peered through the mesh. "Hello, inside."

The man appeared and flicked on the back porch light. He was barefoot and bare-chested, with a dark braid of hair hanging over one tanned shoulder. I gazed up into a handsome face with high cheekbones and dark eyes. He gazed down at me as if I were a rabbit and might make a tasty meal. It felt like a compliment. "Yes?" he asked in a wonderful, deep voice.

"Are you going to be the new occupant of Mamie's house?"

"Yes. And you're my neighbor, the granddaughter of the woman who fought with Mamie? The agent warned me about you."

"Fought? No. I mean *Yes.*"

"And what can I do for you?"

"I...I...You have to turn off all that noise. You're polluting the air!"

He smiled. "Really? You have air pollution regulations?"

"Yes, and your air stops at the fence."

He stepped out past me into the yard and looked up at the dark shadow of the mountain behind Mamie's house. The wind was blowing harder now and the night threatened a hard, warm rain. "I don't think so," he said. "We cannot control nature. Mother Earth welcomes her children, the wind and the rain."

"You're an Indian?"

"Cherokee."

"I thought you back-to-nature types preferred living in teepees."

"Actually, I've been living in a condo in Oklahoma."

"But you're here now. Why?"

"Because this is my birthplace. My people are related to the Settles and the Halfacres."

"You were born in Miss Mamie's house?"

"No, in these mountains. In this cove."

"If that's some kind of rain dance you're playing in there, you're going to have to stop. Storms in Mossy Creek can get pretty fierce. They don't need encouragement."

"I'm not bringing the storm. It's coming around that ridge from the north. I think you may be attracting its force."

I gaped at him and absorbed the electric feel that ran before a storm. Thunder was gathering force in the distance. Then the lightning started. The thunder rumbled.

The pecan tree caught the breeze and the two limbs held to each other. The storm that killed its ancestor had come from the north. The one brewing now was approaching from the south. *What goes around, comes around*, Granny had said. It never occurred to me she was talking about storms. I thought she'd meant life.

The storm moved closer. The stranger and I stood our ground. The wind caught my thin robe and nightgown, pressing them against me like an old Betty Davis movie where Betty stood on a cliff, looking into the distance while a storm tried and failed to frighten her. My new neighbor remained staunch beside me, his head cocked a little as if he were listening to something I couldn't hear.

Then the lightning started. The sky cracked open and a bolt hit so close by the ground shook. I turned and ran back to Granny's house as the rain started. The stranger stayed put, his face turned up to the water. Oh yes, he was a Creekite by nature. A lover of water and trouble. I huddled on Granny's back porch and watched as he turned and calmly walked back into Mamie's house. But just as I shivered and started inside my own door he returned.

Lighting flashed again and I saw that he'd changed his jeans for some kind of loin cloth. His unbraided hair hung down his back in dark, wet strands. I put a hand to my heart and stared at the wild, masculine image. And I'd thought *Mamie* was trouble. What would Granny have done about *this*? What am I going to do?

I'll get a dog, I thought. *I'll rebuild the fence. I'll refuse to look at the man. Or think about him.*

In the next moment lightning shimmered around the pecan tree. I held my breath, fearing the worst, but the lightning appeared to arc around the intertwined limbs as if they were shielding each other and nothing could harm them. A few minutes later the storm moved on. My astonishing new neighbor looked over at me. When one last flicker of lightning showed his face, he looked from the pecan tree to me. He nodded. Before I realized I was doing it, I nodded back. He smiled and walked inside his house.

What goes around, comes around.

I told myself I wouldn't follow in Granny's footsteps. Her freezer was still full of pies. The pecan tree wouldn't bear fruit for ten years. And I had wished for a friend, but not a friend so unnerving he made *me* feel I'd been struck by lightning.

The drumbeat started up again. I sighed. On the other hand...

Mossy Creek Gazette

VOLUME III, NO. 2 — **MOSSY CREEK, GEORGIA**

The Bell Ringer

Changes & Choices

by Katie "Tree Hugger" Bell

I'm sorry to announce that Grace Peacock has taken up residence in Magnolia Manor's assisted living quarters. She will be sharing an apartment with her long-time *dear friend* and neighbor Mamie Brown. We wish them all the best. Mrs. Brown's house has been sold. As of this column, your Bell Ringer does not have information on the buyer.

Beginning in the fall, at the request of Opal May Suggs, a class in Spanish will be offered in our continuing education program. Any suggestion that the request has anything to do with ghosts or the unusual amount of thunder from her side of the mountains has been totally discounted by one of our summer residents, recently retired from the weather department of one of the Atlanta television stations. He also says it has nothing to do with Rip Van Winkle or bowling. When questioned, Miss Opal only smiles and invites her friends to open their minds and hearts, lay in a supply of bran flakes and learn Spanish.

Jayne Austen Reynold's baby, young Matthew, has celebrated his first birthday with a party at Jayne's coffee shop. In Matthew's honor there's a sale on at Hamilton's Department Store in the children's clothes, newborns to size five. When submitting the advertisement, Robert Walker, president and general manager of Hamilton's, bemoaned the shortage of young children in Mossy Creek. We do have some weddings planned and hopefully the couples will fill our gaps. After the weddings, please, not before. We're old-fashioned here in Mossy Creek.

Incidentally, last week we had a tree surgeon visit from the University of Georgia. Mrs. Howell called him in to examine one of our lover's lane sites, The Sitting Tree. He said the old maple seems to be in remarkably good shape considering it's in the middle of an open area where the elements can get at it. Mrs. Howell says it has a guardian angel, but I'll let her tell you about that herself.

"A friend is someone who knows the song in your heart and can sing it back to you when you have forgotten the words."

— *unknown*

SADIE and ETTA

Chapter Four

It's been just over fifty years since the summer Etta Jones Howell insisted I come to Mossy Creek for a visit. She kept begging me even though she knew I didn't like to leave my neat, tiny, post-war apartment in Atlanta. In the end I gave in. Etta was my very best friend. How could I refuse her?

At the time, I didn't know she was dying.

I can hear her now. "Sadie Johnson, I will not allow you to waste your life any longer. I know you better 'n anybody else and I've got a plan."

Listening to her back then, my curiosity rose, though Etta and a secluded mountain town named Mossy Creek seemed a distant cry from my ordinary, daily routines as a single career woman, which is what people called a young, unmarried elementary school teacher in the late 1940s.

Etta added something she knew would work.

"I've got a surprise or two for you."

"Are they good?" I asked.

"One of them is very good. Maybe the best."

"Well," I began...hooked in spite of myself.

Etta let out a sigh of satisfaction.

"Okay, that's settled then. You have the whole summer

off. Pack up your things and head north as soon as you can." Her voice changed, became a little sad. "And, Sadie, plan to stay for quite a while."

As I pulled together some things for the trip, my thoughts flew back to the fall of my third grade year, when Etta came into my life.

❦ ❦ ❦

That school year was as difficult for me as the first two had been in the small town in South Georgia where I lived. The clothes I wore were either too small or too large and always second-hand. My hair was a nest of snarls amid burnished red curls. My nose was scattered with freckles that seemed to shriek aloud that I worked outside in the hot sun digging in the dirt, growing vegetables for my foster family to sell. It was bad enough that my outside announced to every one in town that I was poor and unkempt.

My inside was in even worse shape and would, I suspected, always be that way. Moving from foster home to foster home had left me with the enormity of being unwanted. I was too dumb, too smart for my own good, too ugly, too beautiful beyond my ken and on and on. I couldn't understand why it was that no one loved me enough to keep me. That constant ugly lump of knowledge was something I carefully kept inside.

One day my teacher, Mrs. Sampson, announced we were going to have a new girl in our class.

"She will arrive tomorrow," she said.

"Please welcome her and make her feel at home."

The year was 1933, and newcomers were a rarity in the small-town South. That night I went to bed wondering what this new girl would be like. Maybe, I thought, she would be nice to me. Not like the others.

In the morning I brushed my hair carefully, scrubbed

my hands and straightened my oversized dress. This new girl, whoever she was, had to like me. She just had to!

Etta walked into the room like she owned the place. It wasn't a strut exactly but mighty close to one. She stood with her arms crossed and a frown on her pretty face that made her look downright annoyed to have to be in school. Her blue-eyed gaze, beneath a stray lock of blond hair, swept across the kids sitting at their desks and came to rest on me. I gave her a shy smile and held my breath.

"You may choose someone in the class to be your partner until you learn our rules," the teacher said.

Etta pointed directly at me. "I'll take *her*."

My surprise was matched by the expressions on the faces of my classmates. My cheeks burned and my heart warmed. Someone had chosen me!

From that moment on, I gave my heart to Etta. With her I was someone special. Not just the poor, dirty, unwanted child everyone knew about. I was a different version of me, proud and tall. I was Sadie Johnson, Etta Jones' best friend.

Even now, many years later, recalling that moment, I cannot help the tears of gratitude that fill my eyes. She would always be my best friend.

❦ ❦ ❦

Not long after Etta called, I headed to Mossy Creek for the summer. My little blue Ford was filled with clothes and books and all the paraphernalia of a long-term stay, as if I knew what lay ahead.

Driving into the mountains above Bigelow, my heart lifted. I understood why Etta loved this place. There was something about the fresh air, the blue sky and puffy white clouds around Mossy Creek that made me think of fresh beginnings. One of the pleasant aspects of teaching was having the whole summer to myself. I cherished those times.

I was a loner, and though I missed the children I taught, I embraced each summer with the joy of knowing my days were my own.

Mossy Creek greeted me like an old friend. In 1947, Main Street had just received its first street lamp and the traffic was so light that I had to circumvent two sleeping dogs in the middle of South Bigelow Road. I drove past Hamilton's Department Store, the town hall and all the other landmarks I remembered from my last visit. Mossy Creek felt special, quiet and gathered-together, unlike the crowded life I'd left behind in Atlanta.

On the outskirts of town I turned onto a sidestreet and found my way up a long, graveled driveway that led to Etta's house. Howell Lane, as the little street sign named it, was a mark of pride for her.

"Can you imagine," she once said to me. "We have our very own road with our very own name on it. Not many people can claim that, can they?"

Etta got such pleasure out of the simple things in life. I wish more people would.

At the end of the driveway sat a small, two-story house with clapboard siding painted a bright yellow. Dark-green shutters edged the multi-paned windows. A long, wide porch in front, lined with comfortable rocking chairs, invited visitors to set a spell.

I got out of the car as Belle, a yellow lab, hefted herself to her feet and ambled down the front steps to greet me. I smiled at Etta's long-time companion and gave her a pat on the head. Her tail wagged a hello and her mouth opened into what promised to be a canine smile.

"You're here!" Etta called through the screen door. "Hold on! I'll get Ben to help you with your things."

I stood a moment and drew in a deep breath. I heard the sound of bees going about their tasks among the flowers clustered in colorful bunches along the lattice work beneath the porch. Yes, I thought, this would be a pleasant, peaceful time. No worries to think about. Just time to enjoy being with Etta and Ben, her husband.

Etta reappeared at the door, Ben in tow. She crossed the porch and hurried down the steps to greet me. I rushed forward, filled with questions. Why was Etta so thin? I hugged her and felt the absence of flesh in the body my arms surrounded.

Alarmed, I asked, "Are you ill? You're so thin. And you look tired."

Etta's laugh was not the hearty one I knew. "Oh, I've been feeling poorly but now that you are here, it's going to help." Her eyes filled with tears. "I'm so glad you came."

I glanced at Ben standing behind Etta, one hand on her shoulder. His lanky body towered above her small, round frame. She reached up and stroked his craggy features. Ben smiled at her but turned to me with a troubled expression.

"How are you?" I said.

He nodded. "F-f-fine."

I looked at him and knew he wasn't fine at all. He was stuttering and that happened when he was under stress. What, I wondered, was going on?

As if he heard my unspoken question, he silently shook his head, warning me to keep quiet. My heart sank. Something was terribly wrong.

Etta's smile was bright. "Come on in. We've got your room all ready for you."

I followed her, carrying some of my bags up the stairs and automatically turned left into the bedroom I had always loved. The sloping ceiling, flowered wallpaper and big double bed were perfect for me—and Etta knew it. I liked to keep things the same. I suppose it was the instability in my life growing up that made me that way.

"Just the way you left it from your last visit," said Etta with a knowing grin.

"It looks wonderful. And thank you for the wild flowers." I bent over to smell them and then turned to her.

"Are we going to have a chance to talk soon? I think you're hiding something from me."

She nodded and looked to see if Ben was outside, in the hall. "For now, let's have a nice lunch. I don't like to worry Ben. You know what a gentle soul he is."

Ben entered the room only a minute later. "Got your bags, Sadie. Mighty heavy, too." His blue eyes twinkled. "Glad to know you're going to stay a while. Etta perks up when you're around."

I chuckled. "You know Etta. Once she makes up her mind to something there's no stopping her."

He put his arm around Etta. "Yessir, she's got a stubborn streak in her."

Etta looked up at him, a loving smile on her face. "If I wasn't that way, Benjamin Howell, you would never have asked me to marry you. That was your lucky day!"

Ben grinned. "Don't I just know it."

Watching the interchange between them, I was filled with a jumble of emotions. I guess I'd have to say a good deal of it was envy. A love like hers and Ben's was hard to find.

The next few days passed quickly as the three of us settled into a routine, although Etta avoided telling me anything more interesting than the color of the mums she hoped to plant for fall blooms. I arose early in the morning and headed outdoors, walked down to the bottom of the drive and out onto East Mossy Creek, the main drag that headed toward the small-big mountain city of Gainesville, over an hour's drive away on bumpy country roads. I loved the peace and quiet of those early morning strolls. When I got back from my walk, Ben and I sipped coffee in the kitchen and then I would fix us breakfast. Etta remained in bed until midmorning. Another warning sign. But each time I'd ask Ben about her, he'd just shake his head.

"I can't say nothin' about it. I promised Etta I wouldn't. She'll talk to you when she's ready."

In those first mornings I enjoyed Ben's company more than I ever realized before. He was a good man and an ambitious, self-educated leader who managed the huge dairy at Hamilton Farms. Time off he spent at home, maintaining a large garden, a henhouse full of chickens and the pretty house he and Etta had inherited from his grandmother.

I wasn't comfortable with many people, especially men. Ben knew that and was as gentle with me as he would be with a nervous calf. I'd always been grateful to him for his understanding.

One morning Etta came into the kitchen as Ben was leaving for work. "It's a beautiful day!" Her smile was wobbly but broad. "Sadie, let's pack a picnic and take a drive over to our favorite meadow."

"I like that idea."

While Etta got dressed, I fixed egg salad sandwiches, filled a big jar with sweet tea and wrapped up some of my homemade sugar cookies Etta liked so much. Etta came out of her bedroom and sat down at the kitchen table. A chill went up my spine when I realized she was winded just from the effort of getting dressed.

We loaded up my little Ford and headed out. A few miles north of town a breathtaking meadow grew in the shadow of huge, blue-green mountains. I pulled off a dirt road and drove deep into the swaying grass.

"Where are you going?" squealed Etta.

I laughed.

"I'm driving you up to our Sitting Tree. I don't feel like walking the whole way today." Etta had named the broad, umbrella-shaped maple the Sitting Tree the first time I came to picnic with her in Mossy Creek.

Etta began to chuckle.

"Why, Sadie Johnson, I do declare you've got a wild side to you, after all. I find it dee-lightful."

"I don't know exactly what's going on," I said quietly, "but we're going to have a double dee-lightful day."

Etta squeezed my hand at the familiar language of our childhood. Only then a double dee-lightful day meant a trip to the candy store and hiding out in my bedroom with a few books.

"Today," she said now, "my delight will be in having you here with me, bringing back good memories."

I heard the sadness in her voice and blinked back tears. "Hang on!" I cried. "I'm going to see if I can make it all the way up the hill!"

I gunned the engine. The car rumbled and shook as I drove toward the tree.

Etta clapped. "Hooray! I think we're going to make it!"

About then, the car's tires sank into a soft spot left by a summer storm the day before. I rocked the car back and forth, until we were so stuck we knew we'd have to get a tractor to pull us out.

"What will we do now?" asked Etta, chuckling softly.

"We're going to have our picnic." I got out of the car, raced around to her side and opened the door. "Come, Madame, a luscious repast of egg salad awaits you."

Etta laughed and took my arm. I walked her up to the tree and raced back down to the car to collect a blanket and the picnic basket. I glanced at the road, certain someone in the area would discover the car and come to our rescue. We weren't far from the Bailey Mill community and the Bailey family's famous Sweet Hope Apple orchards.

Etta sat down on the blanket I spread out beneath the tree and leaned back against its broad trunk. She closed her eyes and let out a tremulous sigh. Tears slid down her cheeks.

I sat down beside her and took her hand. "Please, don't wait any longer. Tell me what's wrong."

She opened her eyes and gazed at me sadly. "I'm dying, Sadie. Way before I want to. The doctors say the cancer has spread too far to be able to help me. I was hopin' they were wrong but I get weaker each day. Benjamin thinks it's going to take a while, but, Sadie, it's happening real fast."

I gripped her hands tightly, as if I could will my good health into her. I tried to speak, but couldn't.

"Sadie," she said gently, "That's why I asked you to stay the summer. I don't think I'll make it to fall."

I inhaled and tried to control the misery that rose inside me. "I'll stay," I said. "As long as you need me to."

She patted my hand. "It's for both of us. Ben will need you, too."

I put my arms around her, willing myself to stay strong for Etta's sake. Inside, I shook with a grief that tore me to pieces.

🌱🌱🌱

After Etta took a nap, we had our picnic. Neither of us were hungry, but Etta was determined to make the day as normal as possible.

"Remember the time we decided to try mascara?" she asked. "I got so much on my lashes I could hardly open my eyes."

I managed a smile. "When I went home, Mrs. Redmond swatted me so hard I couldn't sit down for supper. She called me a painted whore." I shook my head. "My foster mother was one mean woman." With some sense of revenge, I added, "I still paint myself up, as she would say."

"Never to excess. You always look nice and put together. In fact, you're beautiful." She waved her hand, knowing I was about to protest. "I know, I know, you don't want to hear anything like that..." Her expression became very quiet, very serious. "Sadie, while you're here it's important for you

96

to get to know some of the people of Mossy Creek."

I frowned. "Of course, I enjoy meeting your neighbors—"

"That's not quite what I mean." Etta went right on, as
she usually did when she got an idea in her head. "Before
long, I won't be well enough to get out of the house. You'll
need to go to the bakery, the department store and other
places in town, to do the errands. That will be a good chance
for you to meet people and feel like part of the town."

"Now, Etta..." I began.

"Hush, now," she said. "You're not going to deny a dying woman her wish, are you?"

I gazed into her determined eyes and sighed. Etta was
going to get her own way come hell or high water.

"All right," I said. "Somehow I'll manage to be sociable,
instead of a cranky old maid."

Etta patted me on the shoulder. "It'll be for the best.
You'll see."

We heard an engine, and turned to look. A tractor made
its way up the dirt road alongside the meadow. The old-man
driver stopped near my car. He cupped his hands around
his mouth and hollered, "Y'all need help?"

I stood. "Sure do! I'm stuck!"

"Go on down and talk to him up close," said Etta. "I'll
wait here."

"Better stand back," the grizzled rescuer shouted as I
reached him. He guided the tractor, a metal-wheeled, smoke-
puffing monster, toward my car, hooked up a chain, then
dragged my car out of the field and onto the road as if he'd
done the same for more than a few city folk.

"Thank you for your help," I said as he cut the engine
and climbed down. I held out my hand. "I'm..."

"Yes, Miss, I know who you are. Etta Howell's best friend
come for a visit. School teacher, they say." He laughed at my
surprise. "My name's Mobeley. Curtis Mobeley. I work for

the Baileys. Just happened by."

"Nice to meet you," I replied tentatively.

"Don't be surprised I know all about you. In these here parts everybody knows everybody else's business. By tomorrow they'll all know how you tried to drive your car up to that tree to carry Miss Etta to a picnic. Gonna be a few jokes about it. But I imagine folks will be impressed by your dedication, too."

I felt my cheeks growing hot. He shook his head. "Don't you worry about the talk none. It's all friendly. Just the way things are in Mossy Creek."

I thanked him again, made sure everything about my car was still working properly, then headed up the hill to get Etta and our picnic things. The whole time my mind was whirling. How was I going to keep my promise to be sociable when I was heartbroken over Etta's news and the privacy to grieve was the thing I valued most?

Etta gave me a knowing smile when I relayed the old man's remarks to her. "Talk is harmless. Everybody likes to keep track of everybody else's business around here."

"Then you're going to tell everyone you're...sick?" I couldn't make myself say dying.

"Not exactly. Over time, they'll realize the truth, but for now they will just know I'm feeling poorly. I've got to get used to the whole idea, first."

"Me, too," I said, and held her hand again.

❧ ❧ ❧

When Ben came home that evening, he glanced from Etta to me. "I told her," Etta said simply. "She'll stay for as long as we need her."

Ben put his arm around me. "Thanks, Sadie. It means a lot. To both of us."

I blinked rapidly and nodded, too emotional to do or

say much. Etta was my best friend, my only friend, and she was dying.

The summer days heated up as Etta's time on earth ebbed. Every evening, the three of us would sit on the front porch, rocking back and forth in rhythm, letting the breezes cool us off. As often as they'd let me, I left Etta and Ben on the porch to talk in private. But more often than not, Etta would call me back, saying we were a family now and families should stick together during times like this.

I never asked Ben how he felt about such a statement, but he didn't seem to object when I returned to the porch.

We talked about our childhoods during those long summer evenings. As mortality becomes a reality, some people flee to the past. It was easier for Etta to do that than it was for either Ben or me.

"I remember the first time I met you," she said softly, one evening. "Your hair was so curly. I can't remember what you wore. Just the way you smiled at me, as if you wanted me to like you. I knew then we'd be best friends."

Etta had a knack for making people feel comfortable about themselves. She seemed to thrive on bringing out the best in the folks around her—and bringing them together. Around her, Ben never stuttered and as the summer went on, he grew that comfortable with me, too.

During the hot afternoons in late August, Etta napped on the couch in the living room. If I tiptoed through the room in an effort to be quiet, she invariably roused herself.

"Don't you go getting quiet on me. I want to hear life around me." When I banged a pot or two in the kitchen on purpose, she laughed.

Mornings often found me in town, getting groceries and doing other errands. Just as Curtis Mobeley had warned me, people I didn't even know greeted me by name and asked after Etta. The awkwardness I felt at being so exposed to curious strangers began to fade. I could tell that, more often than not, their questions were asked out of caring. Some-times blatant curiosity coated the words. Then I was careful what I said, skirting the issue of Etta's dying until she was ready for the word to be out.

Late one afternoon, Etta asked Ben to help her to the porch. "There's something I need to talk over with you," she said to him.

This time I knew I should give them privacy. I got into my car, drove into town and parked. Slowly, I walked up one side of the street and down the other. The shops were laid out in an orderly, comforting fashion. I knew the names of the owners. They knew my favorite purchases. A bittersweet sense of satisfaction washed over me. Mossy Creek had become home for me.

When I got back to the house, Ben and Etta were wait-ing in the living room. "I want all three of us to go visit the Sitting Tree," Etta said. "Right now."

I stared at her. "Are you sure? You're not too tired?"

"It's what I want," said Etta, leaving no doubt in my mind that if she wanted it, it was going to happen.

Ben, his eyes tear-stained, carefully lifted Etta in his arms. Not a word was said as Ben drove us to the meadow. A glorious red-and-gold sunset colored the mountain rims. Ben gingerly lifted Etta in his arms, again, and carried her up the hill to the tree. I raced ahead, carrying a blanket and a soft pillow for Etta's head. Ben lowered her to the blanket and fixed the pillow against the tree trunk so she could lean back comfortably. "I'll be back in a while," he announced suddenly.

Before I knew what to say he descended the hill, one strong stride after another.

Etta touched my hand. "He's a good man, Sadie. The best anyone could want. He doesn't talk much to strangers. He's shy with women, because of his stutter. But I know you like him, and he likes you, too. Remember when I told you I had a plan? Well, I feel convinced it's going to work out, now. You are comfortable here in Mossy Creek, with Ben, aren't you? You do love it...here?"

I nodded, but tried not to think of where this conversation was going. She smiled. "I can't leave my Ben unless I know he'll be all right. You know how he is, how much he needs someone to care for him...to love him."

She cried. Her tears were matched by my own. I swiped at my cheeks with a fist. "I wish things were different," I managed to say. "I would trade places with you if I could. I would die for you, Etta."

She squeezed my hand. "That's not what I want you to do, Sadie. I want you to live for me. And love for me. I want you stay here and take care of Ben after I'm gone."

The pounding of my heart echoed in my ears. Surely I hadn't heard right. Me, an old maid and Ben?

"But I... what will people say? What does Ben say?"

"He doesn't want to talk about it," said Etta. "I've made him promise to say nothing to you until you want to talk about it."

"It seems so cold, so callous."

"Do you love him? Be honest with me, Sadie."

After a long moment, I put my head on her shoulder. "Yes, I do."

Etta lifted my chin and gave me a beautiful smile. "Good. Don't you see? That makes me happy—the two people I love most in all the world, helping each other, loving each other. Because I believe Ben will love you back after I'm gone, Sadie."

We turned and watched Ben climb the hill. Shock coiled through me at the impact of Etta's words. I averted my gaze when Ben glanced my way, then turned to Etta.

"Ready to go, sweetheart?"

"I am now," said Etta.

❦❦❦

Neither Ben nor I said a word about that afternoon as Etta's final days came to a close. Her funeral was just as sweet and sad and open as she would have wanted. Everyone in town showed up for the service. Wildflowers filled the church and reminded me of the first day of my visit that summer. Etta Jones Howell, my best friend, had died and left me a legacy and a husband.

❦❦❦

I moved out of Etta's home and took a room at the Hamilton Inn. People in Mossy Creek would have nothing bad to say about either Ben or me, I vowed. Besides, I wanted to give Ben time to make his own decision about any future with me. Etta, bless her heart, had a plan, but I needed to know Ben had one of his own.

I got a job teaching third grade at Mossy Creek Elementary. Parents in town were delighted to have someone from the big city of Atlanta teaching at their school. Big Miss Ida Hamilton—grandmother of our future mayor, Ida Walker—introduced me at a school board meeting as "a fine young woman who has Etta's blessing." It made me smile to think those Creekites thought I knew something they didn't. The truth was, they were the ones teaching me a thing or two. Like trusting others, joining in various activities and feeling comfortable about myself at last. It would have pleased Etta no end.

As the weeks went by I began to wonder if Etta's plan for Ben and me was nothing more than her own whimsical idea. Ben arrived at the inn promptly at six o'clock every Saturday evening for our weekly "meeting." We didn't call it a date. We often ate at the inn then strolled awkwardly around the square, catching up on each other's activities. In the beginning we talked of Etta a lot. But as time passed the conversation turned more and more to my stories from school and Ben's stories from the Hamilton dairy farm.

One spring evening, when the setting sun glowed orange and the smell of new green grass tickled my nose, Ben met me on the inn's front verandah carrying a small bouquet of flowers.

"Why, Ben! How lovely," I said as he handed them to me with a smile.

"Like you," he answered. Then, after a long, somber moment when his throat worked and I put a hand to my heart, he added, "Now, I think we need to go ahead with this plan of Etta's..."

I cried and nodded and smiled. He threw his arms around me, hugging me tightly while a small crowd of guests and locals peered at us from the windows of the inn's parlor. They burst into applause.

🌷🌷🌷

My teenaged granddaughter looked up at me from her perch on the front steps of the porch where Etta, Ben and I had rocked many years before. Her lips spread in a knowing grin.

"And so *that's* why you named Mother *Etta*."

I smiled. "Yes. And to keep the name going, she changed it just a little and named you Lor-etta. *Loretta*. I've always felt it was a gift to all of us that she did so." I checked my watch and rose on legs that felt their age. It was hard to believe so many years had fled, leaving me an old woman closer to eighty than I cared to think about. "It's time to go. I don't want to keep him waiting. We do this every year, as the afternoon draws to a close."

"I'll get the blanket," Loretta said.

I slowly made my way down the porch steps and Loretta

helped me into her SUV. She took me out of town and up into the mountains to the meadow. I began to chuckle as I remembered the time I drove my 1940s blue Ford with Etta into the meadow and we got stuck. *Etta*, I thought, *cars are made to go anywhere in Mossy Creek, nowadays.*

Loretta turned off the road and drove the SUV into the meadow and right on up to the Sitting Tree. I got out of the giant vehicle and waited under the tree's deep shade.

"See you later, Grandmother," Loretta said, gave me a peck on the cheek, then drove away.

A minute later, a pretty red pickup truck pulled off the road and stopped. A tall, lanky, handsome, gray-haired man emerged and I felt a smile spread across my face. He carried a bouquet of wildflowers, as I knew he would.

Ben climbed the hill and gave me a small wave. The gentle look on his face filled me with deep joy. He handed me the flowers. "Happy anniversary, Sweetheart."

"I love you, Ben Howell," I said as his arms came around me. We held each other tightly as a gentle breeze caressed us. Then we bent and placed the flowers on Etta's grave.

I thought of the priceless gift I had been given, looked up at the clear evening sky and whispered softly, "Thank you, dear friend."

Mossy Creek Gazette

VOLUME III, NO. 3   MOSSY CREEK, GEORGIA

The Bell Ringer

Millicent Steals Another Heart

by Katie Bell

The lovely wedding of Millicent Hart, 80, and Tyrone Lavender, 81, was held at Magnolia Manor Nursing Home on Sunday afternoon. All the home's residents and many Creekites attended.

The wedding ceremony was held in the cafeteria (turned into a chapel for the occasion by Swee Purla Designs). The reception was catered by Win Allen, aka Chef Bubba Rice, who provided Millicent's favorite dishes for a hearty buffet, including Tequila Lime Chicken, Broccoli Quiche, and Chicken and Dressing Casserole.

The ceremony was performed by Mayor Ida instead of a minister because Millicent and Tyrone wanted their marriage recognized as official by everyone "except Social Security.'" Mayor Ida assured them her service would be enough for propriety's sake, but not the government's.

The bridesmaids included Millicent's daughter, Maggie Hart, and Tyrone's niece, Anna Rose Lavender. The groomsmen in-

cluded Maggie's fiancé, former Atlanta Falcon linebacker Tag Garner, and Anna Rose's fiancé, Beau Belmondo. Both Anna Rose and Beau interrupted filming on his new action movie, *Death Commando*, to attend. As many of you know, Anna Rose has a small part in Beau's film, playing "the only girlfriend who doesn't get blown up by the bad guy."

Owing to our local celebrities, Police Chief Amos Royden and deputy Sandy Crane caught two photographers from *The National Enquirer* at the wedding. One photographer claimed he was only attempting to retrieve his wallet. The wallet was later found inside Millicent's bouquet.

Millicent looked lovely in a powder-blue dress with a lace collar hand-crocheted by Josie McClure. Rainey Cecil of Goldilocks' Salon did a lovely job on Millicent's hair. It matched the dress beautifully.

In lieu of a honeymoon, the couple spent the next day moving

(continued on page 106)

Welcome to Summer Visitors

(continued from page 105)

Tyrone's furniture into Millicent's assisted-living apartment. When asked, Tyrone said that was about all he could handle at his age.

Millicent only smiled.

The bride's bouquet was caught by Inez Hamilton Hilley, 79, who promptly tossed it back. No one was surprised, as Inez has always been trouble. Read on for more news about Inez.

"Hold a true friend with both your hands."

—*Nigerian proverb*

LUCY BELLE and INEZ

Chapter Five

My name is Lucy Belle Hamilton Gilreath. The Hamilton part is my middle name, not a maiden name, as at forty-five, I am a spinster by Mossy Creek standards. Seeing as how the Hamiltons are as close to aristocracy as you can get in Mossy Creek, if you have a drop of their blood in your veins, you will almost always get Hamilton as part of your name. Hamilton is kind of like the Mossy Creek equivalent of Windsor or Mountbatten. Not that I'm bragging, you understand.

I'm one of those Mossy Creekites who intended to live by the town motto, "Ain't Goin' Nowhere And Don't Want To," but had to leave, anyway. I pursued a career in computer programming—God knows why, looking back on it—and so had to leave town to find a job, as Mossy Creek is not what you'd call a haven for high-tech activity. About the highest Mossy Creek has ever gotten, tech-wise, is the electronic milking machines at Ida Walker's dairy farm, and bovine applications are not my specialty.

But I do come back to Mossy Creek most weekends to spend time with friends and family. It helps me forget the stresses of a demanding job and city living. That is, usually. But home, no matter how humble, can come with stresses of its own. Take my grandmother, Inez Hamilton Hilley, for example. In her day, Grandma was the most formidable woman in town, with the possible exception of her cousin, old Big Ida Hamilton. Now she is tethered to an oxygen machine by a length of plastic tubing because of smoking Camels for more years than she cares to admit.

Her limited mobility does not dim her spirit or mar her mettle. Unfortunately, though, her once boundless energy has diminished, and facing the fact that she can no longer accomplish all she sets out to do leaves her often frustrated and fractious. Even more fractious than in the old days, which was to a considerable degree.

That in mind, I knew I was in trouble when I walked into Grandma's house one hot Friday night after visiting the Bigelow membership warehouse on the way home to Mossy Creek for the weekend. I greeted her and my mother, who were seated at the kitchen table embroidering and watching *Wheel of Fortune*. The kitchen is the center of Grandma's home and where she holds forth from her customary place at the table, her oxygen machine rattling away at her side. I put the items from Grandma's grocery list onto the table and gave her the receipt.

"I put the sack of birdseed on the porch," I said. "They didn't have the kind in the bucket this time."

Her eyebrows shot up like a pair of white doves flushed by a bird dog, and she stopped pawing though her purse for her wallet. "I wanted the kind in the bucket."

"I know you wanted the kind in the bucket," I said patiently. "But they didn't have any of that kind so I got you the kind in the sack."

"She wanted the kind in the bucket," my mother put in for reinforcement, presenting a united front.

I took a deep breath and tried again, enunciating my words carefully. "I realize that Grandma wanted the kind in the bucket. But, as I said, they didn't *have* the kind in the bucket, and I don't know anybody else who sells it in a bucket, so rather than come back empty-handed, I got the kind in the sack *just this once.*"

"I always get the kind in the bucket," Grandma said, staring into her purse as if to make eye contact with a creature as contrary as myself would singe her eyeballs.

"She likes the kind in the bucket because when the bucket's empty she can use it to take her peelings to Hank's compost pile," my mother allowed, not looking up from her embroidery.

Of course I was aware of all of that. I was the one who hauled the bucket next door to my uncle's compost pile after Grandma had deposited a week's worth of scraps in it, after it had started getting nice and putrid. The watermelon rinds are the worst—heavy, juicy and quick to go sour on you, like my mood at present.

I gritted my teeth. "I promise. Next time I'll get the kind in the bucket."

Grandma gave me the sort of withering look she usually reserved for Bigelowans. "The kind in the bucket is the only kind to get, because—" Grandma started.

I could feel my face glowing like neon. "Dammit! Listen here. They didn't have any birdseed in a bucket. If they'd had birdseed in a bucket, I'd have gotten it. If I came back here without any birdseed at all, you'd be on my case telling me I should've gotten the kind in the sack! If you want a bucket, I'll go to the Home Depot down in Bigelow and buy you a plastic five-gallon bucket for five dollars and you can *sit* in it for all I care!"

"Don't talk to your grandmother that way," my mother said seriously, looking down her bifocals at me.

Grandma smirked and slung the money she owed me across the table. "Put that gallon of milk in the ice box for me, would you?"

I chewed my tongue. I was raised to be respectful to my elders. "Sure," I said finally, opening the fridge. "Can I have some of this macaroni and cheese?" When angry, talk about food. It's a Southern tradition.

"Help yourself," Grandma said, and picked up her embroidery hoop.

Did I mention that Grandma loves a good fight? These days her fracases (or is it fraci? I'll have to ask Sue Ora and Katie Bell at the *Mossy Creek Gazette*) are usually only verbal in nature, thank goodness. Mostly she confines herself to railing and shaking her fist at objectionable people she sees on television, such as umpires and Republicans.

Mercifully, arguments with her family members are quickly forgotten. But in the right setting, she can still wring satisfaction out of nursing a grudge, and can still squeeze enjoyment out of fueling a feud. I guess it's the Hamilton in her.

I think she likes to fuss with me most of all, which is just as well, since I am the only one who has the guts to give her back as good as she dishes out. The others—my mother, aunt, uncle and cousins—are too deferential to be much of a challenge for her. That was one reason I had been selected by the whole family to break the news that hot summer night. This was going to be a fight neither of us was going to enjoy.

Grandma got up from her seat at the table, stretched to her full five-feet-even and waddled to the bathroom, trailing her length of plastic tubing behind her. When the door was closed firmly, my mother scrambled, sweeping her embroidery, scissors, thread and thimble into a tote bag and heading for the front door as if an air raid siren had just gone off.

"It's time for you to tell her."

"Tell me again why I have to be the one to do this?" I queried as Mama raced by me.

Pausing at the door, she looked back and said simply, "It'll be better coming from you. You're not just her granddaughter. You're her best friend." Then she disappeared like a wraith.

I knew Mama was right. I was the one who needed to tell Grandma that, for her own health, she had to do something that would be, for her, a fate worse than death. Her pulmonary problems had been worsening and after a few near-fainting incidents, something had to be done to ensure that she wouldn't harm herself. It was going to be hard, but she would have to face facts.

Grandma shuffled back from the bathroom, sat down, aimed the remote at the television and tuned in the Braves game. I took my mother's vacated place opposite her.

"Grandma, we've got to talk."

"Talk away."

"You know you've been getting weaker lately," I began. "And the family, well, we think you should take things easy from now on."

Grandma's thinning white hair, which normally stuck out in all directions anyway, took a sudden notion to stand on end like the comb of some strange albino rooster. She eyed me darkly. "What is that supposed to mean?"

I took a deep breath. There was nothing to do but plow onward. "We don't think you should get yourself all exhausted working up an entry for the chow-chow competition at the Bigelow County Fair this fall."

Right about now, dear reader, I figure you were thinking that I was about to tell Grandma that she had to go into Magnolia Manor nursing home. Oh, heavens no. I wouldn't ride up to Grandma's house with that proposal if you gave me a Humvee and a flame-thrower to protect myself.

"No!" Grandma slammed her fist down on the table. "This is the year. This is the year I'm going to beat Ardaleen Bigelow at her own game!"

I sighed as Grandma began to tell me the story again.

🐾🐾🐾

The feud between her and her younger cousin, Ardaleen, went back fifty years to when Grandma was president of the Bigelow County Home Demonstration Club. Ardaleen had come to Grandma's house on the pretense of attending the club's program on the latest canning techniques.

The county home economist doing the teaching was just out of the University of Georgia with a degree in home economics and a lot of fresh ideas regarding the womanly arts. Ardaleen was newly married to Winston Bigelow and said she was eager to impress her wealthy new in-laws with her homemaking skills. Ardaleen always spoke as if her own clan, the equally wealthy Hamiltons of Mossy Creek, could not hold a shade to the Bigelows of Bigelow. She turned up uninvited at the club meeting, which Grandma could have overlooked, Ardaleen being blood kin and all, if it hadn't been for the pepper pod incident.

The season before, Grandma had received from a distant cousin in Mexico seeds from a rare breed of pepper unrivaled for the ferocity of its hotness. It could peel the pink off your esophagus like turpentine peels paint. Using these fiery little pods and her own culinary creativity, Grandma had slaved over a hot stove until she had produced the perfect chow-chow.

Grandma distributed many jars of this stern stuff to her friends and relatives. Before long, the recipe was being hailed far and wide as the preferred invigorator of boring soups and stews, the stimulator of choice for stagnant deviled eggs, tuna casseroles and chicken salads, and the ideal complement to wieners. The formula had even beaten back stiff Bigelow competition at the county fair that year and won the blue ribbon in the aforementioned pickles and preserves category.

It was probably the Bigelows' loss in the competition that inspired Ardaleen to impress her fancy Bigelowan mother-in-law by executing the most vile and underhanded bit of domestic sabotage ever committed on a Creekite by a denizen of our evil sister city. While refreshments were being served in the parlor, Ardaleen sneaked into Grandma's kitchen and stole the secret chow-chow recipe right out of the metal box Grandma kept on the pantry shelf.

That bit of treachery was not discovered right away, however. Having heard that the rare peppers were the secret ingredient, Ardaleen also pocketed a handful of pods drying on the window sill, the ones containing all the seeds Grandma was planning to use for next year's crop. Then Ardaleen made the mistake of rubbing an itch beneath one demurely mascaraed eye.

Upon making a return visit to the kitchen to fetch a quart of pineapple juice concentrate to replenish the punchbowl, Grandma spied Ardaleen splashing cold water onto her face at the sink. The sill above the sink was as empty of pepper pods as it could be.

"What's wrong with your eyes?" Grandma demanded.

"Oh, I'm just so touched to be back with my kin again," Ardaleen squeaked. "I'm all choked up."

If Ardaleen thought her eyes were bugging out after she'd touched a pepper-stained finger to them, I expect they were prominent indeed after Grandma seized her by the throat. "I'll choke you up. Where are my pepper pods, you stringy-haired, flat-chested hussy? What did you do with them?"

It took the home economist and two neighbor ladies to pry Grandma off Ardaleen, who made a swift getaway before anybody got a chance to shake her down for the pods. It wasn't what you'd call a clean getaway, though, as her baby sister, our future mayor, Ida Hamilton (known as "Little Ida" back then), managed to dump the pineapple concentrate on Ardaleen's head as she was beating it down the back steps. Afterward, Little Ida tried to comfort Grandma the best she could. "Maybe she drew some yellow jackets on the way home," she suggested hopefully.

After that, the hated Bigelows of Bigelow claimed Grandma's recipe and her rare peppers, and she'd been stewing about it ever since. Especially when she found out that Ardaleen had tried to plant the pepper seeds herself the next spring but had let them all die. "Why didn't you just get some more peppers from that Mexico cousin?" people asked Grandma.

"He died at a chili cook-off," she explained mournfully. "Sweated himself to death, they say."

🌶️🌶️🌶️

Fifty years had passed, but Grandma had never forgotten or forgiven the pepper and chow-chow-recipe betrayal. I steepled my hands beneath my chin and sighed. "Grandma, why do you believe you're finally going to beat Ardaleen at her own game this year? After all, neither you nor Ardaleen ever found that variety of hot pepper again."

Grandma pounded the table.

"I've got a spy in Ardaleen's household. It's her maid, Ruthie. Ruthie told me that Ardaleen has found those very peppers. She used Ham's international connections with the Mexican government to track down some seeds."

I did a double take. Our governor, Ardaleen's pompous son, Hamilton Bigelow, had established diplomatic relations between the state of Georgia and the nation of Mexico? "Those Bigelows will do anything to get hot peppers for chow-chow," I deadpanned.

"This is serious. Ardaleen hired a horticulture expert to grow her a few plants and now they're putting out peppers like nobody's business. They're hidden in Ardaleen's fancy garden!"

"But surely Ruthie wouldn't risk her job to steal peppers for you if there's only a couple of plants' worth. It would be too obvious. Too risky."

"No, she wouldn't risk it. But we would." Grandma gave me her best make-it-so look, the kind that always caused the hairs on the back of my neck to stand up.

Sometimes Grandma could make me feel like a failure, whether it was for being an old maid, or for not having children, or for being a worthless bearer of bucketless birdseed. But more often than not, she bragged on me for my accomplishments and made me feel good about myself. (Incidentally, I think this alternation between praise and scorn is a form of mental torture banned by the Geneva Convention.) So because of this, and because I adored her, I had been looking for her approval from the time I was knee-high.

The surest way to get Grandma's approval was to help her execute one of her outlandish schemes—to take one of her harebrained ideas, set it up, flesh it out, breathe life into it and make it happen. So far none of the stunts had landed me in jail, in the hospital, or in the loony bin, but that had mostly been dumb luck. Especially the fourth-of-July fireworks incident in retaliation for Lamar Bigelow's son beating up Grandma's mailbox with a baseball bat. It was a good thing I had escaped unseen. The Bigelow clan were so mad you'd have thought I'd damaged the last Mercedes convertible north of the Atlanta city limits. I'll spare you the details.

As I stared transfixed into Grandma's intense, bird-like eyes, I realized that she'd presented me with the greatest opportunity ever to do her proud, to be her golden grandchild. I could feel a silly grin spreading across my face. Wordlessly, Grandma took a section of the *Mossy Creek Gazette* off the counter and slid it toward me. It was doubled back to a banner headline on the politics page.

Matriarch Throws Summertime Fundraiser.

"It looks like Ardaleen is giving a fancy garden party to raise money for Ham's next run for office."

"Two hundred dollars a plate," I observed, scanning the article. "I'll bet Ardaleen will be putting on the dog but good."

"Yep. She's already got Ruthie polishing silver and starching table linen. Sounds like this luncheon will be the social event of the summer down in Bigelow. I could get tickets, you know." Grandma rubbed her chin and rolled her eyes heavenward, looking like the sweetest little old lady you ever helped across the street.

"Grandma," I said. "What are you doing for lunch next Saturday?"

❦❦❦

Grandma's portable oxygen tank fit nicely onto the back of Casey Blackshear's motorized wheelchair. Casey was happy to make us the loan since she preferred her manual one for daily use. Wheeling the chair helped keep her arms in shape for softball, she said.

Grandma looked as cute as pie in her new cotton dress with flowery print. The big straw hat was a bit much, but she'd decorated it herself with millinery fruit from the Michael's store in Bigelow and was so proud of it that I didn't have the heart to tell her how ridiculous she looked. I myself was clad in a demure suit and pumps.

Our plan came close to being scrapped when Grandma almost dumped herself into the freshly-turned flower garden while practicing doughnuts in her driveway. When I was satisfied that she had mastered the wheelchair's steering mechanism, we loaded it into Grandma's minivan and headed south, to Bigelow.

The elegant, stacked-stone mailbox of Ardaleen's fake English manor house was decorated with an ostentatious floral display. "Where is my baseball bat when I need it?" Grandma muttered.

"No use stewing over that again. We roasted celebratory marshmallows over what was left of the Mercedes, remember?"

She gave me a beatific smile. "I remember."

The shady residential street was lined with fine cars in both directions. Beautiful tents had been set up in Ardaleen's garden. Catering staff hurried among the guests at linen-covered tables. I explained to a valet that I preferred to park the minivan myself to make sure I could maneuver the wheelchair in and out, and he waved me toward a side street bordering Ardaleen's yard. "There's a very accessible entrance through the wrought-iron gate by the peonies, ma'am."

"Thank you. It looks perfect."

"For making a clean getaway, you mean," Grandma said when we were out of earshot.

I neatly backed into a place on the street nearest where the tables were set up, then got Casey's chair out of the back and helped Grandma get seated. I looked down at the elfin old lady in her flowery dress with her huge straw hat that Scarlet O'Hara might have rejected as too gaudy. "Try to be inconspicuous," I said.

"Don't worry. Ardaleen will be so busy she won't notice me at all. And if she does, I'll just create a diversion for you by picking a fight with her and making a big scene."

"Okay," I said, checking my watch. "The guests should all be seated within ten minutes. I'll take the house and you take the garden. Are you sure you won't mire up? The motor makes that chair kind of heavy on sod."

Grandma waved a dismissive, white-gloved hand. "It hasn't rained in ages. I'll meet you back here as soon as I can."

Ducking under the hat brim, I kissed her rouged cheek and watched her roll off toward the cash bar.

❧❧❧

As I slipped into the house, I scanned the crowd of milling guests for Ardaleen, Ham, or anyone else who might recognize me. The coast remained clear as I walked unnoticed through the kitchen, which was bustling with caterers' assistants.

Ruthie, the spying maid, had told Grandma that pepper pods could be swiped from one of two locales. A few pods were ripening on plants tucked among the gardenia shrubs in the garden, and a couple of dozen were drying in a screened porch off the kitchen, where plants were potted and flowers arranged.

Unfortunately, that was also where Ardaleen's surly little dog was locked away to keep him from gnawing the ankles of the guests. At first I took him for a jumpy sort of dustmop. He had that long, stringy hair that obscured his eyes and made you wonder how he could see. But see me he did, because the minute I entered the room, he advanced on me as menacingly as his painted toenails and hair bows would allow. I hadn't seen as sorry a representative of the canine species since Ingrid Beechum's Chihuahua, Bob, got picked up by a hawk and urinated all over Mossy Creek before he was rescued.

"Good dog," I muttered unconvincingly. The dog bared its teeth and issued a throaty growl. He probably had been a good dog before Ardaleen got him groomed to look like the canine equivalent of Liberace and the humiliation just made him turn plumb sour. And if all that wasn't undignified enough, the name etched on his water bowl proclaimed him to be Pierre.

"Chill out, Pierre," I said.

I looked around. Lo and behold, I saw the bunch of chili peppers strung up in a loop and hanging on a peg at eye level. I also saw a broom leaning against the wall just within my reach.

Pierre took my grasping of the broom as a threatening gesture. Either that or just general effrontery. In any case, he poised to charge. I managed to snag the string of peppers off the peg with the broom handle, but when the dog sank his teeth into my shin, I flinched just enough to drop the pepper necklace—right over his head. And I screamed just enough to alert Ruthie, who opened the door from the kitchen to see what was the matter, allowing Pierre to bolt as if he were Cerberus fleeing the gates of hell.

"Good gawd!" Ruthie exclaimed as I raced past her with the broom. Pierre shot across the kitchen amid the startled caterers, executed a tight turn around a chopping block and skittered out a side door, while gnawing on the string of peppers that dangled around his front legs. I followed as quickly as I could, almost upsetting a huge tray of pecan tassies borne by a petite woman who squealed, "Dios Mio!"

I'd lost sight of the dog by the time I got outside so I slowed my pace to a casual saunter. I still had the broom tucked behind my back in case Ardaleen spied her dog and figured out why he was wearing a pepper-pod necklace with his hair bows. Poor Pierre would be feeling the effects of the peppers pretty soon. If he dealt with stress like Bob the Chihuahua, he would be in a nervous urinating frenzy that might put a damper on the flow of political contributions, depending on whose legs got in the way.

That wouldn't bother me. I wouldn't vote for Ham Bigelow for dog-catcher.

As I scanned the tables and milling guests, I saw a fuzzy bit of movement over by the manicured swimming pool. I sidled around the edge of the stone patio toward the pool, still grasping the broom behind my back. Poor Pierre was shaking his head violently, having discovered that his neck was too short to drink from the pool without falling in. He grasped one of the peppers in his teeth and shook his head as if in revenge. I winced for poor Pierre, who began to foam at the mouth.

But that's when I sneaked up on him and, for his own good, mind you, nudged him into the pool with the broom. He went under only for a second, just long enough for the pepper string to float to the top so I could snag it with the broom again and stuff it into my purse. I then got down on my knees and scooped Pierre back onto dry land, hoping the dunking had relieved his stinging eyes, nose and mouth.

I don't know if it accomplished that, but what it did accomplish was to make his humiliation complete. The dunking seemed only to have enraged him all the more, as it plastered his formerly glorious hair to his body, revealing the puniness of his true form. In the course of a few seconds, he went from simply looking like a sissy dog to looking like a sissy, half-drowned, wharf rat.

It was at that point that somebody screamed, "Look! A rabid possum!" I guess the sight of a dripping rodent staggering around the pool with his eyes rolling back in his head and foam forming at his snout was too confusing for genteel visitors from the wildlife-deprived skyscrapers of Atlanta. The sight of Ardaleen pushing her way through the crowd and screeching, "Pierre, darling!" got my feet to moving, and I lit out in search of Grandma.

Darting around the hedgerow that separated the patio area from the rest of the grounds, I looked back over my shoulder and saw Ardaleen bend down to pick up Pierre, who vigorously shook the water off his coat and all over Ardaleen's silk suit.

I spied Grandma in the garden, her wheelchair mired up halfway to the axle, spinning the back wheels, spraying mud all over the general area including herself, and going nowhere. "They've been irrigating, dammit!" she yelled as I reached her.

"Did you find all the plants?" I seized the handles of the

chair and began to drag her out of the mud.

"Yeah. They're in my purse, but I couldn't fit all the peppers in there."

"So what did you—" It was then I looked down and saw lovely, real, green peppers nested amongst the plastic grapes, plums and berries on grandma's hat brim. "You're a genius," I breathed with pure admiration.

"Pshaw," Grandma said with a little wave, her formerly pristine white glove covered with expensive garden loam and Georgia red clay.

We headed for the minivan as fast as we could and nearly made it when Ardaleen planted herself right in front of us. Next came the anxious-looking governor himself, accompanied by two burly state troopers complete with campaign hats, crew cuts and scowls.

"I know what you've done," Ardaleen said imperiously. "Hand over those peppers."

"Whatever do you mean?" Grandma challenged, her chin thrust out defiantly. Her dress, handbag and hat were speckled with mud, and when she tucked a stray strand of hair under her hat brim, she left a reddish streak on her forehead.

"It's as plain as the oxygen-tubed nose on your face that both you and your granddaughter have your bags stuffed with my peppers. Now give them back."

"Now, Mother," Ham soothed, "Mrs. Gilreath has considerable influence in Mossy Creek, and after all the misunderstandings from last fall, we don't want to overreact—"

"She stole my chow-chow peppers!"

Grandma eyed Ardaleen, a decidedly uncomfortable Ham, and the troopers. Then she reared her head back, took as deep a breath as her damaged lungs would allow and yelled as loud as she could, "Let me by! I'm fixin' to have one of my spells!"

I glanced toward the tents. Many of the luncheon attendees were staring our way. Good. I clasped my throat. "She's running out of oxygen and she forgot her inhaler!" My own shout elicited concerned looks from the guests. Then I glared at Ardaleen. "Are you prepared to shake down a little old lady on oxygen in front of your guests, Ardaleen? Governor? How do y'all think that would go over with the campaign contributors?"

Ham linked his arm through Ardaleen's. "Let it go, Mother."

Ardaleen's face contorted into several expressions before finally freezing in a forced smile. Through gritted teeth, she said, "Get out of my garden."

I grabbed the wheelchair's handles and headed Grandma toward the van. From behind us, we heard Ardaleen's parting shot, "That hat looks ridiculous."

Grandma raised a hand in a parting gesture. It was not the Southern beauty queen wave.

❦❦❦

Many have said that Grandma is full of spit and vinegar. I don't know about the spit, but after hours of tasting and perfecting the batch of chow-chow for the fair, I'm reasonably certain that she is, at least, full of vinegar. I know I am. After helping her procure the peppers, I also had to help her prepare the chow-chow, to make sure she wouldn't overdo it and get too tired.

Since her secret recipe had been breached long ago, she had come up with a variation that featured a new secret ingredient, which she decided should be moonshine from a local supplier. The result is quite remarkable, I must admit.

So much so, we not only expect to win the competition at the fair, but we've decided to go into business marketing the chow-chow. Here in town you'll be able to buy it by the pint jar at the Mossy Creek Grocery, Mama's All You Can Eat

Café and various gift shops, but we're working on a deal with Piggly Wiggly to sell it across the southeast.

With that, plus the Internet sales we expect from Grandma's website, we may do well enough for me to quit my programming job and move back to Mossy Creek, living with Grandma, which would just tickle me pink.

We have a lot more fussing to do.

Lady Victoria Salter Stanhope
The Clifts
Seaward Road
St. Ives, Cornwall TR3 7PJ
United Kingdom

Dear Vick:

You aren't going to believe this but one of your long-lost Salter relatives has come home to Mossy Creek. I told you about Mamie Brown going into the Magnolia Manor Retirement Home. Mamie's children put her house up for sale. Then Mamie's long-time "friend" and neighbor Grace Peacock broke her hip. Now Grace shares a suite with Mamie at the nursing home. Grace's granddaughter, Emily had been living with Grace for some time. Now she's decided to stay on in her granny's house since she likes her job as Mayor Ida's assistant. She's getting into the spirit of Creekite life and has even signed up with the new dance teacher to take lessons when the teacher gets her studio open.

But Emily is a little perturbed. Her new neighbor—the new owner of Mamie Brown's house—is Sagan Salter, a handsome young professor of anthropology from the University of Oklahoma. He's related to a Salter who married into the Cherokee Indian tribe over 150 years ago. We're not too clear about what he's doing here. Eventually, I'll get the story. You know how charming I can be. If charm doesn't work, I'll worry it out of him.

The only thing I can say now is that Emily and Mr. Salter seem to be developing the same kind of friendship that their former house occupants enjoyed. In other words, watch out for the fireworks. In the meantime, I'm off to interview a little girl named Therese Stroud. She insists she has a secret to tell me about her family. You know I can't resist a secret. More later.

Katie "Snoop" Bell

"We will be friends forever, just you wait see."

—*Winnie the Pooh*

❦❦

THERESE and the STROUD WOMEN

Chapter Six

Not many people in Mossy Creek could sing every stanza of *I'll Fly Away* without the hymnal and get all the words right. The number steadily decreased when you limited it to people who were only ten-years-old, well, almost ten. I could do it because I was a Stroud woman. At least, that's what my mama said. Personally, I was still not sure if I wanted to be a Stroud woman, or if I'd rather take my chances being known by my daddy's people, the Taylors.

When she married my daddy and they were presented to the congregation as Mr. and Mrs. William Taylor, Mama stopped the preacher dead in his pronouncing tracks and told one and all that she would have nothing to do with changing her name. She said as long as she stayed a Stroud, she had a good idea who she was.

"I'm going to need that name as a reliable excuse for being crazy one day," she said. Besides, she wasn't comfortable giving up who she was, or would be, for any man. Daddy agreed, seeing as how he didn't have much of a choice right there in front of every Stroud from the surrounding counties. It wasn't like it had never been done before, just not in

Mossy Creek. At least his daughters got the Taylor name a few years later.

From what other folks whispered, being a Stroud just meant you were tackier than a flea market and mean as a snake. I'd not lived long enough to be forced to pledge my allegiance one way or the other. It worried me though, because the women on my mama's side—except Mama, of course—all seemed like they got trapped by kids and dirt and lazy husbands who didn't ever make enough money to pay the electric bill. They wore loud clothes and too much perfume, like talismans against failure.

So maybe I'd choose to be a Taylor. I wouldn't wear loud clothes or perfume even if it meant I'd be more famous than Elvis Presley. I figured if I decided to be a Taylor, the worst thing that could be said about me would be that I was boring.

When you're stuck with an eccentric family and only four feet tall, you don't count for much. You can't even ride the good rides at the Bigelow County Fair. Most folks in Mossy Creek didn't pay me much mind. But that was all about to change, because tomorrow I'd have been on the earth for a whole decade, and that meant I was on the verge of Arriving. My family was always talking about people Arriving, like the person doing it had just come into something big. I figured living for ten years ought to get me something, so I was expecting my birthday to be the Arrival of Therese Taylor.

That's me.

❧ ❧ ❧

My mama worked as a teller for Mossy Creek Savings and Loan. She didn't have many close friends except her cousin, Ingrid Beechum, who owned the bakery, but she smiled and waved at everybody we passed on the street. I knew she felt their snubs and knew about their behind-the-hand comments concerning one crazy Stroud act or another. But my mama never bowed her head. I think she wanted better for her girls, wanted them to fit in and be upright citizens that folks wouldn't call troublemakers. The problem with that was my granny, Georgia Stroud. Mama would always be her mother's daughter, no matter how good-willed she might try to be, and there weren't many people who could tolerate my pot-stirring granny.

Including Mama. They fought like ducks snipping at each other's tail feathers with dull bills. Harmless, but annoying.

See, my mama named me "Therese" after a character in a racy romance novel. She read it on the sly when she was a teenager, after finding it in a collection of paperbacks stuffed under Granny's bed. When Mama found out I was on the way, she told Granny she had a name ready to go. This revelation resulted in a quarrel that goes on to this day. Granny swears those romance books were never in her house and that she doesn't read anything but women's magazines and the weekly Sunday school lesson.

Mama had already named my older sister, Sally, after Granny (whose full, formal name is Geraldine Sally Stroud), so she gave me my middle name, Geraldine, to appease Granny. Geraldine was my Great Granny's name. And so it also became my redemption from an existence assuredly headed toward deprivation after being branded with Therese, a fancy name straight from books Granny calls "a hussy's guide to life."

Sally was seventeen and she thought she was queen bee now that she could drive. She had a summer job working for Jayne Reynolds at The Naked Bean. She only got that job because Ingrid Beechum is my mama's cousin on the Stroud side. Ingrid and the owner of the coffee shop are good friends now, but that didn't happen until after they had a dirt-throwing fight right in the middle of town. You can tell Ingrid's my relative that way.

Anyway, my sister, Sally, complained day and night about how she couldn't get the coffee smell out of her hair. Sally was the only person I knew who put raw eggs and mayonnaise on her head as a hair conditioner. She looked at me like I was the crazy one while she waltzed around smelling like long-lost Easter eggs.

My sister had aspirations of becoming the wealthiest woman in Mossy Creek one day and rubbing all our noses in her money. She liked to talk big about going off and becoming famous making shampoo commercials with her long black hair. Her hair made me think of a horse's tail. In fact, a lot about Sally made me think of a horse's tail.

Most of the time Sally was off somewhere with Earl Jenkins, her stupid boyfriend. At night I had to listen to her talk about what a stud he was until I fell asleep. "Earl is such a good kisser, Earl is so strong, Earl's such a great boyfriend, Earl looks so cool on his daddy's tractor..."

It all made me want to throw up, and I said so.

Sally said I'd understand when I was a woman.

"If you're a woman," I shot back, "then I don't have much to look forward to."

She whacked me with her hair brush, but I didn't care. I wasn't sure I'd ever understand the women in my family.

The only adult woman in all of Mossy Creek who understood me was our mayor, Ida Walker. She must be about ten-feet-tall, and she was always dressed up pretty in things like scarves. I didn't know anybody else in Mossy Creek who wore scarves in warm weather. She ran her own show, the scarves flying like silk flags over a fancy country where she was queen. Nobody said anything bad or embarrassing about Miss Ida, and not just because she'd go after them with her gun.

She always patted me on the back, not my head. And

she always said my name right. Not Tur-esa, not Tear-race, but Tha-*reese*. I never had to help her remember how to pronounce it with a "th," like you had a lisp.

Best of all, she often said, "Therese Taylor, you're a bright one."

Last fall at the big reunion picnic I marched right up to her and asked how she ever got people to listen to her, because I needed some tips. Miss Ida said she understood how hard it can be to have big opinions in a small body. She said it would help to get taller, but mostly I'd just have to bide my time and keep my eyes open for Opportunity.

"When Opportunity comes your way, Therese," she explained, "you'll be ready to jump on it and express yourself loud and clear. And then people will listen to you. Always remember: She who hesitates is last. Bide your time and keep your eyes open."

Okay. Since then I'd been biding and watching like a hawk. It turned out, I'd been sitting on top of Opportunity all along. I was living right in the middle of a bunch of criminals.

My grandmother and her sisters. The Stroud women.

❧❧❧

On the eve of my tenth birthday, I was ready to confront them. All I had to do was get out of the house, first.

"Did you brush your teeth, Therese?" Sally asked snidely as she flounced past me in the cramped little bedroom we were forced to inhabit together.

"Yes." I hurried to my side of the room, pulling my shirt over my head and breathing heavily in my sibling's face.

"You did not, you liar!" she bellowed. "I checked your toothbrush and it's not even wet." I ignored her. Teeth were not on my agenda, and neither was my obnoxious teenaged sister.

"Good morning, Daddy." I swiped a kiss on my father's scruffy cheek as I zipped through the kitchen.

"Therese didn't brush her teeth yet!" Sally called down the narrow hallway of our double-wide mobile home. "She already has bad breath, even when her mouth is clean!" She narrowed her eyes at me. "You're so embarrassing!"

"Sally, if you don't have anything better to do than check your sister's toothbrush every morning, maybe you could help your mother out a little more around here, huh?" drawled Dad, his exasperation already evident.

I stuck out my foul little tongue and grinned at her.

"You're just gross, did you know that!" she yelled. "Your teeth are all going to get cavities and fall out of your head and I won't even act like I know who you are."

Big change, I thought. I watched as Daddy scrubbed his face with his hands and yawned, apparently resigned to his eldest daughter's belligerence.

My Daddy worked all day as a lineman for the Mossy Creek EMC Company, and when he got home, he took off his faded, blue, work clothes and headed straight to the bathroom with the weekly edition of the *Mossy Creek Gazette*. The only thing that might slow him down was the need for a new roll of toilet paper or when he spied a new dirt spot on the carpet. We had gotten fancy wall-to-wall carpet in our trailer the spring before. My daddy got pills for his blood pressure not long after. We had to take our shoes off before we could go inside now, even in summertime. I'd tried to tell Daddy that it doesn't matter if you leave your shoes outside when you've been barefoot all day, but he was usually too busy lecturing Sally to listen.

He was always trying to teach her about being proud of what you've got. He said, "Sal, you can tell a lot about a person by the way they take care of their things and appreciate the hard work it took to get them. If you don't learn what it is to work hard for something and be thankful to the good Lord that He sees fit to provide for you, you won't amount to nothing in this world."

He thought he was going to give his family something he called class. I thought he was going to give himself a heart attack by the way his face got red when he talked to Sally. My sister was a big believer in her version of the American way. If she could get rich quick from a lottery ticket at the filling station for a buck, then she saw no reason to worry about making a living some day. She was embarrassed by my dad because he didn't work in an office and we lived in a mobile home. She wanted to be a big shot, like the folks down in Bigelow. The way I saw it, Daddy was probably wasting his time trying to explain to my sister what gives a person class. On my birthday eve, Daddy's morning sermon to my sister and me was no exception.

"...and it wouldn't kill the two of you to have a little pride in what we have here. You could help your mother clean up the place better. She works a hard job all day. She don't need to come in here and have to clean up after you kids, too."

Sally rolled her eyes and let out a long, frustrated sigh. "Daddy, I'm working a summer job, you know. Tell Therese to clean up. She's the pig. Besides, if I came home to clean every evening like some kind of Cinderella, I'd practically never get to go out with Earl. Summer only lasts so long, Daddy. Don't you remember being young? This family is so boring!"

"Young lady!" Daddy bellowed as usual, pounding on the kitchen table so hard the portable TV jumped. On the *Today* show, even Katie Couric looked rattled. Sally knew just the right buttons to push to send Daddy into orbit. I left my sister, my father and Katie to the troubles of the day.

Mama was cooking biscuits for breakfast and changing out the laundry like she did every morning. The aroma drifted through our cramped little house. But I was not really interested in food that morning. I could feel my nerves jangling, anticipating the plans I had for the day. My mouth was a direct link to my conscience and so I started to talk to my mama about anything that came to mind. I jabbered a mile a minute about what I thought I might be doing over the weekend with my cousin, Sue Ann.

Sue Ann had to play with me on the weekends when Mama kept her while her own mother worked. I say if somebody is a playmate by obligation, there just isn't much point. I tried to be Christian to my cousin because of Mama, but mostly I stuck to myself. Everybody in Mossy Creek thought that made me peculiar, but kids my age just had no appreciation for ambition. I didn't have time to waste on piddly, girlie nonsense when I had to be thinking how I was going to put myself on the map. One day, Mossy Creek would be knocking down my door to socialize. Until then, I'd consider Sue Ann babysitting practice.

After about five minutes of my chatter, Mama said she was too busy to listen to me. "Therese, you are the mouth of the South! Get out of here before you give me another one of my headaches with all your jabber!" Mama brushed past me to put away the Crisco. I knew to get out of her way quick if she started to notice me enough to talk to me. Usually, if Mama got a good look at me, she had a fit about the way I was always wearing my favorite pair of cut-off overalls or told me to wet my hair down real good so I didn't look like a scarecrow.

Mama was pretty. She tried real hard to keep her hair all combed down and shiny; it was wild and curly and dark auburn. Not at all like my straw-colored thicket. Mama was always wearing some kind of beauty cream when she got ready for bed. She liked to stay polished and pressed, even if her clothes didn't come from the department stores.

She was like my Granny that way, but you'd better not

say it to her. My mama and my granny don't like anybody saying they had the first thing in common. If they admitted they were so much alike, they might not have any good reasons to hate each other. I didn't think I was like either one of them.

Suddenly, she took a long look at me. Uh oh.

"Therese, you're going to have birds nesting in your hair! If you don't start taking care of it, I'm going to take you into town to see Willy at the barber shop. He'll give you a buzz cut like he gave your cousin Tommy last summer. Then you'll wish you'd brushed that stuff."

Wilburn Hankins was a legend in Mossy Creek. From what I could tell, he was about one-hundred-and-fifty-years-old and blinder than the moles our cat turned up in Mama's flower beds. If there was a threat that could inspire me to spend time yanking knots out of my hair, it was a trip to see Willy and his enthusiastic shears. Everybody in Mossy Creek remembered my cousin Tommy's summer haircut. His head looked like an eraser on the end of a pencil that had been chewed up.

So I tolerated the short haircut Mama had Miss Rainey give me at Goldilocks. Rainey said I looked like some ice skater who was real famous about a hundred years ago, I guess. Lucky me. That was about all Mama could do to pretty up my fuzzy head, or the rest of me. I wished she'd eventually give up and figure out I'd never be beautiful like Sally.

"I'll brush," I promised Mama.

"Good. Now go on outside and play. Enjoy the summer."

"Okay! I'm going to Granny's."

"Then go."

Perfect. I'd made it past the periodontal police, the minister of work ethics and the hair inspector. I'd hung around long enough to keep suspicion at bay, so I waltzed out the front door. There was only one problem. Mama followed. As I hopped on my bike, she called, "You better brush that hair before your Granny sees you! I don't want to hear from her after she sees you wearing a rat's nest!"

"I'll brush! I promise!"

"I just bet! Come back here and let me put some mousse on that hair!"

I pretended I didn't hear. It was a good thing I was already on the road, seated on my bike and peddling like mad. My mama had long arms that could catch me with a fly swat at a thousand feet, if she wanted to.

She was a tough Stroud woman, for sure.

❦ ❦ ❦

The summer air was sticky and thick with humidity. I could feel a trickle of sweat rolling down the middle of my back as I peddled all the way into town. I had to save my family's reputation.

I'd single-handedly bring my family to redemption. I'd start a new breed of Strouds and Taylors that the citizens of Mossy Creek would all want to have over for dinner with the real cloth napkins.

I zoomed down North Bigelow Road, crossed the creek at the North Bigelow bridge, and was in downtown Mossy Creek at eight o'clock a.m. My ride into town had made me thirsty and my mouth was dry from more than anxiety. I felt nauseous with excitement. I thought maybe it hadn't been such a good idea to leave without breakfast, after all.

Sandy Crane's pickup truck was already parked out front of the police station. I felt a rush at the prospect of setting my plans into action. I parked my rusty purple bike and scampered up the building's creekstone steps.

Sandy stood at the front counter, stirring her coffee and eyeing a box of pastries from Cousin Ingrid's shop. Sandy always showed up first at the office. I didn't want to risk running into Chief Royden or anyone else. For one thing, I had a crush on the chief, like most females in Mossy Creek.

Sandy grinned at me. "Hey there, sweetie. What you doing out so early? You got a cat up a tree or something?" Sandy leaned over the counter to look down at me.

"No, ma'am. It's bigger than a cat."

"What is it then?"

"This is about my granny and my great aunts."

Sandy came around the counter to me. Her expression changed to a more serious one. She sat us down in a couple of chairs. "Are they all fighting again? Is it over your Great Uncle Hogue? Is he okay?"

"Nobody's hurt, Miss Sandy. I'm here because I need to report a crime. Well, actually it's a crime that hasn't happened yet. But I want to report it to you later today, after it happens. That's why I came here this morning. I need your help to set up a bust."

Her eyebrows furrowed. "Now, Teresa, are you sure about this, honey? What exactly are you talking about? What do you mean a bust? Have you been watching your daddy's detective shows on TV again?"

I had, but she was missing the point.

"No, ma'am," I lied. "What I'm talking about is a real crime. My granny and my great aunts are about to break the law. Today. At the old Baptist cemetery outside town."

"Do tell!"

I spoke in hushed tones. "Miss Sandy, I'm a law-abiding person. I believe in being good. And even if it means turning in my own kin, I want to make people think well of the Strouds and the Taylors from now on. I ain't got no choice but to hand over my granny if I ever want to be able to live with myself. I've heard my mama say granny ought to be locked up, so I think she approves."

I finished dramatically, covering my face with my hands like I had seen a distraught actress do on *Law and Order* the week before. It had worked for her. They had started working on her case really fast. I peeked through my fingers to see if Sandy was won over.

She looked skeptical. "I believe I'll need more details," she said in a solemn tone.

I sighed. "They're good women, really. They're just Strouds, is all. Everybody knows that makes them crazy. But I'm part Taylor. I'm not crazy. And I want to be a good citizen of Mossy Creek. Maybe someday I'll even be respectable enough to get a job as your assistant, Officer Crane."

Sandy sat up tall in her chair, apparently moved by my performance, and took me by the hands. "Sweetie, you be brave and go on and tell Miss Sandy exactly what has you so worried about your granny and her sisters. I'm listening."

The magic words! She was listening! I beamed and let it fly.

"They're grave robbers!"

Miss Sandy bit her lower lip. "Grave robbers?"

"I've never seen them, but I've heard my mama talk about how they go down to that old cemetery south of town where the Baptist church used to be, and they say they're going to clean it up, but they never clean up! They steal the flowers right off the graves. My mama says they've been doing it as long as she can remember. They bring 'em home and plant 'em right in their own yards, as proud as you please. She says they don't ever bring her anything, though. Before she married my daddy she used to go with them, but one day she got in a fight with my granny and her aunts and after that Granny and her aunts never took her with them again! But they're taking me today! For the first time! I'll see it all, and I'll bring them right straight to you!"

Miss Sandy sat back, staring at me. I guess it took her a minute to process all the critical information. I figured she was trying to decide how to charge them in her report. Finally she got herself together. "Miss Taylor," she addressed me formally, "You sure are a good citizen, and I'll tell the chief all about this as soon as he gets in this morning. Probably after he has his coffee and doughnuts. Don't worry. We'll be sure to look into this."

She stood up from her chair. She hadn't made any notes or started a file or anything.

"But you don't understand! I can bring them here this evening. They'll probably have a car-load full of plants by then! I can do the leg work for you!" Leg work was another crime term I had gleaned.

"Now, listen, Teresa." There that name was again. "You keep your eyes open, but don't say a word. You just go enjoy your day and let us handle things from here. I promise, we will." She began ushering me toward the door. "Tell your mama I said hello, sweetie."

She patted me on the head as she deposited me on the front step. I took a deep, disappointed breath. The town was beginning to stir. Mr. Garner, who owned the art shop, was out sweeping his sidewalk. He waved to me and I waved back, even though he had blue hair and I knew that probably made him someone I shouldn't wave to. He was a fellow crime-stopper. He had nabbed his own prospective mother-in-law, Miss Millicent Hart, on numerous occasions. Well, if he could do it, I thought, and him with blue hair and not even born in Mossy Creek, then so can I.

I'd just have to do it alone. And why not? I did everything else that way.

❧ ❧ ❧

Granny Georgie wasn't the sort of grandmother who teaches you how to make perfect biscuits or takes you to the roller rink and sits there for hours while you wobble around to loud rock-n-roll music. In fact, I wasn't even sure if she liked me. But whether she liked me or not, Granny

Georgie was determined to indoctrinate me with all the Stroud family history, according to her. She was also training me in the finer points of feminine beauty according to Mary Kay cosmetics. Stroud traditions and Mary Kay were both held sacred by my grandmother.

I never knew my granddaddy. His name was Claude and he died back when Mama was still a kid. Granny still missed him, and in her way, she continued to honor him. For example, in recent years she had bought a used male mannequin from Mr. Hamilton at the department store and dressed it up in Granddaddy's clothes. She often put that dummy in the passenger seat of her Buick so she wouldn't be a lady traveling unescorted when she took a road trip to see her cousin, Irene, who lived way down on the coast, in Savannah.

Granny was a die-hard Braves fan, so on one trip to see Irene she stopped off in Atlanta to catch a baseball game. I don't know if she left the dummy in the car or if he went to the game alongside her, but she said that mannequin made the best company she had ever had on a vacation.

Thus far, my summertime days with Granny and her Claude mannequin had been fairly quiet, filled with stringing beans on her back porch while she rolled my short hair in tiny curlers and slathered some kind of pink lotion on me, which drew every bug in the county.

Now I watched as Granny Georgie whizzed past me in a flurry of floral house dress, looking like a Banty hen in a fizz. She primped up for the monthly trip to the graveyard. Every third Wednesday she and her sisters went to clean up the graves of our forgotten relatives, since the Baptist church had moved into town fifty years ago. Most days, by the time I got to her house Granny was already on the telephone with one of her sisters, planning the day's trip and gossiping. They would argue about the local Southern Baptist congregation or argue about the gossip Granny hasn't been the first to hear.

But today was not a day for casual telephone calls. Today was the day another well-organized heist would take place, and finally, for the first time, I would be allowed to go along and see it, in person.

I parked myself on Granny's big, maroon sofa, which was covered in plastic so Granny could keep it clean for the "good" company. I did my best to blend into the big, pink peonies on the wallpaper behind it, not moving a muscle. The plastic stuck to my legs in the humid, eighty-degree air of the living room, but I knew if I budged I would draw attention to myself. With that one crunch or squeak, Granny might change her mind about taking me along to the cemetery, and then I wouldn't get The Scoop.

I learned about The Scoop from overhearing Sue Ora Salter, publisher of our town newspaper, talking to Mama at the bank one day about some fiasco down in Bigelow. Anything about the city of Bigelow, the Bigelow family, or Bigelowans in general was a real attention-getter around Mossy Creek. Despite being married to a Bigelow herself (in fact, her husband was president of the Bigelow County Bank, the biggest competition for the Mossy Creek Savings and Loan), Sue Ora (who kept her maiden name, just like Mama) put the scandal right out on the front page of the *Mossy Creek Gazette*. Then our town gossip columnist, Katie Bell, would dig into the story and keep it going on the front page for weeks at a time. Katie Bell was still writing about the reunion events from last fall and the plans Governor Bigelow had announced back then—under suspicious circumstances—for rebuilding Mossy Creek High School.

If I turned in Granny and her sisters for grave robbing, Katie Bell and Sue Ora would have the whole town talking about me. I studied my worn-out sneakers and thrilled to thoughts of a parade featuring me on top of the Mossy Creek

Volunteer Fire Department's ladder truck, just like old Mr. Brady sat on top during the Christmas parade every year, dressed up like Santa. I'd be a celebrity, get to ride on top of the truck and I wouldn't even have to wear a Santa suit.

Granny got dressed in a pair of cotton capri pants that made her ankles look even more like chicken legs. Then she pulled on her long, narrow Keds, complaining that they covered up her fuchsia toenails, but saying she couldn't see wearing sandals to work in the cemetery. I almost snorted at the idea of my prissy grandmother doing anything that might threaten to make her break a sweat.

Fifteen long minutes later Granny emerged from her bathroom in a cloud of aerosol fumes, all ready to go, bottle-red hair teased and sprayed generously with Aqua Net, her skin smelling strongly of Oscar de la Renta perfume.

"Come on, Therese! What are you doing just sitting there? You're going to make us late!"

I peeled my legs off the sofa cover, straightened my cut-offs and followed her out to her enormous, baby-blue Buick. We barreled down the road.

My grandmother's incessant need to be on time consistently provided me with opportunities to be thrown from a moving vehicle. I'd learned it was best to sit close to the door in the back seat. That way, I could hold onto the door knob to keep from being slung all over the place. Clinging to the door with all the strength in my scrawny little arms, I pushed my feet into the floor board to keep from slamming into the back of Granny's seat. We came to a screeching halt at the one traffic light in Mossy Creek that never failed to turn red upon our approach.

"That blame thing catches me every time!" Granny complained. "It's beyond me why Amos Royden thinks we need it. You see anybody coming either way, Therese?"

Before Granny could make a break for it, the light changed and she gunned the engine. Being that I was on a mission to catch my grandmother up to no good, the adrenaline was coursing through my skinny little body at such a speed that I felt light-headed. I was relieved she had been spared a chance to incriminate herself so early in the day.

We shot down the street like bandits.

❦❦❦

I was relieved to tear into Great Aunt Burt's gravel driveway, a cloud of dust roiling up behind us. Granny honked the horn long and hard. The Buick's horn sounded like a freighter docking. She honked again, then flipped down the vanity mirror to check her hot-pink lipstick. Loud, pink colors were a big thing for Granny.

Granny sat stewing and growing increasingly agitated. It would be another ten minutes before her sister, Burt, lumbered out her screen door to resume their on-going disagreement about the time of departure. By then, Granny would be worked into such a dither that no rational comment would be heard until kingdom come. I couldn't figure out how you could be late to visit dead relatives.

Aunt Burt shared my opinion on this topic.

Her given name is Coretta, but no one could remember, or would admit to remembering, how she came to be known as Burt. Aunt Burt was a short, broad woman with a sharp nose and an easy smile. Her salt-and-pepper hair was cut short like a man's, and she went barefoot in her blue jeans most days. She wore no-nonsense, button-down shirts that pulled tight across her massive bosom. She set no value in the painstaking beauty regimen Granny insisted upon. Burt's fingers are always stained with different colors from her oil pastels.

She lived alone in a house behind the public library, with a couple of parrots and a blue-tick hound dog named Rufus, who she rescued from the Bigelow County Pound.

Burt had never been married, and no one ventured any opinions—at least not in front of me—as to why she remained single. She always seems content enough to me, and she was my favorite great aunt. Burt had a big, boisterous laugh and she was always full of funny stories. She was always in a good mood, she was always casual and she was always, always late.

All of which provoked my dandied-up, precise little Granny into a fit of nervous indignity.

"You're late!" Granny yelled as Burt lumbered to the Buick.

"You're on time," Burt shot back, and grinned.

She got into the car and they began to argue like professional commentators at a wrestling match. Granny volleyed something about Burt's lack of self-respect and appearance. Burt hefted back a joke about Granny's increasingly wider rear end. All the while Burt cast glances my way, conspiratorially grinning at my grandmother's rage.

We arrived at Great Aunt Darcey's mobile home ten minutes later to find her waiting on her front stoop. She gracefully took one last, long drag from her non-filtered cigarette before crushing it underfoot on her way to the car. I couldn't help admiring her rebellious swagger.

Aunt Darcey's hair was always a riot of nondescript curls, like my own, only brown instead of yellow. She wore her blue jeans just a bit too snug, according to Granny. I didn't mind her tight pants. In fact, if I grew up lucky enough to have a skinny butt like Darcey's instead of my mama's wide hips, I'd wear my jeans tight, too.

Darcey was the baby sister in the group, but she looked older because her marriage to my Great Uncle Hogue had not been easy. Her youth had gone the way of hard work in a chicken-processing plant way over in Gainesville. She had miscarried two babies buried before they took their first sweet breath. She never had any more children, after that. I was a little afraid of Aunt Darcey. She squinted wickedly when she smoked her cigarettes, and she never apologized to any living soul for any reason.

"Lord, I thought you all were probably in a ditch somewhere," she growled at Granny and Burt. "What took you so long? Burt, as usual?"

"Who knows what ever takes Burt so long," Granny snapped. "Next time, I'll just come pick you up and we'll get on out to the cemetery on time. Let Burt wait all morning wondering where we are, for a change."

Aunt Burt winked at me. She and I both knew they wouldn't leave her at home.

She brought the lunch.

"How's Hogue?" my Granny asked as she drove. Darcey let out a short blast of air.

I waited on tender hooks. If she had finally murdered him in his sleep with a kitchen knife or poisoned him with crushed up rat poison in the cornbread, I was a shoe-in for town detective.

"He's as stupid as ever. We had a Big One this morning before he left for work. "Big One was our family's slang for a brawl that usually involved cooking utensils. "I don't know how a man can lose money like he does. I know it ain't falling out of his pockets, cause I check 'em for holes regularly." Darcey fluffed her hair with her long, lethal fingers.

"Is he drinkin' again?" asked Aunt Burt. From the scowl on her face it was just luck that Great Uncle Hogue wasn't already stuffed in a trunk somewhere.

Darcey snorted. "Is he ever not drinking? It's not that. I mean, I don't mind if he stops in to set a spell at the pub. At least I know where he is then. I just don't like the way he's alley-cattin' around up in Chinaberry, lately."

Darcey rolled down her window to let in some cooler air. The plush upholstery in the car was stifling in the summer. There had been no air-conditioning in the Buick since the compressor went out two summers before. With all four of us packed in, it was oppressive and full of the aroma of fleshy, powdered women and whatever we had eaten for breakfast that morning. I clutched the door handle and gratefully inhaled the blast of sweet, warm air.

"What's Hogue doing up in Chinaberry?" asked Granny.

"He says it's something about some job a man over at Bailey Mill told him about. There ain't a job, and I know it." When Aunt Darcey was angry, she tended to sound like a saw blade. She was often angry. She continued on a tirade of accusations with a livid baring of her not-so-white teeth. I crouched down in my corner, listening for any information that might come in handy when I would surely have to testify as an accomplice to homicide.

When Darcey came to a halt in her tantrum and put her face in her hands, I was surprised to see a look of sympathy on Granny's face.

"Well, there's no use making trouble where there ain't none." Aunt Burt interjected. "If he gets himself a better job, it could be good for the two of you. And if it ain't a job, then you can always get that frying pan after his head again."

Granny, Burt and Darcey traded a look, then smiled in sinister unison.

I was riding down the road to hell in a Buick full of degenerates.

❦❦❦

The rest of our drive was an unending cackle of community hear-say. When we bumped into the cemetery along the worn gravel path that led to our family plot, I assumed my best bird-dog vigilance.

The cemetery sat on a hill overlooking a little branch of Mossy Creek called Baptist Creek, since the Baptists used to divert it into a little pond for their baptisms. What had once been a beautiful church beside it was now just a stone foundation filled in with mowed grass. The old cemetery had been forgotten.

I got out of the Buick, looking up in amazement into the bower of an enormous tree. Three gigantic oak trees were strategically placed throughout the graveyard, guarding the loved ones resting at their roots. I don't think I had ever considered the reverence of a place that held bones and memories, before that moment. I was almost as impressed by the concrete Jesus, arms also outstretched, looking down at me from a pedestal at the cemetery's center. His fingertips had gone missing long before he and I met. My nose filled with the sweetness of all things green and moist, a loamy sort of scent that was pleasant in the heat. I felt strangely enchanted by the hush.

Granny and her sisters began their monthly perusal of the grounds, wandering about the smooth, cool granite stones. All the while, they spouted long-forgotten stories of ancestors they'd never known and of kin they knew and remembered all too well. They talked about the Stroud women who had married good-for-nothing men and the Stroud men who had been lured away by racy women. Great-Grandmother Stroud's sister, Velda, had "near lost her mind to have run off with a philanderer." Great-Great Uncle Herbert was "always too good for the rest of the family once he married that foreign woman, though that hateful hussy never loved him."

Some Strouds had been fools and lost souls and there was no redemption even in death for them, according to Granny and my great aunts. But none of that talk, fascinating as it was, furthered my mission. I wanted them to get down to business and start robbing graves.

To my great disappointment, Aunt Burt decided it was time for lunch. I scarfed down a bologna sandwich and spent the rest of my time jumping over the graves of my kin while my great aunts and my granny feasted on coleslaw, meatloaf sandwiches and sweet iced tea. They communed together on their old picnic quilt like witches.

Darcey stirred a sprig of mint around in her tea glass with a long fingernail, as if stirring a cauldron. I thought of how convincing she always looked on Halloween, when she would answer her door dressed in a wicked-witch outfit with a fake, green wart on her nose. She, Granny and Aunt Burt huddled together on the picnic quilt like a scene from a Southern version of *Macbeth*. They argued over what kind of accidents and diseases Strouds were most likely to suffer, and which elderly kin or young fool was likely to die next.

Their preoccupation with the morbid side of our heritage had led them straight to a life of crime, I reasoned. Now if they would just get on with it, I would have the evidence I needed to set our women right again. I would put the Strouds back on the Baptist straight and narrow. Granny and her sisters finally finished their meal, folded up their blanket and packed up their Tupperware. I had to stifle a squeal of delight.

The time had come.

❦ ❦ ❦

"Well, let's see," said Granny as she inspected a grave.

"Looks like Bobby Lee's lobelia is gettin' a little overgrown. Burt, do you want a piece to root for your back yard? It would do real nice out there by your crepe myrtle." She took a hand spade from a tote bag and began digging. "I remember when old Bobby Lee told me lobelia was his favorite shrub and asked me to put this here for him one day. Lord, that don't seem no time ago. And me just a little ol' thing."

"He was so hateful, I'd have never guessed he'd have

told you what he liked," said Darcey.

"Well...he wasn't hateful all the time. I can remember when that old man would take me up on his knees some nights and we'd listen for whippoorwills out back of the house."

"How about that sweet little clematis vine on Baby Jane's grave? It has some real nice blooms on it. I think you ought to pull up a piece or two to set out by your stoop, there, Darcey. Want me to walk up there and pull you some?" Darcey and Granny wandered up the hill, their conversation growing faint. I looked around in search of Aunt Burt's round form.

She was at the other side of the cemetery. I found her squatting beside a remnant of a fieldstone wall around a grave plot. She ran her fingers over a stone with a cross engraved at the top. Sgt. Samuel T. Blevins, it read. She looked up at me, and I was surprised to see tears on her cheeks. She reached out and took my hand. I settled beside her on the newly cut grass.

"This here was the love of your crazy old great aunt's life, sweet pea," she said. I gazed at her as though I had never seen her before. "This man was a soldier for us in Korea. He died a long time before you was ever born; that's why you never knew about him. Nobody talks about him, 'cause they think it'll hurt me. I reckon it would. We was sweethearts and best friends all our lives. We was getting married, we thought. I almost married him before he left for the war, but we thought we'd just wait so it wouldn't be so hard."

She traced the shape of the little cross on the tombstone with a stubby finger. "When you're young, you don't ever think the people you love will go away forever. That's why folks love so easy when they're little—like you, pumpkin. You don't have no fear of what can happen."

I couldn't help my heated response. "I'm afraid of everything! Most of all I'm afraid of being a grouchy old Stroud that nobody likes and everybody talks about! That's why I won't admit I love anybody. I'm not even wasting my time." I sat there like a mad, wet bird with my feathers all puffed up.

I had no idea why I'd said any of that or where the words had been hiding inside me. All I knew was that I was going to be ten-years-old and nothing in my life would ever improve. No kids would suddenly write me friendship notes in class or pick me for the games in P.E. because they truly liked me. My family wouldn't find me amusing or wise or worthy of their attention just because I was a year older. And here sat my great aunt, the only one I liked, caring for someone who had been dead all my life. Caring for a grave, while I was planning to turn her in for grave robbing.

Aunt Burt looked hard at me. "Therese, people waste their whole lives on being afraid. That's why you need to keep on lovin', just the same. So when you get old, like me, you won't be sitting here thinkin' how you wished you had. It ain't wastin' time to hang on to the people you care about. It's wasting time to pretend you don't care."

She swiped at her runny nose with the back of her hand and grinned. "One day, you'll be plantin' pretty things on your old Aunt Burt's grave and I'll know you've taken my advice, and that you're taking care of my memories."

I watched as she pulled a little piece of thrift from the base of the soldier's tombstone. "Therese, you take this back home with you." She put the tender plant in my hand. "You give that there to your mama and you help her plant it. You help her remember who she is and that she's a loved woman. She should be out here today planting and picking, just like you. I think maybe that's why she let your granny bring you out here today. Maybe she needs you to help her remember what it's like to be a daughter."

"Did Mama help plant with you?" I asked, suddenly aware that my crime-stopping plan was falling apart. "I mean, did you all put these plants out here?"

"Why yes, what else did you think?" I said nothing. She looked puzzled and somewhat amused. I realized I never wanted her to know what I had been up to all day long. She looked away from me, across the hillside, before speaking again. "We have to take care of our kin's graves. We've been comin' out here most of our lives. I guess we mean to just keep on coming until somebody has to come for us, too." It began to dawn on me, like warm water spreading through my limbs, that I felt proud of my great aunts and my granny for the first time.

They weren't thieves. They weren't grave robbers. Not like I thought. They were more like big-haired, overweight, tobacco-toting good fairies. They weren't anything to be ashamed of; they were the keepers of this realm of forgotten souls. I looked at my stout, squat aunt with admiration and wonder and threw my arms around her thick neck, nearly toppling us over.

"Therese!" She laughed her big, bubbly laugh. "Honey, I guess that means you'll take your mama a plant."

"And Sue Ann too, and even Sally, I guess. They should get one, too. So they know they can come next time." I felt giddy. Like I had surfaced from an exhausting swim up through deep, dark waters.

Darcey and Granny walked up to us about then. They were deep in conversation.

"Won't that be something?" Darcey was saying. "I can tell everybody how this root-sprig of azalea came off the grave of a man who knew *the* Dick Clark. I heard he shook Mr. Clark's hand and had a Coca-Cola with him right there in the restaurant! This azalea has a lot of historical significance, don't it? I wonder, Georgie, if this sort of plant adds value to a house?" Darcey examined a little piece of azalea attached to a spindly root.

"Yeah," Granny said. "You just go on and tell everybody that azalea knows Dick Clark. We'll visit you in the asylum."

Darcey laughed, and so did Burt. She got up and left me sitting by her true love's grave. The three old sisters continued snipping and foraging, filling their pockets with botanical loot and proudly discussing where they would display their bounty. I watched, astonished by what I was seeing. Not because I had found the proof I had been seeking, but because I was seeing a metamorphosis right before my eyes.

They spoke to one another not only in civil tones, but caring and gentle ones. They touched, supporting one another over tough patches of ground and giggling at quiet jokes. I saw Granny pat her baby sister's back and stroke her hair, taking Darcey's head to her shoulder while murmuring reassurances. Granny and Burt whooped with laughter over old memories of their mischievous childhood and sat down under a tree together to have a drink of water like old friends.

I couldn't imagine how I had missed the truth before. My prickly, mean-as-snakes Stroud kin weren't grave robbers. They were comrades in the trenches; women who meant something to one another and survived because they stuck together.

I liked the idea that I had been initiated into this secret society. My daddy's Masonic meetings had nothing on this. I could see pieces of my own heart's desires reflected back at me in these goofy ladies. When their pockets were finally full of green stalks and roots, I found myself eagerly cradling a few tufts of thrift. I would plant it in remembrance of so many things—especially that day.

🌱🌱🌱

As we shot back toward Mossy Creek like a baby-blue streak of Buick, I felt like a different person. Granny and my great aunts prattled on as usual, but there was a connection between them I hadn't noticed before. Underneath the pine-knot hard exterior, these women nurtured a tender, inexplicable kinship. And as was their tradition, they sang gospel songs most of the way back into Mossy Creek, admiring their stolen vegetation. I sang along with them. I saw each woman with a new respect. I saw her determination in the face of a lifetime of grub-work, hungry children and misguided men. Mistakenly, I had believed that they didn't care for one another or know their value. In reality, they were courageous and unabashedly devoted friends. They were strong.

We finished up with a jubilant rendition of *I'll Fly Away* just before we dropped off Aunt Darcey. She got out of the car with a smile and a lightness to her step as she walked up the path to her trailer. She looked like a girl again.

When we dropped Aunt Burt off at her old, green house she squeezed out of the back seat and said to my granny, "Call me tomorrow. I've got peas coming in and I need your help shelling on Saturday. You don't need to dress up."

"I'll do it," answered Granny, with a good-natured snarl. "I can't believe it's time to sit out and shell peas again. Seems like we just finished up last year's." She rolled her eyes at Burt. Back to her old, cranky self.

Burt waved her beefy hand at me as I peered out of the back of the Buick.

Granny turned around and eyed me.

"You were awful quiet today, Miss Therese. What's happened to the rattle mouth? You growin' up?"

Burt and I exchanged a knowing look.

Mossy Creek would have to find itself another crime-stopper.

I had been converted.

🐾 🐾 🐾

I gave my mama that piece of thrift. She looked at me with surprise and a question in her eyes. I didn't know what to say, so I just hugged her. Later that evening, I heard her on the phone. She had called and was talking and laughing with my granny, holding an old handkerchief of my grandfather Claude's under her nose. I couldn't remember the last time I had seen my mama cry through a smile. I couldn't remember ever hearing her laugh with my granny. Something deep moved in Mama's puffy eyes when she turned them on me, as I stood in the shadows of the hallway. She looked different to me, in the dim fluorescent light. She looked like her mother.

I had learned the difference between having a name and having a legacy. I would have to earn the latter, whereas the first was a gift from the family in which I was only beginning to find my place. I had learned the value of kin, by blood or by choice, and the blessing of friendship by grace.

That night I lay in my bed, listening to Sally run on about Earl's many virtues while I thought about the day I'd just had. I pulled the sheet up under my chin and sighed. I had followed Miss Ida's advice and kept my eyes open to things I had never taken the time to notice before. I would have to tell her she was right about Opportunity.

I turned my head to look at my sister, sitting up in her bed with her knees tucked under her chin while she talked on the phone, in the dark, to Earl. I knew who we were now, whether she did or not. She was already important, with or without Earl, because I was her sister. Some day, we would be grave tenders and grave robbers, together.

As she lulled me to sleep with her dreams of raising little Earls, I dreamed a sweeter dream. I dreamed of baby blue Buicks and shady cemeteries and dead sergeants and love. The year of my tenth birthday would come and go, but no matter whose name I decided to add to the one I carried behind me now, I would always know who I was.

A Stroud woman.

Lady Victoria Salter Stanhope

The Cliffs, Seaward Road
St. Ives, Cornwall TR3 7PJ
United Kingdom

Katie Bell, *Assistant Editor*
Mossy Creek Gazette
106 Main Street
Mossy Creek, GA 30533
USA

My dear Katie:

I'm thrilled to learn that Sagan Salter has appeared in Mossy Creek. Do keep me posted. I'd love to know more about him. Perhaps in some decade past we might be related. I still haven't been able to find out about my mother's American family. I know she was being reared by the Hamiltons, but I don't know why. Through the Cornwall Genealogical Society I've found out about my English ancestors. But I have a feeling the answer to the Salter mystery is to be found in Mossy Creek.

As for the other residents in your lovely village, I feel as though they're my friends now. My little part of the world is very different. You asked about Cornwall. Let me explain. Cornwall is the southern-most point of land in mainland England. It would be a county such as your Bigelow County. Much like your mountains seem to cuddle your little cove, the Atlantic Ocean embraces the little string of villages that make up our special part of England. I live in St. Ives. In the summer our village is filled with hanging flower baskets, tourists and fishermen. We have cobblestone streets, quaint little shops and friendly Cornishmen ready to invite you to tea. In fact, I'm going to send you my own ingredients for a real English Tea. Maybe your local chef, Bubba Rice, would like to try it.

Yes, we're English but we were originally Cornish. At least my ancestors were. I'll tell you more about that later. For now, let me say *Bolla tay/coffy?* (Cup of tea/coffee?) Until next time, *Gothewhar daa* (Good day).

Your friend,

Victoria

P.S. Let me know about Sagan. If memory serves me, he's the first male Salter in Mossy Creek in years.

"Friendship is one mind in two bodies."

—*Mencius*

LOUISE and JACK

Chapter Seven

Ida Hamilton Walker stuck her head around the kitchen door and said in a frazzled voice, "Louise, we're running out of potato salad."

"Here." My daughter Margaret handed her a Tupperware bowl straight out of the refrigerator. I would have dumped the salad into a crystal bowl, but didn't suggest that. This was Margaret's first foray into the world of Southern post-funeral feasts, so I refrained from correcting her. I doubted those Visigoths eating me out of house and home in the living and dining rooms of Aunt Catherine's little cottage would notice.

I'd only *bought* the ham and the turkey, of course. Half the town had descended on Aunt's house with food the minute they heard she had breathed her last. They brought everything from sweet potato casseroles to homemade coconut cakes. They filled Aunt's refrigerator and mine as well.

Good thing, too. Unlike Moses, I couldn't call down manna from heaven, and after Aunt's funeral, practically the whole town of Mossy Creek came back to her house to chat and eat.

And eat some more. I swan, you'd think it was a church picnic instead of the aftermath of a funeral for a ninety-two-year-old woman. But she had wanted a great big party, and I was glad to help her get her wish.

She was actually my great aunt, and one of my few remaining relatives. I'd been run off my feet arranging the viewing at the funeral home, picking what she was going to wear into eternity, and organizing folks to meet and greet during the viewing at the funeral home before they moved her to the church for the service.

Her old lady friends had demanded an open coffin, and I wasn't prepared to put up with their complaints if I closed it. Lying in state, Aunt looked like a generic "aged crone" from Madame Tussaud's gallery of waxworks, but that was unimportant. She was long gone from that body. She would have been the first to agree that if the empty husk that was left gave pleasure to her friends, it was fine with her.

I also had to get folks to stay at both her house and mine during the actual service and the trek out to the graveside. According to Amos, the Police Chief, thieves actually read the obituaries. Then while the family is away burying old Uncle Victor or whoever, the thieves break into the empty house and steal everything in sight. Talk about tacky.

Despite being the chief mourner, I'd spent most of the last three days in Aunt's kitchen and on the telephone. Thank heaven for my Garden Club. They'd pitched right in with flowers and food, made sure the house stayed presentable, and saw to it that every dish and bowl was labeled and entered so that it could be returned to the right person with a thank-you note. Plus somebody was always available to greet folks who came by either the house or the funeral home.

I've heard men boast that a girl only becomes a woman when she loses her virginity. Typical. As though that frequently uncomfortable and bloody encounter with a male is the defining moment in the female life.

A girl truly becomes a woman when she is first initiated into that cadre of women who keep every sort of ceremony humming from behind the scenes. They are seldom appreciated, except by one another. They are the Marthas who spend most of any event around the kitchen stove and the sink.

I became a member when my mother died. I was only twenty-five, and I hadn't been a virgin since I married Charlie, but I was still a novice until after that event. From then on for the rest of my life I have been a part of that select group, and now my daughter Margaret was following in my footsteps.

I suppose it's like being invited into some secret female earth cult. Men are excluded simply because they don't comprehend either that it exists or that it matters.

So I was trying my darnedest to open the last bottle of watermelon pickles and having no luck at it, when the kitchen door opened and Ida stuck her head in again.

"Louise, somebody out here wants to speak to you."

"In a minute." I slammed the pickles down on the table lid first, heard the pop that said the vacuum had been released, and twisted off the top. "Who is it?" But she'd already gone back to the crowd in the dining room.

I wiped my hands down the front of my apron, pulled it off, settled my hair, and went out with my best funereal smile plastered on to meet whoever special had arrived.

I hadn't had the leisure to grieve for Aunt. She'd taken to her bed only a week earlier after fainting into her gladiolas while she was planting parrot tulips for spring. She refused to go to the hospital. I didn't try to persuade her, although I knew I'd take some flack for that. The woman was ninety-three. If she wanted to die in her own bed in her own time, then I wasn't about to have her poked with needles and sucking air through a tube and generally being treated like a piece of meat while she did it.

I hadn't shed a tear, nor even given more than a fleeting

thought to my loss, although she was the last of her generation and I loved her dearly.

But when I recognized Jack standing on the front porch behind the screen door, so big he cut off all but a tiny bit of light that surrounded him like a nimbus, I lost it. By the time I'd shoved through the folks standing around the dining room table and clustered in the small living room, I was sobbing audibly.

Jack held the screen door open long enough for me to rush out onto the porch and into his arms. He'd always been the sweetest smelling man! Even when he was a teenager—most teenaged boys smell like unwashed goats—he managed to smell as fresh as spring. I felt those big arms of his around me and dug my forehead into his chest and just clung to him for dear life while I keened like an Irish fishwife.

Now, my family does not display emotion in public. Tears may be tolerated if they slide silently down the cheeks. But sobs? Episcopalians, which is what I am, are affronted by any sort of unbridled public display. No doubt many of the funeral guests were horrified.

At that moment I didn't give a damn if the priest himself took me to task.

Jack simply held onto me and let me cry. I have no idea how long we stood like that, blocking the door for anybody else who wanted to leave the house. Finally, I loosened my grip and let him lead me to the swing around the corner of the porch.

I had a momentary qualm when he sat. I don't think the chains that held the swing up had been replaced in my lifetime. I'm no lightweight, and Jack probably weighed well over two hundred and fifty pounds, not an ounce of it fat. I had visions of both of us landing flat on our backsides in the middle of the splinters from swing and ceiling.

The swing groaned, but it held.

"If this thing starts to let go, jump," he said.

"I was just thinking the same thing. Oh, Jack, I'm so glad you came."

"I'm sorry I missed the funeral. I just found out about it yesterday and I was out on the coast at a meeting. Came straight here from the airport."

"You drove from Atlanta?"

"Nope. From Bigelow. Company jet."

I laughed. "Impressive." If I'd given it any thought, I guess I'd figured the limousine I saw standing at the curb in front of Aunt's cottage was a leftover family car from the funeral, but now I took a closer look. "Yours?"

"Rented." He grinned. "I figured the best way to handle this was to put the big pot in the little one and just come on."

"And rub the noses of some of Mossy Creek's finest snobs in it."

"Uh-huh." His gigantic brown hand enveloped mine. Looking down at the two hands entwined, I remembered how as a child I'd always felt so unfinished next to him with his lovely milk chocolate skin. Like God had primed me and never painted on my top coat.

"You should have called me directly when she died," he said.

"I left a message with your secretary or assistant or whatever she is. I know you're busy, Jack. I mean, damn, you're a real captain of industry these days. About the richest man I know. Sure richer than anybody in Mossy Creek." I turned to him. "You remember when you came home from Brown the summer after your freshman year and I asked you to go water-skiing with me?"

"As I recall I said that I had no desire to try to water-ski and wind up in a couple of hundred feet of chain and an anchor or two."

"Miss Virgie went upside your head and said big as you

were, you were not to say things like that in polite company."

"But she knew it was the truth."

"She sat me down after you'd gone off and told me that if you and I were going to stay friends, we'd have to meet up north."

"We're meeting now."

"We met at her funeral, too. I guess that's the last time I've seen you. At your mother's funeral." I managed a laugh. "I never felt so underdressed in my life. I haven't even owned a hat since the Episcopal church decided the Lord didn't really care whether I wore one in church or not."

"Momma would have been pleased at the turnout."

"Aunt leaned over to me and whispered that this was a real celebration of Miss Virgie's life. That's what she wanted when she went, too. I've tried to give it to her, although without the choir and the three-piece combo it lacked a little something."

"Y'all stuffy Episcopalians don't run much to 'yes Jesuses' either."

"I'm sorry we didn't visit Miss Virgie more often those last few years when she was in the nursing home."

"She always did say you were as much her child as your momma and daddy's. I used to tell her that made us as good as brother and sister."

"She taught me how to make beaten biscuits and to soak chicken in buttermilk before you fry it and that you have to add coffee to make decent redeye gravy. Manners, too. I'd probably still be eating my breakfast toast whole if she hadn't taught me it was proper to break it into pieces and eat one at a time." I shoved the porch gently with the toe of my black pump and felt the swing move back with a creak.

"Don't press your luck," Jack said. "Better sit still."

We were silent for a long moment. "How's your family?" I asked.

"Randy's a sophomore at Morehouse, Virginia's at George Washington law school."

"And Peggy?"

"Peggy's Peggy. That woman spends more money than God." He shook his heavy head. For the first time I realized his short hair was steel-gray. "Peggy would have come along to the funeral with me if I'd been driving up from Atlanta."

"No, she wouldn't," I said softly. "Not unless you made her."

He was silent for a moment. "No, she wouldn't. She'll never get over being jealous of you and feeling out of place up here. I've never talked much about you and Mossy Creek, but she knows.

"Besides, she wants everybody to believe I sprang a full blown financial genius from the Harvard Business School, not out of some tobacco patch outside of Mossy Creek. All the time Momma was in the nursing home, I doubt Peggy went to see her once that I didn't drag her." He laughed. "Which was fine with Momma. She finally told me she thought Peggy was the uppity-est paper-sack heifer she'd ever met and that I should never have married a witch who acted like she was doing me a favor marrying a man blacker than she was."

"She didn't! Miss Virgie?"

"Miss Virgie." His big laugh rumbled up from his belly. "So how are you, Louise? Charlie? Your family?"

"Everybody's fine. Hard to believe I'm a grandmother. Oh, Jack, when did everybody get to be so old?"

"You and me, we don't get old. It's just those other folks get crows feet and pot bellies. You like being a grandmother?"

"Better than being a mother. I can send them home when I get tired of them. But I try to be patient and teach them things the way Aunt and Miss Virgie taught you and me. I'm content in Mossy Creek."

"Content? How about happy?"

"Happy, too. I guess. Most of the time, anyway. Aren't you?"

"Most of the time. I got to admit I like being rich. If it hadn't been for Miss Catherine, I'd probably be teaching school in some ghetto in Atlanta and driving a ten-year-old clunker."

"She paid your tuition because she loved Miss Virgie."

"That wasn't the only reason."

"She knew you were brilliant."

"Not that either."

I let that lie and went on quickly. "Those two women were closer than sisters. When I was going through Aunt's closet I found a couple of shoeboxes full of letters from Miss Virgie that she wrote from the nursing home."

"I found the same thing in Momma's stuff. I held onto 'em. I should have sent them back to you. My mind doesn't always recognize what's important."

"Would you like Miss Virgie's letters? I can give them to you now if you'll wait."

He shook his head. "You hang onto them. I'm not sure I could take that much of Momma's honesty."

I had to laugh. "Then you hang onto Aunt's for the same reason. I don't imagine they're going to be many scholars investigating two old ladies for a biography." I leaned back and closed my eyes. "Aunt Catherine never got over Miss Virgie's death. Life started trickling out of her when Miss Virgie died. It's taken all this time for the last little bit of sand to drop through the hour glass."

"Louise, dear, we'll be going." Eleanor Abercrombie and her husband came around the corner of the porch. She didn't miss a step when she saw Jack.

Jack stood.

"My goodness! Don't tell me this is little Jack, Virgie's boy. Why, I barely recognized you."

After they had left and Jack had carefully resumed his

seat on the swing, I snickered. "What'd she expect? International banker coming home in bib overalls and a baseball cap?"

"She might have been more comfortable if I had." Jack stood and pulled me to my feet. "I got to go, Louise."

"You've only been here a little minute!" I wailed.

"I know, but I've got—hell, no, I haven't got a meeting to go to. I still feel weird in Mossy Creek, I guess."

"Things have really changed, Jack."

"Some folks never did need changing. The others? I don't know." He shrugged.

I slipped my arm through his and walked with him to the porch steps. Out on the street across the lawn and the sidewalk Jack's chauffeur slid out of the front seat of the limousine and opened the passenger door for his boss.

"Call me when you come to Atlanta," Jack said, and kissed me on the forehead—my cheek was down way too far for him to reach. "We can have lunch."

"Sure." I knew I wouldn't. So did he.

He turned from the top step and took both my hands in his dark ones. "I don't think it would work even now, Louise. I sure as hell know it wouldn't have worked back then."

I felt the tears start again. "I know," I whispered. "Doesn't change the way I feel about you. Always will."

"You know that old Southern saying? The races can be friends until puberty, then it's segregation of the sexes until death." He touched my cheek. "I'll love you until the day I die."

Then he turned and loped down the stairs and across the lawn. A minute later he was gone.

I turned back to the house. I knew tongues would be wagging inside. It's not every day we get a multi-millionaire in Mossy Creek, and certainly not one like Jack.

I was in and out of Aunt's house all the time I was growing up, but I only saw Jack in the summer. We went to different schools. Back then that was the norm. He started coming with Miss Virgie when she *did* for Aunt, and after we got to be friends, he came most days every summer. I was a loner and so was he, so we spent much of the summer being alone together. We read books together on the front porch when it rained and even rode that old horse out at his granddaddy's farm bareback when Miss Virgie took me out there for the day.

He taught me to play chess, which I hated—still do. I taught him to play bridge, which he loved, and he and Miss Virgie and Aunt and I would play until after midnight sometimes during the summer. I suspect that's when Aunt recognized how brilliant he was and started thinking what she could do to help him.

We said goodbye in August of my junior year in high school as good buddies. Christmas Eve I walked into Aunt's kitchen and saw him slicing on the ham. Not a boy any longer. He was a young man, and Lord, he was beautiful! He turned around and offered me a piece of ham and all of a sudden I was Juliet looking at Romeo for the first time.

When he finally got around to admitting he felt the same way about me, he said we should be thinking more in terms of Desdemona and Othello. "And you know what happened to *them*," he said. "All Romeo and Juliet had against them was a couple of nitwitted fathers. You and I have practically the whole world against us."

We didn't get much further than a couple of furtive kisses. In this day and age we'd probably have tumbled into bed, but back then I expected to go to my marriage bed a virgin. I didn't inquire about Jack and he didn't volunteer the information.

Miss Virgie and Aunt realized how Jack and I felt about one another almost before we knew it ourselves. They must have talked about us, but they kept very quiet until they planned their strategy.

When they sat us down and talked to us both that long ago afternoon in January, we didn't want to admit they were right.

"Miss Catherine and I agree that it won't do, Louise," Miss Virgie said.

"So far we have kept your parents from hearing about the two of you, but it's only a matter of time now that school is in session. You will be a scandal."

"That's bad enough," Aunt Catherine continued. "Jack, however, will be in real physical danger. Are you willing to be responsible for that?"

We blustered that we weren't doing anything wrong, that times were changing, but in our hearts we knew they were right. We were already scared half to death.

"This is what will happen now," Aunt said. "The two of you will not meet—not here in this house, nor secretly."

I felt as though the heart had been torn out of my body. I know I was crying. Jack held my hand hard. I didn't dare look at him.

"Jack, Virgie and I had already planned for me to send you up north to a good Ivy League school after you graduate."

Jack started to say something, but she stopped him with a hand. "This is not a bribe, but an opportunity. We will simply move the timetable up. I will get you enrolled in a good prep school in the north for your senior year. That should make your entrance into a good university simpler."

"Y'all won't talk on the telephone or write letters in the meantime either," Miss Virgie added, then her face softened. She leaned over and brushed my cheek with her callused palm. "Oh, child, child, I know this is hard, but it'll get easier, I promise."

Aunt Catherine patted Jack's hand, the one that was covering mine. "We should'a seen this coming. Pair of old fools is what we are. You know how much we love you both.

Maybe in twenty years or forty or a hundred it won't matter—Lord, I hope it won't. Right now it matters a lot. And not just to Louise's people. Virgie's people would be horrified."

Virgie nodded. "That's right, Louise. It just won't do, child. You know it won't."

So in the end we agreed to their terms. I went back to my school. Jack went back to his. He stayed away from Aunt Catherine's house and I stayed on my side of town.

That fall Aunt sent Jack off to a Yankee boarding school for his last year of high school and then on to Brown.

The summer after his freshman year he came home to visit, and one of my friends brought him to a lawn party over in Bigelow. He had already integrated a previously all-white fraternity at Brown, and at least on the surface things seemed to be changing. We both tried to act like casual old friends meeting after a long absence. That was when I asked him to go water-skiing with me. He knew enough to refuse.

Seeing him again was only marginally less painful.

He never came back again. He graduated from Brown and the Harvard Business School. After that he was on his way up the ladder to multi-millionaire-hood.

He paid Aunt back a billion times over, not just in money. And last year he set up a whopping trust fund in the name of Aunt and Miss Virgie to help other smart kids get the education they need.

Oh, Aunt took care of me, too. A good college, Millsaps, but not up north. Not close to Jack.

Aunt and Miss Virgie were doing what they thought was best for us both. If we'd tried to stay together, we would both have had to leave Mossy Creek. Instead, Jack gave me Mossy Creek and took upon himself the role of exile. A rich exile, maybe, but still an exile.

I know now that relationships between the sexes, and certainly marriages, are tough enough when you have everything in common the way Charlie and I do—background, religion, schooling, same friends and neighbors, same view of the world, same goals—on and on. With every difference between you, marriage becomes just that little bit tougher. No matter how much we loved each other, Aunt and Miss Virgie felt those obstacles would have destroyed Jack and me in time. In the end, they prevailed.

Could we have made it? Lord knows.

But there are days like today when I wish to God we'd tried.

Mossy Creek Gazette

VOLUME III, No. 4 — MOSSY CREEK, GEORGIA

The Bell Ringer

Christmas in July

by Katie Bell

It may be ninety degrees outside but in our hearts it's already starting to snow. Auditions for the fall and winter play season will be held at the Mossy Creek Theater on Friday and Saturday beginning at ten a.m. each day. Maggie Hart will be directing *Blue Ridge Santa*, an original play by Jess Bottoms.

Everyone will be happy to know that Ed Brady has already agreed to play Santa in Mossy Creek again this winter, marking his fiftieth consecutive year on top of the fire truck throwing candy to the kids. In honor of his late wife, Ellie, Ed and son Ed Jr. will decorate a special version of Ellie's beloved "Ugly Tree" for the residents of Magnolia Manor.

To get a six-month jump on the mall down in Bigelow, Swee Purla announces she will be offering artificial Christmas trees professionally decorated. Choose your theme early.

Casey and Dr. Hank Blackshear have already ordered an "animal tree" for the veterinary clinic. I assume they mean a tree decorated with animal ornaments. I can't imagine how even Swee could get the cats and dogs to be still long enough.

Incidentally, giving kittens and pups for surprise Christmas gifts is not a good idea, Hank says. Be a responsible Creekite pet owner and follow the advice of the Mossy Creek Humane Society's "spokesbird," Tweedle Dee the parakeet. "True Love For A Pet Is Never Cheep."

Now, wipe off the perspiration and think snow. Only six months until Christmas!

"Friendship with oneself is all important, because without it one cannot be friends with anyone else in the world."

—*Eleanor Roosevelt*

SARA-BETH and CAROLEE

Chapter Eight

Reconciliation and absolution crept up on me in the middle of a heat-singed Mossy Creek day. I didn't see it coming and I definitely felt no need for it and yet, after that day there would be no place else to lay the blame.

She (I had long ago stopped using her name) snuck up on me like kudzu: a meaningless weed whose roots needed to be pulled from my life. She had stolen my high school love; she had been my best friend; and she had made me hoard and distrust all the happiness I'd earned since then. I, Sara-Beth Connelly, had not been able to ever fully let go of the anger I'd felt toward her, Carolee Langford, for over twenty years.

Not long before she returned I was helping my daughter with a book report on C.S. Lewis's *The Lion, Witch and Wardrobe*, when I read, out loud, a quote that caught me off guard.

Friendship is born at the moment when one man says to another "What! You too? I thought that no one but myself..."

I locked myself in the bathroom and wept for the *You too?* I'd never find again.

I had a full and beautiful life, and even if I did not trust anyone to be my best friend, I did have a friend for every occasion. My life had turned out just fine, thank you. Fine. A loving husband, three beautiful children, good health. And I, at least, had remained in Mossy Creek after college, unlike Carolee, who left in shame, along with my boyfriend.

She had become, through the years, a scapegoat for all things unplanned, for all things gone wrong. She had become less real, more a cartoon-like character of betrayal than the event itself. Carolee and I were more than the silly *BFF* (best friends forever) of Mossy Creek High School. More than the "What are you gonna wear today?" kind of best friends. We knew, really knew each other. What is better when you are seventeen, or any age for that matter, than knowing another person understands you perfectly? Neither of us needed to escape a cold, cruel world or divulge deep dark family secrets. We didn't have them. We were, plain and simple, loved by our families and each other. We were the fortress of friendship that others wanted and most never have. I observed life, she described it.

We had that rare bond C.S. Lewis talked of. The *You too?*

It was as if she became a black-ink outline of childhood faith. She was the reason I never truly trusted a best friend, again

❦ ❦ ❦

Carolee and I were seniors at Mossy Creek High School the year before it burned to the ground. BJ Carter lived south of Mossy Creek and thus attended Bigelow County High, instead. He played football, quarterback to be precise, but we did not care that he played for the enemy. No one did. He was loved by all with his James Dean coolness, his languid blue eyes and deep, slow voice. It all came easy to him, or seemed to, and that was all that mattered. He and I dated all through senior year. Carolee and I graduated. BJ didn't.

He blamed his non-graduation on the rigors of football and academia together. Oh, he was so cute in his football pants. He'd have to repeat senior year, but he was cute. Carolee's grades were respectable but not good enough to get her into the university, so she entered Bigelow Community College. I went off to the University of Georgia and left her behind to take care of BJ.

BJ and I wrote every day. I avoided all fraternity parties and all hints of impropriety in the college scene. I was a promised woman. I belonged willingly and lovingly to the best-looking, smartest, most-adored boy in all of Bigelow County. All of those were my own evaluations—none of which were wholly true.

We planned a life that included BJ playing pro football while I indulged my pottery hobby by running a chic craft store in whatever big city was lucky enough to get BJ for their football team. Of course we would eventually return to Mossy Creek, but only after our major victories out in the real world. We would retire with a fortune acquired through football and pottery and I would open a pottery store in Mossy Creek.

I came home that frigid winter quarter with a raging case of the flu. I could not stand even one more day of the barren campus trees, the drunken roommates, the laboring midterms. I bundled up in my Chevy and made the long drive home for some chicken noodle soup, a grilled cheese sandwich and some clean laundry that would smell like my mother's house, like my own bedroom. And, of course, I headed home to surprise the love of my life, the future, my only man: the one I pledged my body and soul to.

How silly of me.

I'm still not sure why I didn't recognize Carolee's car in the driveway of BJ's house. Maybe it was the 103-degree fever. Maybe it was the dehydration. I should have gone to my own home first. If I had gone home first, I would not

have known about them. Turn left here, turn right there—
we don't realize that the small turns in life may be a disaster
averted or met head on.

I met this one, well, head on.

I didn't knock on the cut-glass door of his parents'
porched home. I never did. I was family, or at least promised family. I stood on the white painted boards of the front
porch and picked a dead leaf off his mother's dead resurrec-
tion fern. She, in her beautiful, hippie-like beauty couldn't
garden worth a damn. Not a good skill to lack in Mossy Creek.
She tried. I covered up for her often, bringing living plants
from mother's garden to replace her own brown and wilted
ones. I loved BJ, I loved his silly mama and I adored his big
construction worker daddy.

As I opened the front door I could tell his parents weren't
home. If they were, there would be the blaring sound of Janis
Joplin from the stereo, the smell of Gardenia perfume radi-
ating from the parlor, the soft swish of his mother's cotton
broomstick skirts across the floor as she came to sweep me
in her arms and offer me a Coca-Cola with a cherry in it.

A wave of nausea and dizziness washed over me. I
closed my eyes to balance, reached for the banister of the
foyer stairs, then heard a soft noise. I turned, blinking slowly,
and looked into the living room. There they were, Carolee
and BJ, caught in a compromising situation, all opened buttons and hidden hands.

The yelp that came from me was animalistic.

BJ jumped up. "Sarah-Beth."

Carolee did not move. She covered her face and
moaned.

I ran out the front door. Neither of them followed me.

After I stayed in bed for five full days, my mother told
the university I would not return to finish the semester. They
did not know what was wrong with me...they had thought it
the simple flu, she told them, but I was still not well and

they were running some tests. I did not care what the doctors did to me as long as I never had to see my best friend or boyfriend again. Both Carolee and BJ tried to visit me, but Mother turned them away at my request.

In the weeks and months after I found them, life blurred between the solid and the vaporous. I finally transferred the stone in my gut and lodged it in my heart where trust had once resided: a rock set in memorial to Carolee and BJ's betrayal. I went back to college and told no one I was a different person, now.

It was easier to forget BJ's betrayal than Carolee's.

🌱🌱🌱

Carolee—or a stranger who looked very much like Carolee must look at thirty-seven—now stood beneath the trees in the middle of Mossy Creek's town square, as real and solid as the blister forming inside my new shoes.

I froze outside Goldlilocks Hair Salon, feeling seventeen-years-old again and betrayed. I stared. I didn't want to, but I did. She was beautiful in a white linen dress, her long brunette hair falling over her shoulders. She looked around with a nervous smile.

"Sara-Beth...are you all right?"

My friend Izzy Mullins prodded me with her shopping bag.

"Izzy..." I lowered my voice. "I think that's Carolee Langford."

Izzy squinted and leaned forward. "No. Carolee...hasn't been seen in what? Thirty years?"

"Twenty."

"I'm going to walk right on up there and prove to you that that is not her."

Izzy bounded across Main Street. A Mossy Creek police cruiser screeched to a halt inches from her Capri pants.

Sandy Crane poked her head out the driver's window and yelled, "Izzy, I oughta give you a ticket for not wearing your glasses!"

Izzy smiled. "Sorry."

Sandy harumphed her best harumph and drove off. She was not the first, nor would she be the last to melt a tire or two trying not to kill Izzy.

I was still staring at The Woman. She turned her back to me and headed across the square toward Hamilton's Department Store. A mixture of disappointment and relief settled inside me. Izzy threw up both hands in defeat and followed me up the sidewalk. "I need a glass of wine," I said. I rushed into O'Day's Pub. Michael Connors came out from behind the bar, said something about me looking a little flushed, and led Izzy and me to a table near an air conditioning vent.

We sat down and I shoved my purse under the seat. Izzy began a rambling dissertation on laser eye surgery, which she was considering as a solution to her nearsightedness and forever-lost glasses. I bent my head over the pub's menu and tried to concentrate. Until I heard the unmistakable sound of high-heeled shoes on the pub's wooden floor.

"Sara-Beth," a dulcet female voice said. "Is that you?"

The Carolee lookalike in white linen stood there.

"Carolee," I said. Amazingly, I smiled and rose to shake her hand. Ah, how deep and wide politeness can be, when needed.

She hugged me. I knew then that every etiquette class, every *yes ma'am* and *no sir*, every snip and snap from my mother and me-maw had been embedded marrow-deep, because I hugged back and retained my smile. A Creekite woman must not be rude. Strong, yes. Smart-ass, more so. Carry a loaded gun, often. But never, ever rude.

"How are you?" I heard my own voice asking.

"Fine, just fine, thank you. I was hoping I would run into you."

"What are you doing back in my Mossy Creek, Carolee?" I hoped she noticed that I called it my Mossy Creek, not our Mossy Creek.

"My great aunt died."

"I'm sorry."

"Her funeral service was this morning at First Baptist. I've just been walking around town since then. Remembering...looking around. It doesn't look much different, you know? It looks a little smaller to me, but I know that is because I am bigger. Taller and..." She laughed, a nervous silver tinkle that fell quickly at our feet. "...bigger."

Yes, she was bigger. Not obese at all, but not the slim-waisted, waifish girl of high school, either. I even saw a hint of silver in her chestnut hair, and a few fine lines around her eyes.

Izzy looked back and forth between us, then at her watch. She opened her mouth in very poor acting style. "You know, I have got to get home. I had no idea what time it was...Carolee, here you take my place." Izzy stood and patted the worn wooden seat of her chair.

"Oh, no...no."

"Really, I have just got to go. Carolee, don't let Sara-Beth eat all alone. Time just got away from me...along with my durned glasses. I think I left them at Goldilocks. I'll go there first." Izzy turned to Carolee. "So good to see you. Y'all take care now." Izzy picked up her bag and left me there with Carolee.

"May I?" Carolee asked and pointed to Izzy's chair.

"Please." I sat back down. I would eat fast, pay the bill, go home, forget about all this. I would not let her bring up the past. This was all definitely twenty years late and a tear-drop short.

"Sara-Beth, you look great. How are you, really?"

"Fine, just fine." I began to rattle off the statistics of my life that proved how fine I really was. The names of my three children, including pictures of them at the beach. I told her about my husband, James, and his prominent position as a doctor down at Bigelow County Hospital.

As I talked I could see the air between us as if it contained the energy force of betrayal. I wanted to reach my hand to the middle of the table and swipe at it although I knew it was just the air-conditioned air mixing with the pressed and shaken humidity of the day. I wanted to go home.

"And now, Carolee...how are you?"

"I'm good. Well...doing okay. My husband...died...this year and...it's been hard. My kids are still young, at home and all."

"BJ died?" My heart began a slow roll, a nauseating lurch that brought my hand to my throat.

"BJ? God, no." She leaned forward. "You thought I was still married to BJ?"

"Yes." My voice was small, tight.

"Oh, Sara-Beth. No."

"What?" I was as confused as if I had found myself on another planet. I was blinking, blinded.

"Okay...okay. Let's start over here. Sara-Beth, I thought you knew. We were only married a year."

"No, I didn't know that." My voice seemed to come from far away.

"I knew I should have called you. I needed to talk to you so long ago...oh, God, why haven't I called you? You thought I was still married to BJ?" She choked on the end of her sentence and put her head in her hands.

Okay, so now the conversation began. BJ's name hung above us, bloated and full of enough poison to fill the conversations at all the pub's tables, much less just ours. She looked at me and I saw her eyes fill with tears. I stared back in genuine shock. Tears. "I'm sorry. So sorry...about your husband...the one who died." Nothing was coming out right.

"I know what you're thinking, Sara-Beth. I do. I would be the same: what goes around comes around...all that...karma."

"No...no."

"Yes. I came here for my great aunt's memorial, but I really came to look for you. I tried to get up the courage to call you over the years. I wanted to talk to you. Really."

"To tell me that you and BJ were only married for a year...you sought me out for that?"

"No. No. Not that. I have, for so many sad years, wanted, needed just to hear your voice. But, what would I say when you answered? Hi...it's me, the friend who stabbed you in the back?" She sighed. "The longer I waited to call, the more impossible it became."

Michael appeared with a bottle of wine and two glasses. "You look you need this," he said simply. As he set the drinks down and returned to the bar I rubbed my forehead, trying to ease skin that had pulled painfully tight. "We don't need to rehash this. Why don't you tell me about your kids, your husband—we do not, I mean it, do not need to talk about BJ."

"But you don't know what happened."

"I know exactly what happened." I lowered my voice, "I came home from college sick as a dog and found you wrapped around BJ. That is all I need to know. Please, please drop this. It really is all so simple at its base, Carolee. You two fell in love. Beginning of story. End of story."

She started to cry. "It's not that simple. Please, let me tell you. You never have to talk to me again, or ...but let me tell you."

I leaned back in the chair and forced a swallow of wine.

"I'm listening. That's all I can promise."

"That's all I ask."

Carolee took a long swallow of her own wine. "Here

goes..." She sighed and looked up at me. "I missed you so terribly when you went off to the university. Here I was, stuck at Bigelow Community College because I needed to improve my grades. There was a hole of disappointment inside of me I could not seem to fill up with your letters and phone calls. I was missing out all the fun of a real college. I missed *you*. I began to resent you. I know that doesn't make much sense. But it's an honest description."

She paused. I said nothing. I wanted to hear the rest, I wanted to know the final destination of this rushing river of words and confessions.

Carolee continued. "Daddy came home from work one miserable day to tell me that we would be moving—that the army was making us go back to Fort Bragg. He couldn't afford for me to live here and stay in the community college. I'd have to move with the family. I called you right away, called your dorm to sob, cry, tell you about it. I needed you to fix it...I don't know, I guess I just needed you to understand. I thought you would know what to do, what to say." She choked on a small cry. "But I couldn't find you. Your roommate said you had left for Mossy Creek hours earlier. I ran to BJ's house thinking you might be there."

"I hadn't told anyone I was coming home. I was sick...the flu."

"BJ was home and I told him my tale of woe, and how I needed to talk to you about it, but I couldn't find you at the university. BJ said you were probably out with some guy."

"What?"

"Sara-Beth, he was so insecure about you going to the university. So jealous. He was often in a rage, especially after a few beers, about you away at college with all those boys and the frat parties. He hated the wild college stories that other Creekite kids came home with...I was constantly soothing him in those days...telling him that you weren't doing any of those things."

"I wasn't."

"I know you weren't. But that day when I couldn't find you, when I desperately needed a friend...BJ and I found some bizarre common ground in missing you, in envying you, in feeling left behind. I accepted BJ's offer from his parents' liquor cabinet, and...Sara-Beth, these are not excuses, just facts. I want you to know I am not giving you excuses. I have none left for anything in my life, for any of my choices."

I held up my hand in defeat but her words were beginning to cover me with the slow blanket-warmth of the truth. She leaned closer, across twenty-plus years, to let me see her stark, urgent eyes. "Sara-Beth, we got drunk and talked about how you were getting on with your life...how we were stuck here without you, how we really had no idea what your life was like or what you were doing. BJ began to imagine, really imagine this life of yours, and he went into a downward spiral until...between his imagination and his daddy's Jack Daniel's, we had you..."

"Had me what? Going to school getting my physical therapy degree...driving home with the flu?"

"No...we had you living and loving without us."

"What then?" Almost yelling, I slapped the table top. "You decided it was time to live and love without me?"

Carolee put her face in her hands and sobbed. Around us at the pub tables, the bar and the dart boards, the lunchtime crowd began to stare.

"Stop crying," I whispered.

"I can't help it. Doesn't any of this make you sad? Ever make you cry?"

"No, I don't cry about this anymore, Carolee. Did I then? Oh, yes. For days, weeks, months. Does that make you feel better? That I cried? That I almost died in a pity party of immense proportions? Does knowing that make you feel better?"

For over twenty years I had not looked behind the old

wall of rage. I did not want to look, now.

"No, no it doesn't make me feel better. Stop." She held up her hand. "None of this is coming out right, though I practiced and practiced."

"Carolee, let's stop this now. You and BJ found solace in missing me. I'm flattered. Okay...okay..."

"Please hear me. After you came in BJ's house and...after that...it was as if we had entered a dark cave we could not find our way out of. You had seen us and both of us knew, although we never discussed it, we knew nothing could ever be the same, that there would be no forgiveness. I believe that if you had not come in, if you hadn't found us, that we would have stopped there...before...before...we did. But, af ter you saw us..."

"Spare me the details, please." I rubbed my eyes.

"I got pregnant that day. Pregnant...and the cave door disappeared behind an immovable boulder."

I sat back, stunned. "Pregnant?"

"No one knew. Mom and Daddy moved and took me with them. BJ came with us and we had a quiet little wedding ceremony. BJ went off to college in south Georgia to play football and I went with him. Oh Carolee, it was horrible. We lived in the married students dorm and it was cramped and smelled like old beer and there were crying babies all the time, day and night. BJ was taking classes, playing ball. He could not figure out why I was depressed. Wasn't college just the greatest thing in the world? He wasn't cruel or...belittling. He just didn't get it. Then...then baby Billy was born six weeks too early and did not live three days..." She began to weep and the sound of it filled my chest with her sorrow, crowding out any anger still tightly held in my heart.

"Oh dear God, Carolee, you lost the baby?"

She nodded. "BJ left me two weeks later. It wasn't a surprise, Sara-Beth. How could it have been? There was no reason, anymore, to stay with me. He never loved me, and I never loved him. The only common ground we had ever had was loving you—and the baby, who in some way, also came from loving you."

Now I was crying, too. The lost years of miscalculated rage washed over me in a flood of regret. "What did you do?"

"I moved back home with my parents. I lost the baby, I lost you, I lost BJ. There were a few times when I could not move, get up out of the chair to decide what to eat...days I do not want to remember. But, a few years later, I met Austin. It was real love. Real. We'd been married for nineteen years when he passed last summer."

"Carolee. I'm sorry." And I was. "I thought...it doesn't matter what I thought."

"Yes, it does."

"All these years...all of them, I thought that you and BJ were together...behind my back...all through high school. That you were happy when I went to college and left you alone together. That you wanted to get married...actually that you were still married. I have carried that story with me."

"I should have called you when we broke up...I was too embarrassed...humiliated."

"Embarrassed. You were embarrassed? I would have listened. I would have understood. I would have come."

"BJ and I didn't want anyone in Mossy Creek to know what happened to us. Or our baby. Oh, Carolee, the baby is buried in a small plot at a church down in south Georgia. His little gravesite is no bigger than this table..."

"I would have come..." I knew I was repeating myself but I could find no other comfort for Carolee in this new and alien world in which I found us; a world in which my rock-solid assumptions had melted.

She took my hand. "I never forgot you, Sara-Beth. I can't

tell you how many empty times I have picked up the phone to call you...beg you to talk to me...but I knew I was being punished...for what I did to you. I had no right to turn to you for comfort." She whispered now. "Did you, ever, once, want to call me?"

"Yes, but I was too...proud."

She leaned back in her chair. "A deadly cocktail of pride and pain has kept us from this...from us." A silence as long and wide as the years that separated us spread across the table. Then we spoke simultaneously.

"I figured you didn't want me to call..."

"I thought you were happily married to BJ and didn't want me to call "

"You too?"

"You too?"

And there it was. The friendship I used to have, the *You too?* we missed and now held as a precious gift, again.

Our words crossed each other over the table, over the years, over the betrayal I had miscalculated. "Sara-Beth, can you forgive me?"

I took her hands. "Of course. Can you forgive me for not being there...for not...wanting to listen? I missed you, Carolee. No one knows how to describe things, explain life, as you do. I've missed you. Us. I can't believe what you've been through, how I wasn't there for you. I'll make it up to you. I will."

We began to speak in excited torrents, sharing our lives. She talked of meeting Austin, of regret and love and her children and always knowing exactly how old baby Billy would be, to the day. We breached a great divide of time and space and absolution at a small pub table in the town it all started and now ended.

"How long are you staying, Carolee? I want you to meet James and the kids."

"Well, my great aunt left her little house on the square

to her only sane, living relative: Mother...who said I should come here and decide for myself what to do with it."

"Well, what are you going to do with it? It is a great house."

"Well, isn't Mossy Creek still a wonderful place to raise kids?"

"Yes, oh yes. Especially when your best friend has kids the same age."

"Yes, my best friend."

We paid Michael hurriedly and rushed outside in the bright summer sun, hugging and holding hands.

"Look at that cute little girl in the pink dress." I pointed at a toddler crying in earnest, pulling at her mother's hem, pink from her cheeks to her patent leather shoes.

"She looks like she's been sprinkled with the dust of a just-rising pink moon." There she was, describing the feeling again.

My heart squeezed and expanded, filled and emptied. Carolee and I walked down a Mossy Creek sidewalk, as flawed but as strong as our own new friendship. I drew comfort from the imperfect and unplanned unevenness of the Mossy Creek concrete. Everything felt lighter, more solid and weightless all at the same time. Nothing I could explain, nothing I would ever try to form into words to my family. Carolee would know how to explain this, but I would discover it trivial and insignificant in my own words. Regardless, all was different.

As I drove Carolee to my house, I suddenly threw my head back and laughed. Without even asking why, Carolee began to laugh along with me.

"You, too," she said.

The Bell Ringer

Okay, Nobody's Perfect

by Katie Bell

The notice in last week's paper regarding the "Gospel Singing on the Square" had a typo. It read: "This evening at 7 p.m. the music minister of Mossy Creek First Methodist will lead an old fashioned gospel music sing-along in the park. Bring a blanket and come prepared to sin."

No, we did not intend to leave off the "g."

Those readers who pointed out the error to the *Gazette* may continue to *sing* in public and, as for the other word, well, use your own judgment.

The same Weekend Events column advised Creekite women "not to forget your husbands when you're gathering up items to donate to the Jaycees' yard sale."

Yours truly composed the column and can only plead for forgiveness. I'm developing several major stories to share with you, dear readers, before summer's end, and my brain is fried. I apologize to all the husbands and anyone who wanted to sing but not sin.

In other news: Michael Conners has announced this week's Creekite Who Deserves His Own Drink Named After Him at the Pub. After the recent small hubbub involving two of our town's more colorful young women, their husbands asked Michael to name the peach margaritas a "What Do We Do Now?" The honorees, Emma and Aurrie, are only mildly amused.

"The road to a friend's house is never long."

—*Danish proverb*

EMMA and AURRIE

Chapter Nine

The crickets sang and the summer moon glowed as I sat on my front porch in Grandma Jackie's squeaky, white-washed rocking chair. Our side street was quiet, too quiet, just like the rest of Mossy Creek that night. My old cat, Scarlet, lay sprawled out before me, licking her paws as if all was right with the world. A cool chill crept up my spine. The night seemed peaceful. It seemed calm. But everything was not okay. My son, Keith, and his best friend, Mack, had departed shortly after dinner to hunt rocks for their geology collection. Now it was past ten, darker than the crawl space under the house, and they still hadn't returned. I wanted to throw up. My husband Rick had left to look for them an hour earlier, but as of yet, no word.

The table phone I'd dragged outside rang loudly from its perch on my lap. I longed for the day when cell phones worked reliably inside Mossy Creek's mountainous borders. It always amused visitors that we often had to depend on old-fashioned technology.

I grabbed the phone off its cradle. It had been over five minutes since Aurrie's last call. That was a record for the evening. "Hey, hon," I said weakly.

"I feel physically sick. I do. I'm gonna spank Mack's fanny when he gets home," Aurrie declared, knowing she'd never raise a hand to her only son. "I taught Mack better than this. Checking in is a must. I always say..."

"Mama needs to know," I completed her sentence. Aurrie DuPree had been my best friend since the second grade at Mossy Creek Elementary. There wasn't a thought in her head that I couldn't read, and vice versa.

I'll never forget the day she strutted into Mrs. Willard's classroom. Already towering at five-foot-four, she was the epitome of an eight-year-old trendsetter. She wore a black and white, knee-length polka dot jumper with knee socks and saddle oxfords. Her silky blonde hair was held up by matching polka dot ribbon. Aurrie DuPree was cool with a capital "C." And just as important, she was carrying a Donny Osmond lunch box. To say he was my idol was the understatement of the year. I was in awe of Aurrie and made it my mission to find out everything about her. I succeeded, too. Even in second grade I knew what I wanted and went after it. By the end of the week, Aurrie and me were best buddies.

"I'm freakin' here," Aurrie bellowed now, obviously on the verge of tears. "This sitting by the phone is torture. Where are they? Have you heard from Rick, yet? Burke should have called me by now."

"Haven't heard a word. Come on over. I think it's time to call Chief Royden."

We hung up and I dialed the police station. Sandy Crane answered, asked a slew of questions and said she would send the chief out to find the boys immediately. She also said she'd call me back as soon as she got any news.

Aurrie came jogging down the sidewalk wearing shorts and a knee-length t-shirt, her long, sandy blonde hair in a ponytail. She raced up the three steps that led to my porch. I stood, and we embraced. I could feel her pulse racing, and by the way she squeezed the air out of my lungs, I knew she was just as terrified as I was, but I always felt like anything was possible when Aurrie was around.

She gave my soul hope.

A few minutes later, headlights approached the house, and Amos Royden's Jeep came into view. Aurrie gazed at me with mascara streaks covering her cheeks. "What are we supposed to do now?" she cried.

We had been asking each other that question for years.

❧❧❧

The summer of our pregnancies had been hotter than the chicken wings at Mama's All You Can Eat Café.

It wasn't hard to believe Aurrie and I had attended West Georgia College together, Aurrie majoring in fashion design and I in journalism. Everyone in Mossy Creek was surprised, however, when both us married handsome city guys and then hauled them back to our good ol' hometown.

My husband, Rick, headed up the finance department at Mossy Creek Savings and Loan. And Aurrie's husband, Burke, purchased a small dairy farm up near the Yonder community, though he and Aurrie kept a house in town. It has always been acceptable to bring an Atlanta boy to Mossy Creek, just as long as no part of his family was from Bigelow or related to a Bigelowan. We had done okay.

I don't think anyone ever really expected us to return, we were just so darn sure of our success. Together Aurrie and me had followed our hearts, spoken our minds and ended up just where we started. And that was fine by us.

We strolled into an unsuspecting downtown Mossy Creek. We had spent the entire morning curling and styling each other's hair. Aurrie's sandy blonde hair hung long, curling at the ends. I had also weaved braids on each side of her face. She had maneuvered my shoulder-length auburn hair into a chic spout on top of my head, with a few loose tendrils flowing around my chin. The hour-long make-up session had produced faces that would make Las Vegas showgirls look bland. Our attire was the utmost in comfort: polyester maternity shorts, flowing tops and two-dollar flip-flops completed the ensemble. We were stylin'.

To me, Aurrie looked exotic. Her five-eleven frame was lean and strong. The little cantaloupe under her small boobs was simply adorable. Now I was a different story altogether. At five feet three inches, my stomach was the size of a full-court basketball and my butt was bigger than the barn down at Hamilton's farm. I was due first, but that didn't alleviate my insecurity. However, now with Aurrie by my side, the fabulous hair-do and stunning make up, I felt better.

It really wasn't amazing that Aurrie and I had remained best friends through so many years. We did have a lot in common. Both of us had mouths on us. The term "Mouth of the South" had been used to describe each of us several times. If someone was not facing reality or there was a bully in need of a tongue lashing, one of us would be the first to do it. And believe you me, we were not afraid of anything or anyone. Sugar coating the facts was not our style either. When we were at Bigelow County High we had taken on the responsibility of matchmakers, gossip investigators, and fashion police. As young married women, we continued to strut our stuff.

I placed a hand over my heavily mascaraed eyes.

"The town folk may not be able to handle this." We took a left onto North Bigelow.

The right side of Aurrie's upper lip inched upward. I always called it her Elvis look. "Handle what?" she asked.

"Two big ol' pregnant women strutting through town on their way to Beechum's Bakery just after lunch time on a Tuesday."

"Hogwash, Emma. We look good. We have absolutely nothing to be ashamed of. You're on leave from the *Mossy Creek Gazette* and I'm taking a break from buying for Hamilton's Department Store. We're sort of on vacation and hey, we've always been known as women who know how to make the best of things. Besides we're single-handedly upping the population of Mossy Creek by two." Suddenly she leaned close and whispered, "Look to your left."

I could see Ida Hamilton Walker laughing at us from inside her office window at town hall. She gave us a mayorly wave. My chin rose, and I waved back. I glanced at Aurrie and her hand was up as well. It was rather comical. Us carrying ourselves like beauty queens in a parade. We had the wave down: flat handed, side-to-side. All we needed were lace gloves and a fancy automobile and you'd have thought we were really important.

Sauntering past Mossy Creek Pharmacy, I waved at the druggist, who was laughing at us, too. He held up a soda glass but we shook our heads. "I don't want ice cream," I sighed. "I want a beer. It's been months."

Aurrie nodded. "After we have these babies I'm going to make us the biggest pitcher of frozen peach margaritas you've ever seen. And none of that store-bought fruit, either. I'm going to use the finest peaches in Mossy Creek. That's a promise."

We crossed West Mossy Creek and all the women in Goldilocks Hair Salon waved at us, laughing. My legs were tiring, and a just-off-of-a-roller-coaster feeling took hold of my stomach. "Aurrie, I need to sit."

"Just a minute, Emma. Stick your chest out. Everyone's watching." She was obviously concentrating on the perfect, parade-worthy appearance.

The moment we cleared the gawkers at Goldilocks, she helped me to a small bench outside of Dan McNeil's Fix-It Shop. I plopped down, my belly pushing into what felt like my throat.

"I'm so big," I mustered, my bottom lip beginning to quiver. "I shouldn't be out here. I look ridiculous." Tears began to slide from my eyes. I sobbed loudly, suddenly so embarrassed by my behavior. Aurrie grabbed my chin.

"Great balls of fire. Why are you talkin' this way? You are the most beautiful woman in all of Mossy Creek. Your baby is going to be the next full-fledged citizen. You are glowing, and that's a fact. Your hair is shinier than ever, your nails are perfection and you still have that famous sway to your hips. Marilyn Monroe would be jealous." She took a tissue out of her purse and began wiping my cheeks. "The make-up is a little ruined. But I promise you, as God is my witness, you are lovelier than daisies blooming in the springtime. And what you're doing—what we're doing is just as important or more important than the mundane activities everybody else is doing. You are one hot chick. Now I want to see a smile."

I lifted my arms. "I'm hot," I declared, as I moved my elbows up and down like a chicken in an attempt to air out my soaked armpits. "Maybe it's just hormones. I think I need..."

"Chocolate," she completed my thought.

"And a..."

"Coca-Cola," she said, rising. "Well, come on friend. We didn't walk all this way for nothin'. And we're almost there."

I stood up, feeling stronger. By golly, I was a valuable part of this community, and there was no greater responsibility than bringing a child into the world. We walked quickly to Beechum's, entering the bakery like two determined Olympians crossing the finish line in first place. Hallelujah. I purchased a half-pound of chocolate covered peanuts and Aurrie bought a half-pound of peanut brittle. It was the pregnant equivalent to a gold medal. The first bite was more glorious than I can explain, like cotton candy at the state fair or hot chili on a cold winter's night. Definitely comfort food. I popped my Coke and took a big swig. Life was sweet.

As we walked and munched and munched and walked, we forgot about all the grinning town folk, our demeanor and our appearance. The treats from that bakery were that good.

"Aurrie, do you think our babies will be friends?" I asked.

"Of course. They'll be best friends, like us."

"What if I have a girl and you have a boy, or you have a girl and I have a boy?"

Aurrie placed her arm around my shoulder. "Then they will get married and we'll be kin."

"Awww. Good thinking." I reached into her bag of peanut brittle. She brought her arms down and seized the opportunity to grab a handful of my chocolate covered peanuts. Truth be known, we really didn't care what everyone else said about us. We knew we were sassy and our bloated condition was only temporary. But just for good measure, I put a hand on my hip and swayed from side to side as we made our way. With Aurrie's encouragement, I felt beautiful in any condition.

As I tackled the three steps that led to my front porch, I felt a small trickle of water flow down my leg. "Aurrie!" I screamed.

She glanced at my drenched flip-flops. "No more chocolate for you," she laughed.

"It's time! It's time," I shouted. "What are we supposed to do now?"

🐾 🐾 🐾

I exhaled, staring at my beautiful baby boy, Keith, lying on the floor atop Grandma Jackie's hand-made blue quilt. His ear-splitting shrieks had been going on for over an hour. Aurrie sat beside me, her eyes fixed on her equally beautiful baby boy, Mack, as he howled just as loud. An onlooker would have thought it was a competition to see who could squeal the loudest, a four-month-old or a three-month-old. It was purely awful.

My new kitten, Scarlet, sat perched on the windowsill looking in from the outside. She'd barely entered the house since little Keith had made his boisterous debut.

Aurrie and I had changed Keith and Mack's diapers, fed them, sung Patsy Cline melodies to them, rocked them and yet they still bellowed like kids on booster-shot day. And worst of all, they didn't even seem to be tiring.

I sighed. It was almost humorous. But I noticed that Aurrie looked pale and deeply disturbed. I brushed the hair from her forehead.

"Everything's alright, hon, they're just exercising their little lungs."

A tear cascaded down her cheek. "What are we supposed to do now?"

That was it. I couldn't watch the most self-assured chick in Mossy Creek be brought down by a twelve-pounder, no matter how adorable he was. Time for Aurrie to get her groove back. I jumped up, darted to the hallway closet and located the enormous box containing my brand-spankin' new stroller. I got the contraption open and pushed it into the family room.

Aurrie crossed her arms. "Emma, it's November."

I put my hands on my happy-to-be-in-denim, hips. "I don't care if it's thirty degrees below zero. We're going for a walk."

"They'll catch colds," she complained.

"Hogwash. They're going to get sore throats at this rate."

"We only have one stroller here."

"We'll strap them in side by side. They'll love it and maybe, just maybe, they'll shut up, for goodness sakes." I watched as Aurrie brought her un-manicured hands up to cover her face. I lifted Keith first, bundled him and placed him in the stroller on his back. Then I picked up Mack and wrapped him in a flannel blanket, situated him beside Keith and belted them in snugly.

"That should do it," I shouted over the babies, and then pointed to my sneakers. "These boots are made for walkin'. Let's go." I opened my hand and she cautiously placed hers inside and slowly came to her feet.

"I look horrible. I didn't get a shower this morning. I haven't slept in weeks and I still have ten pounds to lose."

I pushed the stroller near the front door, put my coat on and handed Aurrie hers. "Nonsense. You're a mama, now. You can look haggard whenever you please. It's one of the perks of motherhood." I shoved her arms into the coat and buttoned her up tightly. I ran to the kitchen, retrieved a bottle for Keith, placed it into my green polka-dot diaper bag and tossed it into the basket on the back of the stroller. Then I grabbed Aurrie's well-stocked, blue-checked diaper bag and put it in the basket too. "Now open the door and help me get the dudes down the front steps."

She did as she was told, and I marveled at how well she was taking my orders. That was a first. By the time we reached the sidewalk, the cool air had already begun to have an effect on the little ones. The intensity of their squeals dropped to a lower octave. I pulled Aurrie to my side and entwined our arms. We both gripped the stroller and giggled. "We're off to see the wizard," I joked.

"Lions, tigers and bears would be more like it."

Falling into step, we glided down the street and then onto North Bigelow. The cool breeze lifted my spirits and I could tell Aurrie's mood was improving too. Before we reached the town square, Keith and Mack were sleeping like teeny angels. Aurrie and I didn't talk too much. The silence was refreshing and beyond golden.

When we reached Goldilocks Salon, all the women, some in curlers, others with a head of aluminum foil, rushed outside to see the precious babies. "Little pink darlin's," Rainey Cecil cooed, dabbling her teasing comb at the boys. She was only in her early twenties then, about our age, and it was so easy to see she wanted kids of her own. Aurrie and I beamed as Rainey and her customers raved over our adorable young-uns. And there they lay, as peaceful as newborn kittens, their little mouths closed in tender slumber. Foolin' folks already, I concluded. Those were our boys all right. Everyone ranted about how calm and relaxed the babies were, insisting that we were definitely doing something right and that motherhood really agreed with us. My eyes met Aurrie's and we chuckled softly.

It was then that I saw something I had never seen before. Aurrie had always been a proud woman, but at that moment she was practically overflowing with pride. I peeked down at the babies and also felt that magical satisfaction. Keith was the most spectacular thing I had ever done. I felt as if my feet had just lifted off the pavement. The adoration was simply wonderful. The boys were beautiful and I felt so honored to be sharing this moment with my best friend in the world, Aurrie.

The ladies began to worry that the chemicals on their hair might have been on a tad too long, and hurried back into the salon. Aurrie and I solemnly passed Beechum's Bakery. "Next time we're in town, we'll pick up some fudge," I said. "Right now I don't think I can fit one more pound into these jeans."

"Ditto, here," Aurrie admitted.

We paced ourselves through the square and back toward home, still shoulder-to-shoulder. When we reached my house, Aurrie seemed lost in thought. "What's up?" I asked.

She peeked at the babies as they began squirming in the stroller. "Come on, let's get to my house. We can make it before they wake up."

I shrugged. "Okay." We boogied the two blocks and just as we trotted up her drive the screaming began again. "Dinner time," I observed.

I unhooked the safety belt and lifted Keith out and Aurrie

grabbed Mack. We rushed inside, turned on the TV and fed the ravenous infants.

After they finished eating, I burped Keith and Aurrie burped Mack. Then Aurrie flashed a good ol' I'm-back-to-my-normal-self grin.

She laid a blanket on the floor and placed Mack on top. "Can you watch 'em for a minute? I'm going to make us something very special."

"Ohhhkay," I said. A few minutes later, I was scowling at the television and dangling rattles in front of the boys. "Be careful. I wouldn't want your brain to explode," Aurrie joked, as she entered the room.

I gazed up to find her carrying a tray containing two large, frozen, peach margaritas and a pile of wheat crackers.

"Yeah, baby," I gushed.

She sat on the floor, handed me a glass and raised hers in the air. "I'd like to make a toast," she began, "to walking with friends."

Tilting my head, I giggled and lightly touched my glass to hers. "To walking with friends."

🐾🐾🐾

My heart pounded in my ears as Aurrie and I ran to meet Chief Royden.

"Have you found Mack and Keith?" Aurrie called.

Our handsome police chief smiled and nodded toward the shadowy street behind him. Suddenly, the sound of whistling pierced the air, followed by laughter. I peered up the sidewalk and saw four dark forms—two tall, two short—approaching.

Aurrie stepped forward, her chin jutting outward, her hands on her hips. "There better be a good explanation."

Rick and Burke came into view under a street lamp, arm-in-arm, singing the Ray Charles' tune, *Georgia*, like they didn't have a care in the world. Keith and Mack meandered a few steps behind them, each carrying a bucket.

"Hi, honey," Rick began. "Look who I ran into." He motioned toward Burke.

"Thank God," I exhaled. Then my chin dropped and I crossed my arms tightly over my chest.

Without so much as a glance, Aurrie followed suit.

"Explanations," she repeated.

Keith's eye grew wide.'"We found so many awesome rocks, and then we stopped at Beechum's Bakery for a snack."

"Chocolate cupcakes," Mack added with raised eyebrows. "And a..."

"Coca-Cola," Keith finished. "That's when we ran into our dads."

Aurrie pointed at Burke. "Why didn't you call me, and where on earth have y'all been?"

Burke stepped forward. "Darling, I tried to call from the pub a hundred times. The line was busy."

"I have call-waiting," she reminded him.

Burke glanced at Rick. "I did try to call."

Rick nodded vigorously, gazing at me. "I tried too. Over and over. When we couldn't get through, Burke and I decided to share a couple of beers, play some darts and catch up on world events. Plus the boys were having a lot of fun showing off their rock finds to the other customers."

"A couple of beers," I repeated, and pressed my lips together. "Phone trouble. You couldn't call in, but we could call out."

Aurrie glared at the four of them. Mack held up his bucket. "Mom, look. Don't be mad. We found some citrines, a few crystals and an agate, one amazonite and lots of mica."

"And some pyrite, too," Keith added, looking at me hopefully. "All the folks in O'Day's were impressed. Dad tried to call you. Really. The phones aren't working."

A telephone truck came down our street as if on cue. Chief Royden nodded to the technician driving it. The man called out his open window, "I'll have y'all back on line in no time." The chief smiled at us. "Glad everyone's accounted for. You folks have a nice evening."

"Thanks, Amos," I said weakly.

"Yes, thank you for fetching our men and our sons," Aurrie said, still not certain she wasn't mad.

Amos gave the guys a look that said, "You're on your own now," then climbed into his patrol car and drove away.

Aurrie and I stood tall, guarding our dignity like Dobermans in a junkyard. We wanted a bit of sympathy for our hours of worry.

Rick shifted from one foot to the other. Burke inspected the stars in the sky and chewed on his lower lip. Keith and Mack stared at each other, as if communicating by mental telepathy. Scarlet walked leisurely in front of us. The only brave soul, I thought.

Then Keith and Mack squared their shoulders and stepped forward. "Listen Mom," Keith began. "We weren't doing anything wrong."

"We got some great rocks," Mack insisted.

"And ate a few chocolates," Keith added. He gestured toward the others. "We were just walking with friends. It's a hobby we learned from certain wives I could name."

Aurrie glanced at me, her Elvis lip rising and her eyes openly amused.

My shoulders slumped, but I smiled. "What are we supposed to do now?" I intoned.

We hugged our boys, our husbands and then each other.

Lady Victoria Salter Stanhope

The Cliffs, Seaward Road
St. Ives, Cornwall TR3 7PJ
United Kingdom

Metten das (Good morning) Katie:

I'm anxious for tales of the cooking competitions you Americans seem to enjoy. You promised to tell me about the summer culinary contests in Mossy Creek. Now, do tell! My mouth is watering. Before I forget, I promised you the recipe for an English tea.

You might like to know the English custom of High Tea started in the 1700s. Back then, they had only two meals a day: breakfast and dinner. Dinner was served very late so the Duchess of Bedford invented an afternoon tea to keep her going until dinner. She invited friends to join her and it became a very pleasant custom. That's where sandwiches started, too, but they didn't call them that.

I've attached a copy of the recipe to the second sheet of my note. First, you must use fresh-cut flowers and real bone china, artfully arranged on a crisp tablecloth. Prepare a silver teapot filled with piping hot tea and scones.

The scones should be split horizontally so that no knives or forks are needed. Clotted cream and jam should be placed in some sort of lovely glass container. Though I expect you can't find clotted cream in the States, for it's made from unpasteurized milk. Perhaps you could ask Bubba Rice if he has a recipe for making a mock spread. Now that I think about it, the making of scones may be of interest to other Creekites. I'd be glad to send it to them on email if they'll just address the request to my attention at your BelleBooks.com address. For those without the modern convenience just send it to P.O. Box 67, Smyrna, GA 30081 and I'll send it along. You don't have time, Katie and if I do it, I'll get to know you all better.

By the way what have you heard more about Sagan Salter? I'm waiting with bated breath.

Keep in touch.

Vick

Who is trying to determine how many scones make a "mess."

"A friend is one who knows all about you
and likes you anyway."

—*Christi Mary Warner*

LILA and FRYZEEN

Chapter Ten

Fryzeen Sneerly has been the queen of pickled beets in greater Mossy Creek and the rest of Bigelow County ever since Jimmy Carter retired from peanut farming to run the big fifty. Each year—from braces to engagement ring to fifteen years of wedded bliss with Lorn Spivy, my ownliest—I've tried my darnedest to beat that old big-haired, pickled gerkin, and still I've come up empty-handed. Yours truly, Lila Spivy, has been beat by the beet queen for over a quarter of a century.

This summer was supposed to be different. I was going to do me some good old-fashioned research to prove that Fryzeen was a charlatan, even if had to plant video surveillance in her trailer for the month before the contest. I didn't care what it would cost.

That's the thing about being a champion pickler. Pickling is something you do in the privacy of your own home. Yes, you have to get good beets from either a neighboring farmer or grow them yourself. That's one of the rules. I haven't been able to prove it yet, but I'm sure Fryzeen's been getting those organic beets from a farmer outside the county. She grows a decoy crop in her backyard every year, so I'll have to catch her on video buying the tainted goods.

I've been preparing for my investigation for almost a year. I'd casually stop by Fryzeen's place when she was out spading her garden. "Things sure are looking nice over there," I'd say, real sweetlike. "I love the way you planted multicolored zinnias all around the edges of your garden to make everything look prettier. You know how ugly vegetables can look in your front yard?"

She'd nod, suspicious of my every good intention, I'm sure. I understood her reticence, though, since I had been the only surviving pickling competitor to continue to come in second place behind her for the past five years. Marta Jean Plunkett and Tasha Zellhart both passed on last winter in a freak ice storm. Both ladies crashed in a head-on collision with each other at the intersection of North Bigelow and Main, no less, the poor dears, leaving just me to be Fryzeen's only real rival in Mossy Creek.

After the eighth month of drop-by visits and small talk, I finally got bold and invited Fryzeen over for a cup of coffee and homemade biscuits. No one in town can refuse coffee and my homemade anything, especially a widow with no friends and no children in the surrounding Southern states. She was reluctant, but when I wooed her with my homemade strawberry preserves, she finally agreed.

Early Wednesday morning on an August day just thirty days prior to the fair, before the sun started scorching down so hot we could've had a skin-fry, I wheeled out the breakfast cart to my verandah and waited for Fryzeen to arrive on her Schwinn bicycle, complete with training wheels. Imagine having a hairdo three times bigger than her head, covered in a mangy old Blue Willow-looking scarf and wearing clothes she wore before anyone was able to buy the original Charlie's Angels woman's designer clothes at the Wal-Mart down in Bigelow. This was the picture of Fryzeen.

She pulled up at my front gate exactly two minutes after nine. When I let her in, I tried to act surprised that she had in her hand a jar of her apple butter. It didn't take much of an effort to look shocked, because I had had a case of heartburn like after you eat Mexican for three days in a row. Every time I took a deep breath, I had to grab my heart. Looking surprised and having gas kind of look the same.

I sort of figured Fryzeen would bring apple butter, since she always enters that contest, too. But Pearl Quinlan never loses that one. Landsakes, I won't even think about entering the apple butter competition. I don't have the energy to try to knock two old birds out of their nests. Besides, Pearl is one of the nicest women I know. Her and her sister Spiva, who belongs to that Cherubs Are Chubby club, do such good work with the sick and elderly.

I hadn't really spent enough time in Fryzeen's presence to know the first thing about her. All I knew was what I'd heard from gossip. You can only trust gossip so far. Taking time to add or subtract so much from the truth just to get close to the facts, it's hardly worth listening to.

In a small town like Mossy Creek, gossip got to almost everyone in about two hours. The girls down at Goldilocks spread the news to Rosie at Mama's All You Can Eat Café. Rosie tells Sandy Crane, who dispatches the news to her brother Mutt. Mutt then tells Father Mike at O'Day's. From there, the news travels by phone like a prayer chain. Only thing was, no one ever breathes a word to the one who is being gossiped about—even if it is family.

Fryzeen probably already heard what everybody else in town was murmuring about her. Maybe that's why she kept to herself. To tell you the truth, no one I knew had really spoken with her since her husband died in eighty-five. Even then, only ten people showed up at the funeral. The whole Sneerly family kept to themselves. Carlos was from Honduras, and though we all tried to understand him at Fourth of July picnics, no one really could make heads or tails out of what he said. In fact, I heard that Fryzeen and her kids kept her maiden name to keep the kids from being picked on for being foreign. Carlos and the kids would always come to those functions without Fryzeen. He was a nice man, from what I remembered of him. He worked with my Lorn over at Brewers' Coffins in Gainesville.

Lorn said that the guys at work used to ask Carlos questions, but besides tending to the interior coffin designs, the fabrics and such, no one much knew what he was chattering about.

Lorn did tell me that more than once Carlos came into work with bruises or a broken finger. Once he even had a cast on his leg. The guys would ask him what was wrong, but he just shook his head and mumbled something about Fryzeen having fits.

Well, I planned on getting the truth right from the horse's mouth. No better way existed to find out what I needed to know than to get that woman smeared from the face of pickled beet competitions forever.

🐾🐾🐾

"Morning." A raspy whisper floated toward me from beneath the hand Fryzeen held directly in front of her mouth. In that moment, I realized that I really had never heard the woman speak. She would listen and nod a lot, but almost never utter a thing.

"Come on in, dear. I've been expecting you." She leaned her bike against the fence and hobbled toward me.

I swear, when she looked at the little breakfast I made, tears came to her eyes. "Thank you for inviting me."

"Well, welcome to Lorn's and my humble abode." Without thinking, I took her by the arm and led her to the Adirondack chairs in the center of my pseudo-English garden just beyond the verandah. My dahlias and asters and marigolds looked like small sets of multicolored eyes witnessing our little tea party.

Believe me, they stared when they saw Fryzeen.

Fryzeen's flowery, orange-and-yellow dress looked like frayed drapes someone had forgotten to mend over the years. Her rough hands reflected about seven decades of toil in the hardest of conditions.

I thought about my own cushy life, with never much more than a day's menu to worry about. We Spivys never went hungry, always had clothes, pretty outfits right from Hamilton's and the little shops in town.

"How are your kids doing?" I asked.

Her eyes averted. "Jimmy's overseas, and Melba and her three kids just moved again "

I'd heard about her son being in the armed forces, but I didn't know a thing about her daughter. "Where is she moving this time?" I offered Fryzeen a biscuit.

She looked at the biscuit like it was made of gold. Her eyes opened wide, and I could see she was imagining what it would taste like before she even bit into it. "They're up in Niagara Falls now. Her husband, Milo, has to stay close to the water, seeing he's a fisherman and all."

"Oh, that's right." I pretended to know.

"And your kids, Lila?" she asked.

"We sent Missy up to Tennessee State to study physical therapy so she'd be close to her brother, Travis, who is trying desperately to break into the music business in Nashville. He's a drummer, you know. Lord forgive me, I spent half my life listening to him pound on those darned noise traps. He'd sure as hell better do something with it."

Fryzeen held her hand over her mouth again and actually laughed, I think, because I let out a teeniny swear word. Her laugh wasn't hardy. More like a chortle. But I could see the sides of her mouth turning up, bordering each side of her hand.

"Kids," I said, holding my heart again. I felt like I couldn't take a good breath. "How old are yours now?"

"Jimmy's pertinear forty and Melba is a year younger."

"Do you get to see your grandkids much?"

Now Fryzeen's single moment of happiness turned to severity. Tears collected in her eyes, and she reverted back to her inner silence, shaking her head in dismay.

I put my coffee down and touched her leathery hand. For the first time in a long time, I didn't know what to say. I don't know what I would do if I couldn't see my children. And if my kids had kids, I'd sell my home to go see them. But I don't suppose Fryzeen's old trailer would bring in enough to get her to Lexington, Kentucky, let alone across the continent.

She started to cry real hard, now.

"What's wrong, dear?" I asked, patting her back.

After a moment, she stared up at me. Heavy silence fell on the both of us. She looked into my eyes, her chin quivering so bad her teeth chattered.

"No one has touched me in ten years," she said, folding her hands over mine like the last bit of dough in a nut roll, trying to seal off the inner filling.

I did something I never thought I would do in a million years. I reached for her and hugged her. I held her so tight I thought she was going to have to ask me to loosen it up so she could breathe. She was as fragile as a little baby bird. The only thing on the woman that had any body was her hair. Because I'm allergic to Aqua Net, my own eyes got a little teary.

Suddenly I thought about what the neighbors would think if they saw me hugging the Elmira Gulch of Mossy Creek, and I kind of backed away. But she held on tight.

I finally pulled away a bit to hand her my grandmother's embroidered handkerchief. Fryzeen didn't know it, and I didn't realize it until it left my hand, but that was the first time I ever let anyone else in the world touch that handkerchief. It was the last thing Grandmother gave to me, and I've cherished it and kept it with me daily.

Fryzeen looked at me like she didn't know what to do with it.

"Here, dear. Use this to wipe your eyes." I helped her hand up to her face and dabbed the tears from her sagging cheeks. "My grandmother told me once that this handkerchief was part of a prize she won for being Woman of the Year at First Baptist Church in Yonder."

"It's so pretty, Lila," she said. "Are you sure?"

"Yes, yes," I assured her, "it's just an old thing. Don't you worry about a thing." I closed her hand around it, feeling a little shaky the entire time, like the first day I left my infant daughter with a babysitter.

Again, she wept.

Well, my investigation had gone awry in the first fifteen minutes. How could I bring up pickled beets now? The woman was a sobbing mess, and I had no idea what to say to make her feel any better.

Ply her with food, I thought. Food always, without a shadow of a doubt, makes me feel better. The last time Lorn and me got into a fight, I ate my way through an entire box of double-fudge Oreos and a half-gallon of that Purity vanilla bean ice cream. It was just the perfect amount of chocolate with just the right amount of vanilla to make it go down like Drano. So, when Lorn came back from his mother's house, I was already sleeping it off. I don't think I woke up till an hour after he left for work the next morning. Now that's food doing its job.

I gathered Fryzeen's half-eaten biscuit and put a spoon of strawberry preserves on it and handed it back to her. "Have a little of this. It'll make you feel better. I promise."

I had to steady her hand around the napkin. She broke off a little piece with her left hand and put it in her mouth.

What do you ask a woman who hasn't really spoken to or touched anyone in ten years? I felt like I just needed to be sitting there and keep rubbing her back or something, but I was too uncomfortable for that.

As much as Lorn and I barely speak to each other, let alone touch anymore, I still couldn't get through the week without that peck on the cheek each morning, or that big lug hugging me tight just before we get up in the morning. If he weren't there, I'd be lost. I know it.

What I didn't understand is why Fryzeen didn't ever move on with her life after Carlos died. Why she didn't go to women's groups or volunteer at Magnolia Manor, or something to get out and be around people. Then it occurred to me when she made a frail attempt at a smile. This time with her hand occupied, she couldn't hide her mouth. She had no teeth left. Not one.

The poor thing was probably embarrassed to be out and about without any teeth. I know I would be.

No wonder the biscuits looked like the perfect feast.

I tried not to stare.

"So, how do you like your coffee?"

"Three sugars, please, and light."

For company I like to use sugar cubes and my sterling silver tongs. I felt almost like I was flaunting my wealth in her face now. Everything I touched, I wanted to give to her, just to appease the feelings of guilt for having too much, too easily.

I handed her the coffee cup and saucer. "So, your garden looks to be the best in the neighborhood."

"If we don't get some rain soon, everything will die."

I tried to remember if I'd ever seen Fryzeen water her garden, or if there was even a hose in her yard. My goodness, I don't believe there was one.

"You know," I said, "I was just going through some of my old clothes before you came over. I was going to take them to the church. If I'm not mistaken, I remember a couple of dresses in there I've never even worn, that I think would fit you perfect. I'm too fat to get in them now. I swear, if I don't stop with this gaining weight, I'm going to have to get rid of every shred of clothes I have and start over again. This time with all moo moos."

"No thank you, dear. You give them to the church like you planned. I'm sure many folks are lot worse off than me."

"No, really," I said, "after we're finished with our coffee, come in and just take a look. I'm trying to remember, but I think the one dress kind of looks similar to the one you have on now, real flowery and pretty. I'm sure Preacher Hickman won't miss a thing. It's not like he's ever been in my closet, to know the difference."

"We'll see," she said, with calm resign. She held Grandmother's handkerchief tight and tucked it in the pocket at the front of her dress. "Thank you for this."

I just about choked on the gulp of coffee I had in my throat. Fryzeen actually thought I had given her grandmother's heirloom handkerchief. I didn't know what to do or say. My blood pressure shot up faster than a dog trying to tree a squirrel. "But...I..." Nothing that made sense came out of my mouth. All those years of being Southern and saying only what was proper and right put a noose around my tongue so tight, I could hardly breathe.

Fryzeen gulped down half a cup of coffee, then held the warm cup to her heart. "You think that I might have just a little more to heat this up?" she asked.

When I tried to pick up the urn, pain shot down my left arm. I looked at Fryzeen, and there were two of her—really—both faces staring at me with grave concern.

Before I could utter a word, the coffee urn crashed to the glass table and smashed it into a hundred pieces. Hot coffee splashed all over me. Only I didn't feel it.

I watched myself, like in a movie, as I dropped to one

knee. Then my head hit the table. After that, I don't remember a thing.

❦❦❦

When my eyes popped open, my first real look at the world seemed vague and blurry. I heard heart monitors like on those television doctor shows. I smelled something like isopropyl alcohol. The white sheets were tucked so tight around me I felt like a bound baby.

Then I saw Fryzeen, her purse in her lap, staring at me with such concern it hurt. How quickly I'd judged her and how much I wanted to steal the only glory she probably had ever had in her life. Now, she was the one who had saved my life. Imagine that. How ironic.

She touched my hand and patted it. "How you feeling, honey?"

I tried to talk, but the words didn't seem to want to come out. Though I felt Fryzeen's hand on mine, I couldn't rightly move it, at least not without a struggle. I didn't have the energy for any fight. Not then.

"Where's Lorn?" I finally eked out.

"He's down in the cafeteria getting us both some coffee," she said, fluffing my pillow and easing the tension in the sheets, like she'd heard my thoughts.

"I'm going to go call the nurse. They said to tell them when you wake."

When Fryzeen left the room, I noticed that there was a mirror on the top of the bed frame, like the kind you see over the cooking area of a chef's demonstration. I could see my body, my face. My permanent was still intact, thank gosh, but I looked as though a child had gone wild with pastels and a smudge tool.

I had a black eye and a nasty headache that made my skull feel like someone used a jackhammer on it. What on

God's green earth happened to me?

Lorn came in just before two nurses. He rushed to the bed, setting the coffee down before he grabbed my hand. "Honey, I was so worried."

"What happened to me?" I whispered.

The nurse answered from behind him. "Mrs. Spivy, you had a heart attack. You're on heart monitors now and as soon as we can get a doctor in here to talk with you, we'll give you the rest of the test result."

Lorn asked the nurse, "So, how long is she going to have to stay here?"

"It depends," she said, opening the drapes for some much-needed sunlight, "on whether the doctors think that surgery is necessary."

Surgery, I thought. *How could I need heart surgery? I'm only fifty-one. I've never smoked. The only habit I have is eating too much.*

I reached for Lorn's hand and tried to hold it tightly, but I was too weak. I felt a tear roll across my face to the pillow.

Fryzeen handed Lorn a handkerchief. I'm sure he didn't even recognize that it was Grandmother's. He wiped my eyes. "Shhh, now. It'll be okay." He kissed my forehead. "We're gonna get you all well and perfect, like new. Okay?"

The nurse left the room. I overheard Fryzeen ask her, "If Mrs. Spivy needs surgery, do you think she'll be well enough in three or four weeks to do anything strenuous?"

Suddenly, a cold rush of anger rolled down my back. That mean old woman. How could she? Wishing me to be out of commission, just so I wouldn't be ready for the pickled beets contest at the county fair.

Well, I was going to show her. I've never been one to stay sick for long. If it took every bit of three weeks to get back on my feet, I'd be picking and pickling and *beeting the tarnation* out of her, this year and every year we're both still alive.

Lorn yelped. I must have been digging my nails into his hand. "I think Lila's coming back already." He laughed, then kissed my hand. "Everything's going to be all right, honey. I'll be here. And Mrs. Sneerly said she could come over to help with housekeeping when I'm at work." I held onto Grandmother's handkerchief for dear life.

If I had the energy to yell, I would have screamed at the top of my lungs, That woman will never tend to me. I'm going to do some tending to her skinny butt when I get my strength back.

Imagine.

Oh, the pickled humanity.

❦❦❦

The first week home I couldn't do much of anything for myself, which meant having to let go of more control than I was willing to. I looked green around the gills and felt more depressed than I'd ever had before, like a U-Haul truck backed over me.

Despite my reluctance for Fryzeen to help, neither of my kids could come home, Lorn could only take off three sick days before we'd start losing money, and every person in the ladies' auxiliary at Mossy Creek Methodist was in bed with the flu. Fryzeen was not only my sole choice, she was the only one willing to help.

Lord knows, I tried to be nice and appreciative, but every part of my body ached to beat the band, and I wanted to take the dinner knife and slit my wrists from boredom. I swear, I was that low. Nothing anyone could say made me feel better. All I could think about that even remotely made me feel better was getting well enough to beat the pants off of Fryzeen in the pickling contest.

Fortunately for me, she wasn't a big talker. In fact, she never even tried to initiate a conversation. She simply came in when Lorn left for work, cleaned up a bit while I slept, then she would try to feed me some soup or crackers or something salt-free and tasteless for lunch. I'd fall back to sleep from all the medication while she knitted on the couch. I'd wake up just in time to see Lorn walk her to the front gate.

I think Fryzeen knew I didn't trust her. She never pushed the issue. She just helped and tended, like a good friend or even family. Nothing was expected, but everything was given so freely. After the second week, when I started to feel good enough to get up and start to get my life going, I felt the desire to trust her again. I suppose the Prozac helped a bit. I thought, *How silly could I have been to distrust the very person who has selflessly helped me since I got sick?*

That afternoon I couldn't take a nap after a not-so-bad bowl of lentil soup, which I think Fryzeen actually made from scratch. You don't get a nice fresh taste like that from a can. So, I actually set out to talk with her. "How did you make the broth so good?"

"My daughter's one of them vegans, and she showed me. You got to roast the vegetables first to make the broth, the onions and celery and peppers." She got behind the bed and fluffed my pillows. "You want to sit up?"

"That would be nice," I answered.

"You look like you're feeling better today."

"A bit."

"Good."

She left me alone and went to the kitchen. The physical therapists from Bigelow County Hospital had been coming in once a day for the last week or so and making me exercise. I knew just about how much I could do, but pretended, especially around Fryzeen, that I could do a lot less. Even Lorn didn't know that I could get up and go to the bathroom by myself. However, while they were home, I did as little as possible. Suddenly, it felt good to have someone wait on me for a change.

About ten minutes before five, I just got the itch to go into the kitchen. I don't know why. Call it instinct or being led by the spirit, I wasn't sure. But I slid my legs over to the side of the bed, like the therapist showed me, then I used the stool to inch my way to the floor. I was in my stocking feet because my circulation was real poor since the operation, so I tiptoed to the kitchen door without much of a sound. With one large swoop, I pushed open the door, and bam, I caught Fryzeen red-handed rifling through my recipe box.

"What exactly do you think you're doing, Missy?" I asked.

Fryzeen dropped the three recipes that were in her hand on to the table.

"I...I was just trying to find your lentil soup recipe. I was going to add what I told you, so you'd have it for the next time."

It took every bit of energy I had to lift my right arm, but I did and pointed to the door. "I don't care what you've done for me for the last week and a half. You have gone way beyond your boundaries. I think it's time for you to leave!"

She knew I was on to her innocent-helper scheme. She wanted my pickled beet recipe so bad she had actually pretended to nurse me all week. And I had actually begun to trust her.

Fryzeen waved a recipe at me. "See," she said, "it's the lentil soup recipe. That's what I was looking for."

Just as I hobbled to the table to check, we both looked down. There on the table, staring up at us like a teenager caught with a smoke, was my secret pickled beets recipe.

Fryzeen looked horrified—terrified that I caught her cheating, no doubt. Imagine that. She comes into my home on the premise of helping me, and then she takes the opportunity to find out my secrets to keep herself at the top of the pickling community. In my eyes, in that moment, humanity had sunk to an all-time low.

Her head and eyes lowered. "I swear," she whispered, "I didn't know your pickling recipe was there."

I didn't say another word. Just pointed to the door.

🐛🐛🐛

Two more weeks went by. The therapy lessened, and I got stronger without the help of anyone except an occasional visit from one of my ladies' auxiliary friends. They all seemed to feel better at the exact same time, just when I no longer was in desperate need of their help. Imagine that.

Still, anyone was better than Fryzeen, even a not-so-willing friend kind of forced to do me a favor was an improvement over an impostor. Anyway, I was sure I'd be paying my fellow Creekites back for the next ten years for all the meals people brought for Lorn and me. Even Mayor Walker sent over a pot of venison stew. Probably from a deer she shot, herself. I think the whole county figured out Lorn only knew how to make a meal with a pre-made mix, a crock pot and a can of beer. Chili. And he only did that one time a year, on Super Bowl Sunday.

Men.

The county fair was just three days away, and I was nowhere near ready for the contest. But finally, I felt energetic enough to get busy. I'd have to get the beets from the Gooseberry Farm over at Yonder, but it didn't matter. Charlie Gooseberry's beets were a lot better tasting than mine, anyway.

I asked Sandy Crane to help me prepare the jars and carry the pressure cooker up from the basement. However, not even Sandy was going to witness me using my secret recipe. She helped me get ready for the event, but during the actual making of the beets, she had to wait in the living room.

This year's beets had to be different, somehow. After all, Fryzeen knew now that I only used fresh dill, just a pinch of dried mustard and honey instead of sugar. I had to alter the recipe just a tad here and there. Otherwise, she'd enter the contest twice and use mine and her recipe. Contestants could enter up to three times. She was just the type to be so greedy.

It took me all day and night to prepare the new and best beet stock ever, but I was finally ready for the big contest.

Let the best beets win.

🌱🌱🌱

When Lorn helped me from our truck, sixteen of my best Creekite friends were all standing around the judges' table right in front of the statue of General Hamilton on the town square. Every one of them began cheering me on.

I noticed Fryzeen standing by herself near the back of the small crowd. The judges were to announce the winner at three o'clock exactly. This year was going to be a little different; people were actually going to be able to taste the winning three picks. Each participant had to prepare two extra jars for just that purpose. I had my extras in the truck bed in a cardboard box, figuring I'd at least get up there in the top two.

At a quarter till three, I saw Lorn inching his way over to Fryzeen after I forbade him to talk to her. Men just don't know how to be supportive. You just don't be nice to a woman who has been trying to steal your glory for all these years. "She's a cheat," I'd told him.

He'd said to me, "Why on earth would a woman steal a second-place recipe when her recipe came in first place the last twenty-five years? Why, Lila? Why?"

Well, the truth is, there was no good reason, except that she was just curious. But curiosity killed the cat. And I was the cat.

While I was conversing with a few of the ladies, I noticed Lorn shaking Fryzeen's hand. I wasn't close enough to hear the exchange between them, but I did see him handing her something on the sly.

My God, I wanted to run over to them and give them both a piece of my mind. Lord knows, if I could have, I would have read them both the riot act. My own husband betraying me right before my big moment, with Fryzeen, no less.

But Sandy had me hooked to her arm and was going on about how Pearl Quinlan wasn't going to be in the Apple Butter Contest this year, so everyone was real curious who was going to win that. The crowd's excitement, considering the beet controversy and the apple shake-up, was so thick you could cut it with a paring knife.

Next thing you know, the three judges from neighboring Lumpkin County paraded out in front of the crowd. Betsy Josselyn Joe, the ladies' auxiliary president, stepped up to the microphone first, wearing her god-awful lime-green pillbox hat, bobby-pinned to purple hair. You'd think her mother would've taught her that you just don't wear lime green with purple or yell like she did into a microphone: "It's been a great year for beets, hasn't it?"

Everyone clapped like at a golf tournament, real quiet.

"We're here today to announce the winner of this year's Pickled Beets Contest, a much-coveted prize at the Bigelow County Fair. To do the honor, we've chosen the six-year winner of the Lumpkin County contest, Billy Kay Portman."

Again the soft clapping.

Get on with it, I was thinking. *Just say my name. Say my name.*

Lorn was suddenly by my side, but I didn't even want him to touch me, let alone link his arm to mine, like he did. Dressed in a green plaid kilt, trying to make a statement, I guess, Billy Kay walked up to the microphone and cleared his throat. "Pickling isn't just for farmers anymore. It's for all those folks wanting to preserve their fresh garden vegetables for use during the winter months. So, not only are we picking a winner for the farmer in us all, but we're picking a winner for the future of pickling everywhere."

Get on with it, I murmured to myself, before I have my second heart attack in thirty days.

"Huh?" Lorn asked. "Whattid you say?"

"Just shut up, Lorn, and pray," I whispered, "because I swear, if I don't win this year, I'm going to march right over there, with a defective heart and all, and tear out every bit of Fryzeen's football-helmet hair."

"And second runner up goes to..." Billy Kay said, "a newcomer to the contest, our police dispatcher, Ms. Sandy Crane."

I couldn't believe what I had just heard. Sandy hadn't even told me she was entering. The humanity.

Sandy smiled at me and held up her jar of beets as everyone clapped.

"This is exciting," Billy Kay whispered to Betsy Jocelyn Joe just loud enough for everyone to hear. "And first runner up goes to..."

I thought my heart was going to beat right out of my chest, I wanted not to hear my name so bad.

"...Mrs. Fryzeen Sneerly." Billy Kay looked back at the sheet of paper, like he didn't even know who had won. "Yes, that's what it says. Mrs. Fryzeen Sneerly."

The entire audience gasped, as every eye turned to me.

"And so the winner," Billy Kay bellowed, "of this year's Bigelow County Pickled Beet Queen is...our own little heart-attack, quadruple-bypass-surgery survivor, Mrs. Lila Spivy."

I suddenly felt faint. The words I longed to hear so badly for twenty-five years were finally being spoken. Without realizing it, old Fryzeen had given me her own pickling secret. I had roasted my vegetables before I made my beet stock, just like her vegan daughter taught her.

Lorn helped me up the step to the stage, and before I knew it, Betsy Josselyn Joe was handing me the coveted Pickled Beet First Place trophy.

As customary, the winner shakes the hands of everyone on stage. I shook Betsy's hand, then Billy Kay's hand. Sandy reached out to kiss my cheek. Then suddenly I was face-to-face with my nemesis, the woman who would have tried anything she could to keep me from her crown.

Fryzeen looked at me with tears in her eyes as she held out her hand.

"Congratulations, Lila," she whispered, barely opening her mouth.

"I'm so glad for you. You truly deserve it."

Suddenly, I realized who my nemesis was.

I turned to the crowd.

"Speech, speech," they all chanted as Betsy Josselyn Joe shoved the microphone in my face.

I cleared my throat, something I promised myself I would never do if I ever had the chance to speak in public. But I couldn't help it. I seriously didn't know what to say. I was as shocked as everyone else there.

I hadn't believed I was good enough to win. Just like I hadn't believed I was old enough to have a heart attack. Just like I thought there needed to be a loser, so that I could be a winner.

But one lonely woman, with nothing but a stupid pickled beet recipe, made me realize I was strong—strong enough to get over more pain than I ever thought I could face, more insurmountable fears than I thought I had, more of own my crummy judgment, of her, and everyone else in my life—including Lorn, including myself.

I turned away from the crowd and faced Fryzeen and smiled. I'm sorry, I mouthed in her direction.

It was then I noticed what Lorn had given to Fryzeen just minutes before the contest winners were announced. She still had it in her hand.

It was a thank-you card with a big sailboat on the front. I recognized it, because I'd bought a box of them on sale at the Dollar Store down in Bigelow. I noticed her eyes welling up, but I was certain in my heart that it wasn't because she lost. No, I believe that Fryzeen Sneerly, the queen of pickled beets five years running, was actually crying because she was happy I finally won.

Imagine.

I'm sure no one in the entire county knew what I was doing. But I left the podium, right in the middle of my speech.

I went over to Fryzeen and hugged her real tight. I felt tears coming down my own eyes, so I grabbed Grandmother's Woman-of-the-Year handkerchief. Just as my hands went to dry my cheek, I gazed into Fryzeen's innocent eyes.

In that moment, my heart made a three-sixty. I wanted to sell my car and buy her a plane ticket to see her children. I wanted to help her get involved in some women's activities in Mossy Creek. I wanted to throw a fundraiser to help get her the cash to have her teeth fixed. I wanted to give her a makeover. I wanted to find her a home with running water and new everything.

But I knew the Fryzeen standing next to me was much too proud for any of that nonsense. What she needed to make her happy, I had all right. And it was standing in my own two-inch pumps and holding on to trivial things much too tightly.

Before I lost my nerve, I put Grandmother's handkerchief in the hand of the only woman in all of Bigelow County who actually deserved it, Fryzeen Sneerly.

Mossy Creek Gazette

VOLUME III, No. 6 **MOSSY CREEK, GEORGIA**

Young Poetry Winner Opines On The Great Beyond

As always, the *Gazette* is pleased to print contributions from younger Creekites. Here is the winner of our *Summer Rhymes With Bummer* poetry contest. It was submitted by Lucy DeLong, eight, great-great granddaughter of Eula Mae Whit.

On Passing Over

Granny Eula says that Jesus calls
those he needs in heaven.
She says that means when a person
loses, he will still win.
There's no waiting line to get in.

I don't much like to go to funerals.
Too much hugging and tears.
But afterward there's food for all.
And cookies chase away fears.
Because there's no hungry folks in heaven.

Near every week someone goes on
To the other side, they say.
Granny says that all their trouble's gone.
If it's all the same, I'll stay.
I'm thinking there's no room in heaven, anyway.

"I want you to live to be a hundred. I want to live to be a hundred minus one day, so I never have to live without you."

—*Winnie the Pooh*

LAURIE and TWEEDLE DEE

Chapter Eleven

The year I turned thirty-seven, my life got hit by a bus, which is how Tweedle Dee and I ended up in Mossy Creek.

Actually, the bus started barreling my way the previous spring when David, my husband, politely informed me that he wanted to move on to greener pastures. So the next few months were spent dividing "ours" into "yours" and "mine," meeting with lawyers to deal with the paperwork that left a greasy film on my heart and finding a place to live that I could afford on my own.

The whole thing put enough strain on my health to push me into seeing the doctor. Nothing was found on the tests, so my "not feeling sick but not feeling well" was put down to stress, and friends gently suggested that, since David had already found his greener pastures, maybe some I should start looking for companionship too. I knew what they meant, but I was feeling too fragile to entertain the idea of Men. Still, after slogging through the workday, it was also hard to come back to an apartment that felt too empty to be a home.

I tried a few adult education classes, but meeting people who were transient acquaintances made me feel lonelier than being alone, so I stopped going. The only thing I stayed with was the storytelling meetings. I loved storytelling. I attended the workshops the group offered, bought suggested books for beginning storytellers, practiced diligently in the evenings, listened avidly when the other members told stories at the monthly meetings—and never had the nerve to put my name on the sign-up sheet to tell a story of my own.

As the long Thanksgiving weekend suddenly loomed before me, the idea of a companion became more appealing. So, one evening on my way home from work, I stopped at a strip mall and walked into the pet store. An hour later, I walked out with a cage, a variety of food, several toys, a book...and Tweedle Dee, a blue, baby parakeet.

I spent most of that long weekend sitting next to the cage and talking to him while I read the budgie book to learn about my new little friend. What I learned very quickly was that Tweedle Dee had his own ideas about the world. He wouldn't sit on a finger. He'd sit on a wrist, an arm, a shoulder, or any other part of me he deemed a suitable perch, but the only time he would sit on a finger was when he wanted to do kisses—that is, have me lift him up so that he could gently nibble on my chin. He was perfectly happy playing with his own toys during the day, but when I got home, he wanted out so that he could play with his person.

I tried to teach him to say, "Tweedle Dee and me," once he started vocalizing more, but what he learned to say was "Tweedle Dee is me." Which actually made more sense. So I'd come home to happy chirps followed by, "Tweedle Dee, Tweedle Dee, Tweedle Dee is me."

For Christmas that year, I bought myself an Irish whistle. I loved Celtic music and thought it would be fun to learn to play some. Besides, the Irish whistle was also within my budget, which a lot of other instruments weren't.

Now, if I'd been a more experienced bird owner, I might have realized that a baby parakeet who was learning to vocalize in his own selective way and an Irish whistle in the hands of a very novice player were not necessarily the best combination. But I didn't realize, so I happily practiced each evening while Tweedle Dee perched nearby to listen.

The first song in the instruction book was "Twinkle Twinkle Little Star." Since I had trouble covering the whistle's holes to get a clear note, it tended to come out as Da-da, da-da, da-da sour note. Da-da, da-da, da-da sour note.

Which is exactly how Tweedle Dee learned to whistle it—and what Tweedle Dee knew, he knew and there was no changing it. I progressed to other songs, and we ended up with these strange duets. He'd wait for me to hold a long note in the song I was working on, then chime in with da-da, da-da, da-da sour note.

No one else had to listen to it, and it entertained both of us. At that point in my life, that was all that mattered.

❦ ❦ ❦

As winter gave way to spring, I went back to the doctor because I hadn't been able to shake that "not well" feeling. In fact, that feeling had been getting stronger. There was another checkup and more tests, which I didn't expect to come out any differently than the last set. But that was before I understood that my feet were stuck to the pavement and the bus was heading my way.

The same week the divorce was finalized, David married his greener pastures, the company I'd worked for downsized my job out of existence and I got the results of the tests.

As I sat in my living room, with Tweedle Dee perched on my shoulder making worried little chirpy sounds when nothing he did produced a response, I thought, *If I got hit by a bus tomorrow, what would I regret not having done?*

The answer was easy. I loved stories. I'd always wanted to write stories. I'd dreamed of a life beyond the nine-to-five routine, where the days would flow instead of being cut up into segments. There would be routine, sure, but not the same routine. Maybe a walk to a coffee shop, where I would sit for an hour making notes and watching the world. Then home to write for hours and hours if inspiration struck, or to read or dream if that's what the day called for. Time for work, time for friends, time to simply be.

I could do it. There was enough money from the sale of the house for me to live on until my retirement fund was sent to me, and since old age wasn't something I had to save up for anymore, there was no reason for me not to use the money.

I could do it. But not here. I'd taken the apartment because I'd needed a place to live, but I didn't like it, had never felt comfortable in it and didn't want to stay there. I didn't even want to stay in the area, even though that would have been the prudent thing to do. No, I wanted a clean start for this pocket of time where I would live out a dream.

So I had a yard sale, and what I couldn't sell, I donated or gave away. By the time I was done and packing up my old Toyota hatchback, which was literally held together in places with duct tape, I had a box that had a set of sheets, some towels and a few plates, mugs, glasses and silverware; three boxes of books, one of the new paperbacks I hadn't read yet, one filled with storytelling books, and the last with favorite books I wanted to revisit; a file box with all the important papers I would need; a couple of shoe boxes of my favorite CDs and cassette tapes; two suitcases stuffed with clothes and toiletries; my Irish whistle and music books...and Tweedle Dee.

We trundled out of western New York on a fine spring morning and headed south to visit my friend Nadine, who had relocated to Richmond, Virginia, a few years before. It took two days to get there since I didn't want to push my luck—or the Toyota, loaded down as it was—by trying to make the drive all in one day. But we got there and had a lovely visit. When we left several days later, Nadine's insistence that I call her on a regular basis was the only indication that she was concerned about this road trip I was taking from life. I hadn't wanted to spoil the visit by telling her about the bus heading my way, so I promised to call and trundled out of Richmond, heading south.

Tweedle Dee was a terrific companion, but he was a lousy navigator, which is why we ended up in Georgia on our way to South Carolina.

It was late in the afternoon when, shaky and finally admitting that we were very, very lost, I passed a white silo with the words "Ain't goin' nowhere and don't want to" painted on it. It made me smile and gave my heart a little lift. I was still smiling when I drove into Mossy Creek and found a place to park near Mama's All You Can Eat Café.

I got out of the car, not sure if my leg muscles were going to stretch all the way after driving for so long, and looked around. The town square was an enticing bit of green, and I spotted a bench. Now if Mama's provided takeout, I'd be all set. I'd been living on takeout since we'd left Nadine's simply because it was a whole lot warmer down South at that time of year than it was in western New York, and I couldn't leave Tweedle Dee locked in the car while I went inside someplace to eat. I had these horrible visions of coming out after an hour and finding baked budgie. But I really needed to eat, so I went inside, hoping I could get something to go.

I could, and did, along with a large Coke for me, a small cup of water for Tweedle and a copy of the *Mossy Creek Gazette*.

As I stared at the passenger door while Tweedle Dee made his *cht cht cht* scoldy noise because I was doing nothing when I obviously should have been doing something, I realized I had a slight problem.

"Need a hand?" a male voice asked.

That was exactly what I needed, but there I was, feeling limp and looking wilted, and there he was, wearing that nice uniform with a badge pinned on it.

"Umm..."

"The square's a nice place to have a bite to eat."

"That's what I thought," I muttered.

Cht cht cht!

"Doesn't sound like he wants to be left behind." There was laughter in that voice.

I sighed quietly, handed over the food and the *Gazette*, got Tweedle Dee out of the car and followed the officer to the bench in the square, with Tweedle chirping at the top of his little lungs to let the whole town know he had arrived.

I put Tweedle's cage on the bench, took my lunch and paper from the nice officer, and set that on the bench, too.

Feeling awkward, I smiled at the man who was still watching me. "Thanks for your help, officer."

"Chief, actually," he said. "I'm Amos Royden, Chief of Police here in Mossy Creek." He looked at me expectantly.

"I'm Laurie Grey."

Cht cht cht!

"And that's Tweedle Dee."

I thought I detected a twinkle in Chief Royden's eyes as he said, "Hey, Tweedle Dee."

Tweedle hopped from perch to bars, studied the man who was studying him, and said, "Tweedle Dee, Tweedle Dee, Tweedle Dee is me." Then the scolding started in earnest.

"Hush!" I said sternly. "You'll get your French fry."

Yep, there was a definite twinkle in those eyes. The man probably thought I was a lunatic. Or, at the very least, eccentric. Couldn't blame him. Right about then, I was wondering about me, too.

"Welcome to Mossy Creek, Ms. Grey," Chief Royden said. "Hope you enjoy your visit."

"I'm sure I will," I replied, trying a smile I hoped made me look like a normal person.

I breathed a sigh of relief when he went away, then settled down to my meal. Before Tweedle could start up again and possibly get us arrested for disturbing the peace, I broke open a French fry, blew on it to cool it off so he wouldn't burn his tongue and slipped it into the treat dish.

As we ate, I looked around—and felt the tightly coiled tension inside me ease.

Have you ever gone to a place you'd never been before and recognized, on some level, that you'd come home? As I looked around, that's what occurred to me. I'd come home.

I opened the *Gazette* and began scanning the pages for an ad for a bed and breakfast or an inn or someplace I could stay that wouldn't object to my having a fluffy blue roommate.

Sometimes Fate just takes you by the hand. I did find an ad for the Hamilton Inn, but I also found a small notice about a cottage for rent, fully furnished. The notice said to call Mac Campbell and gave a phone number. I flipped back to the front page to check the paper's date. Today. Maybe...

I stuffed the debris from our meal into a nearby trash receptacle, grabbed the paper and Tweedle Dee, stuffed him back in the car, then went into the café to use the pay phone. Yes, the cottage was still available, and Mac Campbell would meet me in an hour to take me over and show me the place.

I had an hour to kill, so I retrieved Tweedle Dee, tossed the paper in the car and the two of us took a stroll. So what if people noticed that I was walking down Main Street carrying a budgie in a cage? I'd just be that eccentric Yankee.

Well, people did notice—hard not to with Tweedle happily chirping at the whole world. I just hadn't been in town long enough to realize that little stroll had pretty much assured my welcome in the Mossy Creek community.

I met Mac Campbell, saw the cottage...and before the

sun had gone down, I had signed a lease, had a set of keys, directions to the Piggly Wiggly (which, Mac explained with admirable self-control when I stared at him, was the grocery store) and a promise that he'd call first thing Monday morning to arrange to have the phone turned on.

So I unpacked the Toyota—and almost heard the poor car groan with relief—made up the bed so that I could fall into it as soon as I needed to, left a protesting Tweedle Dee in the living room, and trundled off to the Piggly Wiggly to get enough of the basics and frozen dinners to last me at least through the weekend.

I stayed vertical long enough to put the groceries away, make sure Tweedle had food and water, pull the most recent Sharyn McCrumb paperback out of the to-be-read box, and crawled into bed. I didn't manage to finish reading the back cover copy before I was sound asleep.

Over the weekend, Tweedle and I got acquainted with our new home. One room had a desk, two small bookcases and a phone jack—just about everything a wanna-be writer needed. I also went over to Hamilton's Department Store. When I trundled back to the cottage, my groaning Toyota held a small microwave, a CD/cassette/radio boom box, a touch-tone phone and a laptop computer and printer.

As soon as the phone was turned on the following week, I called Nadine to give her my new address and phone number.

"You're where?" Nadine said.

"Mossy Creek. In Georgia."

"Why are you in Georgia?"

"I was going to South Carolina, remember?"

"I remember. Where is Mossy Creek?"

"In Georgia," I repeated patiently.

"Where in Georgia?"

Long pause.

"Sorry," Nadine said. "Forgot who I was talking to. I'll

look it up on a map. Tell me about the cottage and the town."

So I did. I told her about the little screened porch off the kitchen and the flower beds I could play in. I told her about the bookstore and the library, the potpourri and candle shop, the bookstore, the beauty salon, the coffee shop next door to a bakery and the bookstore.

"Sounds like you'll have everything you need," Nadine said, laughing. "And it sounds like you can't get too lost."

"Most of it's on Main Street."

"Uh huh."

I couldn't really take offense at this lack of optimism about my getting from one place to another. Before moving to Richmond, Nadine had lived in the same house for several years—and I got lost every single time I went to visit her. Come to think of it, that's probably the real reason she'd insisted that I keep in touch. She'd probably worried that I'd start out for South Carolina and end up in South Dakota.

The conversation ended with my getting her email address and promising to send her mine as soon as I got one.

All in all, it was a good beginning.

♀♀♀

The following Monday, I began my new routine as writer wanna-be. After spending a little time over breakfast and writing an email to Nadine, I put a notebook and a couple of pens in my World Wildlife totebag and walked up to Main Street and the Naked Bean. I chatted a bit with Jayne Austin Reynolds, the owner, while she made my coffee and put shortbread cookies on a plate. Then I settled down at one of the little tables, opened my notebook and got to work.

I wanted to tell a story about romance and magic. I wanted a tall, handsome, dangerous hero. I wanted a powerful heroine who, in spite of herself, would swoon for the hero. Now, all I needed was a story to go with the things I wanted to put in it. I spent a happy hour making notes and getting nowhere. Then I went home for Irish whistle practice because Tweedle tended to get cranky if we didn't have whistle time together. During the afternoon, I did practical, mundane things, made more story notes, had dinner, then spent a leisurely evening reading and practicing the stories I had learned. That was my routine for the first week, with added stops at the bakery or bookstore on my way home from the Naked Bean.

The next week, things started to change, but I didn't recognize the moment when it happened.

I was in the Naked Bean, on my second cup of coffee, busily scribbling notes for my fantasy romance, when a woman and two children came in. The boy started making a commotion, waving his arms around and telling his sister something about being "this big."

I glanced up, saw the distracted look on Jayne's and the mother's faces and said to the boy, "I knew of a frog once that tried to puff himself up to be 'this big.' It didn't turn out well for him."

"Yeah?" the boy challenged.

So I launched into the Aesop's Fable about the frog who tried to prove to other frogs that he could puff himself up as big as a cow and puffed himself up so much he blew up.

The girl made a face and said, "Ewwww."

The boy wanted to know how far the frog's guts splattered.

"Far," I said solemnly. "Really, really far."

He grinned at me.

The mother, having concluded her transaction with Jayne, gathered up her children and left.

Jayne placed a fresh cup of coffee on the table. "You didn't mention you were a storyteller as well as a story writer."

"Oh, I'm—" Something inside me stifled the denial,

something that asked, If not now, when? "—pretty much a beginner."

"You did real well."

I felt a warm little glow and left the shop without a suspicion in the world.

Shows you how much I knew.

Over the next few days, when a customer came into the Naked Bean while I was there, Jayne would call out,

"Laurie, we were just talking about such-and-such. Do you know a story about that?" A lot of times I did, since I'd learned a goodly number of short folk tales and fables. So I would tell the story and go back to my struggle to do something with my hero and heroine.

Then, one morning, Jayne said, "I was thinking it might be fun to have a little story program here one evening. Just a few stories, some coffee and treats. Something like that."

"That does sound like fun," I said enthusiastically.

"How's Thursday evening?"

"Sounds good. Who's telling stories?"

"You are." Jayne went back to her counter.

I bolted from my chair and followed her. "But...But I've never actually told to an audience before."

"Won't be an audience. Just a few people I'll mention it to when they come into the shop. You can just tell the stories you've already told."

"But I've already told them."

"Only one or two people have heard each one. So the other stories will be new. Besides, it would be a little something extra for the shop."

That clinched it. I hadn't known her long, but I thought of Jayne as a friend, and I could do this to help a friend.

I trotted home to email a couple of people from the storytelling group I belonged to, asking for tips on telling to an audience—which it wouldn't be, since, as Jayne had pointed out, the news about the storytelling program would be spread by word of mouth.

Jayne hadn't mentioned that all it took was telling the right person or two for the whole town to know about it.

So Thursday evening arrived. So did the audience. My nerves bounced on the ceiling as the place began to fill with people. There was Maggie Hart and her mother, Millicent, as well as Maggie's friend, Tag Garner. There was Hank and Casey Blackshear. There was Sandy Crane and her husband Jess, who had come in his capacity as a reporter for the *Mossy Creek Gazette.* There was Pearl Quinlan, who owned the bookstore, and Ingrid Beechum, who had provided some of the treats for the evening. Even Ida Hamilton Walker, the mayor, showed up. So did Amos Royden, Chief of Police. There were more people there, way too many people there, but I didn't know them. I wasn't sure which was worse— making a debut in front of strangers, or telling stories to the people I knew.

The one thing I was sure of is I would have run out the door and kept going if I could have gotten through the crowd. Which is probably why Jayne had put the "stage" area as far from the door as possible.

So I told my stories. And I survived telling my stories. And people made a point of telling me they'd enjoyed the stories—including Chief Royden, who also inquired after Tweedle Dee. I even survived people saying they were looking forward to coming back next Thursday.

"Next Thursday?" I whispered frantically to Jayne.

"We'll talk about it when you come by in the morning."

I had a pretty good idea how the conversation would go—and it did. I had a week to come up with a new set of stories. Oh, help.

❦ ❦ ❦

The Saturday after my storytelling debut, I stared at

my laptop's screen, then slumped in frustration.

"My hero is tall, dark and dangerous," I muttered. "How could he be boring?"

Cht, mumbled Tweedle Dee. He was busy tugging on the gold chain attached to the tiger-eye pendant.

"Right," I said sourly. "He's not small, blue and fluffy. How could he not be boring?"

Cht.

I'd been wearing that pendant, along with a long, scooped-neck dress, to try to get into the heroine's skin, so to speak. But Tweedle couldn't resist playing with my jewelry and kept landing on my chest. Unfortunately, bare skin doesn't provide anything to hold onto. After the second time he slid headfirst into my bra, I took off the pendant and put it on the desk for him to play with.

So there he was, giving me his best innocent look with his beak and one foot filled with gold chain.

And something clicked.

I opened a new file and my fingers danced on the keyboard as I wrote the story of "Tweedle Dee and the Jewel Thieves." I had the setup (visiting my aunt, who owned a bed and breakfast on the coast of Maine). I had secondary characters (the sheriff, who was a friend of my aunt's, and two gentlemen, who were staying at the B&B while touring the area to research the water-worn caves that, according to local lore, had been used by pirates of old). I had the problem (a series of jewel heists in the surrounding towns). And I had Tweedle Dee, the Houdini of parakeets, who always managed to escape from his cage and hide somewhere convenient in order to go on an outing with me.

I had my second setup (a picnic on the small beach that was part of the B&B property). I had danger (Tweedle attracting the attention of a hungry gull and taking shelter in one of the caves). I had suspense (one of the guests entering that same cave and, upon whistling a particular sequence of notes, opening a hidden entrance behind which was a secret chamber filled with loot). I had more danger (the other gentlemen revealing A Clue that made my aunt and me realize her boarders were the jewel thieves) and an attempt to call for help on my aunt's cell phone, which was thwarted when the thieves realized they'd been found out. Then there was the climax, with the thieves threatening my aunt and me, and Tweedle, sensing his people were in danger, bravely leaving the cave and, flying for his life while being chased by a whole flock of gulls, zipping past one of the thieves at the same moment I flung the plate piled with the picnic scraps at one thief and my aunt scooped up a handful of potato salad and hit the other one right between the eyes. The gulls, having lost sight of the blue budgie lunch special, weren't about to give up the scraps, and the resulting food fight and birdy free-for-all successfully distracted the thieves until the sheriff's timely arrival with his deputies. The thieves were taken into custody, the cave was located and Tweedle was able to whistle the particular sequence of notes that opened the hidden door, thus revealing the secret chamber and helping the sheriff recover the loot.

It was the wee hours of the morning when, exhausted and gleeful, I ran off a copy of the story and made a backup copy on a disk. I put Tweedle back in his cage (he'd fallen asleep perched on top of the pendant) and fell into bed.

The next morning, I read the story. It stretched reality to the point of being a tall tale, and I doubted there was an editor anywhere who would take it, but...maybe I could tell it at the next Thursday evening storytelling program at the Naked Bean.

Energized by that thought, I spent most of the day working through the story while Tweedle preened his feathers and chirped encouragement.

On Monday, I went to the Naked Bean just to take a

walk and get out of the cottage for a while. But I didn't stay as long as usual, being too eager to get back to working on the story.

By late morning, I took a break for whistle time, mostly because Tweedle Dee was making such a racket I couldn't talk over him. So I started out with the first songs—— "Twinkle Twinkle Little Star," "On Top of Old Smokey," and "The Water Is Wide." They were the songs Tweedle whistled with me, joining in as a duet whenever I held a long note. Then I progressed to some of the new songs I was practicing. Or tried to. I was still having a lot of trouble hitting the notes in the next octave. Giving in to a need to vent a little, I took a deep breath and blew into the whistle, which sent Tweedle into a tizzy.

Or maybe it was the banging on the front door that set him off.

I dropped the whistle on a chair and hurried to the front door, reaching it at the same time Amos Royden, Chief of Police, opened the door and started to step into my little hallway.

We stared at each other.

"I was passing by and heard your smoke alarm go off," Chief Royden said. "I thought you might need some help."

"Smoke alarm?" I said blankly.

He frowned. "It's stopped now."

I felt my face get really really hot. "Oh. That wasn't the smoke alarm. That was 'D.'"

He looked puzzled. "Dee? The bird?"

Cht cht cht.

A free-flying budgie and an open door weren't a good combination, so I stepped back and said, "Won't you come in, Chief Royden?"

Leading the way into the living room, I picked up the whistle. I played a note. Or tried to. "D."

He didn't look puzzled any more. But he didn't have

time to say anything because Tweedle Dee shot off the top of his cage and flew toward us at a height that would have let him land on the top of my head but was a collision course with Chief Royden's nose.

The Chief ducked. As he straightened up, Tweedle circled around to land on his shoulder.

"Tweedle Dee, Tweedle Dee, Tweedle Dee is me," Tweedle Dee said happily.

"Hey, Tweedle Dee," Chief Royden replied cautiously.

Deciding to show his favor, Tweedle whistled "Twinkle Twinkle Little Star," sour notes and all. Then, having done his share of entertaining our guest, he flew back to his cage to see if I'd put anything in the treat dish since the last time he'd checked.

"Are you going to arrest me?" I asked.

His eyes were twinkling again. "For imitating a smoke alarm with a penny whistle?"

"No, for assaulting a police officer with a budgie."

Amos Royden laughed. "I like you, Laurie Grey."

I like you, too. "Thanks for stopping by, Chief."

He accepted the dismissal and left.

I knew I was giving mixed signals, and I knew he was puzzled by it. It wasn't because I didn't like him, it was because I did. But that wasn't something I wanted to explain, so if I couldn't help giving mixed signals, I could be kind enough to keep my distance whenever possible.

🐦🐦🐦

Tweedle Dee and the Jewel Thieves was a rousing success on Thursday evening. Amos Royden was there, but he left after telling me it was a fine story. I didn't think anyone else paid attention to his quick departure.

Shows you how much I knew about things like that.

The next morning, still feeling that warm little glow of

success, I sauntered up to the Naked Bean and noticed the new sign in the window.

LAURIE GREY, STORYTELLER
THURSDAY EVENINGS AT 7 P.M.

That was definitely a warm fuzzy. It was the rest of the sign that had me whimpering.

FOLK TALES
FABLES
FURTHER ADVENTURES OF TWEEDLE DEE

As I rushed into the shop, Jayne looked at me and grinned. "Morning, Laurie. How do you like the sign?"

"It's great," I stammered. "It's wonderful. Really. But..."

"But?"

"But I don't have another Tweedle Dee story," I wailed.

Now, a rational, reasonable person who was also a friend would say something like, "Oh. Golly. I didn't think of that. I'll change the sign right away." Or, "I just needed to fill up the space. No one will notice what stories you tell."

A rational, reasonable person who was also a friend would say something like that, wouldn't she?

What Jayne said was, "Then you'd better sit down and start writing, because folks are expecting another Tweedle Dee story on Thursday."

I slumped my way to "my" table, opened my notebook and stared at a page as blank as my mind.

Actually, my mind was blanker. At least the page had those nice blue lines running across it.

I drew a square and filled it in. I turned the square into a box and cross-hatched the other sides for shading. I drew a few spirals. I was working on something viney going all the way up the margin when Jayne brought over a cup of her specialty coffee and a couple of shortbread cookies.

"You're not writing," she said.

"I'm thinking."

"You're not thinking, you're just doodling."

"These are thinking doodles," I said darkly.

Guess I don't do darkly well, because Jayne just said "Uh huh" and went about her work.

I filled three pages with thinking doodles before I gave up and sulked my way back home to face an empty screen that didn't even have nice blue lines going across it. But the laptop did have a paint program, so I spent the afternoon making computer-generated doodles.

Over the weekend, I heard a whisper of something that gave me hope of finding another Tweedle Dee story, so Monday morning I was at the Naked Bean almost as soon as Jayne opened her doors. Amos Royden had gotten there before me.

Sure that he would have the answer, I practically pounced on him—which he didn't seem to mind until I said, "What do you know about the Ten-Cent Gypsy?"

Jayne spilled coffee beans all over the counter, and Amos Royden got this look on his face, like someone who thought he'd been given a cookie and just discovered he'd swallowed a small toad.

Before I could explain that I'd overheard the words "Ten-Cent Gypsy" and thought I could use it in a Tweedle-goes-adventuring-at-a-carnival story if I could just find out what it was, Amos muttered something that sounded like, "ThankyouGladtobehere," and was out the door.

Turning to Jayne, I said, "What did he say?"

Apparently cleaning up spilled coffee beans causes temporary deafness because all I got at the Naked Bean that morning was coffee and too many shortbread cookies.

I decided to try again on Tuesday afternoon when I did a storytelling program at the Magnolia Manor Nursing Home—an engagement that had been arranged by Eustene

Oscar, whose mother was a resident of the home.

After the program, I stopped to chat with Eustene, who just happened to be visiting her mother in time for the storytelling program. I tried to steer the conversation to the Ten-Cent Gypsy while Eustene kept steering it toward what a fine—and unattached—man Amos Royden was.

Finally, I sighed. "You're not going to tell me, are you?" Eustene just smiled.

"It's because I'm a Yankee, isn't it?"

She patted my arm and said, "You're too Southern to be a Yankee."

On the way home, I kept thinking that would be a great line for a story if I could figure out what it meant.

ϖϖϖ

Tuesday evening, I was channel surfing, which usually drives me batty, and muttering about people who put road-blocks in the way of creative flow.

"You started this," I told Tweedle Dee, who was fluffed and comfy on the arm of the couch. "You come up with something."

He didn't even *cht* at me, so I went back to channel surfing—until I came to an old Western. I have no idea what it was, but there were cowboys and cattle and—

"That's it!" I yelled, jumping up and startling Tweedle so much he fell off the couch.

I shut off the TV, ran into the other room and fired up the laptop, completely ignoring Tweedle as he chittered and scolded me for scaring him.

That evening I wrote "Tweedle Dee and the Stampede," about how, during a visit to a friend who was working on a cattle ranch one summer, Tweedle prevented a troop of Boy Scouts doing an overnight Boy Scout thingie from being trampled by a herd of cattle by bravely flying off into the night to soothe the restless herd by whistling "Twinkle Twinkle Little Star" all night long.

When I told that story on Thursday night, I had a good idea of how many people in the audience had heard Tweedle whistle that tune by how hard they laughed.

I called Nadine over the weekend, and when I got done telling her the story, she said, "How come I don't get to be in a Tweedle Dee story?" So I wrote one about Tweedle staying with Nadine while I went off to a storytelling workshop and she got to play Dr. Watson to a little blue Sherlock Holmes. Or maybe it was a little blue Lassie. It was hard to tell sometimes.

I sent her a copy of it and got back an email full of those shorthand thingies emailers use that I could never completely translate, but the gist of it was she liked the story.

That story also established me as Mossy Creek's resident storyteller. Besides weekly programs at the Naked Bean and Magnolia Manor, I started doing an every-other-week storytime at the library. I told stories during the Fourth of July festivities and a ghost story night in the town square in August. As the seasons changed, I did programs at the school, told Halloween stories at Pearl Quinlan's bookstore, told Thanksgiving stories at a special storytime at the library—and I was there to celebrate a Mossy Creek Christmas.

I spent Christmas evening quietly at home with Tweedle Dee, having already made merry for most of the day. While I lay on the couch watching *It's a Wonderful Life*, with Tweedle snuggled up on my chest so that his little head rested against my chin, I realized I'd gotten the gift I'd wanted most. I'd gotten my pocket of time. And while I never did write that romantic epic, I'd written my Tweedle Dee stories, sweet and silly things that they were, and had amused and entertained people with them—and had been able to see and share that pleasure with the people who had become so very special to me.

And I tried not to wonder too much about what Amos Royden thought of the Christmas present I'd left for him at the police station. It was one of my favorite Celtic CDs. I wasn't even sure why I'd given it to him, except that I sometimes found myself wishing for a different ending, and I wanted to leave something for him to remember me by.

I wanted to leave something for the rest of Mossy Creek, too—some tangible legacy that wouldn't fade away with memory.

Just before I dozed off, I realized I could do just that.

❦❦❦

All through the winter months, I wrote Tweedle Dee stories. I polished them and practiced them, preparing each one to add to my legacy. I told friends I was indulging in a "creative hiberation" as a way to explain why I was spending more and more time at home—and also as a way of explaining why I was doing storytelling programs every other week at the Naked Bean and Magnolia Manor Nursing home and why, with regret, I was turning down other requests for storytelling programs. I still went to the Naked Bean a couple mornings a week to sit for an hour and watch the world, but I drove over instead of walking the short distance. And if Jayne or another friend asked if I was feeling all right, I would smile and say I was tired, just tired.

The grace of a lie—and the grace of friends who accept it while suspecting it's a lie.

And then came the day when I barely had the strength to get out of bed. Too many storytelling programs. Too many late nights. I'd been working too hard. I was tired, just tired. That's what I told myself while I used the walls to support my unsteady progress to the bathroom and then to the kitchen.

I knew that wasn't true. I hadn't expected to see another Christmas, let alone ring in another new year or see the spring flowers bloom. Now there was no denying that the bus on the Reaper & Scythe line only had a few more stops before it got to me.

But there was still enough time. There had to be enough time.

I felt a little stronger after some toast and orange juice—strong enough to call the sound studio in Bigelow and arrange to have the use of a recording room and a sound engineer for the three days I estimated I would need for what I wanted to do. They couldn't accommodate me until the following week, so I made the other phone calls—one to Dr. Champion's office to set up an appointment as soon as possible, one to my former doctor's office to have my medical records available and one to Mac Campbell.

While I waited to go to the various appointments, I made out careful lists.

I saw Dr. Champion. There was nothing he could do except be the physician of record for what would come.

I saw Mac Campbell. There were things he could do—and he did them.

I also stopped at the police station and gave Sandy, the police dispatcher, a set of keys to the cottage.

"I'm going out of town for a few days," I said in explanation, "and I'd feel better if someone had a spare set."

Neither of us mentioned that Mac, as the attorney for the cottage's owner, already had a spare set.

"Do you need someone to feed Tweedle Dee?" Sandy asked.

"No, I won't be gone for more than two or three days. He'll have plenty of food and water for that long."

And we left it at that.

❦ ❦ ❦

The following week, I set off bright and early one morning and made the twenty-minute drive to Bigelow. I'd found a hotel a few blocks from the sound studio and had booked a room so that I could save my strength. It was a wise thing to do. I worked hard during those days, and crawled back to the hotel each evening. By the afternoon of the third day, I'd done what I'd wanted to do.

And when it was done, I told the men in the studio what I wanted, and when I needed to have it. And I told them why.

Now, I'd heard enough to know about the feud between Bigelowans and Mossy Creekites, but I received nothing but courtesy from those men. Maybe it's because I was a transplanted Yankee and not a native Mossy Creekite. Maybe it's because they couldn't look into my eyes without seeing the truth of what I was saying. Or maybe it's because there are some things even a long-standing feud stands aside for. Whatever the reason, they promised I would have everything I needed by the agreed-upon date.

So I packed my bag, checked out of the hotel and went home.

Tweedle Dee was frantically happy to see me, since he'd never been left alone before. I let him out, gave him fresh food and water, and got into a clean nightgown. He followed me from room to room, as if he didn't trust me not to disappear again.

I forced myself to heat up and eat a bowl of soup. Then I crawled into bed.

Tweedle settled on the pillow beside my head. As I fell asleep, I felt him give my chin a little nibble kiss and heard him softly whistling "Twinkle Twinkle Little Star."

❦ ❦ ❦

I hoarded my strength like a miser over the next few weeks, and when help was offered, I didn't turn it down.

Sandy Crane came by and helped me clean the cottage. Or, rather, she cleaned and I helped by staying out of the way. Jayne came by with rolls from Beechum's bakery, and shortbread cookies and chamomile tea from the Naked Bean. Pearl came by with new paperbacks and meals from Mama's All You Can Eat Café.

And Mac Campbell came by with the papers I needed to sign, assuring me he'd already taken care of the other things I'd asked of him.

I didn't see Amos Royden. I wasn't sure I wanted to. Besides, from what Jayne and Sandy had told me, Amos had his own problems in the form of a close encounter with the furry kind.

Finally, the evening came when I called Nadine. A hard phone call for both of us, but I was glad to talk to her one last time.

❦ ❦ ❦

The package from the sound studio arrived on the promised day. I called Mac, and he picked up the package and promised to mail the padded envelope I'd addressed to Nadine.

That night, I packed a small bag with a clean nightgown, a change of clothes and two favorite paperbacks. I hung my favorite dress and the tiger-eye pendant on the closet door where they would be easy to find.

The next morning, I called Sandy at the police station.

"Morning, Laurie," Sandy said.

"Do you still have that extra set of keys I gave you?"

There was a slight hesitation before she said, "We've got them." Which made me wonder who had them.

"Laurie? Is there something I can do for you?"

"You could call the paramedics—and Dr. Champion, if you wouldn't mind."

She didn't ask me why. She didn't have to.

"Boo and Andy will be there as soon as they can," Sandy said.

"Thanks. Good-bye, Sandy."

I put down the phone and gathered my strength. I had one more good-bye to make.

Tweedle Dee was silent when I opened his cage. He didn't hop out as he usually did. He just politely stepped up on my offered finger. I lifted him up so that we could look at each other.

"You've been a good friend, Tweedle Dee," I said softly. "I wish I could have stayed around longer for you. But these are good people. You'll do all right here."

As I started to lower my arm, he stretched his neck in order to give my chin a last nibble kiss.

I put him back in his cage. As I closed the cage door, I heard Boo and Andy pulling into the driveway.

🐦 🐦 🐦

Seeing Hank Blackshear heading toward me, I waited on the sidewalk outside the police station, dreading the conversation I'd already had a dozen times that day.

"Afternoon, Amos," Hank said.

"Afternoon, Hank."

Hank scuffed his shoe on the hot summer sidewalk. "It was a nice service."

"Yeah."

"We were all pleased that her friend could make it down for the funeral."

"Yeah. Nadine is a nice lady."

"Mac said you asked him to play the bagpipes at the service."

"Laurie liked Celtic music. It wasn't an Irish whistle, but it was the best we could do." I waited, knowing the question I dreaded most was coming.

"How's Tweedle Dee?"

Because Hank was Mossy Creek's vet, I told the truth for the first time that day. "He's grieving. He was all right, pretty much, for those few days she was in the hospital. I think he thought he was just visiting until she came back. But…" I sighed. "He stopped eating the day of the funeral. He just went into a corner of his cage and hasn't come out since."

Hank shook his head sadly. "Little bird like that won't last long once he stops eating."

"I know it."

"Have you…Have you thought about finding him another place to live?"

I shook my head. "He's all right where he is—at least until we know if he's going to stay around."

"You need anything, you call me."

I just nodded, got into my Jeep and went home. I had already lost Dog that summer. I wasn't going to give up on Tweedle Dee easily. I walked into my living room slowly. Not that it would make any difference. Crouching down in front of the cage, I said softly, "Hey, Tweedle Dee."

No response. Tweedle Dee just continued to face the back corner of his cage.

"She wouldn't have wanted you to grieve like this. She wouldn't want you joining her so soon. It would break her heart to see you like this."

Nothing.

Sighing, I stood up, went into the kitchen for a beer, then came back to the living room.

Laurie had made five sets of the two CDs that contained her Tweedle Dee stories. One set had been mailed to her friend Nadine. One set, with a CD player Mac had purchased at her request, had gone to Jayne at the Naked Bean. Another set with CD player had gone to Magnolia Manor. Another, along with a CD player and all of her books, had been donated to the library. The last set hadn't been specified for a particular person, so I'd taken them.

I thought I understood now why she'd given me the CD of Celtic music at Christmas. Her way of sharing something of herself in the only way she felt she could under the circumstances.

Nothing I could do about that, but...

I went over to the table that held Tweedle Dee's inheritance.

She'd set up a trust fund for her little friend so that his new person wouldn't have to worry about covering any vet bills down the road. Besides that, the inheritance was an Irish whistle and songbooks, a CD player...and a CD that was simply labeled, for Tweedle Dee.

Setting down my beer, I opened the jewel case, put the CD in the player and turned it on.

A few seconds of silence...then an Irish whistle playing "Twinkle Twinkle Little Star."

I looked over at the cage.

No response from Tweedle Dee.

I listened for a few minutes as one song followed another. Then I couldn't listen anymore and walked out of the room.

But I kept coming back during the evening to turn the CD on again.

Disappointed that the little bird didn't respond, I finally went to bed.

The next morning, before I left for work, I turned on the CD. When I got home that night and went to give Tweedle Dee fresh food and water, I noticed the bird was still in the back corner, but there was a small bare patch on the spray of millet attached to the side of the cage, and there were seed husks in the food dish. Not many, but enough to give me hope.

For the rest of the week, I turned on the CD before I left for work. Each evening, Tweedle Dee was still in the corner, still wouldn't respond, but there were more bare patches on the spray of millet and more seed husks in the dish.

On Saturday, I turned on the coffee maker before going into the living room to give Tweedle Dee fresh food and water. I turned on the CD, then went back to the kitchen for my coffee.

By the time I got back to the doorway of the living room, the song was "The Water is Wide." As the Irish whistle held a long note, I heard a soft, hesitant da-da, da-da, da-da sour note.

I stayed where I was, out of sight. As the songs progressed to the Irish/Celtic tunes Laurie had learned more recently, there were no more whistling duets. But in the pauses between the songs, I heard the scratching of a beak selectively picking out seeds.

Finally, when the CD ended, I heard a quiet, sad two-note chirrup, like a question that had been asked over and over again—and an answer was no longer expected.

Setting my coffee mug on the floor, I slowly walked into the living room. Tweedle Dee, perched on his food dish, just watched me.

I crouched in front of the cage.

"Tweedle Dee, Tweedle Dee, Tweedle Dee is me," said Tweedle Dee in a hesitant little voice.

Smiling, I said, "Hey, Tweedle Dee."

Mossy Creek Gazette

VOLUME III, No. 7   **MOSSY CREEK, GEORGIA**

The Bell Ringer

When We Look At The Stars

by Katie Bell

There's a legend in Mossy Creek that I'd like to share with newcomers before you read any further. This land belonged to the Cherokee Indians before we drove them out. Only a few Cherokee families managed to stay here. But that's a story for another column.

Legend has it that a pioneer girl was rescued from bandits by the Cherokees. The Indians took her in, named her Shooting Star, and claimed her as their own. She grew up as the chief's favorite daughter, married a man of royal blood and together they ruled their tribe. She became a Beloved Woman, which is a title of great respect among the Cherokee.

The night she died, a flock of tiny, bright-colored birds came down from the sky and settled in the trees. When night fell, instead of roosting, they began to chatter, flew across the full moon and disappeared. Some say they were singing as they escorted her soul to the land of her ancestors. I prefer to think she followed them into the sky and began dancing among the stars.

The storytellers of Mossy Creek claim that's where the children's nursery rhyme, *Twinkle, twinkle little star* came from.

I don't know about that, but I can definitely tell you that there's a lot happening in Mossy Creek this summer, and so maybe a little star-gazing can help us see the light.

"A friend is someone who knows the song in your heart and can sing it back to you when you have forgotten the words."

— *Unknown*

❦❦

HOPE and MARLE

Chapter Twelve

My name is Hope Bailey Stanton, and I'm the reason part of Mossy Creek no longer flows to the sea. When I was seventeen years old my father, Lucas Bailey, climbed into our farm's bulldozer, drove it through the back woods to a beautiful, fairytale glen just above the old Bailey Mill Road and Bailey covered bridge and there destroyed the God-given Mossy Creek tributary our Bailey ancestors had named Bailey Branch. Until then Bailey Branch flowed south to southeast through the mountains of the Bailey Mill community before merging again with its mother, Mossy Creek, just past the Mossy Creek town limits at Hamilton Farm.

"That branch is nothing but a lure for the innocent," Papa announced when he sent the waters of Bailey Branch off into a wooded hollow to form Bailey Swamp. He hoped the branch would just fade into the earth, but it wept into that hollow with endless grief. Marle Settles and I had found each other and lost our hearts in its waters. In my mind, Bailey Branch cried for us.

Just as Bailey Branch is a defiant daughter of Mossy Creek, the community of Bailey Mill is to the *town* of Mossy Creek as Brooklyn is to Manhattan—the no-nonsense cotton panties under a silk skirt. Like other Creekite burbs—

Lookover, Yonder and Chinaberry—Bailey Mill has its own mindset, its own culture and traditions. Say *I'm a Bailey Millite* and people know you'd rather chew your own hand off than hold it out for help. Only a few hundred hardy, apple-loving souls are tucked into our ridges and hollows. New-comers, like Ida's "friend," retired Lieutenant-Colonel Del Jackson, move here for the challenge and the mountainous beauty. Apples like cold, high views from majestic hillsides, and so do Millites.

What's not to love?

The Bailey Mill community includes our famous *Sweet Hope* Apple Orchards, Inc., several fancy "barns" where we sell apples and apple products to thousands of visitors each fall, the historic Bailey grist mill, what's left of Bailey Branch (a trickle through a swampy pond behind the big earthen dam my father built), Bailey Mill Road (a fading pioneer wagon trail) and finally, most notoriously, the Bailey Mill covered bridge, a fantastic local landmark the Mossy Creek Historical Society lists on its tour route. The bridge is more of a notorious curiosity than a dignified historical site, since it's sat high and dry, a marooned ship on a dry mountain sea, for more than two decades.

Thanks to me and Marle Settles making love beneath its sweet old timbers.

"Bailey Mill Bridge has gone unwatered for twenty-two years," I said today, then marked off the early September date on the calendar in the farm office overlooking the or-chards. Shaking a little, I put my head in my hands. A plaque on my desk, given to me by my college-student twins, Joel and Samantha, and my late husband, Rev. Charles Stanton, swam in my vision.

HOPE BAILEY STANTON
PRESIDENT OF SWEET HOPE ORCHARDS
THE APPLE OF OUR EYE

The apple of their eye. Respected mother, wife, apple farmer. (And devoted daughter of Lucas Bailey, despite his stern control over my life after my mother died young.) A year ago Charles had turned to me in our front porch rockers one evening, put a hand to his chest and said in a pained voice, "My heart, Hope, my heart," as if I held it, had always held it. I tried to save him, got him to Doc Champion's over in town, then to the hospital down in Bigelow, but he was gone. Only in his early forties, and gone. I mourned him. I'd come to love Charlie, though not as much as he loved me. He was the best husband, the best father for her children a woman could want. I hadn't wanted him, at first, but that had been my mistake, not his. Whether it's people or apples, we Baileys have a history of loving slow and forever.

I'm the fourth Hope Bailey named after the *Sweet Hope* apple since 1895, when my great-great-great grandmother, the first Hope, crossed a luscious *Sweet Hush* apple from our McGillan kin's famous orchards, up in Chocinaw County, with a hard, tart Mossy Creek *Thunker*. The nationally famous *Sweet Hush* is a wonderful lady of an apple, while the Mossy Creek *Thunker* is the wild frontiersman of fruit—more than friendly with the wild mountain crabapples, and, according to proud Creekites, only good for two things: making apple liquor and throwing at somebody.

"You want to know how to knock a grown man down with a *Thunker*?" my grandfather, Albert Hope Bailey, was fond of telling reporters from the regional travel magazines who came to write articles on *Sweet Hope* Orchards. "Give him a pint of *Thunker* brandy, or—" Grandfather Bailey would rear back with a sly twinkle in his Bailey blues— "hit him right between the eyes with the apple itself."

Like most unlikely but destined matings, the *Thunker* and the *Sweet Hush* mingled the best of themselves to produce the sturdy, delectable *Sweet Hope*, and the rest, as they say at the National Society of Apple Growers, is history.

Generations of *Sweet Hope* apple harvests have made the Bailey orchards and mountain farm one of the most prosperous businesses in all of Bigelow County, and the weekend festivities at *Sweet Hope* Orchards draw thousands of free-spending tourists to greater Mossy Creek every fall from September to after Thanksgiving. Ida has threatened to shoot me if I ever close the orchards. Seriously, she knows I never would. No Bailey has ever been accused of deserting the Bailey legacy of *Sweet Hope*. Even if it meant giving up the boy she loved. As I did, twenty-two years ago, when Bailey Branch went dry.

After I marked the dark anniversary on my desk calendar, I bent my head lower and whispered the prayer I'd spoken at the end of every summer since I was seventeen.

Please God, take care of Marle Settles and forgive me for still loving him. But this September I added a new line. *And after I see him today please make him leave forever, this time.*

❦ ❦ ❦

I opened my eyes every morning for twenty-two years knowing that one day I'd go home to Hope. Not that I expected her to welcome me back, and I wouldn't have blamed her if she told me to go fly my Piper Cub into the side of Mossy Creek's Colchik Mountain. There were more than a few people in greater Mossy Creek who probably wished I had died along with my brother, Creighton, and more than a few who'd have trouble believing yours truly, Marle Settles, was now Lieutenant-Colonel Settles, decorated vet and newly retired fighter pilot, United States Marine Corp.

But here I was, standing in the shadows of the Bailey Mill covered bridge where a 19 year old boy with a bad past and a shaky future had made love to the only person who'd never doubted him—Hope Bailey, named after a famous apple, the pride of the famous Baileys, an apple-pie girl. That boy—me, Marle Settles—thought giving her up had been the right thing to do. Looking back on it, I still say I did the right thing. Helluva note, being right but miserable for two decades.

Now I listened to the dry silence, the rustle of ferns and weeds growing where the creek had once whispered to us. *Water always finds its way back where it belongs*, I told myself. *And so will we.*

I heard footsteps in the leaves of the forest floor. A tall, auburn-haired woman stepped out of the woods and stood, silhouetted, framed by the trees, the mountains, the arching timber roof of the old bridge. An incredible sight. Hope Bailey Stanton—Charles's widow, Joel and Samantha Stanton's mother, my childhood love—was dressed in thigh-hugging faded jeans, a soft red sweater and an aura of September sunshine. She took a few halting, weak-kneed steps toward me.

I took the same toward her. We stopped at the same time.

"Let's keep some root room between us," she said in a shaky voice.

She still talked in apple metaphors. All Baileys did. I slid my hands in the pockets of my khakis and tried to look like a man who'd flown in battle many times without breaking a sweat or rattling words. "Your voice is the same."

She put a hand to her heart. "So is yours."

"I hope not. I sounded like a hillbilly when you made me read books out loud to you."

"You had a deep, beautiful drawl and a way with words that had nothing to do with good grammar. You spoke from the heart. And I loved—" She stopped. Her hand clenched over her heart, squeezing my heart along with hers.

We looked at each other in the pieces of light and shadow that made the old bridge feel like a doorway between this world and memories. She was nearly forty and still the most beautiful girl I'd ever seen in my life. I was just over forty but felt nineteen again.

"I spent years wondering how this would feel," I said finally.

"So did I."

"I was sorry to hear about Charlie. I swear to you. Sorry."

"It's been a year. How long have you known?"

"A year."

Silence. With two words I'd exposed the fact that I'd kept close tabs on her life. Her expression froze. "I should have known Ida would let you know."

"Incredible lady. I stayed in touch with her—and she let me."

"I know," Hope said. "I asked her to send you things."

Now the surprised silence belonged to me. I had scrap-books full of mementos Ida had mailed to me wherever I was stationed over the years—articles from the *Mossy Creek Gazette* about Hope Bailey Stanton, CEO of *Sweet Hope* Or-chards, Inc., pictures of Joel and Samantha when they won some award or trophy at school and casual snapshots of them grinning alongside Hope as she and they worked in the orchards during the colorful fall apple season. My throat tightened. "Thank you," I finally said.

By then, Hope was knotting her hands in her sweater, as if holding onto her control for dear life. "It was only right. And Ida was glad to help. She knew you weren't to blame for what Creighton did to her husband."

Inside, deep down where the boy who had been Creighton Settles' younger brother still lived, I flinched. Creighton had gone down in local history as the reason Ida Hamilton Walker's legendary husband had died in a heli-copter crash up on Colchick Mountain. And I had gone down in local history as the boy who tracked his own worthless brother down and brought him to justice.

More silence. One heartbeat, then two. Hope studied

me with tears in her eyes. I nearly moved toward her again, but she stood at attention, warning me off. "Why have you come back now?" she whispered.

"I want to make my family's name good here, again." I took my eyes off her long enough to indicate the majestic bridge of chestnut logs and creek stone. "When my great grandfather was hired to build this bridge for your great grandfather, the Settles name was respected."

"You have nothing to prove. I always told you that. Families fall on hard times. People understand that."

"Not the people who warned me to leave the county after Creighton—"

"Those people don't matter. There are always a few rotten apples, even in the best barrels."

"Your own father was one of them. And he was *right* to want me gone."

"Marle. *Marle.*" She said my name for the first time in twenty-two years, once with soft rebuke, the next with a harder tone. Regardless, the sound of my name on her lips made me dizzy. I held out a hand. "I want to buy this piece of land from you. The bridge, the old creek bed, a few acres around it. I want to build a house here. I want a *home*, here. But it's your decision."

"You're asking me to make an impossible choice."

"I'll give you as much time as you need to decide. And if the answer's no, I'll leave without an argument."

She made a hoarse sound. "I've left this bridge the way my father wanted it, high and dry, for a reason. No amount of water can wash away the consequences—"

"I'm not asking you to baptize me in Bailey Branch so I can start over as if nothing else mattered."

Hope studied me with an intensity that made my knees weak. "You'll leave if I tell you I believe it's best?"

"Yes."

She held onto the creek stone piling, braced her legs,

sagged a little. "You don't deserve to be cast out again—"

"Consult with your children about it. Tell them an old friend of yours and Charlie's wants to be your neighbor again. That's the truth."

She shut her eyes for a moment. "I'll talk to them."

I turned to leave.

Hope spoke very quietly. "*Because they're your children, too.*"

I took a second to make sure my voice was okay. I have this stupid thing about upholding the tough-ass image of the military. "That's one of the secret joys of my life," I said finally. "But I never want them to know it."

She began to cry. The Hope Bailey I remembered would rather be barbecued than seen crying.

I left before I cried, too.

❦❦❦

That night, tossing in the big applewood bedstead Charlie carved as a gift for our twentieth anniversary, I pressed the sweet, raw cider from memories of Marle I had tried to forget.

We were no more than ten years old, laying flat on our stomachs on the floor of the covered bridge, watching through a crack as the silver water of Bailey Branch swirled below us. "I'm gonna follow the water all the way to the other side of the world some day," Marle drawled. Bold talk for a poor boy who lived in a rusty house trailer with his mean, sleazy, teenaged brother and a half-crazy old grandma who drank too much. But I believed in him. I was bound to earth. He had the sky in his eyes.

"You're not going anywhere, " I announced firmly. "You pick apples for my daddy and that means you belong to *me*, and when we grow up I'll marry you and you'll stay right here."

He turned somber, silver-blue eyes on me beneath golden brown hair. "I ain't no apple farmer. I'm going to fly planes. Mr. Walker down at Hamilton Farm says he'll teach me. He's gonna take me out to his air strip and teach me to fly crop dusters and Pipers and even his helicopter. So someday I'm gonna fly along the path of this here creek all the way to the ocean, and out to the great beyond." He took a deep breath, then finished, "And you'll belong to *me*, and you'll sure enough have to come along wherever I say."

"I can't leave my apples! I'm named after them! I'm *Sweet Hope* Bailey!"

"I'll marry you and then you'll be *Sweet Hope* Settles. So you can sneak off, and your apples ain't gonna know it was you that left."

That argument made no sense, but I was flattered anyway. I punched him on one shoulder like a kiss. We grinned and went back to watching the creek.

Another memory: I was seventeen and he was nineteen. We were naked and wrapped in each other's arms on an old patchwork quilt. Overhead, the mossy timbers of the covered bridge made a bower of spring shadows. The bridge had been our sanctuary and secret meeting place for so many years, it seemed only right that we should make love there the first time. I was scared and happy and full of plans for the future. Marle held me tightly against his chest and whispered, "You okay? You sure?"

I looked up at him and smiled. "I'm a woman now. You're a man. We're together. I feel perfect."

"Good. Will you marry me?"

I sat up, hugging a corner of the blanket over my breasts, suddenly shy, then smiling. "We've been engaged since we were kids. Of course you'll marry me!"

He feigned a frown. "Now, hold on, you've got that backward. I do the asking and you do the accepting. I don't pick apples for your Papa anymore. I'm a certified pilot and a newly accepted college boy, going to Georgia famous Tech to be an aviation engineer, *and I do the engagement asking.*"

I punched him on the shoulder, and he laughed. I kissed him. "You belong to me and my apples," I whispered, "and that's all that matters."

Giving a dramatic sigh that became a soft, deep sound of pleasure, he made love to me, again. It was one of the happiest days of my life, his life, our life.

Another memory: "Hope! Hope, where are you!" Charlie Stanton yelled like a Banshee as he leapt out of the Stanton family van and ran inside the apple barns later that same summer. I was knee-deep in empty apple baskets, counting the supply and trying to decide how to tell Marle my period was two weeks late. Not to mention telling Papa. No, Marle and I would get married, first, then tell Papa. Problem was, Papa didn't realize Marle and I were more than princess-and-the-peasant friends. Bailey girls didn't marry the hired help. Even the former hired help who was going to college. Thunder rumbled outside the big barn, and a high wind raked the orchards. The air smelled of tornadoes. I looked up weakly, feeling a little sick at my stomach. "Hi, Charlie. What's up?" Charlie, Marle and I had been friends since first grade at Mossy Creek Elementary. I couldn't muster much curiosity about his harried entrance. Charlie was always intense.

Charlie slid to a stop, breathing hard. "Gimme...a second." He pulled an asthma inhaler from his jeans' pocket and took a quick drag on it. Charlie was tall and gawky, the only son of a smart, thoughtful family over in town. His father was the minister of Mossy Creek Methodist, and Charlie was headed for Methodist college to follow in his father's footsteps. The second the inhaler took effect, he leaned down and grabbed me by the shoulders. "About an hour ago, Creighton robbed Hamilton's Department Store."

I dropped an apple basket. "Oh, no." After years of trouble with the law, serving time in juvenile lock-ups before graduating to state prisons, Marle's older brother had finally hit the big-time. "Has Chief Royden caught him?" Battle Royden would make Creighton wish he'd never been born.

"No. Hope, he stole a car down in Bigelow and two county sheriff's deputies chased him up on Colchick. They ran off the road up there at Big Sky Overlook. Their patrol car was totaled. They were hurt bad. Creighton got away. They say he's hiding somewhere up on Colchick."

"Oh my God."

I stood. "We have to find Marle. Jeb Walker sent him down to Bigelow to pick up a part for one of the planes. He's probably almost back to Hamilton Farm by now."

Charlie trembled. "Listen to me. You don't understand. Chief Royden needed help getting those injured deputies out of the ravine. Jeb Walker flew his helicopter up there in a thunderstorm. He airlifted the deputies to the road. They're going to be fine. But...but Hope...the wind caught his helicopter. It crashed. He's dead. Jeb Walker is dead. *Because of Marle's brother.*"

I swayed. My cousin Ida's husband, the handsome and beloved and respected Jeb Walker. Dead. Because of Creighton Settles. Jeb Walker had been Marle's idol. A combination of father-figure and adopted big brother. The news swirled in my head, making me dizzy. *Jeb Walker was dead, and Marle's brother was the reason.*

"I have to find Marle," I said.

Charlie shook his head. "I'm trying to tell you. Marle got the news already, and he's gone into the mountains to track down Creighton. He said he's going to kill him."

By the time Charlie and I got up to Big Sky Overlook— a wide parking area along the sheer edges of a two-lane that wound up and over Colchik Mountain—two dozen police cars, ambulances and forest-ranger trucks lined the high mountain road. Gusts of wind bent the fir forest and twisted the old hardwoods. Massive, dark clouds scudded through the peaks, and silver mists filled the valleys below. Somewhere deep in the fog along the boulders and laurel of the ravine below us lay the pieces of Jeb Walker's helicopter.

I saw grown Creekite men crying, tough men I'd known all my life. "Ida got here before he died. She kissed him while he took his last breath," one of them told the others. "She said she could breathe for him if he'd just let her."

"Little Rob's only ten years old," another said. "He'll never get over losing his daddy this way. He saw him. Saw him on the stretcher all...broken. Poor little feller nearly went crazy. Held onto Ida like he was protecting her from the sight, and all the time she was trying to cover his eyes with her hands."

I threw up in the roadside bushes then staggered to Chief Royden's squad car. Marle, bloody and bruised, sat in the back with his head bowed and his eyes shut. Creighton had nearly beaten Marle to death when he tried to bring Creighton in. I knelt in the open doorway. "Marle." He opened his eyes as if he couldn't quite focus on me. I took his bloody face between my hands. "Marle."

He pulled my hands into his, curled them away from him. "Stay away," he said hoarsely "Get away I mean it You can't be seen with somebody like me. A Settles."

"Don't talk crazy. I don't care what anyone thinks. You're not to blame for what happened."

"I took a pistol away from Creighton. I shot him."

A big, gentle hand clasped my shoulder from behind. Dazed, I turned and looked up at Chief Royden. To me he had always been a John Wayne kind of man. My father lived by the books—the *Farmer's Almanac*, the accounting ledger, the family Bible. But Chief Royden didn't do anything by the book. Any book. There was a little bit of larceny in him. "What Marle did was self defense," he said. If Battle Royden said one brother was justified for killing another in Mossy Creek, it was so.

I felt a temporary rush of relief. "Sir, I want to go with Marle to the hospital. There are some things I need to tell my Papa, and tell Marle—"

"I have a bad feeling whatever you have to say ought to wait a year until you're eighteen and legal." He pulled me out of the way and shut the patrol car's door between Marle and me.

I looked back at Marle desperately. I was his girl. His woman. He'd get out of the car and fight for me and his own self-respect, the right to have Hope Bailey believe in him. So what if he'd shot his own brother for being a no-account? So what if Creighton was responsible for injuring two Bigelow County Sheriff's deputies and causing Jeb Walker's death in a helicopter crash?

I loved Marle and Marle loved me. We could still have a life among Creekites who revered Jeb Walker. We could still tell Papa we were getting married. We could still birth the next generation of Bailey Mill's *Sweet Hope* apple farmers. The creek waters still ran under our sacred bridge.

"Marle," I called, crying.

He stared straight ahead, bloody and beaten up by his own brother in a fight to the death, having served justice, but at a terrible price. He didn't lift a finger to stop Chief Royden from leading me away. I knew why, and so did he. No Settles would be welcome in Mossy Creek or Bailey Mill after that day. Marle believed that, and there was nothing I could do to change it.

I should have told Marle I was pregnant. But he couldn't stay and I, being a Bailey, couldn't leave.

You have a twin son and daughter, I wrote to Marle a year later. He'd given up on college and joined the marines. I tracked him down at a base on the west coast.

I named them Joel and Samantha. He has your eyes. She has my hair. I have married Charlie and we let everyone be-lieve they're his children. Papa figured out the truth and I con-

fessed to Ida, but no one else knows. Charlie loves them and me, but we've agreed on what's the right thing to do. Say the word now and we'll tell Samantha and Joel who their father is as soon as they're old enough to understand. We'll tell everyone in Mossy Creek and Bailey Mill and the whole world, too. Say the word. They're your children. I wanted to tell you before you left, but I knew you couldn't stay and I couldn't go. Papa is having trouble with his heart again and I'm managing the farm.

Marle wrote back. His letter was this short.

"Our kids deserve better than my name. And so do you. Tell Charlie I'll never try to take his place. I love you and I love the babies without even knowing them, but that's how it ought to stay until some day when I can just be their friend, and yours."

Just their friend. And just mine. To me, the world is one big apple tree and every one of us is trying hard to bloom. Either we grow an apple, or we shrivel up and die. You harvest your love, or you don't. *And there is no such thing as just friends.*

Memories. Miseries. I finally fell asleep in the bed Charlie made for me. But I dreamed guilty dreams of Marle, of making love to him beneath the covered bridge at Bailey Branch, and I dreamed of lost hope and of lost Hope, the naïve girl I had been. My conscience whispered to me as I slept.

Send Marle away for the sake of your kids, who don't suspect the truth. You're the apple of their eye, but so was Charlie. You owe it to Charlie to let them go on thinking he was their father.

But Marle deserves a chance to know them. They'll accept him as just a friend of this family.

Too risky. You're being selfish. You want him to stay because you still love him.

Shut up, you apple-worm of a conscience.

Just after dawn, I got dressed and went to see Ida.

She was the only living person in greater Mossy Creek who knew my twin apples hadn't fallen far from Marle Settle's tree.

❦❦❦

Most women my age would be happy to look like Ida Hamilton Walker at her age, which is nearly twenty years older than me. It's almost unnerving the way she looks at almost sixty; there have been more than a few whispers over the years about hunting for shriveled-up portraits of her in her attic. The Hamilton clan have auburn-haired good-looking genes like their Bailey cousins, but maybe it's something about living in Mossy Creek, too. Something in the water, so to say. Or maybe it's her timeless talent for keeping the rest of us invested in life.

"You're got a tough *Thunker*-apple soul," Ida said as her housekeeper, Jane McEvers, ushered me into the study at Hamilton Farm. "I wondered if you'd come to see me yesterday, after meeting Marle. But no, you sweated out the night, thinking about what's the right thing to do before you came to ask me for my opinion. You have *Thunker* strength of character. That's why you're my favorite baby cousin."

"You say that to *all* your baby cousins."

"Yes, but in your case, I mean it." Ida smiled beneath somber green eyes. Her auburn hair was pinned up in a swoop of tortoise-shell combs and her tall, curvy body seemed both stately and alluring in a silk kimono Del Jackson had given her. I suspected the retired army colonel had given her other bedroom-related gifts, but she'd have threatened to shoot me if I asked her to confirm that. People whispered that Ida wasn't serious about him, but Ida was *always* serious about her men. I sank down in an overstuffed leather chair and shook my head when she offered me a shot of bourbon with my tea. "Not before breakfast."

"Then I'll tell Jane to bring you a biscuit and sliced ham. Voila. Breakfast."

"Okay, so I'll have the bourbon. I was only trying to feign respectability."

"Naturally. You're a Bailey."

"That feels like an insult."

"No, just a warning. A person should always celebrate her family's best traits but never forget their worst ones. You Baileys tend to be prudish, then overreact and throw out the babies with the branch water."

That remark hit below the belt. After a quick, tearful blink or two, I inhaled sharply and recovered. "I took care of my children the best way I knew how. By keeping them at Bailey Mill. I wanted Marle to stay, too, but he felt he had no future there. Maybe he was right. What should I have done differently? And don't say I should have followed him, because he didn't want me to follow him. He had to go off and prove his worth all by himself."

"You think I don't understand that? Hah. You've just identified the best and the worst trait of the Hamiltons as well as the Settles family. Pride. But what do you really know about Marle's people?"

"I know his great grandpa was the only *special* one. At least, that's what Marle always said when we were kids. He didn't like to talk about it." I paused. "To me, Marle was the special one, but I never convinced him to believe that."

"Well, let me tell you, then. Marle's great grandfather was a Cherokee Indian. His family stayed in these mountains despite all the government's efforts to send them out west when the rest of the Cherokees were driven away. Like the Halfacre family over in town, they *sat down* on their native land and wouldn't budge. They'd been settled here forever, they said. Half of them died fighting the army during the removal and a few, I'm sorry to say, were killed by white pioneer families around here.

"My great grandparents knew Marle's great grandfather as Settin' Down Joe. His Cherokee-white name. Settin' Down Joe was a master carpenter and it was him who turned the big log cabin here on this spot..." Ida jabbed a long, clear-polished nail at the Turkish rug, "...into the Victorian showplace it became by the turn of the century. By then Settin' Down Joe was known as Joe Settles, a Creekite of means and respect. He built most of the bridges in Mossy Creek, including yours up at Bailey Mill. He owned a fine home, property, the Settles sawmill. He had a beloved wife from a good family—who happened to be white. No one threatened him or his mixed-race children. It took a will of steel and more courage than most of us will ever have for Joe Settles to stay here and fit in and prosper."

Ida sighed. "But it was that same tough pride that led his son, Marle's grandfather, Payson Settles, to reject anything that smacked of 'charity' after he lost a leg in a sawmill accident in the nineteen-twenties. That wonderful, terrible Settles' pride ruined their family. Marle's grandfather wouldn't accept help so he lost the sawmill, lost all his money, lost the family homestead, his wife left him, his children began to run wild—everything went wrong. That was the beginning of the end for the Settles' dynasty in Mossy Creek. Hard times bring out the worst in people, and the Settles became a perfect example of that."

"Until now," I said quietly. "Marle intends to redeem his family name."

"Yes. And he will. I don't doubt it."

Jane delivered sliced ham and a biscuit the size of my hand. Ida doused my steaming cup of tea with liquor the color of old wood. I sipped the potent brew in silence. After Jane left us alone in the study behind discreetly closed double doors, Ida ordered, "Eat, drink, be merry." Then she moved around the elegant office as if she'd forgotten I was there. She straightened paperwork for Hamilton Farm's dairy operation atop a gilt-edged desk and flicked dust motes off a wall filled with framed commendations from various civic groups for her work as mayor of Mossy Creek over the past two decades.

I was dutifully swallowing a bite of ham washed down with bourbon tea when she stopped before a large, framed, black and white photograph from the late 1960s. A handsome, dark-haired man in khakis and a black aviator's jacket smiled at her. The jacket hung around his shoulders with one sleeve free for the white sling that held his right arm. He smiled despite the injured arm and the fact that he was standing among the wreckage of his favorite small plane. In the background, several hundred fat dairy cows grazed the pastures of Hamilton Farm, and Colchik Mountain towered in the distance.

The cocky, injured pilot was Jeb Walker, and he was smiling at 25-year-old Ida Hamilton, who had found him and his downed plane in her cow pasture the day after she graduated from college and returned home to take charge of the Hamilton businesses. Her father had just died. Her mother was long dead. Ida was whispered to be too young and reckless to run the farm, the department store and the Hamilton real estate holdings. The last thing she needed was public consternation over her private life.

That fact never stopped her from loving Jeb Walker the second she pulled him from the wreckage and he kissed her as a thank-you.

Jeb, the notorious, 30-ish son of a wealthy Savannah family down on the Georgia coast, had been an Air Force pilot and was a decorated vet of the Korean War. He owned five high-powered stunt planes and was on his way to yet another air show or wild adventure who-knew-where. Then the sky bluntly dropped him into Ida's hands, and she refused to give him back.

Ida had already proved her ability to get what she

wanted and protect what was hers. She'd bested her graspy, much-older sister, Ardaleen, for control of the family's Mossy Creek legacy—no small victory, considering that Ardaleen had married into the powerful Bigelow clan and was already the mother of a smug little baby boy named Hamilton Bigelow, the future governor of Georgia. The Ida-Ardaleen war had raged through the courts, the newspapers, the whispered waterfalls of local gossip—in essence, through the heart, soul and divided loyalties of every related Hamilton/Bigelow family in Bigelow County. But finally Ida had come out on top—to the joy of Creekites who detested Bigelowans. Her fellow small-town citizens immediately began to refer to her as "Big Miss Ida," the title her legendary grandmother had worn as a title of respect.

Jeb Walker, with his courage, his money, his charm and his utter devotion to passions he embraced—which immediately included Ida and her entire realm—was no less and no more than a perfect match. That first Creekite-kingdom photograph of him said it all: The intense expression in his eyes showed he'd found where he belonged and who he belonged to, and that "who" was only a few feet away, in jeans and a tie-dyed silk blouse, flirting with him as she snapped his picture.

Ida married him two weeks later. For more than a decade, they ruled as the royal couple of the mountains—not just Mossy Creek, but all the Southern mountains, from Georgia to Virginia. Ardaleen and no other Bigelow even came close in terms of sheer popularity and personal charisma. Rob was their crown prince, their darling; with baby Rob in tow, Ida ran the businesses while Jeb flew everything from crop dusters to experimental gliders to rescue helicopters. He saved at least a dozen Creekite lives over the years—helping the forestry service search for lost hikers, airlifting the sick and injured to the hospital down in Bigelow. No man was more willing to fly into a bad situation if someone needed his help. He always made it back to Ida's earth-hugging arms, until Marle's brother robbed Hamilton's, two county deputies crashed in a ravine up on Colchik and Jeb flew his helicopter there to help them. Creighton Settle's crime brought Jeb up the mountaintop on a day full of storms and fate. It was as if the sky had always planned to take him back from Ida.

And it did.

After Jeb died, we all feared she'd kill herself within the first year. If she hadn't had Rob to think of, I believe she wouldn't be here, now. In a way, Mossy Creek helped save her. In the middle of her worst grief, our high school burned down. As everyone knows, the circumstances were bizarre and there were wild rumors attached. The loss of the school threw the whole town into civic chaos. There was dire talk of no one running for mayor that next year; of the town's franchise being revoked by the state legislature, of The Creek, as people called Mossy Creek combined with its four outlying communities, being dis-incorporated to await a terrible future when its big, bloated sister-city of Bigelow would annex the unallied Creekites like a snake eating scattered chicks.

Ida stood up at a town hall meeting and said, to put it simply:

Not as long as there's breath in my body.

She pulled us all together. She ran for mayor and won the election with 97 percent of the vote. (One percent went to Elvis and two percent went to Jesus—a Creekite electoral tradition.) Ida had found a calling big enough to keep her focused on living. She made Mossy Creek her lover, husband and second child. Rob made the town his mission in life, too, though I have never understood why salvaging Hamilton's Department Store helped him cope with his father's death. It was as if he had to take charge of the place that had played a part in the crime that led Jeb into the stormy sky above Colchik.

The swirl of memories made me dizzy. I finished choking down a section of breakfast biscuit and ham, took another deep swallow of liquored tea and blinked back tears. Over by the photograph of Jeb, Ida stood as if held by his spell. Maybe that's why she didn't seem to age like normal women. Maybe love can hold us still in time. One way or the other, for good or for bad, I believe that's possible.

I shifted miserably and gave a polite cough. Ida moved away from Jeb's photograph, took and released a deep breath, fluffed her sofa pillows, adjusted a crooked rose in a vase and trailed one hand along a sleepy gray housecat stretched across an antique English side table. Every move was a symphony of sensual restoration.

Suddenly I understood. She mourned, but she lived.

She was giving me a good long look at her serenity and strength. At her life two decades after losing the man she had loved more than life itself. At how well she had survived. That she was no victim, and neither was I.

"I'm about to get drunk and philosophical," I announced.

She turned slightly and nodded, regal and wise and smiling with just the slightest bawdy humor. "That was the point of giving you bourbon at seven a.m."

"You didn't fall into grief and bitterness when Jeb died. You never stooped to taking revenge on Marle for what his brother did. You kept your principles and your priorities straight. So you're telling me that now I have to do the same thing. That I should welcome Marle home even at the risk of our children learning that I hid the truth from them about their real father, because it's the right thing to do."

Ida froze. The sassy, sly woman was gone. Once again, she became the young widow who had buried a dearly loved husband. "You're wrong. I *was* bitter. I did fall into grief and revenge. Do you think I'd have let poor Marle—just nineteen years old and not to blame for his brother's crime—be driven out of town if I'd been in my right mind? No. At the time, I was *glad* there were no more Settles in Mossy Creek. I wanted Marle gone." She flung out an angry hand toward the photograph of Jeb. "Even now, I still miss Jeb, and I'll always be bitter over losing him. And I'll never forgive Creighton Settles for being the cause—even indirectly—of Jeb's death."

My tea cup rattled as I set it down. "So how can you help Marle? If you can't forgive his brother and you hate—"

Ida said a few disgusted words I won't repeat. Let's just not forget that she is an educated woman with a wide vocabulary that includes language mountaineers use when they're wrestling bears. "Don't be ridiculous," she summed up more politely. "I don't 'hate' Marle and have never hated him. I've told him so. Don't you understand what I'm saying to you? We use every crude and not-necessarily-noble method we know to keep ourselves alive after we lose someone we love. We fight the loss in pathetic and sometimes destructive ways, but we go on breathing and we learn to love again. It's never the same kind of love but it's love. You loved Charlie, even if it wasn't the same wild feeling you had for Marle. You mourned Marle but went on living. That didn't mean Marle was dead to you—and it didn't mean you could or should forget him, any more than he forgot you."

She rushed over to me, grabbed me by the shoulders, and practically forced me to my feet. "He's a good man and he deserves to be where he belongs, and he belongs here. Jeb would want me to welcome him back. This is one of the few ways I can keep Jeb's memory alive. By doing the right thing."

"Ida, I'm honored that you've taken this fight as your own, but—"

"It's not *my* fight. It's yours. It's Marle's. It's a fight for the children you have together. For the future of Settin' Down Joe's descendants." She shook me lightly. "Don't deprive your kids of their family heritage. Don't deprive them of their father. Yes, Charlie loved them and he was a father to them and you don't ever want them to think of him as less. But they need a father for the *rest* of their lives, too, and Charlie's gone. Listen, my father died young and that changed me forever. Then my son's father died young, too—and it has changed Rob forever. He's decided to live his life based on some warped notion of how a man takes care of his family—by not taking any risks, not ever taking the chance that they might lose him. I cannot get across to Rob that life is a balancing act and Jeb would want him to risk falling off the edge of the sky. Don't deprive your children of that risk, either—the risk of loving—or even hating—Marle. Give them an opportunity to make the choice themselves. If you're lucky, they can love Charlie and Marle, too. They can love two fathers—and if they're smart they'll come to understand how much they need Marle now that Charlie is gone. Trust me. Trust them. Trust your own heart. You realize why, don't you? To put it in terms you Baileys love—you're as tough as a *Thunker* but your heart is a *Sweet Hope*."

I held onto her, shaking. "I hate when my heart talks to me like an apple. Don't *you* understand *my* point? My heart is telling me to throw caution to the wind and say 'Yes, Marle, *stay*. Yes, we'll tell the kids the truth about us.' Because my *Sweet Hope* heart says, 'You grew these kids from good stock. They'll give you good fruit.' But Ida, Ida…my heart can't promise they'll give Marle unconditional love and forgive me for letting them believe Charlie was their biological father all these years. What if they hate us both and turn their backs on us? What if I lose my children? *What if Marle and I plant a Sweet Hope tree but get a Thunker harvest?*"

Ida rolled her eyes at yet another apple metaphor. "Spoken like a true Bailey. Look, there are *never* any guarantees in life and certainly no promises that you'll get the harvest you want from your personal orchard. But there *is* one thing you can count on. That you're doing the right thing for the man you love and the children you created together. Just as I'm trying to do. I can't bring Jeb home, and I can't stop Rob from living his life in Jeb's shadow, but I *can* help you bring Marle home and *keep your children in the light.*"

She hugged me.

I cried my *Sweet Hope* heart out.

❦ ❦ ❦

There's something about a twenty-foot granite statue of a Confederate general that makes a man a little defensive. General Hamilton, Mossy Creek's Civil War symbol of stone *cajones*, stared down his granite nose at me as if I was a traitor who'd escaped a good old-fashioned firing squad. I stood there in the center of the town square as the first fall leaves drifted down, pretending to scrutinize the old Rebel but in fact just letting every Creekite on Main Street take a long, hard look at me. And they did.

Mossy Creek. After living all over the world, I could have laughed at my hometown, but the joke would be on me. The town was still a beacon for quirky mountaineers, loners, lovers and people who liked giving the rest of the world the old five-fingered nose-thumb salute. Mossy Creek was a place I had loved, and still loved. My great grandfather built the town hall and the row of shops on the west side of the square, where a coffee shop called The Naked Bean now shared space with Beechum's Bakery.

I glimpsed people craning their heads to stare at me from the doors and windows of those shops and everywhere else around the square—in front of Mama's diner, the town hall, the pub, the jail and even peering at me from behind the gazebo on the other side of the park from General Hamilton—men, women and children, old and young, black, white, pink, brown and everything in between. They were all Creekites United In Eyeballing.

Did I look that threatening? Big and lean and hulking, maybe, but I'd deliberately dressed *friendly* in hiking boots, jeans and an old chambray shirt—the uniform of every Creekite mountain man old enough to ditch his diapers and young enough to, well, ditch his adult diapers. But all right, I knew what everyone was thinking: *There he is, a damned troublemaking Settles. Creighton's brother.* Six-foot-one-inches of Settles-without-a-cause. A man without a Creekite country.

I squinted up at General Hamilton as I tossed the butt of a chewed cigar in a nearby trash can. I didn't even have to look to see I'd made the pitch. Instinctive aim. Great reflexes. A fighter pilot forever. In my retirement, I might take up precision cigar-butt tossing for fun and profit.

I gave the General a casual salute.

Settles, here. Lieutenant-Colonel Settles. Formerly of the Union-Yankee Air Force. Want to fight, you old Reb? No? All right, then does anyone else around here want a piece of me? They're watching me like kittens watching a spider. Bring it on.

I sank my hands in my trouser pockets and debated going over to speak to Ingrid Beechum, an older cousin of mine, four times removed or something like that. A Settles girl had married a Beechum boy about a hundred years ago. Ingrid must be about Ida's age now, sixtyish going on thirty, hell on men of all ages. I remembered as a kid watching a teenaged Ingrid yelling, "You damned worthless Settles are no kin of mine," as she chased Creighton out of her parent's bakery because he'd tried to steal another doughnut. He was maybe eight at the time, but already filching anything that wasn't tied down.

Speaking of which...in my shirt pocket was a long list of Creighton's debts to pay back. First I'd walk into Beechum's

and hand Ingrid a hundred dollar bill. "For all the doughnuts," I'd say. Then I'd hand another C-note to Dempsey at
the I Probably Got It Store, because Creighton pilfered tools
from Dempsey's father, and next I'd give several hundred-
dollar bills to Rosie at Mama's All You Can Eat Café, where
Creighton had bashed out the windows one night after
Rosie's mother fired him from his dishwashing job—because
she caught him stealing tips off the tables. I'd work my way
down the list from there, until no one in Mossy Creek could
say the Settles hadn't settled up, at least in terms of money.
The other debts—Jeb Walker's death, Hope's life without
me, our kids never knowing I was their father—could only
be paid down, never worked off completely.

"Get going," I said aloud. I rolled my shoulders to ease
the tension. Put me in a jet flying over enemy anti-aircraft
sites and I'm as calm as a cat in the sun. Put me on the Creek's
square with every eye on me and I feel like a human tourni-
quet.

"Well, it's about time you showed back up around here,
Marle Settles," a little-old-lady voice said behind me. I turned
and looked down at, well, a little old lady. After mentally
erasing twenty years off her, I realized she was Millicent Hart
Crazy-sweet Miss Millicent had been the only person in
Mossy Creek who stole from more people than my brother
did. At least she hadn't done it out of meanness, and she'd
never deliberately hurt anyone.

"Miss Millicent," I said gruffly. "I'm glad you're still roam-
ing free."

She snorted, then held out a blue-veined hand, palm
up. On it lay a small wood chisel, the handle pockmarked
with termite damage, the blade coated in decades of dust
and rust. "This belonged to your great grandpa," she announced. "When his son went bankrupt after the sawmill
accident, the bank sold off all Joe Settles' tools. I stole this
from the auction. I was just a little girl at the time. I liked old

Joe. He built my parents' house, you know. Now my daughter, Maggie, runs an herbal shop there. She's sleeping with a blue-haired sculptor, you know. They have sex in the very house your great grandpa built. So I thought you should have this chisel."

After a moment, I gave up on logic and said quietly, "I want to buy that chisel from you, Miss Millicent."

"Buy it? Son, you can't buy what the heart loves enough to steal. No, you have to take the heart's gifts as a gift. A gift from Mrs. Hart to your heart." She pressed the chisel in my hand. "Welcome home. Now settle down and make old Joe proud. Go build yourself a life."

She scooted away with the agility of an eighty-something-year-old kleptomaniac who plans her get-aways as carefully as her targets. I took a step after her, then realized people were heading towards me from every side.

It was as if Millicent Hart had broken some spell, and now I was fair game. I slid the heirloom chisel inside my trouser pocket, and waited, head up, legs braced, arms hanging quietly but ready by my sides, ready to stay by my sides, that is. Like most men who've been trained to fight, I never forget how easily I can hurt people. Unlike most men who've been trained to fight, I also never forget that I was capable of wrestling a gun away from my own brother and shooting him. Whatever happened next wouldn't happen because I started it.

"Marle Settles."

"Marle Settles."

"Marle Settles."

My name was spoken by each person as he or she arrived in the inner circle of my homecoming—Ingrid Beechum and Rosie from the café, Dempsy, Dan MacNeil from the Fix-It Shop (I owed his old man a hundred dollars to cover a carburetor Creighton had stolen), Pearl Quinian from the bookstore, Rainey Cecil from Goldilocks, who had been a feisty, red-haired little girl who aimed hairspray at Creighton every time he tried to sneak in her mother's beauty salon. And finally, here came ancient Eula Mae Whit, who had quietly fed me dinner on her back porch when I was a kid wandering around town without a meal but too proud to ask for one; and ancient Zeke Abercrombie, who had been mayor of Mossy Creek back then, and who now kept up the flower beds around General Hamilton's granite, fergit-hell feet.

Like worried ghosts they closed in on me, a little nervous, frowning, throwing me off for a minute until I realized they'd spoken my name without anger, and in fact, were only watching me for a reaction before they moved in any closer. I held up both hands, palm out, like Millicent Hart offering to return the goods. "I don't understand."

"We know you don't, Marle," Ingrid said. "Because you never came back to ask how people really felt about you."

"I don't expect a welcome mat—"

"Looks like you expect to be tarred and feathered, instead," Mr. Abercrombie said. "Marle, we can't promise you that everyone in Mossy Creek is thrilled to see Creighton Settle's brother come home, but we do want you to know you've got friends here."

"You always had friends here, Boy," Eula Mae Whit intoned in a voice as old as parchment. She wrapped her dark, bony hands around my forearm like the talons of a bird coming to roost gently. "You think Creekites forget their own? You think what your brother did is what you did? Last year I turned a hundred and I thought I was ready to die, but then I saw all the folks who didn't want me to die and I said, 'Well, I'm just a plain fool if I don't stay around a while longer.' The way I see it, you looked death right in its face a long time ago, but you haven't yet seen why you got the right to live. Well, I teetered over here today to tell you. You got the right to live, Boy. Welcome home."

Okay, now most of the women were crying and even

Dan MacNeil, who looked like he could bite nails in two, was snuffling. A tight spot grew in the back of my throat and I couldn't come up with any words to get past it. How in the hell had I forgotten that Creekites are always surprising and never take a backseat when it comes to plain, bald-faced, public displays of intent? I'd just gotten the equivalent of a group hug from some of the most important citizens in town, and all under the stony eyes of a Hamilton who'd fought for the wrong side and maybe, just maybe, wanted me to realize what side I belonged on, now.

"I...have a list, here," I said gruffly, then pulled out my notepad of Creighton's petty crimes. "It's something I wish I'd taken care of a long time ago. Things my brother did. If I've forgotten anything my brother stole, or broke, or vandalized, I want you to tell me, because I'm going to do everything I can to repay—"

"Then go down to hell, drag your brother back and let me have five minutes to kill the bastard myself."

Rob Walker finished that entrance by stepping through the startled crowd. I would have recognized Jeb and Ida's tall, dark-haired son anywhere, even after twenty-two years. But it caught me off guard to see him in a pin-striped blue suit and silk tie—the president of Hamilton's Department Store. I'd heard about his likable lawyer wife and nice little daughter. I envied him, but then again, I didn't. One look at the fury in his face and the fists he clenched in front of him told me this was payback day for him. I'd known hardened soldiers in the field with kinder eyes. He didn't see me. He saw my brother.

"Take your best shot," I said quietly.

And he hit me.

It's one thing to be noble; it's another to be lying on the ground feeling as if your jaw just bounced off the inside of your skull, tasting your own blood—and sensing—I have some military experience with the sensation—that the earthquake in your brain is not going away in the next five minutes, because you probably have a concussion. I raised myself to my elbows and became dimly aware of various people shrieking around me. Rob bent over me and wrapped one hand in my shirt. "You're not welcome in my town, and you never will be," he said. "To me, you'll always be Creighton Settles' brother, and nothing else matters. Get up and fight like a man—the way your brother never did."

I grabbed him by the wrist, twisted expertly and popped his hold on me. "One free punch is my limit," I said between bloody lips. Pain whitened his face but he refused to back off. Likewise, I refused to let go of his hand so he could pound me again. We began a free-form arm-wrestling match, me still on the ground and him leaning over me, barely moving but straining every muscle. I was forty-one and could still knock down my weight in marines, but he was most of a decade younger and looked like he spent his time in Hamilton's sporting goods department punching a boxer's bag.

It was no fun.

Someone loomed over us both. Amos Royden, Battle's son and heir to the title of Mossy Creek Police Chief, pulled Rob up by the back of his fine suit. "Take a stroll over to my office," Amos said to Rob. Not a suggestion, the way Amos put it, and the look on Amos's face said he was ready to add another arm to our arm-wrestling match.

Unfortunately, Rob still wanted to kill me. He never even looked at Amos. Didn't seem to hear him. Never took his eyes off me. "Get up," he repeated through clenched teeth. "It's an insult to my dad's memory for you or any other Settles to come back here expecting to stay. This isn't over."

But for me, suddenly, it was.

I remembered the day Jeb took me and Rob up for our first wild-ass, free-form, trick-diving plane ride. I was a dirt-poor kid who hung around his airplanes absorbing aviation trivia like a sponge, and Rob did the same. The kid was Jeb's proud little look-alike shadow. Jeb loaded us into his restored World War II fighter plane for a hair-raising series of twists and dives over Colchik Mountain.

"Hold onto your lunch, men," Jeb yelled around the unlit butt of a fine cigar. "Marle, after the first roll I'll let you take the controls."

"Yessir, Captain Walker!"

"Rob, you make it through without losing your lunch and I'll let you help land this tub!"

"Yessir, Captain Daddy!"

Jeb never even broke a sweat. He'd flown fighters in Korea as a young honcho straight out of the Air Force academy. He had the first small jet trails of gray at his temples, but he was a legend among mountain pilots. I wanted to be Jeb Walker. Rob, like most little boys, worshipped the ground his daddy walked on. Or flew over.

Rob and I grinned like idiots when we climbed out of the vintage fighter plane. We staggered around then sat down hard on the dirt of the Mossy Creek air strip. But we didn't toss our cookies. To toast our non-puking victory, Jeb stood at attention and saluted us. "You'll both be ace pilots one day," he said. "You've got the stomachs for it."

We saluted back.

Twenty-plus years later, that's what I remembered when I looked up at Rob. I saw a kid who had been more like me than not. A boy who I'd wished had been my baby brother. A kid who'd been grounded by his father's death like a bird who'd lost a wing. Rob had never set foot inside another small plane after Jeb died. It wasn't fear, according to Ida, but some brand of responsibility he'd adopted. He wouldn't risk dying the same way; wouldn't risk hurting his mother again, and later, his wife and kid. Especially his kid. Jeb Walker's son refused to learn to fly. Or forget. I wanted to help him, not hurt him.

I turned my head enough to spit blood, then wiped one hand across my mouth. The world swam in lazy circles. "If it would bring Jeb back I'd let you beat me to death," I said to Rob. "But it won't, and I'm not."

"I just want you out of my town." He strained to get the words out, since Amos was now patiently twisting Rob's arm behind his back. "I mean it. Get up. This isn't over."

I took a slow breath. My head throbbed. There were three Robs, now. I heard an ambulance siren somewhere in another universe. "It won't be over," I told him, "until you have the guts to live the way Jeb wanted you to live. Learn to fly."

Rob made a hoarse sound then. He lurched toward me with his free hand drawn back in another fist. Thankfully, the maneuver helped Amos jerk him off balance. Amos spun Rob around, then calmly pushed him through the crowd. "We'll take that stroll, now," Amos said quietly. Rob looked shaken. All the fight drained out of him. I'd hit him where he lived, without lifting a finger. He let Amos pull him away.

Good. Time to collect a few lost brain cells. I shut my eyes. The Creekite world whirled around me without my participation. Now everyone in town could stare at me while I dozed off in a nice, undignified little faint.

"Did you see the look on Rob's face?" someone whispered in the crowd. "It was like Marle ripped his heart out and handed it to him."

"Well, Marle isn't Creighton, and Rob is just a fool for looking at him that way. Rob Walker's been walking around with his heart on his sleeve for twenty years. Nothing new about that. He needs to have some sense knocked into him."

"Don't you talk about Rob that way!"

"Rainey, we all know you think Rob's perfectly fine since last fall when the reunion mystery was resolved, but he's not fine and he never will be—"

"He went into a rage just now, Rainey. Admit it—there's a dark side to Rob even his wife and his best friends—like you—can't fix."

"Ingrid, I will never perm you again, I swear, if you keep talking that way about one of the most responsible, good-hearted—"

Amidst this weird bickering, I heard the soft scuffle of running feet. Someone knelt beside me. Hands curved around my face gently. I smelled an apple scent mixed with cinnamon and sugar and bourbon, sweet but sexy, clean but not shy. Hope.

"Stand back and stop staring at him, please," I heard her say. "He did the right thing and I'm taking him home."

A man can tolerate hard choices, loneliness and a concussion when the woman he has always loved says that.

❦❦❦

I knew a fact about Marle few other people remembered: his jaw was his Achilles Heel. Creighton had broken it badly during one of their boyhood fistfights, and it hadn't healed quite right, despite Dr. Champion's expert care. So when Rob slammed a fist into Marle's chin, he did more damage than anyone would have predicted. In a way, he *did* bring Creighton back from the dead for a vengeful beating, because he proved Marle could never escape the taint of his brother's crime and violence; the memory lived in Marle's bones.

Marle spent the rest of the day and then the night with his face draped in an ice pack, resting uneasily under warm Bailey-grandma quilts in a guest bed at my farm. I woke him up every few hours and made him count my fingers.

"Four," he said the first time I did it. "And you're not wearing your wedding ring."

"I took it off while I was working in the apple barn yesterday. The season is about to start and...oh, go back to dozing in a coma."

I held up my right hand only after that.

"Check his vision regularly," Doctor Champion ordered, "and talk to him to make sure he's coherent. Just to be on the safe side. A smack in the head like that would have put most men in the hospital."

Oh, Marle was coherent. His vision might be a little fuzzy, his jaw swollen, his tongue raw where his teeth had snapped into it under the force of Rob's fury-fueled punch, but there was no doubt in my mind that he knew every move I made. The mere passage of my hand across his bare chest to smooth the apple-print bedspread drew his half-shut gaze like a magnet. He inhaled deeply every time I bent over him. When I sat in a chair beside the bed and talked to him to help him drift off to sleep, he kept his eyes shut but gingerly angled his head toward my voice. I wrapped an apple-print throw around my jeans and sweater and sat beside him all that night, even when he slept.

"The world is clear again," he said as he walked into my big, marble-countered kitchen the next morning. "I see only one of you. Too bad." He latched the buttons on his blood-speckled shirt. I glanced at the disappearing sight of his bare stomach and darkly haired chest, then looked away with misery. I wanted him just as recklessly as I had when I was a teenager. If love could turn back time, then I would always be seventeen, in Marle's arms.

"Most people will tell you that one of me is more than enough," I said quickly. "I'm picky, demanding, strict—you name it. According to the kids and my employees I'm about as fun-loving and spontaneous as a squirrel hiding nuts for a hard winter." I kept my back to him and finished filling a percolator. "I sent one of my farmhands to fetch a gallon of water from the pond that used to be Bailey Branch. So when you drink this coffee you'll be getting a dose of the old creek.

I believe there's still potent magic in the water. Hmmm, I guess you can add 'silly' to those other descriptions of me. Silly and sentimental and—"

He stepped up behind me and put his hands on my shoulders. I stiffened and relaxed at the same time, lost my breath, felt every inch of my skin blush like the pink-veined flesh of a peeled *Sweet Hope*. Marle was close enough for his warm breath to touch the back of my neck. "You're still the Hope I remember," he said gruffly. "And that girl was perfect, to me."

I pivoted on weak knees, my throat aching, and looked up at him. "If she'd been perfect, she would have followed you. She'd have gone wherever you went, even if you rejected her, and she'd have told you she was pregnant."

"That boy she loved—that boy I was—never gave her a chance. He did the right thing—for that perfect girl, and for the children we made." He held me by the shoulders, pulling me toward him, holding me still, me with my hands reaching for his shirtfront, to pull him close, to keep him at a distance. There were so many obstacles in the thin air between us. "What happened yesterday wasn't good," he said. "If I stay, there'll be more trouble."

"Oh? I saw *plenty* of good. I saw people who cared about you, people who made an effort to welcome you back."

"None of them were named Rob Walker."

"Rob *needs* to fight you. He needs to deal with the past. You're the key to him doing that. Ida knows that—it's one reason she wanted you to come back here. Sorry, but you're stuck. It's messy business, being an icon of redemption. Isn't it?"

"An icon of redemption." He gave the words a sardonic twist and added a mountaineer term or two to seal his disgust. But all the while, he searched my face. "Are you trying to tell me," he said slowly, "that you've decided you want me to stay?"

Silence. We looked at one another in electric sorrow and desire and fierce self-restraint. "We have children to think of." *Children to think of.* "I've called Joel and Samantha at the university. I've told them you're here...Lieutenant-Colonel Settles, our old friend, their father's and mine. Old childhood friend. That you want to buy the bridge and a few acres around it so you can build a house. They both immediately said they'd drive home today and meet you."

"They know my history."

"Of course. Everyone knows the story of—" I halted, wincing.

Marle nodded stiffly. "Everyone knows the story of the trashy Settles family."

I lifted my chin. "They know you were and are considered a good soul and that I have always spoken of you as a dear friend. And they know Charlie felt the same way."

Marle relaxed a little. "All right, then I'll go back to my room at Hamilton Inn and get cleaned up, and you let me know when they get here. I'll come back looking decent, and we'll do the whole 'old friend' scenario and see what they say about me being their family's next-door neighbor."

I uttered a soft sound of defeat. "It's not going to be that simple. Marle...we have to tell them the truth. That you're their father."

Stunned silence. Marle's eyes bored into mine, his expression dark, angry, incredulous. "*No.* Not just no. *Hell, no.* I won't do that to Charlie, to you, to them. No. I didn't come back to hurt them with the truth. It's not your decision to make alone, Hope. I don't want them to know—"

"How can you be a father to them if they don't know you're their father?"

"By being their friend. By being *your* friend. By developing trust and respect and... Hope, I want them to *like* me, for God's sake. That's more than enough for me. I admit I've daydreamed that some day, with luck and a small miracle or two, there might be a way for you and me to tell them. But not now. Not like this."

I shook my head wearily. "If you stay and they find out the truth by accident, they'll never forgive either one of us."

"Ida's the only one who knows I'm their father."

I smiled thinly. "No, Ida's the only one who knows for *certain*. Trying to keep a secret in Mossy Creek is like floating on a sponge. If you stay and we're seen together...the rumors will sink us. Joel and Samantha will hear something. We can't let them find out that way."

"Then I'll leave. Now. I'll get back in my Piper and fly out today and you tell them I've changed my mind about making a home here." He dropped his grip on my shoulders and took a step back.

Misery and grief and rage and longing rose up inside me and spewed out. "Don't you dare be noble and try to desert me *again*," I hissed. "I'll come after you this time. I swear it."

He pulled me into his arms just as I jerked him into mine. We kissed ferociously, him not caring about his bruised mouth and me not letting him care. The kiss quickly began to sink into something far more painful—tender and urgent and filled with memories, then gentle and loving and very, very seductive. He sank a hand in my hair and gently pulled my head back enough for him to look down into my eyes. "I can live the rest of my life alone," he whispered hoarsely, "remembering you right now. I'm leaving, Hope. And you're staying. I know you better than you know yourself. You're not going to ruin their lives by telling them who I really am. I won't let you."

Two pairs of footsteps thudded on my front verandah. Marle and I traded a startled look. "Joel and Samantha are here early," I said hoarsely.

"I want your word. You won't tell them."

The front door opened with the swoosh of oiled hinges

and the slightest melodic jingle of a tiny wind chime dangling from a wooden apple. "Mom?" a strong male voice called, followed by a lilting female voice singing out, "Mother? We're here."

The agony on Marle's face tore me apart. "Give me your word," he repeated.

I clutched a hand to my throat to ease the knot there. "I can only give you my *love* and hope I'm doing the right thing."

He looked as if I'd stabbed him. I turned away. Moving like old people whose bones refuse to bend, we went to meet our children—our harvest of mistakes and love and redemption—together.

❦ ❦ ❦

Our son, Joel Stanton, is a lanky, dark-haired future astronaut. He's finishing a degree in science at the University of Georgia but has already been accepted at Georgia Tech, down in Atlanta, where he plans to get a second bachelor's degree, in engineering.

"Mom, I'll wave to you from Mars someday," he likes to tell me.

"I'll be out in the orchards, and I'll wave back," I always say.

Our daughter, Samantha Stanton, is a tall, sturdy, redheaded farmer. She's finishing a degree in horticulture at UGA, with a minor in business. After that she'll go down to Atlanta and study more business, at Georgia State. After that she'll become my junior partner in *Sweet Hope* Farms.

"We need an expanded, year-round, commercial kitchen to produce *Sweet Hope* apple pies and jellies, Mom," she tells me. "And an on-line catalog with credit-card ordering."

"I'll be out in the orchards," I always repeat. "Waving at Mars."

By which I mean that I'll be content to work my earth

and nurture my trees as long as my children are happy in their own orchards, whatever or wherever those may be. They are the fine harvest of my heart, and Marle's heart, and Charlie's, and all three of us did well by them. I'm so proud of Joel and Samantha I could cry.

Crying was uppermost in my mind all morning, as they politely chatted with Marle, the man they didn't know was their father, the man who gave Joel the heart of an eagle and Samantha the dark, visionary eyes of a Cherokee medicine woman. Sitting on a stiff wicker chair across from them on the back verandah, Marles' stoic expression crystallized in the autumn sunshine. He made nice in return, gruff and formal and straight-backed, a man of means and honors, a military officer of no small rank. I was so proud of him I could cry again. He kept glancing my way like a condemned soldier waiting for the firing squad to pull the trigger. Our unsuspecting children saw a strong-jawed, notorious man of the world; I saw a vulnerable soul depending on me for his future.

Finally, Joel and Samantha traded one of those portentous, semi-psychic looks shared by children who shared a womb. My skin tingled. Charlie and I had had a saying for moments like this. "Look out," one of us would whisper. "The wolf puppies are about to team up for the rabbit hunt."

"Now, hmmm, Lieutenant-Colonel," Joel said in his deepest, most solemn voice, "Let's get down to brass wing nuts and talk about your request to buy property from our mother. You realize, I know, that every acre on this mountain has been in the Bailey family for over one hundred and fifty years. Baileys don't sell their land. Ever. Mother has explained that you're a special case, and of course, we understand that your great-grandfather built the bridge over what used to be Bailey Branch. But still...we have some things to say to you."

Samantha nodded like the CEO of an inquisition. "Yes,

we need to ask you some hard questions, if you don't mind, Lieutenant-Colonel."

Marle leaned forward in the wicker chair, his elbows on his knees, his face calm, ready, slightly sad as he looked at them. "Go ahead. Nothing's off limits. There's no question I won't answer. I respect your loyalty to your heritage."

"No, it's my turn to talk, now," I said. I stepped forward from a tense spot beside the verandah's railing—no way could I have spent that morning sitting calmly in a chair. "Y'all's questions won't matter—or won't be the same questions—after I say what I have to say."

"What we both have to say," Marle corrected gently. He stood and stepped over to stand beside me. "If it has to be said, I want Joel and Samantha to hear it from me. I want all the blame on my shoulders."

I put a hand on his arm. "If we're going to tell them the truth together, then we'll share the blame together, too."

Sorrow and love and regret moved across his face. I nodded. We looked down at our children, who had been perched on the edge of two old wicker rockers all morning, not rocking at all. They were even more still, now, on alert.

"First," Marle said quietly, "I want you two to know that I'd rather die than hurt you or your mother. You have to believe that, if nothing else. I've loved your mother as long as I can remember, and I will always love her, and I've always wanted what's best for her. And for you two. Everything you're about to hear...well, please believe what I just said."

I tightened my hand on his arm. "Y'all know I have a tendency to put things bluntly when need be, and so—" my voice broke, but I gritted my teeth and went on—"so I'm just going to tell you—"

"Mom, don't."

"Mother, it's all right."

Joel and Samantha stood. Both of them were misty-eyed,

and both looked at us with a kind of poignant understanding. When I glanced at Marle he was frowning, bewildered. So was I.

"Mom," Joel said hoarsely. "Lieutenant-Colonel." He nodded to Marle as if greeting him for the first time. Re-introducing himself.

"Mother," Samantha repeated, tears sliding down her cheeks. "Lieutenant-Colonel." She nodded to Marle, too. She and Joel looked at each other, communicated some silent, obviously well-rehearsed signal, then looked at us again. Samantha said simply, "Lieutenant-Colonel, we'd never agree to sell the land at Bailey Branch to anyone outside our family." She paused. "But we'd be honored to *give* that land to our own father."

My knees went weak. I looked at Marle. Amazement softened his face. He snared me around the waist as my legs buckled. He held me up, and turned to look at me with tears in his eyes. I shook my head. "I had no idea," I said brokenly.

Joel cleared his throat, tried to speak, couldn't and so, to my astonishment, simply smiled at us. Samantha put a hand to her heart and smiled at Marle tearfully. "Dad told us about you and Mother a few years ago. Everything. He made us promise never to tell her we knew. He said when Mother told you about our birth, and told you that she'd married him, you swore to him you'd never come back and try to take his place. He told us you started sending money every month, even though Mother had told you not to. Dad invested all that money over the years in our college funds."

Marle's throat worked. He finally said, "Money was all I could give. But I know every award you've won, every good report card, every time you got your pictures in the *Mossy Creek Gazette*. It would take a cargo plane to carry all the scrapbooks I have about the two of you."

Samantha sobbed softly. Joel scrubbed a hand over his eyes. "We have scrapbooks about you, too. Things Dad collected for us. Everywhere you were stationed, every mission you flew in the Gulf War, every medal you won."

I bowed my head. *Charlie, God bless you. I'll always love you, too.*

"He wanted us to know about you in case anything happened to him," Joel went on. "He said if you ever came back here we should be grateful. And that we should try our best to make you feel you have a home, here—for your sake, for our sakes, and most of all, for Mother's."

Joel and Samantha eased toward Marle, who looked at them with an expression I can't describe other than to say the condemned soldier had been set free, cleared of all charges, his honor and his heart safe inside an embrace he'd been fighting to earn all his life. He could not move, he could not breathe, he could only look at his children in wonder. I inched away just far enough to let his arm slide, distracted, back to his side. He needed to stand free and clear so his children could have him to themselves.

Joel and Samantha each held out a hand to him. Slowly, as if in a dream, he reached in return, took his son's hand and his daughter's.

"Welcome home," Joel said hoarsely.

"Welcome home," Samantha whispered.

❦ ❦ ❦

A man doesn't recover from a total transformation overnight. In fact, I'm sure it'll take a lifetime. I'll never be the same, thank God.

"Look at you, just look," Ida Walker said when she came by the farm to see if her son had done any permanent damage to my jaw. "You look *new*."

"Happiness will do that to a face," I said.

"How about me?" Hope asked in exasperation. "How do I look, Ida?"

Ida put an arm around her shoulders, and smiled. "In language Baileys can appreciate, let me put it this way: You've come into bloom."

Hope kissed me.

I checked myself in one of her apple wood mirrors and, for the first time since I was kid, didn't see Creighton Settle's brother. Instead, I saw Joe Settles' great grandson. Even better, I saw Joel and Samantha Stanton's father.

And I saw Hope Bailey's future husband.

But there was something I had to do alone.

I drove one of the farm's pickup trucks up to the Jeb Walker Memorial Air Field, which consists of a small office, a few privately owned hangers and two paved runways. I've rented space for my Piper. The tiny airport is built on a broad, flat ridge top overlooking Mossy Creek. There's no better place to go for a Creekite perspective on life; the view is anchored by the security of the pretty town in the valley below, protected by the mountains all around, and yet the sky spreads over you like an open invitation.

You stay or you go, but you never forget to come back.

A broad, gold sunset was shooting streaks across the mountaintops when I got there, and the light had dimmed to a blue-gray mist. Rob stood at the end of a runway, legs apart, hands hanging in fists by his sides, silhouetted against the incredible sky.

I walked toward him, not knowing what to expect, only that I wouldn't take another punch, but I wouldn't hit him back, either. In the low light, I couldn't read his expression until I was close enough for him to charge me. I halted an arm's length away, balanced on the balls of my feet, ready to wrestle him if I had to. That's when I saw the mixture of determination and gut-jerked unhappiness in his eyes.

"I've been waiting for my father," he said in a low voice, "to come back from the dead and teach me to fly a plane. In my mind, he's been the only man who could do it."

I nodded. "I have a son and a daughter who'll always put their Father's Day cards on Charlie Stanton's gave. With my blessing. But if I could turn back the clock, I'd save your father's life and save *my* life as a father, too. So I'm waiting to *be* a father."

Rob bowed his head for a moment, then said quietly, "But your kids learned to fly without you."

I nodded, again. Couldn't speak. Whether they'd climbed behind the controls of a plane in fact or in spirit, Joel and Samantha had learned to navigate the skies of life without my help. "I wish I'd been there for them," I finally said.

Rob studied me hard as the last of the sunset drew the sky down in dark shades of blue, leaving just a halo of gold to show us the dawn that's always waiting on the far side of every night. "Will you teach me to fly?"

I was so surprised, I faked an interest in the sky, as if gauging the diameter of a huge harvest moon that had begun to edge over the mountains. The air held the good scent of kindling burning in Creekite fireplaces, and the ripe, cold smell that to me would always mean Hope's apples. I would be working with her in the orchards this year, getting to know our trees and our children, growing a new life. Harvest time had come, and all I had to do was welcome it. Welcome the opportunity to plant friendships on fertile ground.

I held out a hand to Rob. "I'd be honored to teach you," I said. "In your father's name."

We shook on it.

Somewhere beyond the gold sunset, I believe Jeb Walker saluted us.

🐾🐾🐾

It was the last day of summer in The Creek. Greater

Mossy Creek, that is. The town and its happy little solar system of outlying communities settled down under a crisp blue September sky, resting at the end of a long, hot, funny-sad Creekite season. Friendships had been formed, lost, or refound; feuds had begun or been resolved; joy and heart-ache had grown into wisdom across the lattice of our joined lives. In other words, it had been an ordinary but extraordinary Creekite summer.

Now Marle and I stood—muddy, sweaty, scented with the diesel scent of a bulldozer, but holding hands happily—in the shallow channel of ferns and shrubs that had once carried the waters of Bailey Branch. We riveted our eyes to a curve in the deep shade of giant hardwoods, where the old creek bed twisted out of sight. Behind us, afternoon sun-light dappled the magnificent covered bridge.

Autumn spiders spun huge webs under its protective eaves. Chickadees and sparrows flitted among its rafters, planning their winter havens. They and the spiders had al-ways known the old bridge would outlast even the longest dry spell. Marle and I waited, barely breathing. We heard the first soft, unmistakable whisper of life.

The water.

Set free, the old branch crept back toward its ancient path like a kitten full of wary awe. For a few minutes, we noticed only the ground turning dark and damp beneath our dusty shoes; then the ferns of the lost creek bed began to move gently, as if a breeze had come up, but there was none. They were moving with the slightest pressure of wa-ter trickling past, no more than an inch deep.

With a soft sigh of trust, the branch surged around the bend. A moment later, the cold, gray-green waters of Bailey Branch surrounded our shoes, our ankles and rose halfway to our knees. Marle and I began to laugh. We turned to watch the water rise around the bridge's stone posts.

Water has a voice, an echo, a soul. Bailey Branch's song

became a throaty laugh as it passed beneath the hewn chestnut logs and mortared stone Joe Settles had built across it. The Branch knew, and remembered.

And so did Marle.

When I looked at him, he had tears like mine in his eyes, but he was smiling. The water would find its way back to the sea, just as we had both come home to ourselves. We held each other, standing there in the happy, flowing branch, and we kissed like young lovers, again.

Summer in Mossy Creek was ending, but the rest of our lives had just begun.

Lady Victoria Salter Stanhope
The Clifts
Seaward Road
St. Ives, Cornwall, TR3 7PJ
United Kingdom

Dear Vick:

Well, another summer in Mossy Creek has come to a close. The Sweet Hope apples are ready for picking. Black cauldrons of boiled peanuts and cheeky orange pumpkins are ready for the tourists heading for the mountains to see the crazy quilt of color. We're all a little older, a little wiser, but a little younger at heart. Life is always full of mixed blessings, isn't it?

What happens next? Well, there's Thanksgiving and the annual Run with the Turkeys 5K road race, followed by a Christmas season that is never less than strange and wonderful in Mossy Creek. Sometimes we get a little snow, but not often. Mayor Ida will host her annual New Year's Eve party, catered by Bubba Rice, aka Win Allen. Everyone is betting that Del Jackson is going to propose to Ida next year. And everyone is betting that Amos will have something to say about it, if that happens.

Other rumors floating around The Creek include whispers about a bizarre new minister at one of the churches, some unexpected babies on the way, some fun weddings, and a few juicy secrets I'll keep to myself for now. Let's just say that between the garden club, the bridge club, the town council, newcomers like Sagan Salter and comebackers like Marle Settles, all I can tell you for a fact is that life in Mossy Creek won't be dull.

I saw a flock of brightly colored birds fly across the harvest moon tonight. *I wish I may, I wish I might, have the wish I wish tonight.* Come and visit, Vick, and I'll tell you what that wish is.

Your friend,
Kalie Bell

MILLICENT AND TYRONE'S WEDDING RECEPTION RECIPES
Courtesy of Chef Bubba Rice

Broccoli Quiche

Remember the old line from the '80s: "real men don't eat quiche?" Or the old joke about the guy getting slapped in the restaurant for telling the waitress that he wanted a "quickie" for lunch? Well, real men do eat quiche...and one who can't pronounce it should probably get slapped around a time or two.

Ingredients:

> 2 nine-inch pie crusts
> 6 large eggs
> 8 strips of bacon
> 12 ounces grated sharp cheddar cheese
> 2 ten-ounce packages frozen chopped broccoli
> 1-1/2 cups milk
> 2 tbsp. flour

Preparation:

Fry the bacon strips crisp, then crumble. Cook the broccoli and drain completely. This part is very important. If the broccoli isn't drained completely, the crusts will be soggy. Whisk the eggs in a large mixing bowl, then add the drained broccoli, the crumbled bacon, 8 ounces of the grated cheddar cheese, the milk and the flour. Mix well and set aside.

Bake the empty pie crusts at 450 degrees for 5 minutes. This is another hint to keep the crust from getting soggy. Then remove the crusts and reduce the temperature to 325 degrees. Evenly divide the filling between the two pie crusts, then top with the remaining cheese. Bake at 325 degrees for approximately 50 minutes. When the quiche is done, you can run a knife blade into the middle and it will come out clean.

Chicken & Dressing Casserole

This one is a favorite for large gatherings...like reunions or parties or wedding receptions. Hmm, imagine that...

Ingredients:

>5 pounds of chicken. You can use all white meat, but I prefer to mix it up because you'll get a better overall flavor from the mixture of light and dark meat. Don't use boned, skinless chicken unless your fond of bland, tasteless food.
>
>2 sixteen-ounce packages of herb flavored stuffing mix
>
>4 ten-ounce cans of cream of chicken soup
>
>1/2 cup of butter
>
>2 sixteen-ounce tubs of fresh sour cream
>
>5 cloves of garlic, minced
>
>1 tsp lemon pepper seasoning
>
>1 tsp salt
>
>4 tbsp olive oil

Preparation:

Put the chicken pieces in a large stock pot and add enough water to cover. Add the salt, lemon pepper seasoning and garlic. Cover and bring to a boil. Reduce heat and simmer for one hour. At the end of one hour, the meat should almost fall off the bone. Remove from the heat and pour off the broth, saving 2 cups. Remove the skin and bone the chicken pieces. Chop the chicken into small pieces. Try for less than one inch square. In a large mixing bowl, mix the cream of chicken soup and the sour cream. Melt the butter. Use the olive oil to grease the bottoms of two large baking dishes.

Divide the chopped chicken between the two dishes and evenly spread around in the dish. Then cover with the soup/sour cream mixture. Top each dish with one of the packages of stuffing mix. Then, pour the melted butter and the chicken broth over the top. Bake at 350 degrees for one hour.

Tequila Lime Chicken

Okay, y'all remember two things... #1) The alcohol cooks out of the marinade, so if you leave staggering, it *ain't* because of the chicken. And #2) as the alcohol is cooking out of the marinade, it can cause flame-ups on your grill. The key here is low heat, a close watch on the chicken as it's cooking, and a full squirt bottle of water close by.

Marinade ingredients:

1/2 cup of tequila. You could buy the cheap stuff, but who's going to drink what you have left over after you make the marinade? Go ahead and spend the extra 3 bucks and buy the good stuff, okay?

1/2 cup of fresh lime juice

2 tbsp. extra virgin olive oil

4 cloves of garlic

1 tsp. lemon pepper seasoning

1 tsp. chopped cilantro

Preparation:

Use a garlic press to mince the 4 cloves of garlic. In a mixing bowl, combine the tequila, lime juice, olive oil, minced garlic, lemon pepper and cilantro. Stir well.

Should make enough marinade for 3 pounds of chicken. Put the chicken pieces in a large freezer bag, then pour in the marinade and seal. Shake well and refrigerate for 2 hours.

About an hour before you're ready to cook, start your fire. I'm assuming that you're using charcoal. You *are*, aren't you? You'll need at least an hour for the temperature to settle down to around 325 degrees. Spread the chicken pieces evenly over the grilling surface. Remember, the alcohol is going to flame up at some point. Be ready with that squirt bottle, or you'll get charred chicken. At 325 degrees, the chicken should take about an hour to cook.

Welcome to Mossy Creek

A Guide to People and Places

Sponsored by the following merchants

Beechum's Bakery

Mama's All You Can Eat Café

Ingrid Beechum & Bob

Blackshear's Veterinary Clinic

Moonheart's Natural Living

Goldilocks Hair, Nail & Tanning

Mossy Creek Books and What-Nots

Hamilton's Department Store

The Mossy Creek Gazette

Hamilton House Inn

The Naked Bean

The I Probably Got It Store

O'Day's Pub

Mossy Creek:
Then and Now

Located in Bigelow County in the beautiful north Georgia Mountains, Mossy Creek was founded in the early 1800s by the Hamilton and Bigelow families and incorporated as a town in 1839. Shortly thereafter, in 1850, the Hamilton House Inn opened as a retreat for wealthy city dwellers. Since its inception, Mossy Creek has been noted for its hospitality, bucolic setting, quaint shops, commanding vistas, and its feud with the neighboring town of Bigelow.

The feud began in 1859, when Isabella Salter, ward of the Hamiltons and fiancé of Lionel Bigelow, up and eloped to England with Surveyor Richard Stanhope. Infuriated by the insult, the Bigelows retaliated by burning crops and killing livestock. The efforts to run the Hamiltons out of the area resulted in the town motto *Ain't Goin' Nowhere, And Don't Want To* being painted on the Hamilton grain silo. The motto, like the feud, has endured to present day. The original Hamilton grain silo may be viewed from most any point in town. The motto is traditionally maintained by a Hamilton matriarch, and it, too, may be viewed from most any point in town.

For further information about the feud and to view artifacts, including a replica of Rose the Elephant's footprint (original footprint at *Ripley's Believe or Not!*) and the welcome sign destroyed by Mayor Walker, contact Adele Clearwater at the Mossy Creek Historical Preservation Society.

If you have a yen to retreat, Mossy Creek's the place to do it. You're welcome to come hike our trails, fish our streams, shop our upscale department store and boutiques, browse our quaint shops around the square, wine and dine and take in live theater, or just sit a spell.

Who's Who
Vital Information, and then some
Not compiled by Katie Bell

Beechum, Ingrid: sixty-ish cousin of Mayor Walker, mother of deceased Charlie, Jr., employer of *Betty Halfacre*, owner of *Bob the Chihuahua* and Beechum's Bakery on the town square. Exacting in personal and professional life. Past grievances with her son's wife led to estrangement and subsequent guilt. Initially objected to *Jayne Austin Reynold's* shop, later empathized with Jayne and embraced the young widow and her infant son.

Beleau, Jasmine: DOB: 1971. Wealthy former high-class call girl from improverished background. Happened upon Mossy Creek, liked the place and settled on Pine Street. Currently, beauty consultant and mentor to young women in need of self-esteem. Good seamstress. Befriended Linda Polk and gained the support and friendship of *Rainey Cecil*. (Drop-dead gorgeous)

Bell, Katie: DOB: 1962. Distant cousin of Salters and *Ida Walker*. Good snoop, snitch, mischief-maker, and mystery-solver. Enjoys bingo, Writes "The Bell Ringer" gossip column, and is Business Manager, Director of Advertising and Assistant Editor of *The Mossy Creek Gazette*. Corresponds with *Lady Victoria Stanhope*. (Rings entirely too many bells)

Bigelow, Governor Hamilton: DOB: 1955. Son of *Ardaleen Hamilton Bigelow*, nephew of Ida Hamilton Walker, Governor of Georgia, former member of Fang and Claw Society, deadly mix of Hamilton charisma and Bigelow slyness, and presidential wannabe. If Mossy Creek were Gotham City, Ham would be the Jester. Uses state convicts to work at family mansion in Bigelow. Notorious for battling Aunt Ida over Mossy Creek's motto. Responsible for Mossy Creek High School fire. (Possum-hearted jackass of a weasel)

Bigelow, John Willingham: DOB: 1963. Lawyer and President of the Bank of Bigelow County. Compassionate man; loving father and husband. Married to *Sue Ora Salter Bigelow*, father of *Willie*, and cousin of *Ham Bigelow*. Semi-reconciled with Sue Ora after a fourteen year separation. Former member of high school Fang and Claw Society; confessed society prank responsible for fiery destruction of Mossy Creek High School in 1981. (Improves with age)

Bigelow, Willie: DOB: 1987. John Willingham Bigelow, Jr. Son of *Sue Ora* and *John*. Joined Fang and Claw Society, got into trouble with alcohol on initiation night. Devoted to parents. Lives disparate life: Willie in plain house in Mossy Creek; John Jr. in Bigelow mansion.

Bigelow, Sue Ora Salter: Mid-thirties. Self-sacrificing mother; practical, hardworking businesswoman and journalist. Last descendent of Salter family left in Mossy Creek. Dreamed of becoming great writer. Wife of John, mother of Willie, niece of *Livy Salter*, cousin of Lady Victoria Stanhope. Owner/Publisher and Editor of *Mossy Creek Gazette*. Married and left John same year (1986). Returned from San Francisco to Mossy Creek in 1990, got loan to buy newspaper in 1995. Learned of John's help with loan in 2000; semi-reconciled with him same year. (Also improves with age)

Blackshear, Cassandra Champion: DOB: 1978. (Casey) Wife of *Hank* (local vet), daughter of *Dr. Chance Champion* (local doctor), owner of Piping Our Pets to Heaven funeral service. Loved Hank since fourteen, attended University of Georgia on softball scholarship, Olympic hopeful until auto crash resulted in leg paralysis. Married Hank in 1998, returned to Mossy Creek in 2000, coached Mossy Creek softball team against Bigelow team and won. Determined. (A slugger)

Blackshear, Dr. Hank: DOB: 1973. Husband of Casey; life-long friend of *Rainey* and *Rob*; owner of *Blackshear's Veterinary Clinic,* member of city council, involved in *Mossy Creek Theater.* Attended University of Georgia. Gave up dream of New York to return to Mossy Creek and take over clinic after father's death in 1999. Casey's coach for everything, everyday, forever. (One of the good guys)

Brady, Ed Sr.: Husband of Ellie (Whitaker), father of *Ed Jr.*, World War II veteran, member of volunteer fire department, owner of Brady Farm (est. 1850). Owner of dog *Possum,* traditional Santa in Mossy Creek Christmas parade. Distant relationship with only son. In 2000, beloved wife had stroke and suffered from Alzheimer's. Lost driver's license due to poor eyesight, then suffers broken leg when run off the road by Ham Bigelow's driver. Stayed in *Magnolia Manor Nursing Home* with Ellie while recovering and having cataracts removed. Ellie died in 2001, and Ed Jr., returned home and mended relationship. (Salt of the earth)

Cecil, Rainey Ann: DOB: 1969. Hair stylist, owner of *Goldilocks Hair, Nail, and Tanning,* life-long friend of *Hank Blackshear* and Rob Walker, and member of Screamin' Meemies big-haired, all female band. A young woman who respects the importance of good hair and good manners, does not believe her customers always know what best suits them, hairwise. Has lots of curly red hair, imitation Oscar de La Renta, and talent with shears. (Should not give up day job)

Conners, Michael: Irish-American from Chicago, opened *O'Day's Pub,* only bar in an otherwise dry county, next to city hall in 1995. Invented Ringers (hot whisky and cranberry drink). Brought dart competition, karaoke, line dancing, and St. Pat's Day parade to Mossy Creek. Blue-eyed Irish charmer. Knows how to laugh and have a good time. Friend of Mayor. (A lot like his whisky)

Crane, Jess: Husband of Sandy Bottoms Crane, friend of Sue Ora. Reporter for *Mossy Creek Gazette* and aspiring fiction writer. (Big ol' teddy bear)

Crane, Sandy Bottoms: Wife of Jess Crane, sister of *Mutt and Boo Bottoms*, and friend to all. Dispatcher and officer of Mossy Creek Police Department. Second cousin of Judge Blakely. Rescued Bob the dog from hungry hawk. Helped crack the case of the Mossy Creek High fire and nailed Ham Bigelow. Efficient, lovable, workaholic who drives *Chief Amos Royden* nuts while making herself indispensable. (A honey bee that just can't light)

Halfacres: Cherokee Indians. Betty works at Beechum's bakers. Very task oriented. Edythe is hairdresser at Goldilocks. Snow is administrator at Magnolia Manor. Wanda is assistant at Goldilock's. From the wilds of Chinaberry Mountain. (Two Acres altogether)

Hart, Maggie: DOB: 1950. Only child of *Millicent Hart*, girlfriend of *Tag Garner*, owner of *Moonheart's Natural Living*, and best friend of *Anna Rose Lavender*. Attended Georgia State University, gardens, makes and sells herbal and floral soaps, candles, toiletries and some new age stuff. Spends time returning items stolen by her semi-sane mother. Operates business in Hart family home on Spruce Street. (Flower child who forgot to yup)

Hart, Millicent: Eighty-something year old mother of Maggie, thief, local celebrity, heroine, friend of Eula Mae Whit. Helped solve Mossy Creek High School fire and appeared on WSB TV. Hides stolen loot in base of General Hamilton's statue in town square. Determined to marry Maggie to Tag Garner and plans wedding before they're engaged. Backseat driver, literally and figuratively. Loving mother and loyal friend. (Heart's in the right place but mind is missing)

McClure, Josie: DOB: 1978. Self-proclaimed wallflower; friend of Jayne Reynolds. Finished last in Miss Bigelow County Pageant. Interested in Chinese and Western astrology, talented napkin folder and Martha Stewart impressionist. Lives on the other side of Bailey Mill. Decorated *Naked Bean*. Crazy in love with *Professor Harold (Bigfoot) Rutherford*. (Liberated from the wall and about to bust with bloom!)

Royden, Amos: DOB: 1964. Chief of Police; son of former Chief *Battle Royden*, friend of *Mac Campbell* and Ida Walker, judge of Miss Bigelow County Pageant, former Atlanta detective. Returned to Mossy Creek after father's death in 2000. Wears himself out defending justice (by the book) and trying to protect his own privacy. Likes the Naked Bean; likes women; doesn't like alcohol. Town's most eligible bachelor and man most sought-after by matchmakers. Rumored to have a crush on a certain older woman. Tough ethics and tender heart. (Won't be MC'ing Miss America Pageant)

Truman, Dwight: President of Mossy Creek Chamber of Commerce, insurance salesman, former teacher, father of Sissy, and friend of Ham (says it all). Spends time haranguing neighbors and sucking up to governor. Shirked guard duty night mascot was stolen and high school burned. Ran for state senate and lost. (Prissy possum-hearted jackass of a weasel)

Walker, Ida Hamilton: DOB: 1944. Has held office of Mayor for twenty-seven years, widow of Jeb Walker, mother of Robert (Rob), mother-in-law of *Teresa*, grandmother of *Little Ida*, sister of Ardaleen, aunt of governor, heir of founding Hamilton family, love interest of retired *Lieutenant-Colonel Del Jackson*, and owner of *Hamilton Farm* (site of famous *grain silo*), *Hamilton Inn*, and most of uptown and downtown Mossy Creek. Loves guns, gardening, politics, racy cars and men (not necessarily in that order). Attended University of Georgia. Founder of Women Are Not Girls feminist organization and Foo Club. Famous for dumping new welcome sign on grounds of Governor's mansion. Determined to remain self-possessed, wealthy, politically active and sexy (not necessarily in that order).

Could have made Who's Who list

(and might in the future)

Allen, Winfield Jefferson: aka Bubba Rice. Wealthy entrepreneur with a cooking show. Famous for his Bubba Rice. In 2001, opened lunch and catering two days a week in Mossy Creek.

Belmount, Beau: DOB: 1963. Hell raiser from wrong side of track. Major movie star. Eloped with *Anna Rose* in 1981, but they were forced apart. Left Mossy Creek but kept in touch with Maggie Hart. Reunited with Anna Rose in 2001 and learned he has 19 year old daughter. (Major hunk)

Bigelow, Ardaleen: Mother of Ham, sister (siseroo) of Ida Walker. Disinherited by Hamiltons for marrying a Bigelow. Hasn't spoken to Ida since 1980. (The woman behind the Ham)

Bottoms, Mutt and Boo: Brothers of Sandy Crane. Boo is firefighter/paramedic. Mutt is police officer who arrested Ida for vandalizing Governor's new sign. (Good ol' boys, both of 'em)

Brady, Ed Jr.: DOB: 1955. Son of Ed and Ellie. Owns computer company. Feared Ham as child. Loathes Ham now, with good reason. Returned to Mossy Creek in 2001. (Nice guy, and eligible)

Brown, Tammy Jo Bigelow: DOB: 1967. Wife of Bunkin, mother of Toby and Chip, countrified former beauty queen. Mauled by dog at nineteen. Moved to Spruce Street after Bunkin was injured and unable to work. Hated Mossy Creek until town pitched in when her boys went missing.

Caldwell, Peggy: DOB: 1936. Widowed English professor. Enjoys mysteries more than Shakespeare. Purchased Ogilvie property prior to husband's death. When pressured to garden, responded with walled garden of poisonous plants. Mother of Marilee.

Campbell, Mac and Patty: Mac is a lawyer and the bagpiper for pet funerals, owner of labs Butler and Maddie. Lives on Elm Street. Best bud of Amos Royden. Patty is small woman unable to bear children.

Champion, Dr. Chance: Father of Casey Blackshear, general practitioner. Played minor league baseball in his youth. Named Casey for famous poem character.

Garner, Tag: Moved to Mossy Creek in 2001. Amour of Maggie Hart, former Atlanta Falcon player, sculptor/owner of Figuratively Speaking. Plays banjo and owns Briard named Giselle.

Jackson, Lieutenant-Colonel Delaware: Ida's Rhett (boyfriend), father and grandfather, retired military, part-time martial arts instructor. Arrested for protecting abused child. Member of Foo Club.

Koomer, Derbert: Proprietor of the I Probably Got It store on town square. Enjoys soap operas, salami and red onion sandwiches, and watching the Feisty Felines run by his store in sports bras.

Lavender, Anna Rose: DOB: 1965. Actress/Director of Mossy Creek Theater, mother of Hermia, lost love of Beau Belmount, friend of Maggie Hart. Now reunited with Beau.

Longstreet, Hanna: DOB: 1969. Librarian. Brilliant, entered high school at twelve. Family moved to Mossy Creek in 1981. Has great love for books.

Looney, Buck: DOB: 1972. Aka Jawbone, coaches football at county high school, coaches women's softball in Mossy Creek, played for Green Bay Packers.

Lyman, Bert: Husband of "Honey, my Board Operator." Runs TV station from barn, runs radio station from kitchen, produces *Cooking with Bubba Rice*.

Martin, Violet: Very old. Shoots at crows and grows her own marijuana for glaucoma pain.

McNeil, Dan: Owner of Fix-It Shope, wired Mimsy's garden to keep pigs out.

Montgomery, Rosie: Cook at Mama's All You Can Eat Café. Makes best chocolate meringue pie. Sends food to townspeople when there is illness or death.

Oscar, Eustene: DOB: 1916. Grandmother of Oscar Oscar, member of Mossy Creek Social Society and the garden club. Plays bingo and makes divinity.

Purla, Swee: Interior Designer/Decorator (and bit of a bully). Owns Purla Interiors.

Quinian, Pearl: Aunt of Francine Quinlan. Owner/Proprietor of Mossy Creek Books & What-Nots. Has a pet ferret, which could be considered an indication of something.

Regina, Regina: Waitress at O'Day's pub.

Royden, Battle: Father of Police Chief Amos Royden and former police chief. Died in 2000.

Rutherford, Harry: Aka Bigfoot. Professor of environmental botany. 6'8" tall, face disfigured by house fire. A recluse who loves Josie McClure.

Salter, Aunt Livy: Great-aunt of Sue Ora Salter. Respects and enjoys a good funeral.

Sawyer, Louise: Helped Sandy Crane and Katie Bell solve Mossy Creek High School fire.

Simple, Orville Gene: DOB: 1960. Wears John Deere cap, decorates front yard with commode. Experienced a profound religious epiphany after lightning struck his enemies (beavers).

Walker, Ida, IV: Aka Ida the Fourth, Little Ida and Rabbit. Daughter of Rob and Teresa. Granddaughter and apple of mayor's eye. Shows early promise of being a chip of the Ida block.

Walker, Robert: DOB: 1968. Only child of Mayor Ida. Serious businessman who lacks his mother's sense of adventure. Best bud of Rainey and Hank.

Walker, Teresa: Wife of Robert. Tax attorney. Represented Ida in Judge Blakely's court.

Whit, Eula Mae: DOB: 1901. Oldest woman in Mossy Creek (and without doubt the wisest). Helped solve Mossy Creek High School fire mystery.

The Mossy Creek Menagerie

Bob, Chihuahua; owns: Ingrid Beechum

Samson, Ram, deceased (school mascot)

Giselle, Briard; owner: Tag Garner

Maddie & Butler, Labs; owner: Mac Campbell

Henry, Banty rooster; deceased hero

Possum, Hound; owner: Ed Brady

Dog, Australian Cattledog; temporary owner: Amos Royden; new owner: Clay Atwood

Rose, Elephant, deceased

Tweedle Dee, Parakeet; spokesbird for Mossy Creek Humane Society

Points of Interest
And Much Known Facts

Bailey Mill: Community located just southwest of Mossy Creek. Panoramic views, nature trails, the famous apple orchards and some of the oldest remaining outhouses in the state. (Home of Hope Bailey Stanton and Del Jackson, among others.)

Bigelow: County Seat.

Chinaberry: Located northwest of Mossy Creek. Panoramic views and nature trails. More satellite dishes per capita than any area in the state. (Site of Neil Delgado's infamous cattle-prod escapade)

Colchick Mountain: One of the highest points in the state and a real natural wonder. Panoramic views and nature trails. Site of ecological study (and stomping grounds of Professor Harry Bigfoot Rutherford).

Fang and Claw Secret Society: Society established during World War II at Bigelow High School. Known for making dangerous mischief. Responsible for physical injuries, damage to private and public property (Mossy Creek High School), and many wounded psyches.

Foo Club: (Mossy Creek Five) Geena Quill, Wolfman Washington, Del Jackson, Nail Deluged, and Ida Hamilton Walker. Refugees from Oscar Seymore's anger-management class. Club founded for the sole purpose of aiding and abetting Ida in the removal of new welcome sign.

Grain Silo: Local landmark located on the Hamilton Farm on South Bigelow Road. Panoramic views. Bears Mossy Creek Motto: Welcome To Mossy Creek, The Town You Can Count On. Ain't Goin' Nowhere, And Don't Want To. Picture post cards available at Mossy Creek Books And What-Nots on the square. (Bone of great contention between Mayor Ida Walker and Governor Ham Bigelow)

Hamilton Farm: Dairy farm located on South Bigelow Road. Owned and operated by Mayor Ida Hamilton Walker. (A real showplace, well worth trying to wangle a tour)

Hamilton House Inn: Established 1850. Located in beautiful uptown Mossy Creek. Site of famous Stanhope collar-pin heist in 1859. Features many amenities, including priceless antique furnishings, one-hundred-fifty-year-old oak tree, rose garden, color TV, library, hot-biscuit breakfast, and swimming hole on Hamilton Street. Reasonable rates.

Magnolia Manor Nursing Home: Located on North Bigelow Street across from the library. Administrator Snow Halfacre. Home to many of Mossy Creek's most notable citizens.

Mossy Creek High School: Gutted ruins of former architectural wonder. Destroyed by fire perpetrated by Fang and Claw Society during elephant rampage with burning sheep mascot in 1981. In the truest Southern tradition, this landmark may yet rise from the ashes. (At least Ham Bigelow promised it would; but then, you know Ham)

Look Over: Northeast of Mossy Creek. Panoramic views, nature trails, and plenty of wildlife. A geological and botanical delight. (Best place to get an overview of Yonder, or Mossy Creek, for that matter)

Yonder: Picturesque. Southeast of Mossy Creek. Panoramic views and nature trails. Famous for the RC Cola sign advertisement and trout fishing. Home to such notables as: Wolfman Washington, Hattie Almond, Principal Doolittle, Rhonda Clifton, and Ulysses, the sheep mascot.

WMOS Radio, TV, Cable: Local network programming and production. Tours not available at this time. For additional information contact Bert or Honey Lyman.

Best Bets for Libation, Recreation, Good Eats, and Souvenirs

Mama's All You Can Eat Café: On the square. Local color and good home cooking with all the fixin's. Feed the whole family three times a day at unbeatable prices. Rosie Montgomery, cook.

Beechum's Bakery: Fresh breads, pastries, and confections for all occasions. Drop by for a little something sweet and take a peak at Bob, the Chihuahua who survived a hawk-napping.

The Naked Bean: Gourmet coffees and teas. If you're into biscotti and cappuccino, or just want a to rub elbows with the local theater actors, this is the place.

O'Day's Pub: True testament to Irish pubbery. Wining, 'Dining, and Darts.

Mossy Creek Theater: Evening and matinee performances. For current production or ticket information phone Anna Rose Lavender or check the playbill outside the theater on the corner of Main Street.

The I Probably Got It Store: For unique souvenirs, check with Derbert Koomer, purveyor of those hard to find items. He's on the square.

Mossy Creek Books And What-Nots: For stationery, bestsellers, cookbooks, greeting and post cards, and nice selection of local crafts. Or just stop in to say hey to Pearl and her pet ferret.

Moonheart's Natural Living: Personalized souvenirs meant to pamper. Handmade herbal and floral soaps, toiletries, candles, and potpourri. Browse the shop or visit Maggie's garden.

The Mossy Creek Storytelling Club

(In order of appearance)

Amos and Dog ....Debra Dixon

Opal and the Suggs Sisters .... Martha Shields

Mamie and Grace .... Sandra Chastain

Sadie and Etta .... Judy Keim

Lucy Belle and Inez .... Susan Goggins

Therese and the Stroud Women............. Kim Brock

Louise and Jack......................... Carolyn McSparren

Sara-Beth and Carolee .... Patti Callahan Henry

Emma and Aurrie .... Shelly Gail Morris

Lila and Fryzeen .... Bo Sebastian

Laurie and Tweedle Dee .... Anne Bishop

Hope and Marle............................... Deborah Smith

Bubba Rice .... Wayne Dixon

The Mossy Creek

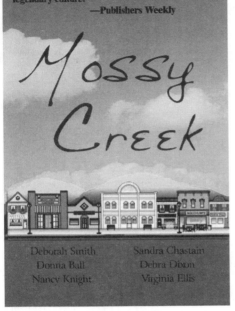

"A sweeter, smoother-edged American South beckons! Conjures up the comfortable if ornery charms of a legendary culture."
—Publishers Weekly

Deborah Smith   Sandra Chastain
Donna Ball   Debra Dixon
Nancy Knight   Virginia Ellis

MOSSY CREEK

Welcome to Mossy Creek, where you'll find a friendly face at every window and a heartfelt story behind every door.

We've got a mayor who sees breaking the law as her civic duty and a by-the-books police chief trying to live up to his father's legend. We've got a bittersweet feud at the coffee shop and heartwarming battles on the softball field. We've got a world-weary Santa with a poignant dream and a flying Chihuahua with a streak of bad luck. You'll meet Millicent, who believes in stealing joy, and the outrageous patrons of O'Day's Pub, who believe there's no such thing as an honest game of darts. You'll want to tune your radio to the Bereavement Report and prop your feet up at Mama's All You Can Eat Café. While you're there, say hello to our local gossip columnist, Katie Bell. She'll make you feel like one of the family and tell you a story that will make you laugh—or smile through your tears. People are like that in Mossy Creek.

Award-winning authors Deborah Smith, Sandra Chastain, Debra Dixon, Virginia Ellis, Nancy Knight and Donna Ball (*Sweet Tea and Jesus Shoes*) now blend their unique voices in a collective novel about the South, the first in a series set in the fictional mountain town of Mossy Creek, Georgia.

So welcome to Mossy Creek, the town that insists it "Ain't goin' nowhere, and don't want to." Welcome Home.

Hometown Series

REUNION AT MOSSY CREEK

Welcome back to Mossy Creek! The warm-hearted but stubborn residents of the small town whose motto is "Ain't goin' nowhere, and don't want to" are once again sorting out the joys, sorrows, and everyday mysteries of life.

This time around they've got the added drama of the big town reunion commemorating the twenty-year-old mystery of the late, great

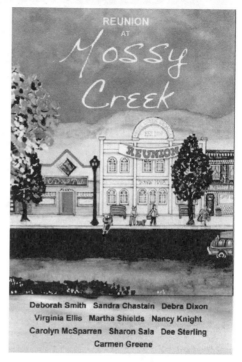

Deborah Smith   Sandra Chastain   Debra Dixon
Virginia Ellis   Martha Shields   Nancy Knight
Carolyn McSparren   Sharon Sala   Dee Sterling
Carmen Greene

Mossy Creek High School, which burned to the ground amid quirky rumors and dark secrets. Are the villains who caused the fire at the grand old school finally ready to come forward?

In the meantime, sassy 100-year-old Creekite Eula Mae Whit is convinced William Scott has put a death curse on her, and Mossy Creek Police Chief Amos Royden is still fighting his reputation as the town's most eligible bachelor. Then there's the new bad girl in town, Jasmine, and more adventures from the old bad girl in town, Mayor Ida Hamilton. And last but not least, Bob the flying Chihuahua finds himself stalked by an amorous lady poodle.

All this and more—including the introduction of Mossy Creek's new recipe section, courtesy of Creekite Chef Bubba Rice—is waiting for readers in the second novel of the Mossy Creek series.

The Mossy Creek Hometown Series

Available in all fine bookstores and direct from BelleBooks

Mossy Creek
Reunion At Mossy Creek
Summer In Mossy Creek

Coming in June 2004
Blessings Of Mossy Creek

Coming soon from BelleBooks
KaseyBelle, The Tiniest Fairy
by Sandra Chastain
Book One in the *Everyone's Special* series—
illustrated children's books with Southern charm

Other BelleBooks Titles
Sweet Tea And Jesus Shoes
Coming in 2004:
More Sweet Tea

New York Times bestselling author
Deborah Smith's *Waterlilies* series
Alice At Heart
Coming: ## Two If By Sea

BelleBooks

770-384-1348
P.O. Box 67 • Smyrna, GA 30081
BelleBooks@BelleBooks.com
visit our website: www.BelleBooks.com